LUKE IRONTREE & THE LAST VAMPIRE WAR

Book 0 - The Centurion Immortal
Book 1 - Dark Fangs Rising - March 22, 2022
Book 2 - Dark Fangs Raging - April 19, 2022
Book 3 - Dark Fangs Descending - May 17, 2022
Book 4 - Blood Empire Reborn - August 23, 2022
Book 5 - Blood Empire Avenged - September 20, 2022
Book 6 - Blood Empire Infiltrated - October 18, 2022
Book 7 - Blood Empire Burning - November 15, 2022
Book 8 - Ancient Sword Falling - March 21, 2023
Book 9 - Ancient Sword Unyielding - August 22, 2023
Book 10 - Ancient Sword Shattering*

The Luke Irontree Historical Adventures
Rise of the Centurio Immortalis - April 5, 2022
Fall of the Centurio Immortalis - May 31, 2022
The Moonlight Centurion*
The Highway Centurion*

*Forthcoming
Titles and release dates may be subject to change.

ANCIENT SWORD FALLING

LUKE IRONTREE & THE LAST VAMPIRE WAR
BOOK 8

C. THOMAS LAFOLLETTE

EDITED BY
SUZANNE LAHNA

ANCIENT SWORD FALLING
C. Thomas Lafollette

A Broken World Publication
13820 NE Airport Way
Suite #K395495
Portland, OR 97251-1158
Ancient Sword Falling
Copyright © 2023 by C. Thomas Lafollette
ISBN 978-1-949410-85-3 (ebook);
ISBN 978-1-949410-86-0 (paperback)

Cover Design: Ravven
Developmental Editing by: Suzanne Lahna
Copy/Line Editing: Alin Silverwood
Proofreading: Amy Cissell

CONTENTS

PRONUNCIATION GUIDE & AUTHOR'S NOTES

Pronunciation: Latin names and words are mentioned throughout the book and are intended to be read with the classical Latin pronunciation. For instance, "c" is always pronounced hard, like a "k." "U" is always a short "oo" sound. "V" typically sounds like a "w." There are plenty of resources on the internet if you wish to learn more about Classical Latin pronunciation.

- Lucius – Loo-kih-oos
- Silvanius – Sihl-wahn-ih-oos
- Ferrata – Fehr-rah-tah
- Jung-sook — Yoong-sook
- Jan - Yeahn
- Roxiustanta - Roks-see-oo-stahn-nah
- Surena - Ser-rehn-nah
- Selene - Sehl-lee-nee
- Le Mousquetaire - Ley Moos-keh-tare

Latin Words: Latin words are used for effect and to add to the "flavor" of the story, not to reflect Latin grammar/declensions/conjugations.

L uke's heart raced as the private jet took off from the small Parisian airport. The last time he'd attempted to board a private jet offered by a European packleader, he'd been tranquilized and kidnapped as he watched his friends fly away, helpless to aid him.

Gripping the armrests, he thought he might rip them from the seat. Roxi did her best to soothe him as his foot tapped nervously on the airplane's floor. He appreciated Roxi's efforts. Though the only thing that worked was gravity pushing him back in his seat as the plane's wheels left the ground. The jet climbing, he took his first deep breath. And once the relief settled in, he felt hollowed out.

He did his best to push the tension away once they leveled out and were safely away from the airport, though he never could break entirely free from it. Next to him, Roxi slept, alternating between resting against the inner wall of the private jet and snuggling up on his shoulder. When she leaned on him, he turned his head and kissed the top of hers, her wild hair tickling his nose. She hadn't had a professional haircut in a long time, according to her, but even when freshly styled, it still liked to fly away. The other bonus of her proximity was her scent. It tantalized and calmed him all at once.

He'd spent months bringing down the three packleaders who'd

betrayed him, exacting bloody vengeance and utterly destroying them. But saving Roxi and reversing Mithras's compulsion ultimately was the most important to him.

If the choice had been Roxi or vengeance, he'd have forsaken his own revenge for her life. Fortunately, he didn't have to do either. Mathis had been taken down then cast out to try to survive; no doubt there were multiple bounties on his head from all those he'd betrayed in his hunt for power and wealth. Without his money and connections, he was useless to his vampire overlords. In fact, he was a loose end for them to tie up. Permanently.

Heinrich Netzke, Cologne's former alpha, had been turned over to his pack for trial and justice. Luke didn't bother asking what that meant in the scheme of things. It wasn't his business. Heidi, the new packleader, could manage her own affairs.

His only regret was that he hadn't been able to bring justice to Jan, the man who'd murdered his own father to gain control of the wealthy Flanders Pack, their control of Belgium and the south of the Netherlands, and the mighty ports in Antwerp and Rotterdam. Luke had helped orchestrate his fall, removing his wealth and leadership of the Pack, but he'd slipped through their fingers and escaped the justice everyone wanted to bring to the patricidal fuckhead.

Luke felt for Pieter, who'd have to wait a bit longer before he could avenge his murdered father. Sometimes Pieter was hard to read. Mostly, he looked weary. Luke would have to get some private time with his Belgian friend for a heart-to-heart when they were both settled after their travels.

With a stop in New York City to refuel, they still had a long day before they landed back home in Portland. Luke couldn't wait to see his girlfriend Maggie—she'd been one of the first to depart after their conference in Paris—and his adopted child Gwen and bestow some well-earned scritches on his cat Alfred.

His life before becoming involved with the North Portland Pack had been a lonely and tedious life with only his cat Alfred to keep him company. At first, he'd feared involving Pablo and Delilah in vampire hunting, but if he'd not given in, he'd probably have been dead multiple times over by now. He'd been reluctant at first, but they'd become so much more than allies of convenience.

He turned in his seat and smiled at Pablo and Delilah. Pablo grinned and winked at him. Delilah nodded, the corners of her lips quirking up. They were family. And knowing them had helped him grow his family further.

He would never have met Maggie. And even though the circumstances of their meeting were dark, he'd never have met Roxi. She'd have died alone in that prison under the arena or in one of their arenas fighting to entertain the soulless bloodsucking monsters.

So many lives intersecting with his would have been irrevocably altered had he not taken the chance and made two new friends. Now, he loved and was loved. He had a girlfriend and, though they hadn't discussed official terms, another budding relationship. He had friends, and he had a young teen he needed to guide to adulthood. He also had a weird dog whose presence locked in one of the high security cells of the arena was still a mystery.

When they hit a patch of rough air, Roxi startled awake, her eyes wide. Her unfocused gaze flicked about as she clung tightly to Luke's hand. When her breathing calmed, she looked a bit sheepish.

"Sorry. I didn't know where I was. I sometimes wake up and think I'm still in that cell under the arena," she mumbled just loud enough for him to hear it.

"That's OK, Roxi. I still struggle with the memory of the arena, too. I haven't had enough time to really unpack it with my therapist, not with the full half year we've had since getting out. It's a lot." Resting his hand on her cheek, he turned her head and kissed her.

"I'm glad I can wake up next to you, even if it's on this rinky-dink plane. It feels more secure to be near you. For so long, you were the only bright light. Now I have more to look forward to than seeing your face through a hole in the stone."

Luke chuckled. "Yeah. It's a bit of an adjustment not being in that cell, but the last few weeks with you have been wonderful. It's weird to say, but I wouldn't trade it for anything."

"Yeah. It's the one good thing I can say about the arena—it brought me you." Roxi kissed his cheek.

"It might be more than just one positive. In all the years I've been doing this, I've never had a target to aim for. I've killed powerful elite vampires by the legion, but I've never had a true target to aim my gladius at. We've brought down some powerful associates of the vampires and spoked the wheel of their plans in Western Europe. We've got a whole bunch of financial intelligence we'll need to sort through, but I think we have a real chance of doing something meaningful and potentially permanently disabling to the vampires." Luke could feel his excitement building at the thought of maybe being able to end it all.

Roxi looked scared and hopeful all at once. "Do…do you really think that's possible? To, you know, end it? For real?"

"I hope so, and for once, that hope might actually have some evidence to back and bolster it." He squeezed Roxi's hand.

"I truly hope you're right, Luke. There is nothing more I long for, well, other than being in your arms, but ending vampires would be a close second."

Luke chuckled at the sweet grin on her face. "Roxi, I love you."

She patted Luke on the cheek. "I know. Now let me out. I need to visit the loo."

He moved out and let her into the narrow walkway, then sat back down. He didn't want to let himself fantasize about a world without vampires, so he forced his brain to lean into the other fantasies he had—home and friends and loved ones. He was still amazed at how domestic his desires had become. Spending time with Gwen talking music or teaching her to fight. Goofing with his friends down at the pub as they shared beers. Kissing a beautiful woman he adored. Sleeping late and being woken by an insistent cat. These had become the goalposts for a good life for him, the things he truly wanted.

Sam squeezed his shoulder, interrupting his wool gathering. "Scoot."

He slid over into Roxi's seat, letting Sam take his spot. "What can I do for you, Sam?"

"Nothing specific. Just wanted to check in with you to see how you're doing. You seemed pretty tense this morning."

"Yeah. I was having some real trouble keeping calm until we got off the ground. I almost had a panic attack. About the only thing that staved it off was Roxi's presence. I was terrified something bad would happen."

Sam squeezed his forearm. "I bet. That was terrible last time. I don't know if anyone told you about the flight back after they saw what happened, but it was a very unhappy crowd of people. A lot of anger and tears. I honestly had some concerns as well, even with an official alliance with Jean-Paul."

Luke nodded. "I'll have to apologize to him if I seemed weird and unappreciative. I'm sure he'll understand."

"Yeah. He seems like a genuinely good man. I'm glad to have met him. He'll make a good ally."

"Plus, he has connections we don't and can get us in contact with other key packs in Europe. Hopefully he can bring them into the cause, or if nothing else, at least assure their neutrality. We can't afford to be fighting big, rich packs and vampires. He's working on a side project for me."

"Oh?" Sam asked, raising an eyebrow.

Luke grinned mischievously. "Just a little surprise in case we need some bigger firepower. The vampires seem to be upping the ante on us."

"You're not wrong there." Sam shook her head before smiling. "We can talk politics later. How are you and Roxi doing?"

Luke nodded and grinned. "We're doing well, I think. We're talking about a future together."

Sam chuckled. "Do you remember the first time we flew to Europe together? When we flew to Belgium?"

"Yeah…" Luke squinted his eyes at Sam, unsure where she was going with the conversation.

"Remember when I asked if you were going to look for someone to date besides Maggie, since you had the option as a person in a poly relationship?" Sam grinned mischievously, her eyes twinkling with mirth.

"Yeah. I do remember that now that you mention it."

"Well, it seems you are ready for a second relationship."

Luke chuckled. "I guess so."

"How do you feel about it?"

"Good but confused. A little anxious." Luke laughed at himself. "I've used 'confused' to describe myself so many times since meeting you all and having Gwen move in, then dating Maggie. Seems like the perpetual state of being with my personal life."

Sam smiled brightly. "It's good, though, right?"

"Yeah. It is. I'm having positive thoughts about the future, and all my fantasies are terribly domestic and simple."

"Luke Irontree, I think you're becoming a real boy!"

"Ha! I'm still a puppet. Haven't managed to cut those divine strings yet. But I can handle feeling more real, more attached to a life of meaning beyond the end of my sword."

"It's a powerful incentive to have meaningful things to fight for, to protect. I know you've been working your whole life to protect humanity, but billions of people are abstract. Maggie and Roxi and Gwen, those are all very tangible and real entities."

"And you, Delilah, and Pablo, and the rest of the crew. But you're right. I feel more integrated into humanity instead of just being an outside observer. I would have never thought it was possible to get to this place, not as old and outside of humanity as I've been, but here I am."

Sam nodded. "Here you are. I'm so proud of you, Luke. I don't mean this to sound condescending, but you've come such a long way since that first time we met. You were such a sad, lonely person. As much as you tried to pretend to be 'normal,' you couldn't hide the pain in your eyes."

Luke sighed and shook his head. "Sometimes I feel like a stray puppy Pablo brought home."

Sam chuckled, patting Luke's knee. "Yeah, he kind of adopted you, but I'm glad he did. You're a wonderful friend and a good man. My life is better for having met you."

"I feel the same about you, too." He leaned over and kissed Sam's forehead.

"So, got any big—"

Sam's question was interrupted by one of the pilots activating the intercom. "Sorry to disturb you, folks. But we're getting some troubling news coming in. We don't have much information yet, but it looks like a plane just crashed near JFK in New York. We're being diverted to an airfield in Maine. I'll let you know more when we can."

"Oh, my." Sam held her hands in front of her mouth.

Luke couldn't find the words and only nodded.

"Um, I see Roxi coming. I'll let her have her seat back." Sam stood up, looking unsteady and unnaturally pale after hearing the tragic news.

Roxi sat down and wrapped her arms around Luke. Feeling the tremble in her body, he pulled her in tightly with one arm while he stroked her hair with his other hand.

"Did...did they say a plane crashed? It was hard to hear in the water closet."

"Yeah. Outside New York near JFK International. Are you OK?"

"I...I don't like flying, even at the best of times."

Luke squeezed her, kissing her forehead. "That's OK. It's understandable."

Holding her in his arms, he hummed the melody to the Gaulish lullaby she liked him to sing to her when she felt down. The simple sound seemed to calm her as she clung to him. He didn't know how long they were supposed to be in the air or how much time had passed since taking off, but landing couldn't come soon enough.

Behind him, the level of noise picked up as people discussed the snippet of news the pilot had given them. Luke wanted to tell them to be quiet as their speculation, loud enough for Roxi with her supernatural ears to hear, caused her to tremble more. He thought he heard her sniffle. It was confirmed when she rubbed her cheeks with her sleeve. A tear fell onto his arm, running down and falling onto his pants.

"Luke, please don't stop humming. If you could sing, it would be better, so I'd have something to concentrate on besides..."

"Sure." Luke kissed the top of her head and started at the beginning of the song, this time with the words.

By now, Roxi had heard it so many times, she knew the melody as well as Luke. It didn't take her long, not as a trained singer. It had been a skill she'd developed as part of her role as an assassin and spy for her father, the Parthian king's general, and for the Parthian Empire. It had also provided a valuable skill to allow her to move through society when women weren't granted much in the way of freedoms. Access to places where people drank allowed her to hunt where vampires preyed.

To focus her mind and distract it from her fear of flying, a fear exacerbated by the news of a plane crash, she played with the simple melody as she hummed along, adding more complex rhythms and tones. While she embellished the song, she made sure her voice enhanced the lyrics Luke sang to her instead of overwhelming them. As he worked his way through the melody, the conversation behind them quieted as people clued in to the music being performed for an audience of two. Yet, Luke didn't mind them eavesdropping on their private moment. It had caused them to quiet their speculation, which would help Roxi's anxiety some, he hoped.

He wished she'd told him she was afraid of flying—not that he could have done much about it. The announcement of the tragedy had clearly upset her coping mechanisms, letting the fear push past her point of tolerance.

The next time the pilot broke in over the intercom, his voice carried a tremble. "Folks, um, we've just gotten word of another commercial jetliner going down. This one in the air over the Atlantic. We still don't know much. We'll be increasing our airspeed to get you on the ground as soon as possible without burning too much fuel. Uh, please buckle up, we're about to head into some rough air. I'll give you an update as soon as we know more."

The second announcement stunned the cabin into silence. The only sounds Luke heard were seatbelts being buckled and someone maneuvering Brutus into his harness.

Roxi shook in Luke's arms, her breath shallow and ragged. One commercial flight going down was exceedingly rare. Two within minutes of each other was virtually unheard of. Whatever it was, he hoped it wasn't something interfering with plane electronics or some other environmental disaster that was affecting planes. He wished he knew which way the second plane had been going—west like them, or east.

It didn't matter; there was little he could do about it. He just hoped they'd get on the ground before anything else happened. Once they were safe from gravity's retribution, they could plan the next stage of their trip home. He sighed, wondering why nothing he was involved in ever seemed to go off without a hitch. Pushing that thought out of his head, he resumed his humming, starting with one of his favorite Parthian melodies.

CHAPTER
TWO

The rest of the flight had been filled with news of several tragedies, reports of more planes going down and the terror it caused. By unspoken agreement, no one talked about it, only looking at watches or phones when the pilots gave a new ETA for their landing in Maine.

Taking Luke and Roxi's examples, people joined them in songs, waiting their turn to sing. Many picked tunes from their childhood. If Luke or Roxi knew it, they'd join along. When Sam broke out an old Japanese lullaby, Luke joined in, singing in harmony with her. When Ahmed picked up an Arabic tune, Roxi provided a melody to accompany it. Occasionally, someone would take up something more modern and well known, and several people would join in, the song often getting loud as people tried to sing along like they were out for karaoke.

As they joined together in song, hoping to distract each other, they provided comfort and touch. Friends held friends' hands or hugged each other, some snuggling into each other to feel the warmth and love of a close companion and family member, of pack. The singing seemed to help Roxi as her body ceased trembling, only returning to it whenever a new announcement was made, though less intensely.

Song had been their refuge while they were trapped in their cells, waiting to die for the amusement of their tormentors and captors. Now, it became the glue that bonded everyone on the plane together as they worked to quell the fear they all felt, hoping they'd make it back to earth the slow way.

Luke imagined a few people were even praying to whatever deity they worshiped. He cast a prayer to Selene. After his words left his mind and entered the ether, he felt her hand upon him and her blessing lightened a bit of the fear he felt, though it couldn't quell it entirely. He hoped Roxi availed herself of the goddess's of the moon's kindness now that she'd a devotee. They both needed the goddess's love and affection, needed her kind guidance as they struggled against a Herculean task—beyond Herculean. Without her, they were two powerful beings adrift. With her, they felt loved and appreciated as they fought to protect humanity from the threat the vampires represented.

When the wheels touched down, they were all jolted in their seats at the impact. Luke exhaled a long, hard breath. Soon, a few laughs broke the silence followed by a ragged cheer as they all celebrated surviving, even if they didn't know what they were surviving. As soon as the plane slowed, people jumped on their phones, making calls to loved ones or to see what extra news they could get since the pilots had been parsimonious with the news after the first few announcements.

"Anyone find any information?" Sam asked.

"I think I found an article with some leaked information from the FAA. Um…" Jung-sook scrolled through her phone, reading the article. "According to this, some passengers went berserk, attacking the plane. Like ripping people apart, then broke into the cockpits."

"Is this just one flight?" Luke asked, a horrible hypothesis idea dawning in his head.

"No," Jung-sook replied.

"Oh, my god," Rhonda said. "So far, at least according to this source, thirty-four planes have gone down worldwide."

"Where are the flights originating from?" Sam asked.

"All over," Rhonda replied. "The US, Europe, Japan, China,

Russia, South Africa, Australia. No one can determine a pattern. It's a variety of airlines. About the only common denominator is that they're all larger planes on longer flights."

Luke nodded to himself. Sam, who'd been watching Luke's face, called for silence.

Once everyone shut up, she looked at Luke. "You have an idea, don't you?"

Nodding, Luke licked his lips. "Vampires."

Some of his friends gave him skeptical looks in return.

Pablo narrowed his eyes. "Are you sure, buddy? It could be any number of things."

"Look, I know. I'm the guy who sees vampires as the origin of most issues—"

Rhonda interrupted Luke. "Would vampires kill themselves like that? They seem pretty attached to their lives."

"Baby vampires would."

Pablo, probably remembering the nursery room he'd helped Luke blow up in Wapato, blanched.

"If they put people about to turn onto flights, then they changed during the flight, it would work. That could be why they wanted longer flights to take out a bit of the variability." He looked around at the faces of his friends. "Most of you haven't seen a vampire nursery. A newly turned vampire has no control, just blood lust. They don't just drink, they destroy. They feed on the horror of their actions as much as on the blood of their victims."

"But those vamps we killed… Didn't they back off when you set them on fire?" Pablo asked, horror and hope in his eyes.

"That was immediate pain—action and reaction. But you put a baby vamp in a plane, and there's no control. A tightly contained space stuffed with tasty humans and no escape? They'd go into a frenzy. They'd probably keep tearing flesh until the moment the plane hit the ground."

Looking at his friends, he saw horror on their faces. They'd seen what vampires did to humans, but really didn't know what a baby vamp could do. He kind of wanted to keep it that way. No one should have that in their memories.

"Why, though?" Sam asked.

Luke shrugged. "I don't know."

Roxi lifted her head and looked around the plane. "It could be anything. Maybe the bosses got bored and wanted some entertainment. Maybe something big is on the horizon. Maybe there's some power play within the ranks of the vampire elites. It's too early to tell at this point."

Sam stood up. "It'll have to be one more bullet point we add to the list of things to investigate. Right now, though, we need to figure out what we're going to do next. There's no way they're going to let this plane take off. Flights will be grounded worldwide."

"I just hope we can get the weaponry offboarded without any officious types looking too deeply. That would be monumentally bad timing," Luke said.

They all turned to the front of the jet when the door separating the cabin and the cockpit opened. "Didn't mean to overhear, but"— he tapped his ear—"wolf ears. Your friend is right. All flight traffic is grounded. I've got a message into Jean-Paul to see if he's got any contacts here with the local wolves. If you have any, it might be best if you reach out as well."

"I'm on it. I'll give Holly a call." Sam dug into her pockets for her phone.

Luke turned to the pilot and offered his hand. "I'm Luke."

"Vincent," the pilot replied. "I'm going to head back up to the cockpit and see if Jean-Paul has gotten back to us."

"Right. We'll knock on the door if we hear anything from our end."

Vincent nodded and ducked back into the cockpit, shutting the door behind him.

"Sam?" Luke asked.

"Sorry, having trouble getting through. The lines are busy."

"I imagine everyone's flooding the system," Rhonda said. "It was the same on 9/11."

Several people nodded, remembering what it had been like then.

Sam held up her hand. "Everyone quiet. It's ringing."

Luke sat back down, tired of hunching over in the short space.

"Hey, Holly. Yeah. We've landed, and the pilots say we're grounded. Do you have any connections with the local wolf packs? We're at a small airport near Portland, Maine."

Everyone waited for Sam's response.

"OK, love you, Holly. I'll be waiting but might want to email as well. Lines seem to be a bit squiffy. Talk to you soon." Sam stuffed her phone back in her pocket.

Vincent stepped out of the cockpit. "Good news. We're at an airport where the local pack has employees. We shouldn't have any problem offloading your gear. They're sending some trucks and vans and have offered sanctuary until you sort out what's happening next."

"Excellent," Luke said. "Our packleader is currently making some calls as well. How long until we're able to deplane?"

Vincent shrugged. "I don't know. The airport is still waiting for guidance from the FAA, but if they're grounding everyone, I imagine they'll want to get people away from airports pretty quickly until they know what's going on. I'll let you know as soon as I make contact with the local pack. I'll go dig up some more snacks and drinks for you all. Please, use the restroom and get comfortable; we could be here for a while."

It was after midnight before they deboarded the plane. After a stressful flight and a long wait on the tarmac, heads drooped with tiredness, though Luke thought everyone bore up well. They'd all gone through hard times together fighting vampires and had become accustomed to the stress. This was just one more event to add to the tally. The local pack settled them into a cheap motel for the night since they'd not had time to come up with better arrangements on short notice. A few other planes, including regional jets, had been sent to the small airport, flooding local accommodations.

Luke and Roxi were given the room with one queen bed, but the rest paired up to share the double-queen-bed rooms so they could get four to a room. Brutus curled up in the corner of Luke and Roxi's room. Luke was unwilling to let the mysterious dog out of his sight. Despite not getting a proper dinner, Luke fell into bed and was asleep almost before the light went out.

It felt like too few hours later when his alarm went off at nine a.m. He and Roxi quickly showered and changed, waiting for the vans to pick them up and take them to a pack property for a catered breakfast. A few people had woken earlier and ventured out for coffee but didn't bring one back for Luke—a fact he found rude. If you're going to bring treats, bring enough for the entire legion.

When they arrived at their destination, a multi-storied old brick building near the central downtown area of Portland, they were escorted in by a few polite folks who were probably members of the local pack. The scent of coffee was the best greeting Luke could have hoped for. As soon as he had a cup in hand, he was ready to face the day as a member of the North Portland Pack Council.

He found Sam, who was talking to a tall, stocky White woman with short brunette hair. She wore a flannel shirt over jeans and boots.

"Ah, Erin. This is Luke. Luke, Erin. She's the packleader here in Portland."

Erin offered her hand and a friendly grin. "So, you're the one who's been kicking the vampire ant hill the last few years?"

Luke was taken aback and paused before jolting himself back into the conversation. "I didn't think I'd developed any kind of reputation here in the states. I've kept my presence pretty quiet."

Erin snorted. "You blew up a jail and sank a freighter. Then had a pitched battle at a famous ski lodge. If you call that quiet, I'd hate to hear what your version of noisy is."

Sam laughed, patting Luke's back. "She's got you there."

Luke smiled politely, unsure how to take Erin's jocularity. Roxi wandered up and stopped next to him, providing a helpful distraction.

"Erin, this is Roxi. Roxi, Erin is the local packleader."

They shook hands.

"She's not a wolf either." Erin looked her up and down.

Luke shook his head. "No, she's more like me. She's a vampire hunter."

"Ah, that's good. We can talk about that when you've been fed, but we might want to use your services since you're in the neighborhood." She swiveled her head over to the wall where the caterers were filling chafing dishes. "Looks like breakfast is ready. Also, we set up a little food and water station for your pooch. There are plenty of pack pets that come through here." She stepped back and raised her voice. "Food's ready! Everyone line up."

His stomach grumbling loudly, Luke nodded politely at Erin—letting Brutus wander to the bowls on the floor—and headed toward the table, getting a spot near the front of the line. He found a table and sat down to dig into his hot food. As others in his leadership group dished up their food, they joined Luke. He was glad they'd sent home a large part of their contingent a few days earlier, or the local pack would have trouble accommodating them while they were stuck here. Luke went back for seconds, as did several of the were-wolves. When they were finished, Erin invited Luke up to a conference room to talk. Luke brought Sam, Pablo, Delilah, Roxi, and Simone with him, leaving Jung-sook and Ahmed in charge of the rest of the wolves.

They were joined by a tall Latino man who Erin introduced as Alejandro, the pack's second.

"I want to start off officially welcoming you as our guests for your stay," Erin said. "We'll get you all housed so we can move you out of that fleabag motel. If you don't mind, we have a couple bed and breakfasts we can set you up in. It's off season, so we'll just need to open them since we only operate them on the weekends this time of year." She turned to Luke. "So, you're the Centurion Immortal. I've heard a bit about you."

Luke raised an eyebrow. "That's a nickname I don't usually hear in the states."

"I have some pack connections in Europe, so I've heard rumors about you before, but Jean-Paul filled me in. He's a good friend."

Sam cleared her throat. "You mentioned something about vampires?"

"Yeah. We've been noticing more in town recently. In the past, we've usually just confronted them and asked them to leave."

"But...something's changed?" Luke asked.

Erin nodded. "Yeah. They've stopped responding. The last time we cornered one, he told us we had the option to leave or be considered part of their herd."

"That's quite bold," Pablo said.

"Right?" Erin shook her head. "My people didn't do anything because the orders were to just deliver the message, but the vamps haven't really made an appearance since, or at least let us catch one."

"Any strange disappearances among the non-pack locals?" Luke asked.

Alejandro nodded. "Yeah. There have been a few. Also, there's been a rise in what the papers are calling 'delinquency.' People getting drunk and sleeping in the streets. I mean, we're a brewery town, but it's been a bit more lately, and it's a bad time of year to sleep outside if you're unprepared. You could die of hypothermia pretty easily."

Luke rubbed the stubble on his jaw. "Let me guess. The people interviewed are reporting not having drank that much, but can't remember anything?"

Alejandro nodded. "Exactly."

Luke looked around the table, seeing several people nodding with knowing expressions on their faces. "Well, that's definitely vampires, and if they've declared you open as prey, it's just a matter of time before one of your pack is taken."

Erin exchanged a look with Alejandro, something passing between them.

"Someone already has, haven't they?" Luke looked between the packleader and her second.

Erin inhaled then exhaled sharply. "Yeah. A young couple. They were out late on a date and didn't show up to work the next day."

Alejandro held up his hand to forestall any questions. "And before you ask the litany of questions, we've already checked with their families to see if maybe they got a wild hair and took off, but there's nothing missing and no signs of elopement or running away. Their suitcases and all their possessions are undisturbed."

"Any witnesses?" Pablo asked.

Alejandro held up his hand and wobbled it side to side. "The server at the restaurant said they paid and left. We canvased the neighborhood and routes between their houses and the restaurant and found a homeless woman who thought she saw a group of people following them, but she couldn't be sure if they actually were following or were just a group heading in the same direction."

"We were able to get a bit of a scent trail, but it dead ended. We've been stymied since," Erin said.

"Yeah, we've even reported them missing to the local cops, though that'll probably go nowhere," Alejandro added.

Luke nodded along, then looked around the table at his leadership team. "We'll see what we can do. Give us tonight to rest, then tomorrow night, we'll see if we can track down your missing pack members."

Erin relaxed, sighing in relief. "Let's get you situated, then we can figure out what all you'll need."

Luke had hoped to be home in Portland, Oregon before he jumped back into the vampire business. He needed some real time off. A week or two so he could move through life without the adrenaline of the fight pumping through his veins, but he'd have to wait a while longer. Despite his mental and physical exhaustion, he did what he always did—shoved it into the background so he could keep at it. Once he found a spare moment, he'd call home and see if he could talk with Gwen and Maggie. It would have to do until he could actually return home.

They split up the teams, mixing three of Luke's people to one of Erin's. She'd wanted to keep their initial involvement small and confined to the leadership team and a few select packmates so they could learn about the process while not being a burden to Luke and his trained hunters.

Luke brought Sam and Pablo along with Erin, while Roxi paired with Delilah, Simone, and Alejandro. They also put out two more teams. The plan was to stay in close contact and converge if they needed to. Erin volunteered to drive, pulling up to the bed-and-breakfast in a Toyota minivan.

Pulling the sliding door open, Luke sat in the back. "Ow!" He pushed off the seat and pulled a pile of Legos out from under his butt. He showed them to Erin. "Yours?"

"Sorry, those are my daughter's. She must have left them there." She took them from Luke and dumped them into a compartment in the center console.

"No worries. Just a bit surprising. I've heard how much Legos hurt, but never experienced it until right then."

"No kids?" Erin asked.

"None of my own. Though I have a young teen living with me."

"Adopted?"

Luke smiled warmly, nodding. "She was a runaway from a bad pack and ended up in Portland. We stumbled upon her when we were trying to track down some vampires."

Pablo laughed. "She basically adopted Luke. She didn't trust werewolves after her pack situation, so she kept turning to Luke for protection. They decided to make it official."

"Where's she at?" Erin asked as she made a turn and looked for a place to park.

"Back in Portland. My girlfriend and her partner have been watching her while I was away."

"Your girlfriend's partner?" She raised an eyebrow.

Sam chuckled. "Luke's a very modern man. He's in a poly relationship."

Erin laughed, then squinted at Luke. "The modern ancient man. Are the rumors really true? About you being a Roman centurion?"

Luke nodded. She hadn't seen him get dressed. He'd just piled into her minivan.

"Go ahead and show her, buddy," Pablo said.

Luke unzipped his hoodie, revealing the armor. Reaching over his shoulder, he grabbed the handle of his gladius and pulled it up a bit, so the blade was partially visible.

"Well, isn't that something?" Erin stared, then shook her head, turning the car off. "This is our starting point. We'll sweep up through town, and that will put us in the center of the teams. We should have the wind blowing in our faces."

Luke nodded. "Good. That'll help the wolves track better."

"How do you track?" Erin asked.

"He can sense vampires," Pablo supplied. "It's like a sixth sense for him."

"Pretty much," Luke said, nodding.

Once the four of them slid out of the Toyota, the fifth person in the van moved into the driver's seat and buckled up, ready to follow and pick them up at a moment's notice. Pablo let Brutus out and grabbed the duffel bag containing a couple shotguns from the trunk area of the van, then slammed the hatch shut.

"What's in the bag?" Erin asked.

"Twelve gauge shotguns," Sam said, grinning mischievously at Erin. "Just a little something if we run into a few more vampires than we'd like.

Luke elaborated, while bending over to scoop up Brutus's leash. "The shells are custom made and contain silver shot and wood. They'll kill a wolf if the shot is right, so don't stand in the way thinking you'll be able to shed off some buckshot. At best, these'll hurt like hell. At worst..."

Sam pulled a backpack off and opened it. She pulled out a handful of stakes and handed them to Pablo and Erin, then grabbed a few more to drop in her coat pockets.

"Doesn't he need a stake?" Erin asked, pointing to Luke.

Pablo chuckled. "Nah, his swords will do the job far more efficiency than these stakes."

Erin looked at the coat pockets and stakes. "What do you all do when it's too hot to wear coats?"

"Sweat," Luke replied.

"Luke, did you get a chance to do an inventory on the shotgun shells?" Sam asked.

"Yeah. We're getting really thin." Luke zipped up his hoodie.

"We might have to make some more," Pablo said.

"Hey, Erin, do you have anyone in the pack who goes hunting that might pack their own ammo?" Sam slung the backpack over her shoulders.

"Honey, it's Maine. A lot of us hunt and fish. I'll put the word out. You'll just need to supply your own packing material. We don't really keep a cache of silver kicking around for some reason."

Luke chuckled. "Fair enough. Wouldn't be the first time we've had to improvise. Might have to hit some thrift shops or pawn shops to see if we can pick up some silver antiques."

With the weapons distributed and hidden, they started down their designated path. Erin peppered them with questions, probably due to nerves. It wasn't often one got to hunt vampires with seasoned pros.

"If we're going to talk, we should probably change the topic to something more mundane or keep our volume to a whisper. Fangers have good hearing, and even though I don't feel any nearby, we don't want to alert them that they're being hunted." Luke stuffed his hands into the pockets of his hoodie to hide his fidgeting.

"Sorry, just anxious, I guess. This is a whole lot of new for me," Erin replied.

Sam patted her shoulder. "Don't worry about it. We all start somewhere."

Instead of vampire-related questions, Erin filled them in on Portland and what they were seeing. None of them had ever visited the other Portland. Erin was proud of her city, pointing out her favorite restaurants, bars, and breweries.

"Hey, Luke. If we get a chance, I'd like to check out a few of the breweries. I've heard amazing things about Allagash," Pablo said.

"You know I like drinking beer." Turning to Erin, he said, "Pablo owns a brewery in Portland. It'll be work research."

"I can hook you up with a tour. One of our packmembers works at the brewery."

Sam held up her hand, pushing her nose into the air as she sniffed. "Hey, Luke, do you feel anything?" she asked quietly. "I think I caught a whiff of stank."

A wisp of cigarette smoke drifted down to Luke. He thought he felt a twinge at the edge of his range. Next to him, Brutus growled quietly, deep in his throat.

Luke waved them in, so they were all practically nose to nose. "I think so, Sam. It's faint. Sounds like Brutus is picking it up, too."

"I think I found the scent, too. I almost didn't notice it with the cigarette smoke," Pablo whispered, sniffing.

Sam nodded. "I think the smoker is our fanger. I got the scents at the same time. I just thought it was particularly cheap tobacco, but I couldn't shake the underlying aroma. Are you getting a direction we can aim for, Luke?"

"Vaguely ahead and to the right."

Erin stepped to the edge of the sidewalk and looked, then waved everyone after her as she crossed to the other sidewalk.

Luke narrowed his eyes and rubbed his chin through his beard. Keeping his voice low, he said, "Yeah, it feels a bit closer. Let's keep going straight, and we can adjust as we go. Someone let the other teams know. Check with the team to the right to see if they're picking it up as well."

"Got it," Pablo said, pulling his phone out. "The right team is also getting it and wants to know if they should stay, converge, or split to do both."

"Stay on course, but we can adjust later. Don't go past it, though." Luke stopped and held up a hand. The vamp was getting closer. The calmness that always descended when he was on the hunt settled on him as the time to fight drew near. "It's shifted directions. I think it's coming back toward us now. Still holding off to the right. Let the other team know. Who's on the right team?"

"That's Roxi, Ahmed, and Jung-sook."

"I thought Roxi was with Delilah and Simone."

"Since Delilah can sense them as well, they decided to put her on one of the other teams so we could keep the teams mixed."

Luke nodded. "Hmmm, it stopped moving. Let's stay on course, and we'll triangulate with Roxi's team. Keep the chatter to a minimum or whisper. We're a ways out, but let's not risk it."

After another block, they stopped to assess the location again.

"Are you doing OK, Erin?" Sam asked.

"I think so. It's all very exciting and scary. I'm hunting vampires with real vampire hunters," she whispered, chuckling nervously.

Luke turned and gave a half-smile. "You're doing great, Erin. I know you're typically the one in charge, but if we have to engage, step back and let us handle it and listen for instructions. Remember, its heart is the kill button."

"Or rip off the head. That's always a personal favorite," Pablo added, a wide grin on his face.

"Or rip the head off." Luke winked at Pablo. "Plus, you can chuck it at another vampire."

"For some reason, that always seems to distract them." Pablo shrugged. "Don't know why…"

Sam shook her head and chuckled. "I wonder."

"Is it always like this? With the banter?" Erin asked.

"Yeah. Though we don't let Luke banter much. He's not that great at it."

Luke shrugged. "I can't be good at everything."

"So, what's the word?" Sam asked, getting them back on task.

"Still not moving. I think maybe the next a block ahead. Have Roxi go two blocks up and cut across. We'll go across and meet in the middle."

Pablo nodded and pulled out his phone to relay the orders. After Pablo sent the instructions, they moseyed over to the next block, allowing Roxi, Ahmed, and Jung-sook time to get the extra block ahead. When they thought they'd waited long enough, they picked up their pace.

"It's straight ahead," Luke said, gesturing with his head to follow him. "Do you know what's coming up, Erin?"

She ran her hand through her short hair. "This is mostly mixed-use neighborhoods. I think an apartment building."

"You picking up more than one?" Sam asked.

"I think it's only one. You still getting the smell of cigarettes?"

Sam stuck her nose up in the air. "I don't think so."

Luke strolled ahead. The trees along the street obscured their view, but Erin's local knowledge proved true as an apartment building loomed over them once they cleared the block.

"I see our team up ahead," Pablo said.

Luke nodded. They met up in the middle of the next block.

"What do you think, Roxi?" Luke asked.

"He's above us." She looked up.

"Right."

"Do we try to get into the apartment building?" Ahmed asked.

"I'm not sure. We may want to let him go and see if we can follow him somewhere more useful. Maybe wherever they're keeping our young couple." Luke looked around to see what they thought.

"It's not really our standard procedure, but novelty might be nice." Jung-sook shrugged.

"Or we could take his phone off his corpse and let Jamaal crack it and check out its location data," Sam replied.

"Would a dead vampire alert the rest?" Erin asked.

"All good thoughts," Luke said. "I'm inclined to go with Sam's option. We could stand here all night waiting for it to come out, then we'd have no guarantee of even being able to follow it." The decision made, Luke shifted into command mode. "Let's circle the building and find the exits. I want two on the front door and two on the back. If we need to hold more ingress points, we can worry about that then."

They found a third entrance and set up a team there. Since two of the doors were within eyesight of each other, he left Pablo and Sam, along with Brutus, to cover one, and Ahmed and Jung-sook took the other. He wanted both of the local wolves with him to observe. He and Roxi could handle anything they'd find with a single vampire.

Someone exiting the building at a fortuitous time let them in without having to resort to more covert methods. Since the feeling was coming from above them, they entered the nearest elevator, pushing the buttons for every floor so they could check each. While they ascended, Luke took a minute to look Roxi over. They'd pushed all the buttons so that the elevator was forced to stop at each floor, though there weren't many. It allowed them a moment to assess if they were on the right level.

"I like the coat." Luke checked out Roxi's stylish knee-length trench coat.

"Yeah, I picked it up in Paris and haven't had a chance to wear it." She lifted the hem, revealing the bronze edging of the bottom of her scale mail then the silver of the scales. "Covers my armor and looks good."

Plucking at his hoodie, he shrugged. "It's cuter than my hoodie, but then I don't feel bad when one of my crappy hoodies gets ruined."

"It didn't cost much. I got it at one of those cheap fashion places."

"Oh, that's good. I lost a few too many good hoodies before I bought these in bulk." Luke hoped the mundane conversation would help settle the nerves of their guests.

Erin seemed even paler than normal, while Alejandro fidgeted excessively, unable to stand still. He almost looked like a kid who needed to use the bathroom.

"Erin, Alejandro. When we get to the right floor, stay behind us. Vampires have claws as well as fangs, so avoid grappling. As a wolf, you can take a fair bit of damage, but a swipe at your throats or eyes could cause some pretty bad injuries or kill you. Roxi and I are equipped to deal with vampires and have killed thousands over the centuries. Let us take care of this pest and show you what the process is like." He looked to Roxi, squeezing her hand. "Let's be careful and get the phone before it gets covered in goo. I don't want to lose the reason we're here. When we get to the floor, avoid talk of anything supernatural. There's probably enough background noise from other apartments, but let's be careful in case this fanger is sharper-eared than most. Once we're off the elevator, find the fire exit first in case we need to escape or follow."

"Of course, dōšagīh." Roxi smiled. The elevator stopped on the fourth floor, and the door opened. "Alright. This is the one. The sense feels a bit more level."

"Yeah." Luke reached out and caught the door before it could close.

The four of them stepped off and let the door close behind them.

Fortunately, the exit was clearly marked with lighted signs and arrows. With a safe exit found, they homed in on the vamp's location. When they found what felt like the right apartment, Luke stepped out of the way, pulling his gladius from its sheath on his back. Roxi drew her sword and stood in front of the door. Erin and Alejandro waited on the other side of the door so that the only person visible through the peephole would be the deadly and heavily armed woman.

Roxi knocked. When no one came to the door, she knocked again. Luke heard a faint metal click.

"Gun," he mouthed to Roxi.

She caught it out of the corner of her eye and gave the faintest of nods. Luke waved Erin and Alejandro further back. The sound of the chain sliding in its frame was far louder. Luke kept his breathing shallow and steady, trying to control the tension in his body. It was ready to uncoil and strike. The door opened a crack. Roxi turned her head, and her face went slack.

"Come in, pretty," the vamp said, his voice oily and seductive. "I love it when they deliver."

The door opened wider, and Roxi stepped in, hiding her blade behind her leg as she entered the room.

"What the hell?" the vamp said.

A moment later, the gun clattered to the ground accompanied by a short scream. Luke stepped into the room, waving his observers in with him. Alejandro pulled the door shut behind him. On the ground, the vampire lay on his back, Roxi's rudis sticking out of his chest. Luke smiled, impressed at her efficiency. She'd sliced his gun-holding hand off, then stabbed him through the heart, all while only getting a small yell. Luke picked up the hand and pried the gun from its grip, pocketing it.

Erin, her face pale and a bit green, raised an eyebrow at him.

"Sorry, standard procedure is to pick up all weapons we find on the vampires. They're usually pretty good quality, and it helps outfit our armory. I'd recommend it, especially if your personal weapons are all registered. Not sure what the gun laws are here, but it's best to have less traceable options if you're going to be fighting vampires. By taking them from the vampires, you can get some impressive hardware."

Roxi smiled at Erin and Alejandro. "You might want to step back. As dumb as this one was, it's likely to be a young vampire. You wouldn't want to mess up your shoes."

Luke took a step back. The Maine wolves followed Luke's

example and stepped back as well. Roxi knelt next to the vampire and wrapped her hands around the hilt of her rudis, placing her forehead on the pommel. She whispered the words of the incantation that activated the rudis Mithras had given her and sent a white light sliding down the hilt into the vamp's body and back up again until it disappeared into her head.

"Hold off on pulling the rudis, Roxi. Search his pockets. Grab his wallet and his phone and any keys you may find." Luke turned to the two werewolves. "Looks like the kitchen is right there and the restroom over there. If you're going to throw up, don't do it on the floor; we don't want to clean it up. Also, try to keep the smell of the vampire in mind, so you can log that in your mental catalog of scents."

Both of them looked a little green around the gills. Stepping back so he wasn't in their way in case they needed to dash to a safe place to throw up, he nodded to Roxi. She stood and pulled the rudis from the vamp's chest, hopped back. The vampire started its decomposition process, sinking in on itself as it lost cohesion, then collapsing into a spreading pile of goo. Luke was surprised when Erin stood still, watching, while Alejandro bolted for the kitchen and vomited in the sink. Roxi moved around the spreading puddle to stand next to Luke. Once Alejandro finished, he rinsed out the sink.

"Wipe your prints off anything you've touched." Luke turned to Roxi. "Find what we were looking for?"

"Yes. He had all three on him, though it wouldn't hurt to sweep the apartment quickly." Roxi searched the living room before checking out the bedroom and bathroom.

Alejandro rejoined them, though he avoided looking at the pile of goo. Remembering a conversation he'd had with Pablo not long after they'd first met, Luke stepped into the kitchen and, with his hands covered, opened the cabinet under the sink and got lucky, finding a box of kitchen garbage bags. Luke snagged two and walked out into the room with the dead vampire.

Opening the bag, he used it to pick up the goo soiled shirt of the vampire and pulled it inside the bag. Then he sealed up the bag and dumped it into the other bag to add a bit of security. Roxi raised an eyebrow but didn't ask.

Once Luke and Roxi had everything they needed, Luke grabbed the doorknob with his hoodie sleeve and held it open for everyone. He followed them out, shutting the door behind him. As his phone buzzed in his pocket, he held up his hand.

"Looks like we need to head down the stairs. Cops are coming up the front way." Luke pointed toward the stairs and took off at a brisk walk. "Someone must have called in a check about the scream. We'll hold up at the bottom to make sure it's clear."

Luke kept his hands inside his sleeves. His three companions followed his example, only touching things with cloth covered hands to avoid laying down fingerprints. They took the stairs quickly without raising a din in the echo-y concrete cinder block stairwell. When they arrived at the bottom, the temperature dropped as the poorly sealed outside door let in a gust. He pulled out his phone to text, receiving the all-clear from Sam.

Luke held the door open, then shut it quietly, joining Sam and Pablo. Brutus wagged his tail at the sight of Luke, though he remained silent. Without a word, their group walked away from the flashing red and blue lights parked out front and back onto the shadowy side streets. They used the cover of the trees to get away from the cops in case they swept the area, though he doubted they would unless they kicked in the apartment door.

Once they made it a few blocks away, they rejoined Jung-sook and Ahmed under a giant, leafless tree. The night breeze created a creaky clacking sound as branches moved against each other. Out of the corner is his eye, Luke checked out Erin and her second. Alejandro was pale but less green than earlier. Erin looked concerned, a wrinkle running down the center of her forehead.

"Anything from the other teams?" Luke asked.

"Nothing. No contacts," Sam replied.

Luke thought about it for a moment, looking at the troubled faces of Erin and Alejandro. "Let's call it for the night. We found one and got what we were looking for."

It was a start. They'd had a relatively easy hunt with a safe and successful conclusion. Their hosts got a firsthand look at what the process was like right down to a decaying vampire. They'd have questions, but those could wait for tomorrow after they had a night to sit. They walked a few more blocks before splitting up into their original groups to return to their vehicles. Erin called their driver.

When they settled into the bed-and-breakfast, Luke and Roxi assisted each other out of their armor, then Luke helped her clean her sword, taking care of the steel one while she cleaned the rudis. When they finished, Luke stuffed the garbage bag with the soiled shirt into the room's mini fridge.

"Why did you grab that shirt?" Roxi asked, finally.

Luke chuckled, scratching behind Brutus's ear. "A while ago, we were trying to find a vamp so we could collect his clothes to train some others on the scent. We couldn't find a single one for weeks. I figured I'd get ahead of that problem in case we needed it."

"Good thinking." Roxi checked the time, then smiled at Luke. "It's still early. Want to find a movie and snuggle in bed?"

Nodding, he leaned over and kissed her. "That sounds perfect."

After breakfast, Alejandro and a local wolf Luke hadn't met picked them up and took them back to the large brick building where they'd had breakfast on their first day. Alejandro explained it was the pack's building, and they used it as a community center and meeting hall. When they arrived, he escorted them upstairs.

Erin was waiting with full pots of coffee. Once everyone was situated, Erin took the spot at the head of the table and leaned forward with her elbows resting on the wood. The troubled look she'd worn since last night hadn't lessened much, if any.

"Last night, that was something," she said. "It was so fast and casual…"

"Between us, Roxi and I have almost thirty-nine hundred years of vampire hunting experience. It doesn't usually go that smoothly. We caught a newer vampire off guard and made him pay for it."

"How do you know how old it was?" Alejandro asked.

"It turned to sludge when it died," Roxi replied.

Nodding, Luke looked at Erin. "I don't have exact ages, because I've only been able to make an educated guess based on accents and language, so it could be off for a number of reasons, but the transition point seems to be around a hundred or so years old. If they're younger, they turn into that nasty goo you saw and smelled last night. Older, they turn into a dusty powder. It's like they become desiccated over time and are only held together by the magic of their kind."

"Are there any good vampires?" Erin asked.

Luke shook his head. "No." He sat back in his chair and stared above Erin's head for a moment. "How much do you know about vampires? How they were created? How a person is turned into a vampire?"

Erin shrugged. "Nothing really concrete… Just what you see in movies or read in books, so nothing real, I guess."

"I'm going to ask for a suspension of disbelief. What I'm about to tell you is a combination of very ancient history and personally witnessed events. The things I didn't see were witnessed by one I trust who was there at the beginnings of it all."

Erin's mouth hung open, her eyes wide in shock. "There's someone older than you?" She blushed. "I'm sorry. I didn't mean to be rude about your age."

Luke chuckled. "I'm not offended by it. To my knowledge, I'm the oldest living human. Roxi is a few years younger than me. I'm including werewolves in this as well, since they still have the piece that makes them fundamentally human — the soul."

He took a drink of his coffee, gathering his thoughts. "There may be vampires older than I am. They've been around a lot longer than I have, but the reason I don't include them is that they aren't human any longer; they no longer possess a soul. When a vampire turns a victim into a new vampire, part of the process is the stripping of the soul. It's ripped violently from the body. The process is excruciating. Have you seen *The Princess Bride*, when Humperdinck moves the lever to fifty on the life-sucking machine?"

Erin nodded.

"It's very much like that, but worse. A vampire's victim isn't mostly dead. They're all the way dead, and to make room for what it needs to become undead, the soul is removed."

"Where does the soul go? And what replaces it?" Alejandro asked.

Luke shrugged. "I don't know where the soul goes. As far as I know, it could be destroyed entirely during the process. But what replaces it? That's a bit of a complex answer, though I don't know the full extent of it. I don't even think my source knows everything that's involved. Let's just say it concerns some very dark gods." Luke wasn't ready to get into a deep philosophical conversation about ancient gods and the evils they committed. He looked around for a carafe of coffee. "Mind if I refill my cup?"

Erin shook her head.

Luke returned to his seat after topping up his coffee, letting the roasty aroma soothe him. "What rises isn't the person who died. They'll have the memories and some of the personality, but all traces of humanity—kindness, decency, compassion—will be gone. Your own mother, if she were turned, would try to feed on you."

"Can werewolves be turned?" Erin asked, fear twisting her features.

"No. The magic that makes the werewolves prevents them from being turned. Also, since we're talking about werewolves, a vampire's glamour won't work on a werewolf—at least I've never seen it. Perhaps if there was a vampire strong enough and a wolf weak enough… Anyway, it's a nice bonus for werewolves."

"If wolves can't be turned, why would they take our people?" Erin asked.

"Food. Vampires like variety in their diet. Also, with a wolf's enhanced healing, a fanger can feed more regularly from one. Vampires also can't get high or drunk, not directly. They can only consume intoxicants via their blood bags. You'll often find vampires running drug dens, giving humans free drugs to get them high so they can then feed on them. There are those who willingly serve and feed vampires—thralls—but a lot of that is the subtle coercion of glamour."

"Silver and wood kill vampires, but you have to stab them in the heart to get the kill." Roxi tapped her chin, thinking. "You can remove their heads, but if someone holds the head in place, the vampire will live. They don't respire, so you can't choke them out. They use air for speaking, but other than that, I don't know what else. It's hard to out-damage a vampire. Your best bet is to remove their weapons—hands and teeth—then they're easier to kill."

"They're fast. Blindingly so. In some cases, they can move faster than werewolves, though I don't know if they can out-muscle a truly powerful werewolf," Sam added.

"Anyway, back to the creation of a vampire. When a new vampire is turned, they are immensely powerful but have no control over their blood lust. They will destroy any living creature." Luke looked at his friends, then leaned a bit closer to Erin. "I think that's what happened on the planes that went down. We saw some leaked reports about 'passengers going berserk' and murdering people, then tearing their way into the cockpit. My guess is they killed every passenger, then went looking for the only living beings left—the pilots."

"They haven't mentioned anything like that on the news," Alejandro said, his voice quiet and weak.

Luke shrugged. "It's hard to tell what a government will release —what's being controlled through natural government secrecy or by vampires controlling the narrative through their pawns. It'll be a matter of reading between the lines."

"You mean there are vampires in the government?" Erin asked, eyes wide.

"Yeah, at least there were in Portland. They were controlling one of the city commissioners and trying to get him elected mayor. He was also the police commissioner, and between the human pawn and the vampires, they'd completely compromised the Portland Police."

Alejandro stood and found a glass and some water. He didn't look like he was taking the news very well, though Erin didn't look much better. Shifting world views so radically can cause a lot of mental trauma.

Erin looked at Sam. "Is this…" She gestured vaguely around her. "Is this all true?"

Luke couldn't blame her for checking in with a werewolf. He'd seen this a few times over his millennia of life when he clued in someone new. The desire to cling to the last vestiges of their comfortable blissful ignorance was nearly universal.

Sam nodded, giving Erin a sympathetic look. "Every word of it. One of the worst aspects is that the vampires have been recruiting werewolf packs as their muscle and underlings. We've been dealing with that for the last couple of years."

Erin startled. "Years?"

Luke nodded. "A couple years ago, my friend Pieter, who was the son of the packleader of the Flanders Pack, asked for help. The vampires were making a major incursion into their southern territory. When we showed up, the vamps orchestrated a kidnapping of the packleader, or so we thought. It turned out that Pieter's brother had betrayed his father to the vampires for his own gain. He murdered his father to secure the support of the vampires."

Sighing, Luke shook his head sadly. "Secretly, he'd been purging non-white members of the pack and, at least on one occasion, trafficked children to the vampires. And this wasn't the only pack the vampires had been taking over." Luke gestured toward Simone.

"Before making their move against Flanders, they took my pack. They provided wealth to those who wanted to replace our leaders and purge our ranks. They killed my parents and gave my little brother to the vampires. We were able to rescue him, but they wiped out all the dissidents. The pack became complete servants of the vampires, serving as their soldiers. Vampires and their pet werewolves do not like the 'other.'"

"We suspect that they also took over several other small packs along the French-Belgian border. They were operating with impunity along the border and launching their assaults into the French-speaking portion of Belgium." Luke took a drink from his coffee, trying to force the jetlag to stay at bay.

Erin's eyes flicked between Alejandro and Sam. "Is this happening in the United States?"

"We haven't seen it yet, at least that we know of," Sam replied. "We've been spreading out and helping wolf packs who want to clean out the vamps from their areas, but we've been operating on a by-request basis. We've not been quiet about what we're doing around Portland and southwest Washington. We've had delegations come in to undergo training, but we haven't tried to move into a city and then met resistance."

"It would probably be best to assume they are. This is a big country with a lot of space." Luke looked at Sam and Pablo. "Correct me if I'm wrong, but the wolf packs here aren't as connected as they are in Europe, where everything is closer and older."

Pablo nodded. "That's a fair assessment."

"It very well could be happening in large numbers, and we're just not aware of it yet." Luke gave Erin an understanding smile. "I'm sorry we've unloaded a whole lot onto you in the last few minutes, but I think your pack is in danger if they're kidnapping your wolves off the streets. It's a hell of a world to have revealed like this. I think big things are afoot, and through a twist of fate, we're in your territory. While we're waiting to learn more about what's going on with the airplanes and airports, we can help you get on a decent footing so you can protect your people."

Sam reached out and patted Erin's forearm. "He's right, Erin. I've known Luke for several years now. He's a good man, and he knows what he's talking about when it comes to vampires. We can't 'live and let live' with vampires because they're coming after us. They're coming after wolves. I haven't seen true horrors like Luke has, but what I've seen is bad enough. Holly speaks highly of you. She says you're a good leader who really cares about her pack and her community. Well, we're here right now, and we can provide the expertise to ensure you can keep on caring for your pack and your community." Sam exchanged a look with Pablo. "Do you have contacts with other local packs? Could you invite them for a meeting so we can bring them in as well?"

"That's a good idea. Get everyone on the same footing all at once," Luke said.

Erin nodded, her face going from scared to sure and determined. "There's a small pack in rural Maine, plus we're on good terms with the New Hampshire and Vermont Packs. There are a few on the other side of the Canadian border that we keep in regular contact with, but there's rumor of the border being closed until they can get more answers about the plane crashes."

"Reach out to them as well. We can teleconference them in or they can go four-paws across the border through the woods. This is really important, Erin." Sam gave her an encouraging smile.

"Alright." Erin looked at Alejandro. "Gather up the rest of the council. I want to meet in an hour. I'll start calling the other pack-leaders and see if we can get something set up for tomorrow or the day after at the latest. I'll impress upon them the urgency."

Luke nodded. "I'll be at your disposal to help explain things and answer questions when you have the other packleaders here." He looked at his friends. "We'll get out of your way while you get things organized. We could use lunch and time to make our own plans. Again, I'm sorry to drop this all on you, but the times aren't gentle."

Luke stood and gestured for everyone to follow. Sam walked over to Erin and squeezed her shoulder, giving her a half hug before joining Luke and the rest of the team.

When they stood outside, Luke turned to the crew. "Let everyone else know they're free to explore the town and have some time off, but be ready to go tonight if Erin wants to take another swing through town."

THEY KEPT business talk to a minimum since the restaurant where they stopped for lunch was full with the local work crowd. They went to Allagash Brewing after lunch, figuring it would be less likely to have a large crowd during the middle of the work week, and they could enjoy one of the popular local institutions while they were there.

"I almost thought we spooked her too hard," Delilah said.

"Yeah, after last night and then dropping a ton of bricks on her, I thought she might ask us to leave so she could go back to living in ignorance." Luke took a drink of his Allagash White.

"She came around at the end," Sam said. "Holly wasn't wrong about her. She's a good leader and a good person. I had faith in her."

"I guess we'll find out for sure later today after she talks to the rest of her pack leadership," Roxi said, taking a tentative sip of her Allagash Tripel.

"Yeah. They could override her, though I doubt they'd go against her and Alejandro," Simone said.

Pablo nodded. "I was watching his face toward the end. We shook him, but he was rallying." Pablo drank deeply from an Allagash White, sighing happily. "You know. This might even be better than my wit, but I guess that's what they're known for." He looked at Luke. "If we have time, I really do want to get that tour she offered to hook us up with."

Luke chuckled. He loved Pablo. His friend worked hard both for his pack and helping Luke slay vampires, but he also liked to play hard. A brewery tour would be a bit of both since he'd invariably get ideas to take back to his own brewery, though with the extended travel, he had less to do with the day-to-day operations lately.

"We should have time, and it's good to get some rest and relaxation to keep us fresh and on our toes. We're going to need to be extra alert since there's a lot going on that we're not privy to. Speaking of which, y'all seen anything new from the available sources regarding the reason we're here in the first place?"

"We've got beers and a quiet table out of the way." Sam looked at her phone. "And a good Wi-Fi connection. Let's do some research. Just be sure you have the security features Jamaal installed active. Wouldn't want to be traced." She made eye contact with everyone, collecting nods of acknowledgment. "I'll see if Holly has updates."

"That's not a bad idea," Luke said, pulling out his phone. "Let's see what we can scrounge up. I'll look through the local and regional news and see if I can find any of the signs that usually precede these kinds of toothy mishaps. Everybody else, hit the national and international news about the crashes."

Luke hit the various news sites for the New England region, including the various small-town papers and local boards, taking a brief break to order another Allagash White before diving back into his research. Sam, who'd brought her laptop, had her nose buried in it as she sent emails bouncing around back home to gather information from her sources in Portland. Occasionally, one of the others would check in to make sure they weren't all looking at the same articles about the crashes.

After a while, Luke called for everyone to set down their devices and report in. He started. "The patterns are right. Something's happening around here or has been a for a while. But it's going slower than it did in Portland when we met."

"I wonder why." Sam pursed her lips contemplatively.

"Could be they decided they went too fast in Portland and got caught, or it could be that this is a less densely populated area, at least until you get into Massachusetts or New York. It was hard to discern at first, but when you look back far enough and you see the consistent pattern, you can tell the vamps are cooking something locally." Luke took a drink of his beer.

"How far does it go?" Pablo asked. "Is it just Maine?"

"No, it's more widespread. I'm seeing disappearances and dead bodies all across the region."

Delilah laughed. "You could teach a course on research. That's some high-level data crunching."

Luke smiled and nodded, acknowledging Delilah's compliment. "Sam, what news from back home?"

"Not much, actually. Holly has the pack on high alert. She's called in extra shifts at the ammo factory to stockpile extras."

"Wish we could get hold of some of that stockpile here. We're looking pretty light on ammo." Pablo looked down at his nearly empty glass and then drained it. "And I'm looking even lighter on my beer."

Luke chuckled. "Yeah. Once Erin talks to the pack, we'll have to see what resources they have and get some more made if we're going to be here for a while. Also, if we're going to have to go cross-country, I don't want to do it without proper precautions. Put a pin in this, but we should start planning our evacuation and look at acquiring vehicles to transport ourselves. If we can, let's purchase so we don't have to deal with rentals, and we can make any mods we need."

"Sounds good. Let's look at tomorrow for a planning meeting

with the rest of the team so we can have all our ducks in a row and assign tasks." Sam typed some notes on her computer.

"What about the rest of you? Pablo?" Luke asked.

"I started with Spanish-language outlets. Lot of confusion, a lot of different statements from different governments. The details are coming together on the various crashes. So far, they all seem to have the same details. One passenger goes wild and brutally starts killing the others before killing the pilots. I don't see any other causes at this point. Saw a few governments not reporting anything. The one thing I started to see, though only a few mentions, was that it might be the work of an unknown terrorist organization. So far, they're saying no one has claimed responsibility for the crashes."

Luke nodded. "Delilah?"

"Largely the same, though I started with US papers and then moved to UK and Australian news sources. I saw a few mentions of possible terrorism there, mostly the US and the UK—the usual governments to always look for terrorists to blame, though they haven't mentioned any of the usual suspects."

Luke nodded. "Simone?"

"Right. I started with French language papers. I'm seeing the same. A few mentions of terrorism. I reached out to a friend in Senegal to see if she'd heard anything... Wait. She just emailed back."

"Go ahead," Luke said.

Simone opened the email. "Sam, I'm sending you a video."

"OK, I'll play it on the screen." She flipped the computer around. "I can't read the script. It looks like Arabic."

"It is," Roxi said. "It says this video was taken when a plane was grounded in Morocco. Oh, my... The vampire didn't activate until they were on the ground and unloading the plane."

The video started on the plane as someone launched from a seat. Soon, screams filled the video as people shoved and dove out of the way. Sam hit the mute button quickly before they drew attention. They could literally see blood flying as the assailant worked its way down the aisle. The angle shifted to someone standing outside the plane in a small group of the already unloaded passengers. They'd turned toward the plane at the sound of screaming people running and shoving to get out of the plane. Soon, the attacker got out of the plane and made straight for the crowd. Whoever was recording kept the camera trained on the attacker for a few more seconds before everything descended into chaos. Luke could see the blood-covered attacker—claws and long fangs dripped with gore and viscera, and its hateful eyes burned with ravenous fury.

"Sam, download that video before it gets scrubbed," Luke said.

"R…r…right." She turned the computer around so she could save the video. "OK. Got it."

Luke's stomach dropped. He took no pleasure in being right. "I don't think we need to see anymore."

There was a palpable sense of relief around the table when Sam closed the video. They'd all seen heavy fighting against vampires, but only Luke and probably Roxi had seen a baby vamp turn into a human shredder. The ferocity and wantonness of it all got to even his hardened vampire slayer's heart. In a way, he was glad for a couple reasons. One, it demonstrated that his friends hadn't become too hardened or jaded to the violence of vampire slaying, and two, it was a good reminder of how dangerous vampires truly could be.

"Now we know for sure it's vampires." Luke shook his head. "That was a brutally coordinated and executed plan. Each turned human was a time bomb waiting to go off." He turned to Simone. "Did your friend know if they took out the vamp?"

"Um, says guards shot it, but it took well over a hundred rounds to 'kill' it."

Luke shook his head, pursing his lips in disgust. "It'll start to heal and keep going, even hungrier because of the need to recuperate and its interrupted first feeding. I don't know if Holly has connections in Morocco, but if there's a pack there, we should tell them how to deal with this."

"We should probably check in with Jean-Paul, too," Simone said. "There are Moroccan wolves in the Parisian pack; they'll know people back home."

"Good thinking, Simone," Delilah said, smiling at her girlfriend.

"If Erin can get the other packleaders here, we have some

compelling evidence for them." Luke lifted his beer and saluted Simone.

"I'm sending it to Holly right now. I'll also email Jean-Paul about his Morocco connections and send him this video." Sam was busy clacking away on her keyboard.

"That wasn't the news we really wanted, but it's good to know. I'm going to buy us a round of research rewards. Be right back." Pablo stood up and walked to the cooler displaying Allagash's specialty bottles.

Pablo made an excited sound and waved Luke over to help him. "Dude! They make lambic-style beers." Pablo started grabbing several off the shelf, handing a few to Luke.

He bought one of the brewery's Gueuze-style "Coolship" beers and dropped them off at the bar for the bartenders to open and serve them.

Once they arrived, he raised his glass. "Here's to surviving another round of hell with the best people I have the privilege of knowing."

"And to new friends and allies!" Sam said.

They touched glasses and took their first tastes of the funky and tart beer. They studiously put away their electronics for the moment and talked lightly, avoiding the darkness of their world for a few minutes. After the brutality of the baby vampire going berserk, they needed a bit of a mental palate cleanser to reset the mood at the table.

Erin had arranged for the local packleaders to visit Portland and meet with Luke. After they'd showed her, Alejandro, and a few of the other leaders of the Portland Pack the video they'd found, she sent it to the other packleaders, increasing the urgency of her appeal. Disturbed by all she'd heard and seen in the video, she asked for another night sweeping Portland to find any traces of vampires and their missing wolves.

Unfortunately, they'd come up empty. They'd even returned to the building, hoping a werewolf nose could pick up fresh vamp scents, but that was a dead end as well. All the scents were either humans or a full day old. Luke could tell Erin was frustrated, even if she understood Luke's explanation. Jamaal was working on the phone and hoped to be able to provide some more information.

The next day, using the large room where they'd first had breakfast in Portland, Luke gathered their entire team together to begin planning their cross-country trip home. Sooner or later, they'd have to leave, and they wanted to be able to do it on a moment's notice. After they laid down the basics of the plan, part of the crew went out to visit sporting goods stores to stock up on the equipment they'd need to manufacture their special anti-vamp shotgun shells. Luke, Delilah, and Roxi, along with help from one of the local wolves to act as a guide, were in charge of hitting up thrift and pawn shops to acquire all the cheap silver they could lay their hands on. They figured the three humans would be the best choice to handle that task. People getting sudden burns from the silver might raise questions around town that they didn't feel like answering. Erin had been gracious enough to provide a small empty building for them to gather materials and manufacture their shells.

After a busy day, Luke wasn't ready to meet with strangers, but he had little choice. A brief shower and a change into nice clothes would have to serve to refresh him. Tonight, he'd planned to bring his leadership team to the dinner Erin had planned at the Pack Hall, as the locals called it. At least he'd have Roxi by his side. When they got the knock on their door announcing their ride, Luke grabbed the case with their swords and armor, and Roxi clipped on Brutus's leash.

Erin picked them up.

"Hey, I wanted to give you a quick brief on who you're meeting tonight," Erin said, putting the minivan into drive. "George McKenzie is the packleader of the Vermont Pack. He's kind of exactly what you'd expect from a Vermonter. He's a little bit old hippy, a lot outdoorsy, and a generally affable guy. I'm quite fond of him. Roger Corbin is the 'alpha' of the New Hampshire Pack. Be careful with him. He's a bit touchy. He's quite wealthy and wants you to know it. He's pretty hoity-toity. I can never get a real gauge on the man or where he stands.

"There's a small pack of rural wolves that span up and down the northern parts of Maine. They're a bit rough around the edges, but Mary Lefevre is a good egg. Don't let her get you into a pool game where money's involved. She'll hustle you right out of your wallet, then try to drink you under the table. As long as you don't piss her off, I don't think you'll have any trouble with her. Offer a vampire to punch, and she'll help ya pick the fight. She and her crew usually get along well with mine. Lots of huntin' and fishin' trips together." She reached over and turned the radio, already low, off.

"I have a couple people comin' up from Bangor as well. They're part of my pack, but they mostly run themselves locally. They're on board already. Don't like the idea of vampires kidnapping their friends and family. We also have a couple Canadian packs that'll be teleconferencing in after we have dinner—the St. Johns Pack from New Brunswick and a smaller Quebecoise pack that operates near the border. The St. Johns Pack are good folks. Their leader used to date Mary for a bit, but they're still good friends. Her name is Rochelle. The Sherbrooke pack has a new leader, and I don't know him well—Maurice Debelier."

"OK. I'll keep all that in mind. Any hot button local issues I should avoid if people try to get me maneuvered into them?" Luke asked.

"No. I'll keep an eye on things and put the kibosh on any off-topic discussions."

When they pulled up, she stopped the car and turned to Luke. "Thank you for all you've done to help us out. I know we're not your pack, and you just happened to land here, but it's appreciated."

Luke bowed his head respectfully. "I'm glad we can be of use. I guess lately I'm in the business of helping and working with were-wolves. Thanks for taking such good care of us while we're here."

"You ready, Luke, Roxi?" Erin asked.

"As we'll ever be. Much better prepped than I'd anticipated. Thanks for all the good details."

"Alrighty, let's do it." Erin opened her door, then opened the rear so they could grab their gear and Brutus.

She took them inside, and they set the gear out of the way but where Luke and Roxi could keep an eye on it. Roxi unclipped Brutus, and he wandered toward the food and water bowl. Erin made brief introductions, merely mentioning that they were from the other Portland. She'd arranged a couple kegs, the Allagash White and a Maine Beer Company Lunch IPA as well as cocktails and wine. Luke and his leadership team—Delilah, Pablo, Sam, Simone, and now Roxi—mingled with the various packleaders and the seconds they'd brought with them. Sam functioned as the lead for the wolves of their group with Pablo as the second. Even though Sam's only position was as a member of the pack's council, she spoke directly for Holly and the pack recognized her as the leader in

Holly's absence. Since she traveled with Luke so much, they'd jokingly referred to her as the out-of-town packleader. Pablo, as always, was content to support Holly or Sam.

When dinner was served, they made their way to their assigned seats. Erin had arranged the assignments so Luke and his people would be spread out among the various visiting werewolves, allowing them to meet as many people as possible and begin the bonding process. The food was excellent and featured local seasonal items and Maine's famous lobsters.

Erin sat Luke next to Mary and Roger. Mary flirted with him outrageously, trying to make him blush, while Roger spent most of the time rolling his eyes and making sounds of disgust at Mary's antics. Luke couldn't be sure, but he guessed Mary's flirtation was in large part to irritate the New Hampshire packleader. Although Luke was typically awkward with such sallies at him, he enjoyed her outrageous flare, even if he spent too much time blushing.

When they finished dinner, Erin called a brief pause to clear the tables and for everyone to take a bathroom break or to refresh their beverages. Luke and his friends gathered out of the way to do a quick check in.

"First impressions?" Luke asked.

"I like George. He's a likable fellow," Sam said. "Mary's a lot of troublemaker, but I'd sure like to go out drinking with her. Brutus likes her." She pointed to where Mary was giving the giant dog a good leg thumping back scratch. "Not sure I'm a fan of Roger or his second. Sorry. *'Beta.'*" She rolled her eyes.

"Not a fan of the term 'beta'?" Simone asked.

"Depends on who's using it. Roger seems like the alphahole type and so is his beta." Sam shook her head.

"You sat next to him at dinner. What are your thoughts?" Delilah asked Luke.

"That he's stuffy and arrogant. He doesn't think much of Mary, so Mary tries to be outrageous to push his buttons."

"She's sure doing a good job flirting with you," Delilah said, a grin on her face. "She's being so obvious even you couldn't miss it."

Luke chuckled. "I think it's mostly to annoy Roger, but it's always nice to be flirted with." He winked at Roxi, who winked back.

The Portland crew were moving the tables into rows and setting up a wide screen monitor with a camera on top.

"OK, everyone! Five minute warning. Luke, Sam. I have your people here." Erin pointed to a table lined out in a row with all the chairs on one side.

The rest of the tables were lined up, but their chairs all faced toward the tables Luke and his team would be sitting at. The TV was set up, so it was also facing toward their table.

"Looks like they set up a panel and we're the panelists," Delilah said.

Pablo cleared his throat, affecting an annoying voice. "This isn't so much a question as a comment…"

Delilah swatted Pablo's shoulder. "Begone with you, nerd!"

They had a good chuckle, then headed to their table. Luke and Sam took the center two chairs, the rest fanning out to either side. A few minutes later, the screen blinked on, split in half, with two people huddling together on one side and a single person on the other side. Erin introduced the people teleconferencing in. The single person was Maurice, while the two people were Rochelle and her second, Wayne. Rochelle and Wayne seemed friendly and curious. Maurice, on the other hand, looked disinterested and haughty.

After she introduced the new attendees, she gestured toward Sam. "I'd like to formally introduce you to Sam Wakamatsu. She's married to Holly Olsen, the packleader of the North Portland Pack, and she's their leader in the absence of Holly. Pablo Sandoval is the pack second. Simone Ndiaye is a newer member of their pack, originally from France. Sam, I'll let you introduce the rest."

Sam stood up. "Thanks, Erin. Thank you for letting us speak with you. It's been a long, weird trip getting here, and I'm about to make it weirder. First up is Delilah Johnson. She's our pack's unarmed combat instructor. Next to her is Roxi Surena, a vampire hunter. And the man sitting next to me is a council member of our pack and the leader of our expedition. This is Luke. He's a vampire hunter and leads our fight against them. In some circles, he's known as the Centurion Immortal."

After a few moments of stunned silence, the chatter started as people checked with their neighbors. George was the first to look back toward the front, holding his hand up.

Erin held up her hand to bring the room back to attention. "Go ahead, George."

George directed his question to Erin. "Vampire hunters? Two of them? Are they for real?"

"We are for real. Everyone at this table has killed vampires to defend their homes and families. Roxi and I have just been doing it a lot longer than everyone else."

"How long?" Mary asked, her eyes serious for the first time that evening.

"Roxi and I have been doing it for over nineteen-hundred years."

"Combined?" Mary blurted out.

"Each," Roxi replied.

"I've never heard of anyone that old, not even the oldest were-wolf," Roger said, skepticism filling his eyes and dripping from every word. "Do you expect us to believe that?"

"We believe him and follow him," Sam said, her normal bright tone gone, replaced by one backed by pure steel.

When Sam needed to be, she could be utterly ruthless. Apparently when the man who'd annoyed her in the brief time she'd known him called into question their integrity, it brought out that Sam. She stared at him coldly, her face a mask of annoyed resolve.

Lightly clearing his throat, Roger's eyes flicked away, and he forced his body to relax as if it was no big thing, but he'd just backed down from Sam, and the whole room saw it.

Luke tried to hold in a laugh.

Erin cleared her throat. "Let's just act as if what he says is true. I've been on the phone with Jean-Paul of the Paris Pack. He assures me that Luke is who he says he is, and that he is a force to be reckoned with."

For the first time, Maurice spoke up through a thick French-Canadian accent. "I hear he is a force of destruction. So far he has brought down the Luxembourg Pack, facilitated the downfall of the Cologne alpha, replacing him with a puppet, and arranged a war against the Flanders Pack, tumbling the leadership of that pack as well. As one of the leaders involved, I'm not sure Jean-Paul is the most reliable of sources. Are you here to threaten our packs, too?"

Luke felt odd fixing his ire upon a TV screen. "Do you plan to conspire with vampires to sell me into slavery as did the leaders of Luxembourg, Flanders, and Cologne?" Luke let the question hang, allowing the tension to rise while he stared at Maurice.

Finally, Maurice broke. "Well, no… But…"

"If you don't work with vampires, you have nothing to fear from me. I'm not the enemy of werewolves. However, I don't allow betrayal to go unpunished. Let it be an object lesson to you if the vampires come a-knocking looking for an alliance." He looked around the room.

"For the vast majority of my time fighting vampires, I've not involved myself in the lives of the world's werewolf packs. It's only been recently that I've begun working with werewolves because the North Portland Pack was kind and befriended me. They joined my mission because they believed in protecting their community. We freed dozens of houseless people who'd been swept off the streets to feed vampires and to be conscripted into the vampire army as their foot soldiers. Since then, we've swept Portland free of vampires and expanded the safe zone to the neighboring communities."

Sam stood up. "The only reason we're here is a fortune of fate. This is where our plane was grounded after the vampire attacks on the airline industry. Erin asked for our help, and we said 'yes.' Erin cares about you all and wants to make sure that your communities are safe. If you've got any missing people, let us know and we'll keep an eye out for them."

Luke nodded. "Vampires can't turn a werewolf, but you make for tasty snacks when they want variety. Also, they don't need to turn you if they can buy your loyalty. We fought against several werewolf packs that became the jackboots of their fanged masters. I pity the people forced to become vampires—those who didn't choose it. I'll still slay them because I have to protect the living. But werewolves can choose if they join the legions of my enemies. I have little pity or mercy for those who choose to participate in the hateful crimes of vampirism. I'm not here to threaten you. I'm here to assist Erin, and she's looking out for you. Let me help you, but if you don't want it, I'll leave you alone. Unless you join with the vampires. Then you make me your enemy at your own peril."

"We'll give you time to discuss things in private. If you have questions, please save them and we'll answer them when you invite us back in." Sam turned to the rest of the table and signaled for them to follow her out of the room.

Luke bowed his head to Erin, then turned to follow Sam. As he turned, he caught a wink from Mary. Sam led them outside into the brisk night and to the opposite side of the building so there was no chance they'd be overheard.

"I do love it when you start speechifying, buddy." Pablo held his hand up for a high five.

Luke slapped five and smiled, shaking his head at his friend. Roxi sidled up next to him and under his arm, settling it around her shoulder.

"He doesn't speak a lot, but when he does, it's usually pretty good," Roxi said. "You look extra handsome when you're delivering firebrand speeches."

"He's kind of scary when gets ominous with his threats." Simone shivered.

"Yeah, Luke does scary pretty well," Sam said, patting Luke on the shoulder.

"Girl, you do scary yourself," Delilah said, chuckling. "I thought Old Rog was gonna wet his pants after you stared him down."

Simone laughed. "Yeah. It didn't take him long to back down."

"Should I tell Holly that you're now the alpha of the New Hampshire Pack?" Pablo waggled his eyebrows at Sam.

Luke smiled at his friends' good-natured banter. "Delilah's right. Everyone thinks Holly is the intimidating one. She's just reserved and professional. Sam is the real intimidation."

Sam affected an innocent expression. "Who, me? I'm just a fun lovin' gal!" She shook her head, waving her hair about like a ditz. "And it was fun to make that little jackass back down."

Luke appreciated his friends and how they had his back. He'd rarely known a group of people so entirely reliable as them who were good allies and even better friends. And that wasn't even counting the rest of the pack that had joined him to hunt vampires. Many of them he considered just as reliable, even if they weren't as close, but he felt like if he had the time, they'd become good friends as well. Some of his favorite times were these, where they were just goofing around. Times like those almost made him feel like a young and modern man instead of the ancient relic he was. Having a legion of trained hunters behind him like when he ran his own legion would have been nice, but he wouldn't trade this group of friends for anything in the world—even a legion.

"Um, excuse me," Alejandro said to draw their attention. "They're ready for you."

Luke nodded and waved everyone behind him. When they retook their seats, Luke felt a bit like the werewolves in front of them were their judges or juries.

Erin stood up. "There were a few last questions, then I think we can let you know our decisions. Roger?"

He nodded at Erin. "Do we have your assurance that if we choose to remain neutral, you'll leave our packs alone?"

"Yes," Luke replied. "I have no interest in making enemies where neutrality will suffice. Don't aid the vampires, and I'll leave you alone."

"Mary, you're next." Erin gestured toward Mary.

"What are you offering if we do join with you?" Mary looked Luke over like he was a slab of meat.

Luke flushed pink up to his cheeks. "We'll offer training on vampire hunting and slaying and help you set up the infrastructure to coordinate and work together. We'll train you on weapons and how to create anti-vamp ammunition."

Mary stared at Luke. "Any training for nighttime wrestling?"

"Mary, behave. The gentleman has a girlfriend. And if I'm not mistaken, she has a big, shiny, and very sharp sword." Erin shook her head and rolled her eyes. "Don't mind her, Luke. She's harmless."

"Oh, I'm far from harmless, but I'm just having fun."

"Are there any other questions? Or are we at the part of the evening where Mary makes lewd comments?" Erin asked.

"Honey, it's always lewd Mary time." Mary winked at Luke, then nodded at Roxi.

"Well, in that case," Erin proceeded, ignoring Mary, "Let's put it to the vote. The Portland-Bangor Pack will be working with our new friends."

"The Maine North Woods Pack will be joining with our Portland-Bangor friends," Mary said, all business.

"New Hampshire will remain neutral," Roger said, trying to look aloof and tough.

George fidgeted with the end of his long ponytail. "You know us, Erin. We'll help our friends in Maine. Vermont is in."

"St. Johns?" Erin asked.

Rochelle smiled and nodded. "We'll join you as well. Sounds fun."

"Sherbrooke will remain neutral, though we request the right to send an observer in case we change our minds." Maurice tried to look friendly, though his eyes were too hard to pull it off.

Erin looked at Luke. "Luke, Sam, what do you say?"

Sam shrugged.

"We'd welcome Sherbrooke's observer," Luke replied.

"Well, that seals it. I'll send out notes to everyone. St. Johns, do you think you can sneak some people over the border? We'd meet you up there with some vans and spare clothes."

"Sure thing, Erin. We'll send you some details, but plan for tomorrow afternoon." The St. Johns werewolves logged out, as did Maurice.

"Erin, I'll send some folks along tomorrow. I need to get home and report to the pack." George got up and walked toward Luke and his friends. "It's nice to meet y'all. Take good care of my packmates. I'll send them along with some Vermont beer." He shook hands with everyone, then gave Erin a hug before leaving.

Roger deigned to give them a nod before waving at Erin and disappearing. After George, Mary, and Roger left, as well as the associates they'd brought, Erin grabbed beers for everyone as they set up a table to be more cozy and friendly.

"I think that went pretty well." Erin took a deep drink of her beer. "I didn't hold out high hopes for Roger, but neutral is probably a good place for him to be."

"I hope he stays that way," Sam said. "I'd hate to have him start collaborating with vampires. That would split you from the Vermont Pack."

"Oh, I think he'll keep his nose out of things. He's comfortable and doesn't like change. I think you and Luke scare him. The packs you helped bring down are far richer and more powerful than Roger and New Hampshire, even if they think they're pretty swanky. They're nowhere in the same league as the European packs, even most of the medium-sized ones. He'll keep his nose clean because you'll come down like a ton of vengeful bricks on him."

Mary stepped back into the room. "Mind if I join you?"

"Not at all, Mary. As long as you behave yourself." Erin kicked a chair out for Mary.

Mary laughed. "When have I ever behaved myself? That's why you like me, Erin. I'm fun."

"Don't let her meet Owen." Delilah covered her eyes and shook her head.

"Oh, no!" Sam said. "That would be a disaster."

"What, is he stuffy like Roger?" Erin asked.

Pablo laughed. "No. The opposite. More like Mary. Their combined forces of chaos would be formidable."

Luke closed his eyes. "There wouldn't be anything left when they were done."

"Now I'm curious to meet this fella. Is he handsome?" Mary asked, sitting down after getting a full beer.

"You'll get to meet him tomorrow, assuming we don't send him away to prevent you two from joining forces." Sam raised her glass to Mary.

"I don't know. They could hate each other," Roxi said. "Sometimes that happens with people who are too much alike."

Mary looked at Roxi. "So, you're the one who landed this handsome hunk of a man?"

Roxi nodded.

"Good for you." Mary reached over and tapped Roxi's glass.

"He's also dating one of the pack doctors," Pablo added, winking at Luke.

"Got you a little harem, eh?" Mary barked a laugh. "You other Portlanders live up to your reputation. I'll have to remember that if I'm feeling lonely some night."

Luke choked on his beer, spluttering. Roxi patted him on the back while Mary laughed uproariously. Luke was going to have to keep an eye out for Mary. If nothing else, she'd make life interesting if he could keep from choking to death with well-timed surprises like that.

CHAPTER
SIX

T he leadership sent out a few teams to sweep through various neighborhoods, but they came up empty-handed again without even a sniff of a vamp. Luke and his team continued their planning while they waited for the late afternoon's first meeting with the combined pack alliance they'd forged. With time on their hands, they placed a few online orders for some items they were having trouble coming up with locally to be delivered, then they started combing the used car lots and local "for sale" boards to find what they'd need to build a caravan to move across country.

Erin organized a meeting outside town at one of the pack member's properties. It was a big, wooded area in the hills with plenty of privacy and a small shooting range. Luke wasn't sure how many people had experience with shotguns, but he still wanted to drill them on shotgun combat, which was a whole different game than sport shooting or hunting.

While they waited for everyone, Luke set up a course and wrote a list of supplies they'd need, including standard load twelve-gauge buckshot and slugs so they wouldn't have to waste their limited supply of anti-vamp ordnance. Periodically, he quirked an ear toward the driveway, anxious to get started but nervous about introducing more innocents to the deadly world of vampire hunting.

Once the various people who'd volunteered or been selected to train showed up, Luke ran them through the basics of anti-vampire weapons from the humble stake to their Winchester M12s.

"These are our preferred weapons when we're able to use guns. This is the Winchester M12 Trench Gun edition. It's got a shorter barrel which is great for confined spaces. Six rounds in the magazine. Best of all…" Luke lowered the ear shields and waited for everyone else to follow suit, then pulled the trigger and held it down, firing off all six rounds just by slamming the pump. When he lifted his ear protection, he waited until everyone else had. "…is the slam fire. Pull the trigger and slam shells into the firing chamber."

"Do you ever really need that kind of firepower?" a wolf asked.

"It's come in handy a few times. Vampires like to swarm. Our anti-vamp shells don't have as long of a range as a regular shotgun shell filled with buckshot, but if you can get some of the shot into a vamp's heart, you'll end their career real fast. Even if you miss the heart, it'll buy you time."

"Can't you get a newer shotgun?" a wolf Luke didn't know yet asked.

"Probably, though not many with slam firing available these days. But whatever works best. I recommend twelve-gauge because you'll want as much of the special anti-vamp shot as possible. Don't be dainty when it comes to killing vampires. Waste them before they waste you. I also carry a pair of sawed-off double barrels on occasion. They've saved my bacon on more than one occasion."

He looked around at everyone's rapt faces. "Think of it this way. Gather up all the tools you'll need and figure out how to conceal and use them. The more variety in weapons you can collect, the better chances of your survival in a variety of situations. But, as werewolves, you'll be able to rely on your strength and speed. That and a stake will do just about everything you'll need."

"If we can tear up a vampire, why do we need a stake?" another wolf asked.

"Give them enough time, and they'll heal. A stake to the heart will take care of the final details and send them on their way perma-nently." He looked to his team, gathered together off to the side. "Can you grab that shirt?"

Roxi pulled out a small cooler and withdrew the garbage bags. Opening them but leaving the shirt in, she handed it to Luke.

As the stench of the dead vampire wafted from the bag, a spike of adrenaline pumped into his veins. Even though there was no danger, his body was apparently hardwired to react to the presence of a vampire—even a dead one. "This is a shirt soaked in the remains of a young vampire. We kept it so you could learn the scent. Pablo?"

Pablo stepped forward. "The scent of a live vampire will have elements of the same smell as a dead vampire. The dead one is obvi-ously more pungent, but you'll be able to pick up the same notes. It's the surest way to identify a vampire before you see their claws and fangs. If you get to the point where they've deployed claws and fangs, be careful. They're lightning fast and strong. Unlike their former human selves, they have supernatural powers, so consider them on par with yourselves, or maybe faster. Better to overestimate them and crush them than underestimate them and pay for it in your own blood and pain."

Luke took the bag and handed it to one of the wolf trainees. "Take a sniff and pass it around."

A few people poked their noses in deeply and inhaled hard, causing themselves to gag to the delight of the people who hadn't had a turn at the bag yet. Their turn to sniff quickly ended their laughter.

"That, my friends, is the stank of a vampire," Pablo said. "Stick that stink in your brain and remember it. It'll help you track the fanged fuckers."

They'd set up a couple sandbag dummies on a quickly built frame. After they finished with the first round of informational classes, Luke and the team took them over to the dummies and lined them up.

"Time for stake training!" Pablo called.

The team ran down the line, giving everyone a stake as Luke watched, wondering if they'd all survive.

After all the trainees had stakes, he stepped to the fore, twirling a stake in his hand, and approached a dummy. "You're going to have to stab hard. Ribs are designed to protect the innards, and stakes aren't exactly knife sharp." He turned and plunged it into the dummy where the heart would be. "Also, you're going to have to get through a flailing vampire."

"I'm a big fan of ripping their heads off. Sometimes their arms, too," Pablo supplied.

Delilah stepped up. "A good machete is a nice addition to your kit. You can hack off pieces of the vamp, then stake them later. Disabling a vampire is a great way to stay alive."

Luke nodded along with his friends. "Pablo and Delilah are right. If you can lop off the head, you essentially deactivate the vamp. Don't let the head roll back, or it can reattach."

"Luke," Pablo said, grinning like he was about to mess with his friend. "Have you ever taken the head from one vampire and stuck it on another vampire to see what would happen? Like when C3PO's head got welded onto that battle droid?"

Luke shook his head.

"Dude, Imma try it next time we get a chance." Pablo grinned eagerly.

"Pablo, we're not trying to teach our trainees bad habits." Sam patted Pablo on the shoulder and turned to the trainees. "You'll have to forgive Pablo—he's got a warped sense of humor. Listen to Delilah and Luke. Disable them, then stake them. Do not play with them."

Luke chuckled and stepped to the back of the crowd, letting Delilah, Pablo, Sam, and Simone lead the trainees while he and Roxi watched. Roxi bent from side to side, twisting.

"Feel like a workout while the kids play?" Roxi asked. "I need to stretch my muscles."

"What did you have in mind?"

"We have our swords and our armor. Feel like crossing blades?" Roxi smiled, raising her eyebrows.

"We've never had a chance to do that before. I was kind of afraid they'd pit us against each other in the arena. Then after, you were never well enough for it. I think I would like to get a bit of exercise."

He offered Roxi his hand. A round of combat with Roxi might go a ways toward lowering the tension tightening up his body.

Hand in hand, they walked back to Erin's van and opened the back, pulling out the crate they transported their gear in. Brutus trailed along behind them. In a couple of minutes, they helped each other on with their armor padding and armor before settling their sheathed swords into place on their hips.

They walked away from the group of wolves training and around to the backside of a nearby hill, so they'd have privacy. Finding a bit of shade under a bush, the dog yawned and stretched out on his side for a nap.

"Helmets?" Luke lifted his helmet from the crate.

"Probably better, so we don't get our bells rung." Roxi grabbed hers.

"Yeah. I've had to heal from too many concussions the last few years. I know the rudis takes care of it, but it still sucks."

"Oof, don't you know it." She strapped her helmet into place. "Start slow with some basics to warm up the muscles?" Roxi asked, pulling her Parthian sword.

Luke unsheathed his gladius and swung it around slowly to get the blood flowing. When he was ready, he and Roxi stepped toward each other. Luke lifted his sword and saluted her. She mimicked the gesture and stepped into the en garde position. He readied himself.

Roxi started with a slow swing telegraphing its path and destination. Matching her speed, Luke parried it aside and countered with a backhanded slash at chest height. Roxi easily pushed it aside and countered with a thrust at shoulder height. With a quick pivot, Luke blocked her thrust and slashed with another backhand. The slash ducked, Roxi stepped into Luke, shouldering him aside.

Luke's heel caught on a stone, and he stumbled backward, windmilling his arms slightly as he worked to keep his balance; Roxi stepped back, disengaging until he steadied.

"You good to go again?" Roxi asked.

His answer was a wink and a quick jab toward her stomach. Parrying it, Roxi spun down Luke's arm and shoved him away, bringing her sword around in a slash toward his waist. He leapt to the side, arching his body as the sword passed within a finger's breadth of his steel-covered side. He followed by bringing his sword around in an awkward downward swipe to help push her sword around and away from his body.

"Nice move, dōšagīh." Roxi grinned at him.

Pivoting, Luke moved his body, so he was back into position and carried the momentum of his sword around to cut a slash toward Roxi's stomach. She, using her sword to push his through, stepped into him so their sword arms were trapped between their bodies. Luke grinned, exerting his strength to push her back. Roxi, her face full of mischief, leaned in and kissed him, then spun around and swatted him on the ass with the flat of her blade, her laughter ringing clear and bright. He couldn't help but smile even as his ass stung from the hit.

"You're a menace, Roxiustana." Luke spun to face her, a broad grin on his face.

Roxi had stepped back so she could laugh unimpeded. "You better hope the vampires don't discover all it takes to get you off your game is a kiss."

"Oh, I think I'm safe. Not sure I've ever been attracted to a vampire. Those fangs aren't exactly kiss worthy in my book."

"You're right. That might just be my advantage to use." She stepped in and stabbed toward Luke's stomach.

Luke parried it away and countered. After their first few sallies and the interruption of the kiss, they cast aside intentional slowness and attacked and defended in earnest, though not to the true speed and power both of them could bring to bear. As they battled, their swords sent up a clamor of clangs and scrapes as they blocked and countered each other.

This was the first time he'd seen her at full speed under good health. Even though she'd fought hard and valiantly in the vampire's arena, she'd been months without full nutrition or a rudis recharge. Here, she'd had months of good health and vampires to drain, though Luke knew she still wasn't up to one hundred percent. He wasn't either. It was taking a long time to recover fully from the deprivations of the arena and the painful attack of the dark entity during his rescue of Roxi. And she was even further behind after the compulsion worked to destroy her body and health. As gloriously as she fought now, he couldn't wait until they were both truly fully recovered and back in fighting condition.

After a particularly intense pass, Luke managed to get a light swat with the flat of his blade on her shoulder. Puffing for breath, they stepped back and took a breather by mutual silent agreement. Roxi bent over, her hands on her knees as she breathed hard, trying to catch her breath. When she straightened, she turned her head toward her left, drawing Luke's attention to the top of the hill that separated them from where they'd left their trainees.

"Dōšagīh, it would appear we have an audience."

"So, it seems." He straightened up and arched his back, stretching out the muscles. "Shall we call it?"

"No. We're still tied one hit each." Darting in with a high downward slash, she didn't give him time to reset as she went back on the offensive.

Roxi attacked, tapping into her full speed. Not set, Luke backpedaled, struggling to get his sword into position. Her eyes were narrowed as she pushed with all her power, harnessing the full two thousand years of her experience, mixing in a variety of techniques and forms she'd learned over the years, many of which Luke only had a passing familiarity with.

Once he managed to turn her and open some space, he set and attacked, drawing on all his various experiences. This time, he drove Roxi back, her eyes narrowed in concentration, a faint smile playing across her sweat-covered face. He should have known he was in trouble when he saw the smile broaden just before she ducked down and rolled under his slash, coming out on her knees just to the side and behind him. He yelped as she spanked him with the flat of her blade.

He hopped away, rubbing his butt with his free hand. "That's gonna leave a welt."

"It wasn't that hard," Roxi gasped.

Once the thunder of his hard breathing and pumping blood settled, applause rolled down the hill to greet their ears. Roxi stood up and bowed elegantly toward their audience. Shaking his head, he bowed to Roxi.

"I do believe this engagement is yours, two hits to one." He stepped into Roxi, pushing her sword aside and pulled her into a kiss. Even though his butt hurt, he felt a bit more relaxed after the vigorous exercise.

Leering cheers and hoots drew a burning blush to Luke's cheeks as he stepped back from Roxi.

"Maybe seeing your prowess with a sword will keep Mary from flirting with me," Luke said, winking at Roxi.

She laughed. "I doubt it. It'll probably just add extra spice to it. If you ask nicely, she'll probably stop. She's fun, but she also seems to be a nice person."

"Yeah, probably." He sheathed his sword. "I suppose we better go rejoin the group now that we've given them a show."

She sheathed her sword and followed him up the hill.

"Damn, Roxi. That was some fine sword work. Maybe we can cross swords sometime if you're feeling up to it," Delilah said as soon as they rejoined the group on top of the hill.

Roxi nodded. "I'd like that, Delilah."

Pablo pointed at Luke and gave his best Nelson Muntz "Ha, ha" laugh. "She spanked your ass, literally!"

Luke shrugged. "She's a supremely talented fighter and beat me."

Two circles formed around them—the inner circle of their close friends and an outer circle of the trainees.

"You better mind your p's and q's, Mary, or that lady'll skewer ya for messing with her man," Erin chided.

"Just added spice, Erin." Mary winked at Roxi.

"I don't think I've ever seen anyone fight that fast," a wolf said.

"Me, either," another said.

"They weren't even going at full speed," Pablo added. "I've seen Luke at full speed, and it's frightening."

"They can go faster?" a wolf asked, jaw dropping, eyes widening.

"Yup." Pablo nodded emphatically.

"Can you teach us to fight like that?" Alejandro asked.

"I'm not sure it'll be terribly useful, and we have centuries of practice and skills learned from dozens of cultures, but we can prob-ably teach you some basic unarmed and armed combat, so you know how to use your bodies, your machetes, and your stakes and how to defend yourself in some basic ways."

"We can start on that tomorrow, though," Sam said. "We need to break for dinner, and then afterward, we're going to put everyone out on the streets so we can sweep this entire town. Leaders, pair up your people. Erin and I will have assignments for you after dinner, and we'll assign your Portland team leaders for tonight's training session."

"Go get cleaned up, y'all. We'll have dinner at the Pack Hall in ninety minutes," Erin called.

The trainees seemed excited after receiving a bit of education on the uses of a stake and getting a free show from Roxi and Luke. He just hoped they'd sustain that excitement, and it translated into purpose and determination when things became tedious, as they often were on long-term hunts, or when the excitement trended toward dangerous or deadly. Those were the times when naïve enthusiasm would fail a person if they also didn't have the fortitude to push through when needed.

"That really was quite the display," Sam said, putting a hand on each of their shoulders as they walked back to their vehicles. "I don't know if you planned it, but it couldn't have worked out better. Your exhibition showed them why they should listen to you and that you're not just talk."

"Yeah, they're a walking history lesson." Delilah quirked up an eyebrow and grabbed a bottle of water, tipping it back. "Though Sam is probably right. A little excitement and inspiration will do them good."

Sam and Pablo helped Roxi and Luke strip their armor off and stow it away before everyone piled into the van to head back into town. Tonight, they'd see what the additional bodies could add to their search for the pair of missing wolves. Hopefully, they'd be more help than hindrance.

CHAPTER
SEVEN

The first night went smoothly, even if they didn't find any traces of vampires. With all the extra teams, they were able to orchestrate a wide sweep through Portland, covering areas they'd not had the people to inspect before. The next day when they met for afternoon training, there was a bit of grumbling in the enthusiastic mix, but Luke and his people turned those around as they divided the group into people with some fighting experience and those who were rookies.

Luke, Sam, and Delilah split their people up to go with the two different groups to assess their actual skills and to begin the basic elements of fighting and defense. By the time they called it for the afternoon, there were a lot of new bruises and abrasions. The trainees were less rowdy as they were given time to clean up for their evening's communal dinner before another night of sweeps.

If they didn't find anything tonight, Luke was considering talking with Erin about splitting up the group to head to some of the nearby towns to add more samplings to their mix. Hell, he'd even considered having his werewolves drive around some country lanes with their heads hanging out of windows like excited dogs to see if they could pick up any hints out in the world.

He wanted to find the missing couple, but even a single vampire would have been good. He needed to give the trainees a little taste of danger and success. Tonight, the Sherbrooke observer would be in attendance. A little victory might persuade them to shift from neutral toward helping out their neighbors in Maine. Unfortunately, they came up empty yet another time. That was the way of hunting. Luke knew his people would relay this information and the fact that they were still doing good work, protecting their community from vampire attacks. The observer listened but maintained a stiff neutrality.

The next day, they assembled for another round of training, followed by the communal dinner. That evening, Luke split off several teams to hit Yarmouth and Freeport on the way to Brunswick. Two teams could each hit the small towns before converging in the bigger town. The rest of his people moved through Portland again, coming up empty once more. With Delilah and Simone in charge of the other teams, Luke headed to bed, knowing they had everything in hand. He liked that he could trust his friends and knew they'd do good work without him there. After several busy days, he and Roxi poured themselves into bed, and Luke fell into a hard sleep.

A SHRILL ALARM ripped Luke from his dreams. As he struggled to get his brain working after the rude awakening, Roxi shook him. He already smelled it before she could say anything.

"Luke, get up! Fire!" Roxi yelled.

Luke shook his head, trying to jumpstart his brain. Once his feet hit the ground, he went into auto pilot yanking on his clothes and pulling out his armor. It was mostly on before Roxi noticed.

"Luke? What are you doing?" She paused, holding a handful of their clothes she was stuffing into a bag.

"What?" He looked down. "Oh. Habit. Alarm went off, brain said attackers at the walls." He finished putting it on anyway, since he was closer to being finished than starting. That way, he wouldn't have to worry about it.

"Shite. Do you feel it, Luke?" Roxi asked.

Luke sighed. "Enemies at the gates." He looked around for Brutus, then remembered he was with Delilah and her team.

He helped Roxi stuff things in a bag, then helped her on with her own armor. Since they had room in the crate, they shoved the rest of their stuff into it. His eyes burned, and he coughed from the invading smoke; across from him, Roxi coughed as well. She grabbed a couple of towels and doused them in water, tossing one to him. He tied it around his lower face, covering his mouth and nose, then pulled his helmet on over it and strapped it down.

"Luke, look!" Roxi, her voice muffled with the towel over her mouth, pointed toward the door.

The smoke rolled under it and the edge looked blackened. She took the rest of the water pitcher and tossed it over the doorknob. It sizzled and sputtered.

"Fuck," Luke muttered.

He looked around the room, spying the window that overlooked the backyard. Running over to it, he peered out but didn't see anything. With their armor crate in hand, Luke used it to bash out the window, then threw it out onto the lawn. Roxi, her sword out, knocked down the remaining shards of glass while Luke grabbed their suitcases, tossing them out and away. After sheathing her sword, Roxi crawled through the window and eased herself down the eaves.

When she placed a hand to move, the roof crumbled under it as flames licked her palm. Hissing, she yanked it back and threw herself off the roof, landing on her feet and rolling away from the house. Luke knew his time in the bed-and-breakfast was short with the flames engulfing it. He dove out the window, sliding down the eave on his stomach. Grabbing at the edge of the gutter, his feet swung around, and he dropped over the side, landing with loose knees, so he tumbled down. Even with the decent landing, his knees hurt, and the wind was knocked from his lungs.

A loud crack like a beam giving way drew his attention back to the house. Flames poured out from the shattered windows as smoke billowed from the roof. He turned around and found Roxi lying on the ground, holding her side.

"Luke…sniper…"

He could barely hear her through the thick towel coupled with the barely audible whisper she'd been forced to use. Sniper? He hit the ground as another crack sounded out. With the fire raging, he didn't know if it was the fire devastating the building as the inferno roared or the sniper taking another crack at them.

He scrambled forward on all fours like an animal. "Roxi. Are you OK?"

She nodded. "Hit my armor."

He cringed. He'd taken a sniper round to the back, and it had broken some ribs.

"Can you move?" he asked.

She grimaced. "No choice."

He helped her roll over and made sure she was moving before lunging toward the luggage and tossing it further from the house. As he lay behind a short hedge, he wondered why the sniper hadn't taken another shot at them. Looking up, his view was blocked by a garage butting up against the narrow alley that ran behind the bed-and-breakfast's backyard. The buildings in this neighborhood weren't all that tall. Perhaps they were in the shadow of the garage enough to block the sniper's view.

He heard shouting but no fire engine sirens, which was troubling —but more troubling were the approaching vampires. He could sense several coming within his sphere.

"Roxi?"

"Yeah, I feel it."

Luke stood up, keeping low to ensure he didn't present a target to the unknown sniper, and helped Roxi up. She groaned, trying to keep it in, still clutching her side. Reaching down, he pulled her sword from her left hip and handed it to her so she wouldn't have to twist across her body to get it.

"Let me engage them. Step in if it's needed. Don't push it if you can avoid it. I don't want you puncturing a lung." He squeezed her hand and gave her a smile he realized she couldn't see since towels still covered both their mouths.

Luke crawled over the hedge and drew both his gladius and rudis, keeping his back to the garage so he could engage both sides of the alley and watch where Roxi hid behind the hedge. Roxi shoved her way through the hedge and put her back up against the garage door. With Roxi to hold his back, he stepped forward and looked over one shoulder then the other, waiting for the vampires.

"Well, shit," Luke mumbled.

The vampires were coming in from both sides. He saw the glint of metal and hoped they weren't carrying firearms. Not wanting to leave the protection of the garage, Luke waited, but the speedy vampires didn't keep him long. The first one, outstripping his comrades, raised a machete.

With a quick sidestep, Luke chopped the vamp's arm off and sent him tumbling toward Roxi. She stabbed it through its heart, ending it. Knowing she had the other side covered, he parried a baseball bat and beheaded its owner, shouldering its headless body into the hedge before lunging out with the rudis, catching the next vampire in the guts. He pivoted and beheaded it, stepping forward and leaving the two headless bodies behind him. He could attend to them later.

His quick handling of the first few fangers inspired their friends to slow up and back off a bit, enough that Luke could toss a quick look over his shoulder. With her arm clamped around her side, Roxi was still more than the vampires could handle, though she mostly wove a defensive pattern to keep vampires from even making it within attack range. A slipped foot in the gravel alerted him to one of the vampires trying to take advantage of his quick check on Roxi.

Waiting until the last moment, he whirled around and stabbed his gladius through its heart. The momentum of the vamp's movement showered Luke in dust as it met its final death. Luke was grateful for the damp towel covering his face. It filtered out the dust and kept him from coughing or sneezing.

Now that only three vampires were left on his side, he waded in. Thinking to take him out with multiple strikes, two of them swung at

Luke. He swatted both swings aside and raked his gladius across the leg of the closest vampire, the sword catching briefly as it met bone. Luke's strength and speed carried it through. The vamp dropped to the ground, cradling a leg that was barely still connected. Lashing out with a vicious kick, Luke caught the second vampire on the knee and heard it snap as it moved in a direction it wasn't designed to go. With two vamps down, Luke turned to the third only to see its back as it fled back down the alley.

Turning his back, he stepped into the shadow of the garage as a shot cracked out. His left arm burned as the shot plowed into it, spinning Luke against the garage door and leaving a dent in its thin aluminum surface. The shot had knocked his rudis out of his hand. He turned to see the vamp that had run away poking around a corner, a pistol in his hands.

Pissed and annoyed, Luke sprinted down the alley, growling loudly as it turned into an anger filled battle cry. The vamp's eyes shot open wide at the sight of the terrible anger on Luke's face. The vamp dropped the gun and ran. Not wanting someone else to grab it, Luke scooped up the pistol and shoved it into his pocket, the handle sticking out, then sprinted back down the alley.

"I'm coming up behind you. Make room," Luke shouted in Middle Persian.

As Roxi stepped aside, he slammed into the front row of the other vampires and laid about with his gladius, not caring what he cut as long as it was vamp flesh. He could finish them up later.

"Roxi, get the two with leg wounds. Drain them to fix your ribs." Again, Luke used the Middle Persian he and Roxi spoke when they needed to communicate secretly.

She'd been expanding his vocabulary and grammar in the language and helping him learn her Parthian dialect. Off in the distance, he heard the first faint sound of a fire engine. They needed to get out of there. He'd taken out another couple of vampires when he heard people approaching from behind, fearing the worst.

"Luke, it's our friends," Roxi called in Persian.

As soon as Pablo and Sam swarmed around him, he stepped back, breathing hard.

"Luke, your arm—it's bleeding." Roxi stood up, looking more limber after draining a couple fangers.

She bent over and picked up his rudis, but instead of handing it to him, she stabbed one of the headless vamps and pointed at it. "Go."

He smiled, holding in a chuckle at her imperious command, and dropped to his knees, speaking the incantation to drain the vampire. The burning in his arm receded but was still there. He grabbed the rudis and found another to drain. Roxi had joined him, deciding she wanted more. Between them, they worked through the downed vampires, draining several each before they just started stabbing them in the hearts to send them on their way.

The last few fighting Sam and Pablo turned and made a break for it. Sam bent and grabbed a shirt from a dusted vamp and wiped her katana clean, then tossed it to Pablo for his machete. Luke grabbed another and wiped his blades down, stowing them in their sheaths after handing the rag to Roxi. Between the four of them, they made quick work of moving the luggage down toward the end of the alley away from the full conflagration, moving clothes out of the crate and into bags so they could quickly strip off their armor and stash it before any official types could show up. Roxi, moving too quickly, got momentarily stuck in her armor as she tried to yank it over her head without loosening the straps enough. Sam, holding back a chuckle, helped pull it all the way off.

"Fuck," Luke mumbled, the armor scraping over the sensitive spot where he'd been shot.

They latched the crate just as a fire engine's lights filled the alley as it pulled in, disgorging its cargo of burly firefighters. Roxi handed Luke a hoodie.

"Put it on. Your arm is covered in blood," she hissed through her teeth.

He slipped it on quickly, starting with this left arm.

"Are you folks OK?" the firefighter—a tall, broad-shouldered woman—asked.

Luke pulled down the towel and nodded. "I think so."

"Anyone else in there we need to know about?" she asked.

"No, our friends made a trip north for the night. It's just the two of us." Luke wiped the sweat from his forehead, leaving a messy smudge of sweat and ash.

"What happened?" she asked.

"We don't know. The alarm woke us up. We tossed our luggage out the window, then followed it because the door was too hot." He gestured toward Sam and Pablo. "Then our friends showed up to check on us. They're staying at a B-and-B a couple blocks away."

"Alright, you should be fine back here. Please stay out of the way." She turned around and jogged back to join her coworkers to battle the blaze.

Sam whistled appreciatively. "I'd like to buy a firefighters' calendar with her in it."

"Sam!" Roxi said, before breaking into a laugh. "I mean, it's true."

"I'm looking respectfully," Sam said, staring after the firefighter.

Pablo shook his head and grinned. "What really happened?"

"That is actually what happened," Luke replied. "Except when we landed, a sniper shot Roxi." He held up his hand to stall any questions. "Hit her armor, probably broke some ribs, but the vamps she drained took care of it. We leapt over the hedge and into the alley when a bunch of vampires attacked. You saw the rest."

Pablo patted Luke's left bicep where he'd been shot, sending a sharp pain through his arm as he cringed away.

"Dude, what's wrong with your arm?"

"Got shot. Didn't check to see if the bullet had gone through." He shook his head at his own hastiness. "Looks like it's still there. I'd appreciate it if you didn't hit that arm again. It pushed the bullet into something."

"Ouch. We'll have to see if there's a surgeon who can cut it out," Sam said.

"Sorry, Luke. I shouldn't have bullied you into draining that vampire," Roxi said.

He waved away her concern. "Don't worry about it. It was the right move at the time. As long as I don't get hit in the arm too much,

I'll be fine. Wouldn't be the first time I've had bullets live inside me for a while."

"Shit, I hope Delilah and Simone didn't have a lot of stuff in their room," Pablo said.

"I didn't even think of that," Luke said.

"We couldn't have done anything about it, dōšagīh. We couldn't even get out of our own door; the fire was so hot." Roxi slid her hand into Luke's, squeezing it.

Luke nodded, staring at the flames rising high into the night. "I know."

"I've been meaning to ask, but I always get distracted, Roxi. You call Luke 'dōšagīh' sometimes. What does it mean?" Sam asked.

Roxi leaned her head against Luke's shoulder. "It means he is my beloved. It's a Parthian endearment."

Pablo raised his eyebrows and smiled at Luke. Sam grabbed his other hand and held it while they stood in the glow of the fire, their sweat drying and chilling them in the cold night air. Tomorrow would be another day, and a more interesting one for all the wrong reasons.

CHAPTER
EIGHT

Eventually, someone had come along to officially collect their statements and get contact details from them, dismissing them after to get what rest they could. By then, word had made it to Erin, who showed up to give them a ride. She'd offered to let them stay at her house, but they refused, citing the attack and the desire to keep her family and home out of danger. She dropped them off at the motel they'd first stayed at after their flight had been grounded.

After a couple of quick showers, Roxi and Luke tucked into bed and passed out. They woke around noon to pounding on their door. Luke, groggy and wary, grabbed his sword and checked the peephole, but only saw Pablo. He unlocked the door and pulled it open, moving out of the way to sit on the bed and rub the sleep from his eyes with his empty hand.

"What's the matter, buddy? Afraid I'm gonna rob you?" Pablo asked.

Luke held up the sword and looked at it before setting it on the nightstand. Roxi, who hadn't bothered throwing on pajamas, held the sheet around her chest.

"Luke, can you toss me a shirt and some shorts?" Roxi asked.

Luke nodded and grabbed them from one of their bags, handing them to her.

"Close your eyes, Pablo," Roxi said.

Pablo closed his eyes and turned around, allowing Roxi to quickly pull the shirt and shorts on.

"I smell coffee, but what's in the box?" Roxi asked by way of letting Pablo know he could turn around.

"Donuts!" Pablo set the box on the small round table by the motel room's window along with a cardboard carafe of coffee.

He grabbed a couple of mugs from the counter, heavy but chipped, and filled them, handing one to Roxi then Luke. Sitting down, he flipped the lid open on the box and pulled out a maple glazed cake donut from The Holy Donut box and took a bite.

"Don't be stealin' my donuts!" Luke stood up and grabbed a garish purple donut that turned out to be a triple berry and sank into the chair on the other side of the table.

Pablo stuck his tongue out. "I bought 'em. I can have one if I want."

Roxi, setting her cup on the nightstand, slipped into the bathroom and reemerged a couple minutes later to grab a donut. Luke stood and let her have the chair, taking the opportunity to visit the restroom himself. Once he finished, he topped off his coffee and grabbed a second donut, sitting on the edge of the bed to eat it since there were only two chairs.

"What's got you pounding on our door so early?" Luke asked.

"Dude, it's noon." He reached into the box and pulled out a maple bacon for himself.

"In case you didn't notice, I had a bit of a busy evening."

Pablo looked at Roxi. "My, he's grumpy this morning."

"The only reason I haven't cut you is you brought coffee and donuts. I mean, you're a friend, so I'd only cut you a little..." Roxi grinned impishly at Pablo.

Pablo chuckled and shook his head. "Damn, that's cold. You two make a good couple."

"Now you see why I love her." Luke grinned groggily at Roxi.

"Anyway, the reason I woke you up is that Erin wants to meet to discuss last night. She's a bit upset for some reason."

"I mean, vampires attacked a pack property and burned it down. I'm sure when the analysis is done, the investigators will find arson, which is going to raise a lot of trouble for her and the pack." Luke sighed. "I don't blame her. Could you reach out to Delilah and let her know I want her to work on our evac plan? We need to be able to bug out in case she decides we've overstayed our welcome."

"Word." Pablo pulled out his phone and started texting Delilah.

"Luke, dear, I'm going to grab a quick shower to wake me up."

"Sure. We've got a few minutes."

Roxi walked over and kissed him on the cheek.

Luke whispered quickly, "Sleep OK?"

Roxi shook her head sadly and headed toward the bathroom. Luke got dressed while Roxi showered and began stowing away their stuff, so they'd be ready to move out when Roxi finished.

"We paid through tomorrow, but I don't think I care to stay here again. We'll have to find another place." He bent over to stow his sword. "Shit. I didn't even think to ask. Did anyone else get hit last night?"

"No. Just your place."

"Huh. That's specific." Luke sat quietly, finishing his coffee while they waited for Roxi to shower.

When she was dressed, they packed up and turned in their key. A few minutes later, they joined the rest of the leadership team as well as Erin, Alejandro, and a few of the other Portland-Bangor pack council members.

As soon as she saw them, Erin strode across the room and hugged them. "Hey, Luke, Roxi. Are you both doing OK?"

"Yeah. Nothing serious as far as injuries. Sorry about the bed-and-breakfast," Luke replied.

She waved a hand at them, dismissing his concern. "We have good insurance."

"Well, the fire investigators will probably find arson as a cause. There's no way a fire burned that hot and fast without some sort of accelerant." Roxi reached over and grabbed a small roll of deli meat to snack on.

"We'll worry about that later. Right now, I just wanted to make sure you two were fine. There's more coffee if you want. It can't make up for a night of short sleep, but it's better than a kick in the shins, that's for sure." Erin gestured toward the table where everyone sat.

Once Luke and Roxi got situated, they all turned to Erin.

She cleared her throat. "Thanks for coming. Sam filled me in on the goings-on last night. So, I guess we found some vampires finally."

Luke chuckled. "You could say that."

"This seems like a pretty direct attack on Luke," Alejandro said.

Several people nodded.

"Yeah, it could be," Luke said. "We have a lot of factors to consider. Was it coincidence that they saw us going into the B-and-B and decided to attack? Did they specifically target me and Roxi? Was it an attack of opportunity? Did they know we'd not have everyone in town last night?"

"That's a lot of questions," Erin replied.

Luke nodded, pursing his lips. "It is. Vampires are good at raising a lot of questions, but rarely give answers—and if you do get answers, they're almost never satisfying."

"I think you're leaving out one important question, dōšagīh." Roxi fixed a serious gaze on Luke. "Were we betrayed?"

Luke's people looked around the table at each other, acknowledging the same question Roxi had just asked. Then Luke widened his gaze, taking in the nervous and awkward looks from the Portland-Bangor Pack. It seemed to be a question they themselves might have thought of but didn't like. He hoped they didn't take offense, at least until they found out if there might be a leak. However, if he found Erin or one of her wolves had betrayed them, he certainly would mean offense when he gave it.

"That's certainly a possibility." Erin looked at Luke, pleading in her eyes. "I'd like to think none of my people would do it, but with some of the stories I've heard out of Western Europe, I can't eliminate the possibility one hundred percent. We'll have to move forward with that in mind. We won't ask you about your security arrangements going forward until we can nip this in the bud. We'll also want to be careful about planning details with our neighbors."

Although she could be a good actor, Luke felt her concern and sadness at the events were genuine. He added a bit more trust back into her column.

"I'll let you decide who from the other packs are trustworthy. We can operate on that validation until they prove otherwise," Luke conceded.

Erin nodded. "The four here I trust with my life and family." She smiled at her packmates. "Of the others, I trust Mary. She's a handful, that's for sure, but I'd trust her to have my back, and I have. She's a good lady to have in a scrap. I'd say George, but I can't vouch for the folks he sent in his stead."

"Is there a reason he's not here leading his own people?" Sam asked.

"George is a good man, but he'd be useless for this kind of stuff. He's good at leading his mix of hippie-dippy granola crunchers, farmers, and outdoors enthusiasts, but he's a hard-core pacifist personally and not good with this kind of stress. I'll have to ask Mary about Rochelle and Wayne and their people. She's much closer to them."

"OK, then. We'll keep the circle of trust to the people at this table, the rest of my people—they've earned my trust more times than I can count—and Mary. Does that sound fair for now?" Luke looked around at everyone.

A wave of relief washed over Erin's face as she smiled around the table. "Good. Now that we've established this. I have some news, or I guess I should say I hope to have some news. When I came over last night to check on the fire, my oldest boy got a whiff of them fangy bastards and went off to follow it."

"By himself?" Pablo asked.

"He called a few friends, and they met him on the edge of town. The trail goes off north. They'll be safe. They're good, strong boys. They go up hunting that way on the two and four. I told him if it looks too dangerous to hightail it back to town and we'd gather up the posse."

"How old is your boy?" Roxi asked, sounding skeptical.

"He's nineteen. He's a smart, sensible boy for a nineteen-year-old."

Pablo looked at Luke, his eyebrows raised. "That could be a big break. A couple of those fangers were hurt pretty badly. They'll be leaking for a while and leave a good trail for them to follow."

"So, what do we do while we wait for Jeremy?" Alejandro asked.

"We stick to the plan. Training this afternoon, dinner, and plan another sweep." Luke turned to Erin. "Do you have any bulk transportation? A bus or the like? If we need to roll out with everyone? If your son finds something."

"We'll have something ready," Erin said.

"Good. Now. I need to borrow my people for some work of our own," Luke said, standing up. "Until later."

LUKE and his people had just sat down for dinner, the crowd quieting as they shoveled food into hungry maws after an intense afternoon of combat training, when a handsome young man burst in through the door before catching himself, blushing as he waved toward Erin. Her shoulders relaxed, and the muscles loosened in her face. She made eye contact with Luke and gestured toward Jeremy.

Luke followed her toward the stairs. Jeremy met them there and followed them up the stairs to a room in the back of the building.

"You can speak freely here. The room's soundproofed. Don't use it much, but it's handy." She shrugged and gave Luke half a smile. "This is my boy, Jeremy. Jer, this Mr. Irontree."

Luke shook the young man's hand.

"Where are your pals at, Jer? I hope they're keeping their lips on the zipped side."

"They're not that dumb, Mom." Jeremy tried and failed to keep an eyeroll contained.

Erin nodded, patting her son's shoulder. "Good boy. I take it by the way you burst in that ya found something?"

"Yeah. We did."

"Well, out with it," Erin prompted.

"I don't know how to describe it. Um, it looked like a summer camp but with razor wire fences and watch towers."

"Like a prison camp?" Luke asked.

"Yeah. Like that. When we got up there, the sun was just about to come up. The wind was blowing all around, but when it was in the right direction, we could smell those dead guys, the vampires." Jeremy shuffled nervously.

"Did you stick around long enough to see who took over guard duty after sunup?" Luke asked, his eyes intense as he held Jeremy's gaze.

The boy nodded. "Yeah. I'm not sure who exactly they are. I think we caught the scent of wolves, but not enough to account for all the people. They were wearing some kind of uniform."

"Police? Prison guards? Army?" Luke asked.

Jeremy shook his head. "Didn't look like Maine cops or military."

Luke frowned, his eyes narrowing.

"You just heard something you don't like," Erin said.

Luke nodded. "Yeah. Jeremy, think carefully. Did they look strong? In good shape?"

Jeremy nodded. "There were some running in formation like you see in army movies. A few were just wearing T-shirts. They looked pretty ripped."

"Fuck." Luke shook his head.

"What's it mean, Luke?" Erin's eyebrows drew closer as worry tightened her face.

"Something new. Werewolves with mercenaries. Probably nasty ones." He frowned and shook his head. "Do you have a piece of paper and pen so he can draw a map of the camp?"

"I can do you one better." Jer pulled out his cell phone and brought up a photo, turning it for Luke to see.

Luke's lips stretched into a smile. "That is better. Send those to your mother, then delete them off your phone when she has them."

"I'll send them to you," Erin said.

"I need to ask you one more favor. Can you loan me your son tonight? I want him to lead me and a few of my team up that way so I can check it out."

The worry that had wiped off her face with the appearance of her son returned. "He's pretty tired after a full day…"

"I'll be fine, Mom," Jeremy protested.

Erin nodded, her anxiety increasing.

"Don't worry, I'll keep him out of trouble. I'm not going up there to pick a fight. I just want to see what's up with my own eyes and survey the terrain if we do need to make a move." Luke turned to Jeremy. "Go grab a bite to eat, then find a place for a nap. We'll grab you when we're ready to move out. I want to wait a bit before rolling out."

"Oh, yeah. That's good thinking. Jer, there's a cot in the closet in my office. Go kip up there when you're done eating. Be a good boy and listen to Mr. Irontree tonight, and don't do anything stupid and get yourself hurt. OK?"

"I promise, Mom."

"Good." She kissed his forehead. "Now go get some food."

Jeremy did as he was told, leaving Luke and Erin alone.

"I'll bring him back whole, Erin."

Erin nodded once. "I know you'll try your darnedest. He's a good boy, just overly enthusiastic sometimes."

Luke chuckled. "He seems like a good young man."

"ABOUT HOW FAR OUT ARE WE, Jer?" Luke asked.

"About five miles, maybe four, Mr. Irontree."

"Jer, call me Luke. It's a lot faster to say, and I'd prefer it." Luke turned back. "Pull over at the next place that's got enough room."

Alejandro saluted.

A few minutes later, he pulled off the dirt and gravel road and put the van in park. The other car that'd been following pulled in behind Alejandro. The teams piled out of the vehicles and assembled in the road. Out this far, there was only the light of the moon and stars with the headlights off.

"Alright. Bravo team, you're protecting the cars. As soon as we bug out, turn them around so they're ready to go. I want someone in the driver's seat at all times. If they need a break, someone else takes their spot. Alpha team, you're with me." Luke put his hand on Jer's shoulder. "You're with us."

"Mr. Ir... Luke, do you mind if I go wolf so I can pick up the scent?"

"Go for it. Hand your clothes to someone with a backpack." Luke pulled out his armor.

Roxi slid over and helped him on with it, then with his swords. Next, he covered it in a heavier black hoodie to keep the shine of the metal covered and to keep him warm in the cold night air. Once he had his armor settled in place, he loaded up a shotgun and ammo belt. The rest of the team was likewise going through their preparations.

Jung-sook was busy testing the scope on her Steyr SSG69 sniper rifle. Judging it good, she slipped it over her back and tightened the strap. Pablo stripped down and changed into his full wolf. Luke picked up his clothes and set them in the pile with Jeremy's. Ahmed grabbed them, along with extra ammo for the shotguns and the Steyr, then stuffed them into the backpack he carried.

While Luke waited for the rest of the team to finish their last preparations, he noticed a stick next to the wheel of the van. Scooping it up, he patted his legs. "Here, Pablo. Here, boy. Wanna fetch the stick?"

Pablo bounced over as if he was excited to dash after a stick, stopping next to Luke.

Chuckling, Luke hurled the stick into the darkness. "Go get it!"

Instead of darting off after it, Pablo chuffed, then lifted his leg as if to pee on Luke's leg.

"Hey!" Luke jumped out of the way.

Chuffing some more, Pablo lowered his leg and walked away.

Several people laughed at their antics. If nothing else, their silliness seemed to have relieved some of the tension.

"Ready?" Luke called.

Ahmed and Jung-sook nodded, as did Pablo and Jeremy in their wolf forms. Jeremy looked more like a traditional silvery-gray timber wolf, where Pablo had a bit more size on the young man and had darker gray-black fur. The two wolves would range ahead, providing double the noses and all the other advantages the hunters could provide. Luke broke into a jog, letting his legs warm up. He could run faster than a normal human, especially after being freshly juiced up the previous night on several vampires, but he'd never be able to keep up with the two wolves if they ran full tilt. He suspected that Ahmed and Jung-sook could run faster than he could in their human forms, but they fell into his pace without a word.

Luke knew how to keep a fast pace and cover rough ground while doing it. He'd been doing it since his days in the legions, though then he did it in caligae instead of the high-end combat-style boots he wore now. Even with the vampires, he still didn't feel up to the conditioning he'd had prior to his abduction two years ago. He'd grin and bear it and run the four-plus miles through the hills to their destination, then run it again. It'd be good for him, he told himself over and over again. Maybe if he repeated it enough, he'd believe it.

Sixty minutes later, they found their wolves huddling at the bottom of a hill. On the other side of the hill, lights glowed into the night.

"That must be our camp," Luke whispered.

Jeremy nodded.

"OK, Jeremy, I want you to stay here and watch our escape trail. We're going to work our way up the hill and take a look. If you hear anything back here, give a little yip."

Jeremy laid down on all fours and moved his head about, keeping a look out. Luke figured he would have argued but was glad he'd listened to the order. Luke took another minute to catch his breath before starting up the hill, carefully picking his path to avoid making too much noise. A few minutes later, they crested the hill and found some bushes to hide under.

Jung-sook unfolded the bipod for the sniper rifle and set it up, sweeping the gun side to side to check out all the sights. Ahmed handed Luke the backpack. Pulling out a set of binoculars, he took his first look at the camp. Pablo settled down on Luke's other side, sweeping his ears, nose, and eyes around to pick up anything the others might miss with their equipment or human-ish faculties.

It did look like a prison camp. There were barracks, some isolated away from the others. The entire thing was surrounded by a high fence composed of various types of wires, including concertina razor wire. Luke guessed it was electrified as well, based on the configuration of the posts and the heavy wiring and cables.

"That'll be a real bitch to get through," Ahmed whispered.

"No shit." Luke swept the binoculars over the entire camp. "Ready to take down some numbers?"

Luke read off distances using the range finding feature of the binoculars. Once they returned to town, they could create a more precise map of the camp and the size of the buildings. After he got the numbers, he settled his gaze on a man who looked like a vampire walking next to a man in the mysterious uniform Jeremy had mentioned. At this distance and in this lighting, Luke couldn't read any of the patches or make out any of the emblems on the man's uniform. They stopped. The changed angle allowed some light to reflect off the vampire's mouth. His fangs were out for all to see. Then the man saluted the vampire and jogged off.

"Looks like the mercs know who their employer is." Luke followed the vampire as he walked into a building.

"How'd they build all this way out here?" Ahmed asked.

Luke grunted. "I think I see a road on the other side leading from a gate. I think it goes west. We should mark the coordinates and see if we can figure out where that road is."

"Yeah. No cell reception out here. Let me grab the GPS." Ahmed perked his head up. "I think we're going to get a breeze."

Luke felt the air stir as at swirled around lightly until it settled into a steady light wind blowing into their faces. Luke's stomach sank. Next to him, a low growl rumbled in Pablo's throat. Reaching out, Luke settled his hand on Pablo's back between his front shoulders.

"What is that stench?" Ahmed asked as he tried to cringe away from the smell.

Ahmed hadn't been at the Wapato assault when Luke first collaborated with the North Portland pack. Only Pablo had gone up that hallway with Luke, though he imagined the wolves near the infirmary hallway couldn't miss the stench even if they wanted to. He didn't know if it was his imagination, or sound carrying on the wind, but Luke thought he heard an agonized scream.

"Death."

CHAPTER
NINE

"Are you sure?" Erin asked.

Luke wiped a hand over his tired eyes. "I wish I wasn't, but I know what that place is. I've seen them too many times over my lifetime. They've taken many forms over the centuries, but that smell is universal. It's a vampire nursery, and it's being guarded by vampires, werewolves, and what looks like mercenaries."

He paced back and forth, his friends and the people Erin approved of watching him. Tension and fear hung heavy in the room. He stopped, resting his hand on the back of a chair.

"Erin. This is bad. I've been scanning the papers for the last few days. There have been a lot of missing people in the region, far more than historical trends dictate. Now your wolves."

Mary sighed. "There are a few from our pack that have gone missing recently. We've been quietly looking but haven't found them."

"I bet whichever pack is providing muscle for that camp sold off those who didn't agree with the arrangements, and they're in that camp in one of those barracks, feeding the vamps. That camp is a death factory. They're turning their captives into brand new vampires and feeding the rest of their captives to them. Dammit all."

Luke's knuckles whitened as he squeezed the top of the chair. "I wish we had the whole team here, but there's no way they can get here in a timely manner."

"We're not trained soldiers, but we can fight and shoot," Mary said. "You'll have my pack."

Erin nodded at Mary.

Luke closed his eyes and took a breath before turning to Mary. "How well do you trust the St. Johns Pack?"

"I'd trust them. They're good folks. They like a good tussle as much as the next wolf, though they'd prefer it be on ice with hockey sticks, but they'll fight if we ask them. If we let them know how bad it is," Mary replied.

Luke stared into Mary's eyes. She held his gaze.

He made the snap decision. "OK. Fill in their packleaders and get them moving this way. Whatever weapons they have, bring them. We're not going to have enough anti-vamp weapons, but you can still do a lot of damage to a vampire with a regular gun, and something's better than nothing.

"Erin? Can you talk to George?" Luke asked.

"Right. I'll do that immediately. I'm guessing we're done sweeping streets?"

Luke caught everyone's eye. "We're done patrolling the streets. We're going to war."

IT TOOK the better part of the rest of the afternoon and the next morning for everyone to filter into town, with the Canadians from the St. Johns Pack arriving last after smuggling what weapons they could across the border and meeting up with Mary and Erin's most trusted people to finish the trip over.

To keep things on the down-low, Luke kept training going and turned out the trainees for nighttime sweeps. With only a handful of the most trusted people outside the joint leadership group knowing the details, Luke and Erin hoped to keep the movements of their reinforcements under wraps. They didn't know who the mole was, or even if there was one, but now was not the time to get sloppy and blow the operation, especially since it was taking so long to assemble his forces. He hated the delay, but they needed people.

While the rest of his team handled the trainees, keeping the routine going, Luke and the people he'd taken out to the vamp camp grabbed a few hours of sleep. When he woke, he met with Erin and Mary to sort out how to organize the influx of new people with the limited intelligence they had about the abilities of those who were showing up. Guns would be useful, but bipedal form werewolves would be better.

Even untrained, they could handle a vampire and take some damage, especially if the enemy wasn't using silver or wood. He hated having to send in green recruits, but time was not on their side with a ticking time bomb on their hands.

He had no idea what the various packleaders told their people. He'd only asked them not to reveal the exact nature of their timeline or the specific destination and mission. He'd insisted their packs seek volunteers for an important and highly dangerous mission that was vital to the safety of their packs and the local region, but he left the rest for them to handle.

Now with the plans set and the personnel on hand, they dipped into Owen's bag of fun acquisitions and loaded everyone into their vehicles. Somehow, Erin had acquired several mini buses. As their improvised army loaded up, Luke had his people activate the cell jammers to ensure whoever the mole might be couldn't get a message off, then briefed their buses as they rolled.

Luke would have to trust to his people. He had a different mission and wouldn't be able to communicate with the others until all units were in place.

"Are you sure this thing is reliable?" Luke asked, as they loaded their weapons into the back of a beat-up box van.

"The engine and suspension are good," Owen said. "It's not pretty, but it'll do what it's made to do, and that's all you can ask of it."

Luke nodded. He stepped back as his assault team finished their final preparation before getting on the road. He missed not seeing Jung-sook, but her sniper rifle would be far more valuable with the other team on the hills overlooking the camp from the back end. Roxi, Pablo, Sam, Ahmed, Owen, and Charlie were reliable people to have on hand and the people he trusted most. The others he truly trusted would lead teams on their own missions. He missed Delilah and Simone's presence, but they were needed elsewhere.

"Mr. Irontree...Luke." Jeremy stood, his hands clasped in front of him as he twisted them.

"Hey, Jer. What can I do for you? Got a message from your mom?" Luke asked.

"No. Um. Can you talk to her, please? She won't let me go. I can fight. You need all the help you can get going up against all that."

Luke's eyes narrowed slightly. "She said no?"

Jeremy nodded.

"You're not my werewolf to command, and I can't countermand your mother. We're her guests and allies."

When Jeremy protested, Luke held up his hand to forestall him. "But. We're meeting briefly for a last check in before we roll out. I will speak to her, but I'm making no promises. Understand?"

Jeremy's face brightened. "Thank you, sir."

"No matter the verdict, you obey her word. Got it?"

"Yes, sir." Jeremy, with a hopeful smile on his face, turned and joined in loading the last of the heavy crates.

As Luke walked away to join the last-minute check in, he stopped Ahmed. "Keep an eye on Jeremy."

"A little over eager?"

"I'm guessing he's already done more than his mother wanted him to do and he's eager for more."

"I'll keep an eye on him," Ahmed replied.

Luke nodded and took off. The vehicle leaders sat around in the living room of the large farm house that sat on the property they'd been using for their training sessions.

"Sorry I was late. Young master Jeremy stopped me and asked

me to intercede on his behalf with the leader of his pack." Luke sank into a chair next to Roxi.

She smiled faintly at him and handed him a can of sparkling water.

"And you told him…?" Erin arched one eyebrow practically into her bangs—the quintessential mom signal that Luke was walking on thin ice.

"That he wasn't my werewolf to command, and that I was a guest and ally of his pack, and then I made him promise that he'd abide by whatever answer I received from you."

Erin stared at him for a few seconds, considering his answer and whether he might have trespassed somehow until finally she nodded. "My answer is the same as when he asked me earlier. He has responsibilities to the pack here."

Luke nodded. "Now that that's settled. Final check in. Owen?"

"You've got all the weapons I could scrounge up. We've already activated the cell phone jammers. Short of someone showing up with a tank, we're as armed as we're going to be."

"Excellent. Erin, all our personnel here are briefed?" Luke asked.

"Yup. They have the stage-one information and are on board. We'll fill them in on everything else on the road."

Twisting in his chair, Luke smiled at Sam. "Do you have the special equipment I asked for?"

"I do. Though I'm not sure what your plan is."

"The vamps changed the name of the game when they brought down those airplanes. It's time to change our approach to meet the new state of affairs." Luke looked toward Erin's second. "Alejandro, you've got your drivers briefed about the first stop and their secondary objectives?"

"Correct. I've got paper maps and GPS units. All the rigs have CBs, and we stocked up on some hand-held radios."

Sam raised her hand.

Luke looked at Sam, tilting his head slightly. "Yes, Sam?"

Her face dead serious, she straightened and looked around the room. "Does everyone have cool CB handles picked yet?"

Luke snorted. Pablo and Delilah chuckled, covering their mouths.

Forcing his face into a semblance of seriousness, he made eye contact with Alejandro. "If you need suggestions on cool CB handles, I suggest you consult with Sam. She is the expert on the topic."

Sam, narrowing her eyes, moved forward to the edge of her seat and looked intently at Alejandro. "Alejandro, you strike me as a 'Rubber Duckie' kind of man…"

Alejandro looked confused, which only increased the poorly contained snickers of Pablo and Delilah.

"Simone, Delilah. You've got your objectives. I'll leave it to you to use your teams as needed when you get within striking distance. And keep an eye on Brutus, though he'll probably be fine." The dog had been a vital part of tracking down Le Mousquetaire a few weeks ago in Paris.

"Are you sure you want to bring him along?" Delilah asked.

He shrugged. "He always refused to be left behind. He's a strange beast."

"Right." Delilah, a smirk on her face from her earlier laughter, saluted Luke. Simone nodded seriously.

"Jung-sook, do you have someone who can use the other Steyr?"

Jung-sook nodded. "Yes. And a few of Mary's folks have some good, well-scoped hunting rifles, so I've got six snipers."

"And that brings me to the last piece. Does everyone have their strip of white cloth and has it been impressed upon them how important it is to wear it, even in wolf forms? Since we don't all know each other by sight, we need to be able to identify each other quickly."

Luke saw a room full of nods. "OK. Let's move out. Good luck and stay sharp."

In ones and twos, people stood up and left to attend to their teams. Standing just out of the way of the exit, Luke pulled Roxi in for a brief kiss.

"What was that for?" Roxi asked, a soft smile on her face.

"Just 'cause." Luke ran his hand along her cheek. "Just taking a moment to appreciate you before we get busy dealing death and destruction."

Roxi chuckled. "It's a weird world we inhabit, dōšagīh. I'm glad to know you."

"Me, too." Luke sighed. "Now I have to go tell a young man that his mom says he can't go to war."

"How old were you when you enlisted in the legions?" Roxi asked, slipping her hand into his as they walked back to the vans.

"Seventeen. But this is a different world, and I can't blame her for wanting to keep her son from going down the same path I did all those years ago."

Roxi laughed. "Hanging out on a corner, smoking cigarettes, and playing with your switchblade?"

Luke shook his head. "I joined the legions, not a 1950s gang of street hoods. I wasn't having a dance fight with the Jets; I was trying to keep Dacians from peeling me out of my armor with a falx. What were you doing, general's daughter? Going to prep school with the other elite girls?"

"If prep school was assassinating my king's rivals and any Roman I could get an arrow into…"

Now it was Luke's turn to laugh. "You and I don't exactly have teen years that translate to modern young people, that's for sure."

Roxi chuckled. "That is a truth."

Seeing them walking up, Jeremy jogged over, an eager expression plastered on his face. When Luke shook his head, the young man's face fell.

"I'm sorry, Jer. She was adamant that you had other responsibilities."

"But… Everyone else gets to go. I'm a grown man…"

"Be that as it may," Roxi said. "She's your mother and your pack-leader. We aren't going to cross her wishes."

Jeremy made a disgusted sound and shook his head. "Fine. I'll go finish loading boxes since that's all I'm good for." He turned and stormed off toward the box van to help with the last of the ordnance.

Luke shook his head as Jeremy stomped away. "I bet my mom wished she could have kept me home from the legions, but I guess I survived, at least physically."

"None of us made it out whole, even if our physical injuries were light," Roxi replied. "It's better he be disappointed today than see what we're about to do."

Luke nodded. "Yeah. It's not going to be pretty in there. What people see in there is going to stick with them far longer than they want." He just hoped they'd all be coming home, no matter the injuries, physical or emotional, they might sustain.

Luke and his team stopped at their designated ready point. Except for the driver of the van, they all climbed out and lined up at the back of the box van. A couple of the werewolves stared at the roll up of the van, eyes narrowed and faces suspicious.

As soon as the driver opened the door, Luke discovered why.

"Jeremy, you're not supposed to be here," Luke said, his face stern.

Jeremy puffed up his chest and straightened his spine. "I want to fight. I want to do my part for the pack."

"Damn it, if anything happens to you, your mother will be crushed, and she'll blame me." Luke shook his head. Ahmed was supposed to be watching him. It was too late to do anything about it now, and there wasn't time for an ass chewing, though that had never been Luke's leadership style, anyway. "Get out of there and go to the van." Luke turned to Charlie. "Keep an eye on him and don't let him slip into the compound."

"Right, Luke. I'm on it."

Luke's nostrils flared as he tried to keep his anger in check, injecting just enough to make sure the boy knew he was serious.

"Jeremy. You can go with him, or I can drag you to the van tied up. It's your choice."

"Ugh." Jeremy climbed out of the back of the box van and got into the back of the passenger van.

Luke thought he heard the kid mumble "fucking asshole" as he walked away. Judging by the amused looks on the wolves with their enhanced hearing, Jeremy probably had. At least the kid and the van would be out of danger, parked a safe distance away until it was time to evacuate the camp.

"I didn't want this complication. Damn it." Luke mumbled, checking his cell phone so he could notify Erin—no signal. He rubbed his hand over his eyes, sighing. "OK. Everyone in the back."

A few people snickered as they climbed into the cargo box of the van, a few shook their heads. Roxi rubbed her hand over Luke's back as she stepped up into the box. When everyone else was in, Luke climbed in. As soon as they were settled with their fake manacles on, Connor shut them in, then climbed into the driver's seat. A moment later, they were bouncing down the rough road.

Roxi snuggled into Luke's side and kissed his cheek. "Please stay alive, dōšagīh."

"You, too." Luke kissed her forehead.

"Shit. I should have volunteered for the other team. This bouncing around is making me motion sick," Pablo said.

Sam looked around and found a small plastic cup someone hadn't disposed of. Holding it in front of Pablo, she said, "If you're going to spew, spew in this."

Pablo snorted, shaking his head. "Don't worry, Garth. I can handle my stomach, even if I don't like it."

Roxi tipped her lips toward Luke's ear. "I don't get it."

Sam's eyes shot wide. "You've never seen *Wayne's World*? Luke, we need to remedy this oversight the next time we have a movie night."

"Party on, Sam," Luke replied.

"Party on, Luke." Sam grinned.

"We're slowing down. Y'all ready?" Luke looked around the box van, receiving the shadows of nods. Luke flicked off the low power camping lamp they'd used for light.

They'd debated about holding until the next day to avoid fighting vampires, but then they'd have to fight in the daylight against the mercenaries when they'd be most comfortable. At night, Luke and his werewolves would have the advantages of their species, and the three humans had supernatural gifts that made them just as dangerous at night.

When the van stopped, they kept still.

"Halt!" someone yelled. "What do you have here?"

"Supplies and snacks," Connor replied.

"Open up." Boots crunched on gravel as Connor and the guard walked around the side to the back.

A moment later, the metal of key against lock snicked open followed by a sudden rush of light. The "snacks" cringed away from the open door. A few people even made frightened noises.

"What do we have here?"

"More werewolves being removed from their packs and a few humans." Connor shined a flashlight around the inside of the van, careful not to hit people in the eyes and mess up their night vision too badly.

"All right. Take them to the Welcome Center for processing."

Connor cleared his throat. "This is my first delivery here. Which one is the Welcome Center?"

Luke held his breath, hoping the question wouldn't ping the suspicions of the guard.

"First building, turn around out here then back through the gate into that loading dock." The guard's voice, which had earlier been intent, now sounded bored at having to do more than the barest minimum of stopping vehicles.

"Right." Connor shut the roll down door, leaving it unlocked, and returned to the cab.

They bounced and swayed as Connor pulled around so he could back into the camp's entrance. Luke's team, now that they'd been properly inspected, shucked their fake manacles and grabbed their weapons from the crates of "supplies."

On cue, Connor stalled out the van. Pablo gripped the handle on the inside, waiting for their next cue.

"Fucking piece of shit van! Couldn't they get one that worked at least some of the time?" Connor cursed, popping the hood.

"Hey, what's going on here?" The guard sounded alert again.

"This piece of shit keeps stalling out on me. If you want to take a look, go ahead. They ain't paying me to fix this thing, not that I can do much, anyway."

"What the hell?!" the guard yelled.

A split second later, a shotgun blast announced the start of violence. Pablo yanked the door up, holding it so it didn't roll back down. The rest of the team sprung out, heading to their targets.

Luke sprinted toward the other guard station and staked the vampire hurriedly trying to get a radio turned on. Connor joined Luke as they dashed across the short open yard toward the Welcome Center. Sam already had the door open, and the rest of the team was in place. Luke was the last through as Sam slammed the door. Just before the door clicked shut, he thought he heard the distant crack of a rifle, though he couldn't tell for sure with the shotguns blasting off around him.

It only took them a couple minutes to sweep through the Welcome Center into the next building. This one looked like some sort of guards' barracks. Ahmed and Connor swept in first, spraying short bursts from their APC9K submachine guns. There must have been human mercs ahead. They were trying to save their limited anti-vamp rounds for the fangers. Luke didn't even want to use them on the enemy werewolves. They weren't quite reliable enough on a werewolf bulked out in their bipedal form.

Their initial assault had caught the camp completely by surprise, but shots were answering back as the vamps and mercs tried to mount a response. Luke worked his way to the front and grabbed a shotgun off his back, looking for the mark he'd made. Wrong shells. He pulled around the other one with the standard shot. He'd gone with a mix of three slugs and three buckshot so he could create more mayhem. Seeing his example when they loaded up, a few others had taken a second weapon for just this situation.

When he neared the front, he snugged up against the wall next to Owen.

"We're getting bogged down here," Owen said. He reached into a pocket and pulled out what looked like a black baseball with a hat on it.

Luke grinned viciously. "Everyone, pull back!"

As soon as the last of his squad pulled out of the barracks, Owen yanked the pin, letting the spoon flip, and counted two seconds before tossing it. Luke ducked, covering his ears. Three seconds later, the grenade detonated, blasting out the windows and sending smoke rolling out the door. Despite clearing two buildings, they still hadn't reached their first objective. Without intelligence from inside the camp, they had to rely on knowledge of basic camp design and Luke.

Ahead, more answering gunfire joined the fight as his people swept up to the next building. Luke's head jerked up as the lights of the camp went out before flickering back on, a loud engine roaring to life.

"Bingo," Owen said.

"I'll cover you. Make straight for the generator." Luke looked around, catching Ahmed's eye. "You clear that building if you can. If it's the control room, you know what to do."

Ahmed nodded, then jogged forward to join Roxi, Pablo, and Sam as they fought their way toward the next structure. Luke peeked around a corner, trying to locate the exact location of the generator. He saw a swarm of people around a bulky, rectangular, short box trailer.

"That's it, Owen." Luke grabbed a couple shells and reloaded his shotgun. "Ready?"

"Let's go," Owen replied.

Luke took off at a quiet run, keeping to the edge of the buildings as he worked his way toward the trailer they suspected was the generator. Once he moved within shotgun range, he opened fire. He couldn't tell who was a human and who was a vamp or wolf; they were just enemies. He fired off the standard shells, then pulled around the other shotgun and fired off its compliments of shells. This was the one occasion he didn't feel bad about wasting the anti-vamp shells as his enemies scattered to get away from the man running toward them and firing wildly.

When he arrived at the generator, he tucked behind it and shoved shells into the magazine. As soon as he had a full gun, he poked his gun around the corner and fired a couple shots toward a few people creeping back toward the generator. They hit the dirt. His head on a swivel, Luke checked all around them to make sure no one was sneaking up behind them.

"It's done!" Owen shouted over the roar of the generator.

Opting for speed, they both burst out from behind the generator and sprinted as fast as they could back the way they'd come, abandoning quiet and stealth for pure speed. Not sure which building they'd selected, they jumped to the side behind its wall for protection.

"Now?" Owen asked.

"Now," Luke replied.

Owen pulled out a detonator, and flipped up the red switch covering the trigger, then depressed it. A moment later, the generator exploded, and the lights went out again. Luke ducked, waiting for debris to rain down on him. When it didn't, he lifted his head and looked at Owen.

"That wasn't very big."

Owen grinned. "It's not the size of the bang, buddy. I just wanted to disable the generator and render it useless. I didn't want to rain junk and fire down all over the camp. We don't know what's in all these buildings."

Luke shook his head, chuckling. "Fair enough."

Taking a moment to reload both shotguns, Luke stood and headed back into the center of the buildings to rejoin their team. With the power cut from the outside and the generator destroyed, Delilah and Simone could bring in the rest of the attack force now that the electric fence was down. A crack bit into the night.

"There's the Steyr," Luke said.

"You really like those things, don't you?"

"It's a good sniper rifle. They were free, or rather stolen from our fangy friends, and we can use common American ammo on it when we can't get or make the regular rounds for it. They've served us well."

Luke's ears perked up as their shotguns barked into the night, the occasional burst coming from one of the subcompact machine guns they'd acquired in Europe. A variety of guns responded. Luke thought he heard a few other machine guns and rifles. They should be hearing an increase in activity with the other teams hitting their points at the wall.

"Luke, I think there coming to provide some payback after we blew up their generator," Owen said.

"You got another grenade? At least one you feel you can spare?" Luke asked.

Owen chuckled. "I have a fair few of my little toys." He reached into his coat and pulled one out and yanked the pin, holding the spoon tight. "Let me know when."

"Now's as good as anytime. As soon as you chuck it, let's move."

Owen peeked around the corner then hurled the grenade, taking off deeper into the camp, Luke hot on his heels. A few seconds later, the grenade detonated, showering them with dirt and debris. Once their ears cleared, they heard a mix of cries and screams of pain. Owen's grenade had done its job. As soon as they rounded a corner, Luke took aim, then pulled the gun, holding it over his head.

"It's us! Don't fire," he called out.

As soon as Luke's team saw it was him and Owen, they returned to their previous targets. Luke waved for Owen to follow, and they ran over to rejoin their friends.

"Update," Luke said.

"We have some vamps and wolves holed up in that building," Roxi said.

"Owen, feel like playing with more grenades?" Luke asked.

"You know it." Owen reached into his coat and pulled one out.

"Make it two. We'll go for the middle window. Throw right and left."

Owen nodded and pulled out a second grenade.

"Let us get into position, then cover us as we go in," Luke commanded.

They slid around the corner, staying back far enough not to be seen. Roxi poked her head around, and Luke gave her a thumbs up. As soon as she tucked her head back in, they laid down a cover barrage.

"Let's go. Stay low," Luke said.

He dashed forward, crouching as he fired off a few shots toward the windows. He saw bodies scramble away from the glass. Luke backed up against the wall of the building as shots thudded above him toward the upper side of the window. His team kept the shotguns away from them, aiming toward the door. Owen slid up next to him and pulled the pins on both his grenades.

Luke aimed up toward the window and fired a shot to clear anyone who might be risking a look. As soon as he did, Owen let go of the spoons on both of his grenades, then popped up, pitching them into the building. Owen dropped, covering his head. Luke curled down and covered his head and ears as the grenades went off, first one, then the other, sending glass and wood shrapnel belching out the windows, followed by billowing smoke.

Shaking his head, he cleared his vision as he saw three of his friends dash out across the gap and break into the building. They fired off a few shots to clear the last of the survivors.

"All clear," came a voice from inside.

Luke sat back and grabbed some shells to reload his shotgun. Roxi ran up, sliding down to sit next to him.

"You alright, Luke?"

Luke nodded. "Yeah. Ears a little weefy, but nothing a vamp won't clear up."

As the rest of the folks moved up to join Luke, Roxi, and Owen, Luke stood up. "Let's be careful now. Watch for the arm bands. We should be seeing our other teams soon. Also, we have to be getting close to the prison barracks, so let's be certain before we blow more shit up—"

The sound of a heavy machine bursting to life interrupted Luke.

"Fuck," Luke mumbled.

He poked his head around the edge of the building. One of the watch towers spewed fire out of the camp toward the hills where Luke and Jeremy had done their recon earlier.

"We need to get on that. Pablo, Owen, you're with me."

"Wolf time?" Pablo asked.

Luke nodded. "Probably best."

Grinning, Pablo pulled off the warm-up jacket and tossed it down, then reached down and grabbed the seams of his pants and yanked. The snap buttons popped like one of their small caliber machine guns.

"Rip. And. Roar." Pablo transformed into his bipedal werewolf.

Luke shook his head, trying to keep his snicker contained, remembering the first time Pablo had demonstrated his rarely used catchphrase. Most people shook their heads, used to Pablo's quirky sense of humor. Sam laughed, probably more at Roxi's expression than Pablo's absurdity. Roxi's jaw hung open as she watched Pablo in his wolf form wiggle his ass in a little dance.

"Let's go, Gene Kelly," Luke said.

Owen stood up and popped Pablo on the butt. "Nice dance there, handsome."

Owen borrowed one of the submachine guns and a couple of magazines as he tucked in behind Luke.

"Let's get to that tower as fast as possible. Pablo, get up that ladder and kill some fuckers. Owen, leave most of your grenades here. I want you to stay up there and crew the gun. Keep an eye on the camp. When we're done. I want that gun," Luke ordered. "Ready?"

He took off, making for the tower but drifting slightly toward the camp. He wanted to be able to intercept anyone going for his wolves. Pablo, using all his wolfy speed, passed Luke on his sprint to the watchtower, Owen just behind him. Luke didn't bother trying to keep up. He couldn't, for one, but he also didn't want to present a nice little group to target. Raising his shotgun, he fired off a round at a head that popped out from behind a building. He wasn't sure if he hit anything, but he didn't see the head anymore.

Periodically casting a glance over his shoulder, he kept up his run, looking out for any other dangers to his two runners. With the other teams closing in, he flicked on his radio. People called into the radio asking for sniper support on the tower. Looking to the tower, Pablo started his climb, scrambling up the ladder like he was on fast forward.

"This is Spartacus. Belay that order. Pooch and Gilligan are already on the southeast tower. Copy?"

"This is Annie Oakley. Copy."

Luke chuckled. Sam did enjoy her CB handles, though the handle worked for Jung-sook who indeed had become an exceptional sharp shooter with so much practice.

As Pablo cleared the top rung, a handgun went off, followed shortly by someone flying over the tower. Whoever it was flew too far to merely have jumped on their own. They probably had an assist from Pablo. They screamed as they fell. Skidding to a halt, Luke pulled his gun around, pointing it at the broken man lying on the ground, his arms and legs bent at odd angles not natural to a body. The man, for he was a human, breathed shallowly, the sound raspy and bubbly.

The man tried to grasp for the pistol that had come down with him, but he couldn't reach it, not with his shattered body.

Luke picked it up. "This won't do you much good."

"Please, Please…" He gasped in a ragged breath. "Don't let them turn me."

Luke nodded, pulled back the hammer on the pistol, and fired a round into the man's head, ending his misery and any shot of being turned. A moment later, the heavy machine gun stopped as another human fell to the ground. This one was dead before it hit, ripped apart by a pissed off werewolf.

Luke shoved the pistol into his pocket and ran to the ladder, making sure the shotgun was secure at his back. He scrambled up. A head popped over.

"It's just me," Owen told Pablo.

A moment later, Owen crested the top and crouched into the corner, popping his head over.

"You all OK?" Luke asked, as he started up the ladder.

Pablo growled and pointed to his arm, a wet patch reflecting in the dim light.

"That first guy Pablo tossed over winged him. He'll live, though. How about you? Heard a gunshot down below," Owen replied.

"Fulfilled a last request." Luke reached into the pouch on his belt and pulled out a small range finding scope and swept the other watch towers to see if and how they were arrayed.

"I see someone moving around in the southwest tower," Luke said.

A shot cracked into the night along with a flash of muzzle flair from the southwest tower.

"Shit, sniper. You about got that gun set up, Owen?"

"Almost." Owen made a disgusted noise, as he wiped shiny liquid off the gun. "Someone was a bit indelicate with the gunner after he got shot."

Pablo held up his clawed paw and curled down his fingers, leaving the middle one up for Owen. Tossing aside a few rounds on an ammo belt, Owen reached into a metal container and pulled out a fresh belt of rounds, laying them into their spot before snapping the lid down. Another sniper shot fired from the southwest tower just as Owen pulled the charging lever.

Owen opened fire with a couple short bursts to find the range, then homed in on the bits of movement that pinpointed the sniper. As the heavy machine gun rounds ripped into the wood of the watchtower and whatever was in it, something rolled out the side and tumbled to the ground, hitting with a slight bounce. Luke watched with his scope. It looked like their shooter. Whoever it was didn't move.

"Nice job, Owen. I'm gonna head back down in a minute. Keep your radio on and watch the ladder. You ready to go back down, Pablo?" Luke swung his scope around to check out the two north towers.

Pablo growled and moved toward the ladder.

"I'll cover your descent, buddy." Luke put away his scope and brought the shotgun loaded with slugs around to cover Pablo as he climbed down. As soon as Pablo's foot hit dirt, Luke returned the shotgun to his back and slid his foot over the end. "Good luck, Owen."

"You, too, Luke." Owen let out a small burst that flew between a couple buildings. "Better hurry, somebody is trying to rally the defenders."

Luke shimmied down the ladder as quickly as he could and landed in a crouch as he pulled around a shotgun. Pablo waited nearby, covering for his friend.

"Well, on to our next objective," Luke whispered to Pablo.

Pablo nodded, turning to scout their next run. So far things had gone relatively smoothly, but they'd barely engaged the number of people this camp could house, nor had they found a single prisoner yet. And that, above all else, worried Luke as he wondered if or when the other shoe would drop.

CHAPTER
ELEVEN

Luke saw shadows moving along the south fence on the other side. He waved Pablo to follow him, then took off in a low crouching run along the fence. The flicks of white cloth in various spots reassured him that his other teams were finally here.

"Delilah?" Luke whispered loudly.

"Hey Luke, how you doing?"

"Good. How about your team?" Luke asked, looking around. "Where's Brutus?"

"Three wounded. They're hiding out behind that hill until it's clear to move in. Your dog is with Simone. He's taken a liking to her. You found any hostages yet?" Delilah grabbed the heavy cable and held on to one end while Erin held onto another section as someone else brought up the bolt cutters and snapped the thick wire in two.

"No. No hostages yet."

Delilah frowned and grunted as she took the weight of the cut cable. She and Erin barely held onto it as it pulled them without the tension holding it. They managed to keep their grips and set the cable down. Prepared this time, they repeated the process on the next cable. All told, they clipped eight cables and made a wide path for their team to enter.

The firefight between Luke's team and the enemy resistance

moved closer as they traded shots along the buildings. An occasional scream or yip of pain punctuated the shots. He knew werewolves healed quickly, but he hoped nothing was serious. Having to undergo a procedure to remove healed-over bullets and shrapnel was not fun. He had plenty of experience with that himself and would again soon.

"What next?" Delilah asked.

"Post a couple people here just to be on the safe side. The rest are on me," Luke said, turning to the nearest building and running toward it.

After the dash across the open space, Luke pressed his back against the wall of the building. Delilah leaned against the wall next to him.

"Have you seen Simone yet?" Delilah asked.

Luke shook his head. "No, but I've not been that way yet."

Delilah nodded.

Off to the west, they heard gunfire break out.

"Sounds like she's arrived." Luke looked around. "Pablo, you're with me. I need five more people. Delilah, you take the rest of your people and sweep this building." Luke patted the wall lightly.

Before Delilah could protest, he took off, dodging to the next building, then the next until he had a clear view of the fence where Simone was currently being prevented from entering. He couldn't see where the opposing shots were coming from, but he had a decent idea from his little jaunt to take out the generator. He grabbed his team and worked their way back to the next alley and peered down.

He saw shadows moving toward the fence. Dashing to the next building, he barreled across the intersecting alley. He checked both ways and waited for the rest of his team to catch up. One by one, they leapfrogged buildings until Luke raised his fist to halt his small team. As he tiptoed silently to the end of the building, leaving everyone behind him, he pulled out the small collapsible periscope from its belt pouch.

With his back against the wall, he poked the periscope around the corner and watched as a few people and vampires kept up a steady barrage of shots toward the fence, using the wreck of the generator as cover. He'd seen enough.

Making his way back down, he rejoined his small team. "You two down to the end and open up fire as soon as you get down there. Go slow so you can space out your ammo. The rest of you are with me."

Luke pulled out the wooden bayonet and attached it to the end of his shotgun. With a quick check to make sure they were clear, he darted around the corner and then the next corner just in time to stake a vampire that had drifted too far back from the action. It dissolved into powder. Shotgun shots rang out, sending those in front of his team ducking at the new threat and distracting Luke and his people. Pablo slid past Luke and snapped the neck of a merc. Then someone staked a vamp. Finally, the defenders noticed the new threat and tried to run away. Luke and his team opened fire, taking them out and sending a few scurrying away to the north, where they'd likely run into the rest of Luke's people.

With the cessation of fire, Simone and her people quickly brought down the cables and joined Luke. He split them up and sent them toward different buildings. With the added weight of two large teams, the resistance crumbled. No mercy was given to vampires. Werewolves were taken aside to be dealt with later. The mercs were tied up and kept under guard.

Luke's frustration was reaching peak levels after finding none of the missing people or wolves, nor any of the trappings of the vampire nursery he thought they'd find. Using the radio, he called for his leadership team to meet at the end of the building under the watchful eye of Owen and the heavy machine gun he still crewed.

"Why haven't we found anything else?" Sam asked.

Luke shrugged. "I don't know. I can feel more vampires near." He turned to Roxi, who nodded, then to Delilah.

"Yeah. I can feel them, too," Delilah replied.

"Then where are they?" Erin asked.

"We're going to need to sweep back through the camp and look for any clues or something we missed," Luke replied. "Let's organize some defensive teams to keep an eye out for any reinforcements coming while we sweep—"

Someone cut in on the radio. "Spartacus. I think you better come check this out. I'll send someone to come find you."

"Copy." Luke headed toward the center and met Ahmed on the way.

"We found something you might want to see, Luke." Ahmed said, then turned and jogged away.

Luke and the leadership team followed him until they came to one of the buildings Owen had tossed grenades into.

"We were searching around for anything usable to salvage, and we picked up some of the furniture that had been blown up. One of the cabinets caught on a rug and pulled it away, revealing this." Ahmed pointed to the floor.

A huge trap door covered a sizable section of the floor. It looked about six feet by six feet. Together, Pablo and Luke opened it, leaning it against the wall. There was some sort of door, or maybe an elevator. Luke put out his hand and someone put a flashlight in it. Dropping to the floor, he shined the light under the floorboards, searching for any kind of indication of what the metal square below him was.

"What is it, Luke?" Erin asked.

"I'm not sure yet." Luke reached in and rubbed his fingers over a shadow, knocking the dirt off of a metal pipe. He followed the line of it to the wall at his feet. "There's a pipe running under the floor to the wall behind me. See if you can find a hidden panel or something."

Behind him, people moved busted up furniture and pulled down curtains and various things hanging on the wall.

"I found something. Looks like a fuse box," Ahmed said.

Luke rolled over and looked. "Open it."

Ahmed pulled the panel open, revealing an up, down, and stop button.

"Shit. We shouldn't have blown up all their power sources," Sam said.

"Let's give it a try, anyway. If it were me, I'd have a redundancy or some extra backup system, so I wouldn't be trapped underground if there was a power outage." Luke moved back so his head was clear of the area.

Ahmed pressed the up button, and something below clanged. "Anything?"

Luke looked down at the edges. They'd risen a slight amount.

"Yeah. Hold the button down."

Slowly, the elevator rose out of the ground until a door was revealed. When it finally stopped, the door popped open, causing several people to jump and aim guns toward it. Fortunately, it was empty. Unfortunately, the charnel stench of death and decay billowed out. People and wolves gagged; several had to leave the building. Luke heard retching from outside.

"We found the nursery," Luke said.

Pablo growled, putting a massive paw reassuringly on Luke's shoulder.

LUKE STEPPED out of the stench of the building and into the fresher air of the surrounding night. "Someone go get that observer. It's time he does some observing."

As they waited, Sam set up a digital video camera with a spotlight, then pulled on a harness she could attach the camera to. When one of Erin's wolves showed up with the observer from the Sherbrooke Pack in tow, Luke addressed his people.

"This is strictly volunteer only. Except for you, Mr. Observer. What you're going to see and smell will be horrific, nightmare-inducing stuff. I don't know how big it is down there, but I'd like to take down ten people."

When he got his volunteers, he had everyone load up on fresh shells and strip down to just weapons and ammo so they could move quick and not get caught if space got tight.

"Alpha team is with me. Bravo team is with Roxi. Delta team is ready if we call for back up. I'm hoping we're going to find some live people down there to rescue, so be ready. We've got medical supplies and sports drinks in the delivery van at the gates." When Luke looked around at his volunteers, he saw faces paling and hands trembling as they prepared to venture into whatever underground hell the vampires had set up.

Luke and his team stepped into the elevator and prepared, some folks kneeling with their guns at the ready, the rest behind them with guns raised.

"OK, team. Lights on." Luke flicked on the head lantern he'd put on.

Once all the head lanterns were on, as well as a few flashlights that'd been taped to their shotguns, Luke nodded at Simone, who pushed the down button. The elevator jolted to life.

As they descended, Luke breathed shallowly, trying to keep his breathing steady and his concentration tight, even though he was having trouble with the latter. His mind kept drifting to the various vampire nursery horrors he'd seen over his life. He still wasn't inured to it. Maggie said his compassion and ability to keep his humanity after all this time was one of the things she loved and admired about him. Right now, he wished he could switch it off, at least for the duration.

Several people looked down at his foot. Under the attention, he stopped tapping it. Usually in the heat of action, his nerves calmed. He didn't like that they'd grown more edgy as they descended into the earth. Even the gentle hand of Roxi on his elbow didn't help.

When the elevator bumped to a stop, safeties were flicked off and everyone tensed, ready to go into action as soon as the door opened. No one met them at the bottom except for an intensification of the stench. A few people gagged, struggling to keep their stomachs under control. The lights were low and dim, as if running on emergency power. An occasional light flickered.

Luke stepped out and swept his gun around, making sure their path was indeed clear. After a short stretch forward from the door, the tunnel took a sharp left turn. Peeking around the corner, Luke stepped around fully when he judged it clear, waiting for the rest of the team to get behind him. The last person out of the elevator ensured the door was shut and found the panel to send it back up. Connor pressed up against the other wall and knelt, aiming down the corridor with Luke while they waited for the second team to join them.

The rattle of the elevator door opening alerted them to the arrival of their friends. Making eye contact with Connor, Luke stalked down the corridor with his gun raised as he swept the barrel in a narrow side-to-side motion to ensure he had everything targeted. Connor proceeded beside him. When they arrived at their next directional change, they had a choice to make—left or right.

"I think the vampires are to the right," Roxi said.

Luke nodded. "I agree."

Delilah pulled out a can of florescent orange spray paint and sprayed a symbol on the wall so they could find their way back in a hurry if they needed. She returned it to a holster on her belt on her right hip. Her jian hung from her left hip.

"Should we leave someone here to guard the way back?" Sam asked.

Luke checked the signal on his radio but got nothing back but static. "Connor, run back and get the backup team and have them hold this passage."

"Right." Connor took off back down the corridor.

"Should we wait?" Delilah asked.

"No, let's move forward. We've got enough werewolves here to hear anything sneaking up on us." Luke waved everyone forward.

Once again, he took point. So far, the sense of vampires didn't seem to be shifting away or nearer, but the stench diminished slightly, or his nose was working overtime to ignore it. As they found no rooms, Luke became more concerned and wondered how big this tunnel system was. He perked up, holding his fist up to stop his team. Vampires were approaching. Rapidly.

"Two-person fire teams, step forward when the team in front of you is out. Advance until I call a halt." Luke knelt and braced his shotgun against his shoulder. Roxi joined him, aiming down the corridor.

The waiting extended interminably, then the vampires burst from an entrance buried deep in the shadows that the team couldn't see. Luke opened fire as did Roxi a split second later. The first vampires went down in a hail of silver and wood, screaming. One splatted to the ground in a wet, noisy mess. Before Luke could empty his magazine, the vampires reversed course, leaving their fallen friends to writhe in the middle of the hallway, screaming in agony as the silver and wood burned their bodies from the inside.

"Next team," Luke said.

Delilah and Mary stepped forward while Luke and Roxi reloaded. With their weapons full, they stood and followed as they crept down the hall until they neared the opening and the wounded vampires. Luke slipped between Delilah and Mary and staked the three vampires with the wooden bayonet at the end of his shotgun, dusting one and gooing the other two. Roxi yanked him back just in time as a bullet thudded into the wall to their left. The vampires had waited until they'd poked their heads into the corridor.

Luke, adrenaline pumping, reached into his pocket and pulled out a grenade, holding it up. He tilted his head to the side, raised his eyebrows, and gave it a little shake. Delilah rolled her eyes but nodded. Luke waved everyone back, then pulled the pin. When he let the spoon fly, he side-arm pitched it down the corridor then ran back, diving onto the ground and covering his head. A second later, the grenade went off. A bit of debris and smoke floated out of the corridor, hitting the wall the bullet had thudded into moments ago.

Standing, Luke jogged back to the side corridor. He pulled off his headlamp and flashed it down the corridor before carefully peeking around when he received no answering fire. The light shined through smoke and dust. When nothing responded, he forced himself further out into the opening.

"Roxi, with me," Luke said.

Roxi tucked up next to him. Together, they had the best armor for surviving bullets. As they slowly worked their way down the corridor, they eventually found the results of the grenade in the twisted bodies of the vampires they'd missed earlier. Together, they took turns staking the vamps, each using their own rudis, and topped off on some energy. Just ahead, a bit of light poured out into the corridor.

Pressing his back against the wall, Luke worked his way to the opening and took a quick look, then spun into the doorway. He kicked the shattered door out of his way and swept the room with his gun. Along one wall, half a dozen bunks were arranged in the tight confines. He took a quick look for anything of value, pocketing a pistol and a couple of magazines before rejoining Roxi in the corridor.

"I think they're just ahead," came a faint voice from further down the corridor.

Luke dropped to his knee, aiming down the corridor.

"Shhh, they'll hear you. Dog ears are just as good as ours," someone else said.

Luke flicked off his headlamp. Roxi, taking her cue from Luke, knelt down and turned off her lamp as well. They hid just outside of the light's reach, waiting in the shadows.

When the first vamp turned the corner, entering their field of fire, Luke held off. More vampires joined the first after no one responded to them entering the corridor. All told, six vampires joined Roxi and Luke in the long hallway, clearly unaware that two hunters waited for them.

Luke wanted to wait until they were committed and had nowhere to go but didn't want to be seen and risk return fire. When Luke judged the time right, he opened fire. Roxi joined him. Between their twelve rounds, only one vampire was left standing, though it had to prop itself against the wall.

Freeing her sword, Roxi dashed down the hall and ended that vampire, then attended to the two that remained corporeal. Luke joined her, turning his light back on. With the dozen vampires they'd just killed, the sense of vampires dropped to a distant twinge. When they reached the end of the corridor, they took the turn into the hall where the last group of vampires had emerged.

They found a series of doors leading into small dorms like the first one they'd found, though these had intact doors since Luke hadn't tossed a grenade nearby. He and Roxi inspected each, finding only a few personal effects and a rifle that Roxi slung over her back. Either these rooms weren't used much, or the vampires belonging to them were elsewhere, possibly even dead from the combat above and below ground.

"Luke, I can hear your teeth grinding," Roxi whispered, squeezing his forearm.

He opened his jaw, stretching the muscles growing sore from tension. "Sorry. Just wondering why we haven't found the nursery yet. I can smell it. I can feel it."

"I know. Me, too. We'll find it."

Luke gave her a weak smile and nodded, gesturing for her to continue down the hall. When they reached a dead end, they jogged back. Just as they poked their head back into the main corridor, they pulled back when a light shined down toward them.

"Luke, is that you?" Sam called.

"Yeah, it's us. Nothing else down this way. Just empty dorm rooms," Luke replied.

"OK. Delilah pressed further down the other corridor, but she left a few people to watch this hall."

Luke nodded. "Let's not keep the woman waiting."

They jogged back to the intersection and then worked their way up the corridor. As they moved closer, gunfire echoed down the hall. Luke picked up his speed until he found the rest of the group, trading fire with either werewolves or mercenaries. They didn't set off Luke's vampire alarms.

"What do we have here?" Luke asked.

"Not sure. They got Amelie in the leg. She'll be alright, but she's hanging back for a moment." Delilah loaded a few more shells into her shotgun.

"Hmm. I'm going to try something." Luke leaned toward the corner. "Hey, you assholes shooting at us. Cease fire. Are you human or werewolf?"

Whoever they were stopped shooting. "Human."

"Listen, human. If you want to live, throw down your weapons and surrender, and you'll leave this camp alive. I'm only really interested in killing vampires, but if you choose to keep fighting, there will be no mercy. You will die, every last one of you. Take a minute or two to chat it over."

Luke looked at Delilah and shrugged. "Worth a shot," he whispered.

A minute later, one of the humans broke the silence. "You'll let us go unharmed?"

"Yes. You will be held here until we leave, then you will be free to go. I suggest you leave quickly when we do, because there won't be anything left here, and you don't want to be around when the vampires come to check out why you failed, or you'll end up in one of their cages, living out the rest of your short life as a juice box."

"And we have your word?"

"Aye. You have my word that you won't be harmed," Luke yelled back.

"OK. What now?"

"All of you toss your weapons out into the corridor where we can see them. Then, I want you to come out two at a time, hands on your heads, and walk this way. How many of you are there?"

"Eight."

"When the last one is here, you'll be our guests. You can show us around. The faster we clear these tunnels, the faster you can be on your merry way. Deal?" Luke asked.

"Deal."

Two by two, the mercenaries walked down the hallway, hands on their heads, and waited patiently as they were thoroughly frisked and relieved of various small weapons, mostly blades. When they were done, Luke had his team gather up their impressive array of hardware, adding it to the pack's armory.

Luke looked over the crowd of nervous men. "Which one of you is the leader?"

A tall white man raised his hand slowly. "I am."

"What's down this corridor?" Luke asked.

"A few rooms we used, then several rooms the vampires slept in during the day," he replied.

"Is that it? Does this open up into anywhere else?"

The man shook his head. "No. It dead ends just past where we were holed up."

"Where do the vampires keep their victims? The people they

kidnap." Luke was getting irritated and, judging by the increase of nervous glances from the mercenaries, they were noticing it. Luke had seen a lot of bad things in this camp, but he knew the worst was yet to come. But even knowing that, not finding it was like a pebble in his shoe that he couldn't find and seemed to grow magically bigger.

"They're back toward the elevator, the other corridor, though we were never allowed too deep into that area, just to the main door."

"Are there any booby traps? In this corridor?" The man shook his head. "The other?" Again, no.

"Delilah, go peek through this area to confirm what they've said." Luke turned back to the men and infused his voice with a dead serious coldness. "OK, we're going to head back toward the elevator. Then, I'm going to have you wait with my friends while your leader and I make a little trip down the other corridor. And just to refresh your memories about the situation…" He raised his shotgun to add emphasis to his words. "If even one of you makes the slightest move to resist, I'll personally hamstring each and every one of you, both legs, and leave you down here to die slowly, assuming you don't get crushed when I blow this place sky high. Do we understand each other?"

The eight men nodded enthusiastically.

Luke smiled mirthlessly. "Good. I hate misunderstandings."

"All clear down here," Delilah said, jogging back to join them.

Luke arranged the team so the mercs were in the middle, guns pointed at them from both angles. When they made it back to the original split, their backup team was holding the corridor.

"Ahmed. We're going to leave our new friends here with you. If they even look at you funny, waste them. Their lives are ours to spend based on their good behavior," Luke instructed.

"Right. Understood." Ahmed saluted.

Luke took their leader and the rest of his two teams down the other corridor. After a turn to the right, they quickly encountered their first obstacle—a locked security door.

"I don't suppose you know the access code to this door?" Luke asked, looking at the merc.

The merc shook his head nervously. "No."

"I thought so." Luke turned to his people. "Roldie? Think you can take this door down?"

Roldie, a short Asian man of Chinese heritage, grinned wickedly. "I think so."

"Make way," Luke commanded.

As the team stepped back, Roldie went to work on the door, stringing explosives around the door at various points.

"You're not going to bring the corridor down on us, are you?" Luke asked.

"Bruh, you threw a grenade back there," Delilah said, shaking her head.

"Nah, this is pretty small and spread out. It should just knock out this door. Maybe a bit of the frame." Roldie gave his work a last look over. "Let's head back down the hall and join our friends."

Nobody had to be told twice. They ran back down the corridor. Just to be safe, Roldie ushered everyone back into the main hall, putting two turns and a lot of feet between them and the door. When he was ready, he twisted the arming key and stuck his arm out into the corridor and pushed the button, yanking his hand back in. A series of loud pops were followed by the sound of metal twisting and a loud thud.

Roldie grinned. "Voila. An open door."

Luke patted him on the shoulder. "Everyone, let's be cautious. Sam, are you ready to record?"

"Yup."

Luke wanted to take a deep breath, but the stench from the door being blown rolled down the corridor. He closed his eyes and tried to calm himself, trying to keep his body steady enough not to spiral into a panic attack. With a nod, he opened his eyes and turned into the hallway, waving his team after him.

The falling door and explosives had twisted the doorframe, pulling it slightly loose from the wall in a few places. Luke and Roldie tipped the door against the wall, clearing their walking space.

Luke kept a close eye out for any booby traps and an ear open for approaching enemies, but the hallway was as silent as a morgue. When they arrived at the first door, Luke held up his fist to stop the advance. Luke closed his eyes and tried to still his mind before turning his head to look into the window framed near the top of the door. As he turned, he held his breath and opened his eyes, exhaling heavily when he saw it was empty.

He tested the doorknob. Unlocked. He pushed it open and looked around. The room appeared recently made up and ready to receive a fresh load of victims. Luke exited and found Roxi looking into the room across the hall. She held her hand up to prompt everyone to stay back.

"This one, Luke," Roxi whispered.

When he looked over Roxi's shoulder, rows of beds filled with the nearly undead strapped to bed frames with heavy cuffs and bands across their bodies and heads, rubber ball gags stuffed in their mouths. Most laid perfectly still, but a few were starting to twitch.

The feeling of vampire—early, distant and weak—grew stronger and more oppressive with each finger that twitched as a new claw formed at the end of it.

"Sam, are you ready with the camera?" Luke asked, weakly.

Sam nodded. "Are you going to be OK, Luke? You look pale as a ghost."

"I'll be fine." He pulled in his strength along with the strength of his friends and Roxi. "Everyone, pull on your ski masks. Make sure you don't have anything identifying out." He turned to the mercenary. "Now, Mr. Blackbag-Merc, you get to see the wages of your sins."

Luke pushed the door open. Grabbing the merc by the scruff of his neck, he shoved him in toward one of the vamps that was stirring to life.

"Look what your masters have sold your soul to do," Luke said, his anger rising.

The merc tried to back away. Luke grabbed him by the neck again and shoved his head down, so it was mere inches from the face of a freshly born vampire. The first sparks of hatred burned in the baby vamp's eyes. It tried lunging at the merc, hungering for the man's blood, burning to consume his life force. Luke held the merc's head steady despite the man's strength as he tried to push away. The fangs slowly descended for the first time. Luke thought he heard the cold-blooded merc whimper.

Yanking the merc back, Luke turned and slammed him into the wall, shoving his face into the merc's face, nose-to-nose. "This is what you protected. This is what your labor made possible. Watch and remember."

Luke turned around and stalked into the middle of the room, collecting himself before turning to face Sam. As instructed, Pablo escorted the Sherbrooke observer in, so he had a front-row seat. Nodding to himself, Luke turned around. "You ready to roll tape?"

"It's a digital camera, Luke, but yes."

"I'll count down five, then go." Luke counted down, waiting for Sam to nod.

Luke exhaled, remembering the script he'd written. "What you're about to see will probably be called a hoax. For those who believe it to be real, it might shake your place in the world and your sense of security. What you're about to see is the birth of a vampire, or in this case, many vampires."

Luke gestured toward the first ones moving. "As you can see, they're already rising. They are strapped to these beds to make the transition from a once-living human to an undead monster, their soul stripped from them, their inner spark of humanity extinguished."

Sam moved in closer to one that was starting to twitch.

Luke continued, "As it awakens, the claws will extend for the first time. Then their fangs will descend but notice the eyes. Notice the lack of humanity in them. Once it senses a live body near it, it will seek to consume it and destroy, to get its first blood as an undead vampire."

The vampire lunged for Sam, shaking the bed violently as it tried to get to her.

"These restraints and heavy beds are meant to protect the handlers. Before a vampire comes into its control, it seeks and hungers, and it must rend flesh and drain its victims of blood. Nothing can stop the hunger until they develop control which could take days or weeks. Watch as they seek out our blood."

The rest of the team spread out in the room, setting up near the most violently active of the newborn vampires.

"Vampires are not friendly neighborhood do-gooders with a quirk for blood. They're not emo sparkly love interests. They are monsters, one hundred percent. They seek to destroy and dominate and drink you dry. If you're lucky, you might escape. But you might also become their thrall—some do willingly—but they can steal your consent. If you're fortunate, you might die and remain dead, your soul yours to take with you to whatever afterlife you believe in. But the unlucky shall be raised into a blood-thirsty monster."

He looked sadly into the camera. "The vampire preys on the weak. Seeks to spread division to exploit the other. All humanity is its cattle. We exist to meet their needs. We exist to be exploited. They don't view humans as equals. They view us as lesser beings whose only value is to serve them."

Luke pulled out his gladius and cut the thick leather straps holding the legs in place. Delilah stepped up and sliced the one holding the vamp's head in place. Together, they cut the wrists free. The vampire rocked violently, still held down at the waist. It clawed at the leather strap holding it down, gouging thick canyons of shredded leather.

Stepping back, Luke slashed the leather waist band, releasing the vampire. The creature practically flew at Sam. Roldie stepped in and staked the vampire in the heart before it got too close. It exploded into a thick mass of blackish-red goo, splattering Sam and Roldie. Sam, the total professional, brought the camera back to Luke.

"The vampire can be slain with a wooden stake to the heart or with silver. You can remove its head to buy some time. Do not underestimate them, or it'll be the last thing you ever do." Luke turned to the next vampire fighting to free itself and stabbed it through the heart.

It dissolved into goo. His team started with the more active ones. These beds and straps looked stronger than the ones at Wapato jail, but Luke didn't want to take a chance. Sam kept the camera rolling until the last body was turned into goo, then she turned the camera off.

"OK, that was gross. But that is some good footage," Sam said. "And nice job on the staking, Roldie."

Roldie nodded. "Thanks, almost panicked for a moment. That's some scary shit when they're unleashed like that."

Luke nodded, too angry and disgusted with the monsters that could do this to a living person to speak. They turned out the lights and left the room, closing the door.

With his hand braced against the wall, Luke stood on the far side of the corridor. "The next rooms will be worse. Baby vamps aren't the cause of that smell."

Pushing away from the wall, Luke stalked down the hall toward the next window. Inside, he found the next stage of the process—the blooding. As soon as one of the fangers noticed a meal on the other side of the door, they bashed against it. Even though Luke was prepared, he still flinched back.

"Everyone, take a look—starting with you, mercenary." Luke stared knives at the merc, then turned to the observer. "Then you."

The mercenary shook his head, trying to back away but running into Pablo's massive wolfy form. A low growl from Pablo's throat halted the man's retreat. Already prepared, Pablo held onto the observer's arm as he tried to tug away. The blood drained from the observer's face as sweat broke out on his forehead.

"You can look willingly, or you can see it from the other side of the door." Luke's voice vibrated with suppressed rage—burning anger a survival method to keep the horror and panic at bay.

Slowly, the merc walked forward, peering into the window. Luke blocked his escape route, so he was forced to lean closely into the security glass as the vampires tried to get to him.

"Look past them at the room and all it contains. Take it all in," Luke instructed.

Luke let the man take in the horror of the room then released him. The merc fell backward onto his butt and shoved himself along on the ground until his back pressed up against the wall. Luke nodded at Sam, making room for her.

Sam lined up so she could get the widest framing possible then nodded at Luke.

"This is the second stage in the young vampire's life," Luke said, narrating the most macabre nature documentary of all time. "The freshly whelped vampires are put into this room for their first blooding and remain here until they can control themselves. Their victims are lowered alive into the room through a trapdoor in the ceiling."

Luke took a moment to summon some saliva into his dry mouth. "The vampires tear into them, feeding on the blood and the victim's terror. Once the human victim is dead, their body is shredded and gnawed on by the vampire for the pure enjoyment of destruction."

Sam let the camera record for a little longer as the vampires, fangs extended and eyes burning with hatred and hunger stared back. Once she stopped recording, she stepped away from the window, making room for others to look in as Pablo guided the observer toward the door. He breathed shakily as he tried to pry Pablo's fingers from his arm.

"We're not going in there, are we?" Roldie asked.

Luke shook his head. "No, it would be too dangerous. General destruction is better."

Delilah stepped up next to Luke. "What was the other door you threatened to show the merc?"

"The one in the ceiling." Luke turned and headed down the hall.

The next door he found led to a small room with a staircase leading up to a platform over the previous room. This was where the victims were transported and fed to the teething vampires.

"When we're ready, we'll use these rooms to deal with the vampires," Luke said, heading deeper into the corridor, the charnel house stench growing thicker.

Stopping by the next door, he peered in, finding the source of the stench. The destroyed bodies of their victims had been unceremoniously discarded in this room. He didn't need to look for more than a few moments. Turning, he pointed at the mercenary and crooked his finger to summon him. The trembling merc stumbled forward, struggling to control his gag reflex.

"Behold, the end result of the innocent people dragged into this hellhole. This is how you earned your paycheck. The innocents either ended up back in that room as one of the monsters or in this room as one of their victims." Luke's voice was deadly quiet.

The merc collapsed onto his knees and crawled away until he heaved his guts out on the side of the wall. Luke ignored him and turned to the observer, who looked pale and shaky.

"Observe," Luke gritted out through clenched teeth.

"No…no…" He shook his head.

"Pablo," Luke said.

Pablo grabbed the observer by the back of his neck and by an arm, walking him toward the room filled with the shattered remnants of innocent humans.

"This is what your neutrality buys, Sherbrooke wolf. In the face of this horror, there is no neutrality. When you choose not to stand, you acquiesce to this."

"I...I...I didn't know..." He breathed heavily, trying to push away. "What have we done..."

"Ah, your neutrality is even more insidious. You're not an observer; you're a spy," Luke said, staring at the observer, his gaze cold and furious. "It's your lucky day. I'm only going to scar you emotionally. Look at your works and think of every loved one mourned. Every life snuffed out before their time. Every child that weeps at the loss of a mother or father or sibling. Those are your legacy, the legacy of your pack. You'll play your roll, observer, and carry word of the atrocities you've stained your souls with."

Luke turned his back and took a few steps away before turning back to face the spy. "And take this message back with you. Every werewolf I find aiding a vampire will meet the same fate as their masters—dead at my hands. You tell them the Centurion Immortal is here, and he's coming for them. I suggest you convince them to take this one chance."

Luke stalked away, heading further down the corridor they'd been working their way through until he reached its end, closed off with another locked security door. He turned and returned to his friends. Sam had just finished with the carcass room, shutting it.

"Roldie, there's another door down at the end of this hall. Unlock it for me, please," Luke said, turning into a corridor they hadn't explored yet.

"Got it." Roldie ran down the hallway as the rest of the team followed Luke.

Roxi caught up with him, taking his hand in hers and giving it a reassuring squeeze. "I'm here with you, Luke. Don't shut us out."

He stopped and held up his hand so everyone stopped, then leaned down and put his lips near Roxi's ear, her head blocking the view of his lips. "If I don't keep the anger coursing through my veins, I won't be able to make it out of here. I'm barely keeping it together."

Roxi caressed the back of his head. "I understand, dōšagīh. Anger is a tool, and if it's the right one for you at the moment, wield it with the strength and grace you wield your gladius."

Luke nodded and continued down the hallway, stopping at the first door. He steeled himself before looking through the window.

Terrified faces stared back at him as they huddled as far from the door as possible, probably thinking him one more of their tormentors.

"Clear!" Roldie yelled.

A half minute later, a series of small explosions announced the death of another door.

Luke turned his head to face down the hall. "Delilah, take a couple people and see where that door goes. Roldie, I need you down here." Luke turned back to the door. "We're here to rescue you. We're getting you out of here."

He wasn't sure if they didn't hear him, didn't understand him, or didn't believe him. He repeated himself louder, then in French and Spanish. Someone separated themselves from the crowd and walked up to the window, pushing their ear against it. Luke repeated his message in all three languages. The person turned their face, a desperate hope filling their eyes.

"Roldie, can you take out this door without hurting the people inside?" Luke asked.

"Yeah, I think so. You sure they're not vamps?" he asked.

"They're not. The only vamps I feel are those back in the way we came," Roxi supplied so Luke wouldn't have to answer.

"Right-o," Roldie said. "This door isn't as gnarly as the security doors, so it shouldn't need much. Jake? I think it's time for that torch."

One of the members of Erin's pack walked up and lowered a backpack that thunked onto the ground. Roldie unzipped it and pulled out a mini torch set up. Unwinding the hose, he turned on the gas and ignited the torch. Luke told the people in the room to get away from the door. Roldie started with the hinges, then ran it down the other side, cutting the locks.

"Stand back." Roldie moved his torch and got out of the way. "If they push it from the middle, it should fall right over. Tell them to stay away from the edges. They'll be hot."

Luke yelled through the door, catching the attention of the person who he'd spoken to earlier, and relayed the instructions. Once he was sure they understood, he stepped out of the way and waited. A moment later, the door thudded to the ground. Inside the room, people screamed. The man who'd pushed the door over saw Pablo and fell backward, scrambling away from the giant werewolf in his scary bipedal form.

"Hey, Pablo, mind heading back a bit? They're a bit skittish," Luke said.

Pablo nodded and headed back to the intersection.

Luke poked his head into the room. "It's OK. He's a friend. He won't harm you. We're going to get you out of here."

"Not with that monster out there, not after what they've done to us," the man said.

Roxi stepped into the room, holding her hands up where they could be seen. "Not all werewolves are bad. Most are good or near enough, just like any other person, but there are some bad ones, too. We've killed or captured the bad ones. We need to get you out of here."

"What about the other monsters, the ones that drink our blood? Are some of you…vampires?" he asked, terror staining his words.

Luke shook his head. "No. No vampires here. There are no good vampires. They're soulless monsters, stripped of their humanity. It's my mission to end their scourge."

The man thought about it for a moment. "OK. We'll go with you."

"Can everyone walk, or do some of you need help?" Roxi asked.

"Some of us are a bit weak after being snacked on for so long."

Roxi poked her head out the door. "Go get those bloody mercenaries. For once in their lives, they'll do something useful." She looked at the man. "We'll get you some help so everyone can get out."

"I'm going to check down the hall." Luke squeezed Roxi's arm, then left her to sort the people out.

He found two more rooms filled with people and summoned Roldie to cut them out. While Luke let Roldie work with his cutting torch, Luke checked at the end of the hall and found one last room, but this one had a heavy-duty door with crossbars on the outside. When he looked in, he found more people, though he guessed they were likely to be werewolves with all the extra precautions.

Two more doors thudding to the ground announced the freedom of the other two rooms.

"What do we have here?" Roldie asked, sidling up next to Luke.

"Can you get them out?" Luke asked.

Roldie peeked into the room. "It's not very big. I can probably… Holy shit, it's the missing two wolves. Oh, my god, we found them." He looked up at Luke. "I'll try cutting them out, but if I have to blast, we can see if a few of them can go wolf and protect the rest. They'll take some shrapnel, but it's probably the best option."

"Do it." Luke stepped back so the man could work. When Roxi joined him, he pulled her in close and embraced her. "We found the two kidnapped wolves from Erin's pack."

"We saved quite a few people tonight, Luke. We did good work."

Luke nodded. "I know." Sighing, he added, "It never feels like enough."

"I know. I truly do, but we have to take the victories when we can. Delilah just reported in. At the end of the hall is a back door out. It opens up just outside the fence. There are stairs and another elevator. It's got power."

"Good. Can you and Delilah take charge of the evacuation? I have another project I want to take care of before we blow this popsicle stand." Luke kissed her forehead, the heat of her skin seeping into his lips and thawing a bit of the cold barrier he'd erected to protect himself in this pit of despair.

"Of course," Roxi replied.

Luke smiled sadly, then walked briskly down the hall toward the exit Delilah had found. Taking the steps two at a time, he was soon at the top, the bit of burn in his thighs reminding him of simple things like his living and breathing muscles. When he found the carefully guarded prisoners, Luke summoned the guards and told them his plan.

In small groups, he took the mercenaries and werewolves downstairs and showed them the results of their work, from the sludge-soaked birthing room, to the ravenous monsters trapped in their teething room, to the carcass locker. Then, he took them back up into the light of the night and grabbed another group. The reactions varied from horrified, to vomiting, to tears, and in a few, amusement. Those people he'd probably have to face again, though next time there would be no mercy. By the time he finished with the groups, the prisoners had been brought up via the elevators and were being moved toward the gate.

Standing in front of the captured mercenaries and werewolves, Luke looked them over, his cold angry stare causing many of them to flinch. "Today, you get mercy. But if I find any of you aiding vampires again, there will be no mercy. You will die with your masters. We have images of each of you, and you'll go into a database. Next time we meet, it better be as allies, for if we meet as enemies, you'll learn why the fangers fear me more than their own vampire lords. Guards, take them in four groups to each of the cardinal directions and let them go." Luke made to walk away but stopped. "If I see any of you near this camp or near our caravan, you will be gunned down without question."

Owen and Roldie ran up to Luke. "We've got everything ready to go."

Luke nodded. "Thanks. Help get everyone evacuated."

"Noooo!" a woman screamed.

"What now?" Luke mumbled, jogging toward the scream. The loud whine of a dog joined the noise as he approached.

He found a small crowd standing in a circle. Shoving his way through, he stumbled at what he saw, his knees nearly giving out on him.

"Oh, no… Why?" Luke stared at the body of Jeremy, his mother on her knees holding his hand and keening in anguish. Brutus stood on the other side, sniffing the boy and whining.

Even though the young man's chest rose and fell weakly, he didn't know how he wasn't dead with a piece of his skull shot away. Luke couldn't see the entry point, but the exit wound looked hideous.

"How did he… What happened?" Luke's breathing grew shallow as his vision blurred around the edges.

Charlie stepped up. "I'm sorry. He snuck out when I planted the explosives on the power lines. I tried to find him, but I had to get to my next objective."

"Someone get a fucking medic," Luke yelled.

As if summoned instantly by his anger, a couple people ran up with a stretcher. Simone squatted next to Erin and helped move her so the medics could put Jeremy on a stretcher and carry him away. It looked like Simone was going to have to carry Erin until she saw Luke.

Fury flared to life in her eyes. She stalked toward him and slapped him, the blow rocking his head around. He stumbled but regained his balance, preparing for the next blow. He heard the grumbling and shifting feet of some of his packmates as he held up his hand to stop them from doing anything. Erin held her arm raised, poised to strike again, but as she stepped into range, she rained down blows on his armor covered shoulders with the heels of her fists, tears streaking down her face as she screamed out her pain in Luke's face.

There was nothing he could say to assuage her anguish, not at the likely mortal wounding of her eldest child. Frankly, he'd rather have taken another slap and more. He'd earned her ire, failing to protect the young man whose path he'd crossed.

As her blows weakened and she sagged into Luke, sobbing on his shoulder, her arms hanging limply by her sides, Luke raised an arm and wrapped it around her shoulder, rubbing his hand comfortingly over her back. It was a wholly inadequate gesture, but there was little else he could do. He ached for Erin and the pain she felt that he'd caused. He felt a pit of emptiness opening inside him, threatening to overwhelm him.

A couple of Erin's packmates took her by the shoulders and walked her away from Luke.

"What are we standing around for? Let's get this place evacuated," Sam ordered.

As everyone went about their tasks, Sam stood by Luke, holding his hand as they watched the victims be loaded into their evac buses while Luke's people loaded all the weapons they'd collected into the back of the box van. Simone stood to the side, holding Brutus on a leash. Based on the stains to his fur, the dog had done his share of fighting to protect his friends. They'd need to give him a good bath when they got back to Portland.

On his other side, he felt a hand slide into his hand. After holding her hand for months on end in their shared prison, he could recognize Roxi's palm instantly, like a lifeline cast to him to keep him from drowning in his own despair.

"Are you OK to do our last recording?" Sam asked, giving his hand a squeeze.

Luke nodded. Pablo, in the driver's seat of an SUV, pulled through the gate and turned around, parking with the nose pointing toward the exit. Delilah ran by the SUV.

She slid to a stop in front of Luke, Roxi, and Sam. "We've got everyone loaded. It's time to get out of here."

Luke nodded. Sam let go of his hand and jogged to the SUV with Delilah before they hugged; Sam climbed into the passenger seat of the SUV, and Delilah jogged off to join Simone in the vehicle they were riding in. Roxi and Luke slid into the backseat of the SUV as they waited for the caravan to roll to life and open up some distance between themselves and the vampires' death camp. Pulling in line at the end, Pablo drove until Sam called a halt.

Together, Luke and Sam set up their last shot with the camp behind Luke in the near distance. Roxi stepped out and stood next to the car, her eyes locked on Luke. In them, he saw all the love and support she could muster for him, to help him hold his strength just a little longer. After Sam set up her camera, she gave Luke the signal to talk.

"Behind me is the camp you saw pieces of. It's sitting in this beautiful forest, hidden from your eyes so you can't see the ugliness of what the vampires do, what they are. They seduce their victims with promises of immortal life and riches. With a promise of belonging, of getting everything they feel they are denied by society. But they only give you death."

Luke looked back at the camp and then back at the camera. "If you are one of the unlucky few selected to be birthed into undeath, like those you saw in this video, then know that I will be the one to bring you death. You will learn why vampires throughout the world have feared the Centurion Immortal for centuries. You will know the name of your doom, and I will bring it upon you furiously."

He twisted the activation key on the remote and pushed the button. One by one, the barracks exploded into fire and debris as the chain of explosives Owen and Roldie had set up detonated. When the last of the barracks exploded, the watch towers went up, collapsing in gouts of flames. Braced for it, Luke still nearly fell when the explosives set up in the underground lair ignited into an inferno erupting from the ground, raining dirt and construction detritus in a wide radius around the crater that had been the camp. Small bits of dirt and slivers made it as far as Luke and his friends, but nothing large enough to do any real damage.

Sam turned off the camera. "I got the chills and tinglies. You're very frightening when you want to be, Luke. If I were your enemy, I'd be seriously reconsidering my allegiances."

Roxi sauntered over, a soft, empathetic smile on her face as she pulled him in for a hug. "You did well, dōšagīh." She brushed some dirt off his shoulder and out of his hair. "You can put away the anger for now. I'm here for you."

Luke nodded weakly and walked to the car. Together, they stripped off their armor quickly and pulled on clean shirts and hoodies before getting in the back seat. Roxi slid in next to him and wrapped an arm around him. He twisted in and buried his face in her shoulder, breathing hard and ragged.

"It's alright, dōšagīh. I'll take care of you," Roxi crooned into his ear.

With a shuddering breath, the tears fell as he sobbed into the soft cloth of her hoodie as she rubbed his back soothingly. They bounced down the gravel road, the faint flicker of burning debris in the background. Luke cried until he felt empty and drained. He no longer felt locked in the embrace of numbness and impotent rage. He'd settle for empty and in Roxi's arms. Empty could be refilled, and Roxi was doing everything in her power to pour her love into him; he soaked it up like a dry sponge.

Drained of energy and exhausted, he sat back, caressing Roxi's cheek. "Thank you, dōšagīh."

"Anything for you." Roxi leaned in and kissed the tip of his nose. "You look tired. Why don't you see if you can catch a nap on the way back to Portland?"

Luke nodded and turned. Sam held her hand out with a travel packet of tissues. He took a few and blew his nose, then leaned up against the window, quickly falling into a bumpy slumber.

LUKE WASN'T sure how long he was out, or if he was awake or just having a dream of his current situation, but the voices of his friends drifted back to him.

"Roxi, mind if I ask you a personal question?" Sam asked.

"Not at all. Please ask away," Roxi replied.

"How are you handling this all better than Luke?"

"Yeah, this seems to fuck him up a lot," Pablo added.

"I don't know, not really. It's not that my brain isn't fucked up after nearly two thousand years of all this, and it's not as if I'm stronger, but we're different people with different life experiences. Different training."

"How would your training matter? Did you learn how to deal with this kind of death and darkness when you were young?" Pablo asked.

"Not as such. I'm an assassin and a spy. That was how I served my family and our Empire. I was trained to do those tasks. As an assassin, you go in, do your mission, then get out. You rarely see the immediate impact of your actions. You're long gone by then if you've done your job well." Roxi paused. "Luke is a soldier and a general. He was trained to think in terms of acceptable losses and attrition, the number of soldiers you had to sacrifice to achieve a victory. When he was just a common legionnaire, it meant taking wounds to stay alive. When he commanded legions, it meant deciding how many men he could afford to lose. Just those two things add up."

She sighed. "Since he left the Roman Empire, he's been fighting an increasingly lonely battle against the vampires. He fights like a general. Meeting his enemies in the field of battle and making calculations of the sacrifices needed for him to win. Except without an army, he takes all the losses. All the attrition is on himself—on his psyche. I'm honestly amazed he's still standing and fighting. I can't calculate how strong a man he is to do all he's done, take all the pain he's felt, and still keep at it, still love as deeply as he does."

Luke felt the warmth and pressure of Roxi's hand on his leg as she rubbed it gently.

"You love him very much, don't you?" Sam asked.

"I do, but so do you two as his friends." Roxi snuggled into his side. "I'd do anything to bear his pain so he wouldn't have to take it all on himself, but since I can't, I'll hold him and let him know he's safe and loved so he knows he's not alone anymore."

"We've all taken up that burden since we met Luke," Pablo said. "There's a reason he's my best friend. He's a good man."

With Roxi's heat against his body and the soothing feel of her hand moving over his leg, lulling him back toward unconscious, he gave up listening to their conversation and fell back to sleep—but not alone. Not with Roxi and Pablo and Sam there with him.

When the car bumped to a stop, Luke peeled his eyes open. The morning sun had drifted over the horizon, illuminating a small city as it woke from its night of blissful ignorance about what had happened in the woods a few hours north. Roxi's weight against him felt comforting as she snored lightly, her head at an odd angle as it rolled off his shoulder at some point.

"Where are we?" Luke asked, quietly.

"Back in Portland. The other Portland," Sam replied, then yawned loudly. "I'm fucking beat."

"Are we home yet?" Roxi stirred next to him, her words groggy and barely intelligible.

"We're close." Luke kissed the top of her head, her messy hair tickling his nose.

Sam twisted in the passenger seat so she could talk to them more easily. "I've got you two in a hotel on the outskirts of town. It looks pretty nice."

Pablo turned his head to the side slightly. "Don't worry about anything for today. We've got everyone taken care of, and we'll stash the weapons van on one of the pack properties. Simone and Delilah have volunteered to keep Brutus. We figured it would be best to avoid the property the spy saw us on."

Pablo slipped away from the caravan and dropped Roxi and Luke off, handing them a key, then sped away. They were still concerned about Luke's safety after the first assassination attempt, and with the outing of a spy, they were right to be.

Luke extended the handle on the rolling carry-on and bent over to grab one handle of the crate. Roxi grabbed the other. Together, they carried their swords and armor up to the room. They took enough time for a couple quick showers, then collapsed into bed, passing out.

THEY WOKE up well after lunchtime. Luke rolled over and checked his phone. Sam had sent him an appointment request for tomorrow at two in the afternoon.

He texted Sam back, *Are you sure there's nothing we can't help with?*

You and Roxi can have the day off. We can assist with the day-after logistics for the rescued prisoners. This is my and Pablo's expertise. If something crops up, we'll interrupt you, but you two have earned a much-needed respite. I know how hard that was for you.

Thanks, Sam. Talk to you soon.

"Looks like we have the rest of today and tomorrow morning off while Sam and the team help the local packs with the logistics. I imagine they'll be trying to talk the packs into replicating what we set up in Portland." Luke flopped back into the king-sized bed, rolling onto his back.

Roxi rolled over and kissed his shoulder. "I can think of some productive ways to spend that time." She kissed his neck. "Assuming you don't have any objections." Her lips brushed the edge of his ear.

"I'm willing to discuss the matter," Luke replied just as Roxi lowered her lips to cover his mouth and stop him from speaking.

They spent the rest of the afternoon indulging in each other's bodies and focusing on the very immediate need to be with each other and express their love and survival to each other.

After the sun disappeared into the west and darkness embraced their little corner of Portland, Maine, they called a taxi and ventured into downtown for dinner and drinks, returning to their hotel when they finished to soak in the large jacuzzi tub before resuming the activities they'd spent the afternoon participating in. Sweaty and satiated, Luke fell into a deep, dreamless sleep and woke late for the second day in a row.

"Is that coffee I smell?" Luke asked, before yawning deeply.

"I slipped out while you had a lay in. I needed a little wake-me-up and thought it would be rude not to bring you something. There's also a lovely scone waiting for you." Roxi shifted out of her chair and bent over, kissing Luke good morning.

He loved the way she pronounced scone "skawn." Her mix of accents always sounded like honey to his ears. Slipping on a robe, he hit the restroom first before tucking into his coffee and scone.

"So, dōšagīh, what shall we do with the rest of our morning?" Roxi asked, running her hand down the edge of her robe, the weight of her hand pulling it open enough to reveal she'd stripped after returning from her morning coffee errand.

Luke pulled her onto his lap and kissed her deeply. "I like your solution to our excess time." He stroked her cheek, tucked an errant curl back into its wild thatch, then rested his cheek against her chest. "I needed this. To feel human and loved." He looked up into her eyes, filling his gaze with all the love and need he could bear to reveal. "Thank you for being there for me."

Roxi kissed his forehead and stood up, taking his hand and leading him to the bed. "I need this too."

PABLO MET them out front at one-thirty and whisked them away to their meeting with Sam. When they arrived at the Portland-Bangor Pack's community center, Alejandro led them up to the soundproof room Luke had met with Erin in a few days ago.

"Erin won't be joining us today," Alejandro said. "She's with Jeremy."

"Any change in his condition?" Roxi asked.

Alejandro shrugged. "The wound has healed a bit, but it still looks bad. He's still breathing, so our doctors say that's a good sign."

Roxi squeezed Luke's hand and reached out to place a reassuring hand on Alejandro's shoulder. "Our thoughts are with them."

"Thoughts and prayers," Luke thought. Maybe there was something more he could do. "Can Roxi and I have a couple minutes? We'll step out."

"No problems," Alejandro replied.

Sam raised an eyebrow at Luke before they walked out. Luke led Roxi into Erin's office and shut the door.

Luke paced in the small space, his brows furrowed in concentration.

"What are you thinking, Luke?" Roxi asked, leaning up against the wall.

"I've asked Selene for her strength a fair few times. She's lent you her strength when you needed it." He stopped and made eye contact, a tiny spark of hope flaring in his eyes. "Do you think she'd help Jeremy?"

Roxi exhaled then pulled her lips in between her teeth. "You know her far better than I, but she seems to love her children even if they don't know she exists. It can't hurt to ask her. My only concern would be if Erin or the pack are firmly monotheistic, they may be less open to welcoming a pagan goddess into their midst."

"That's always a problem in this time and age." Luke shook his head. "I'll speak to Alejandro."

Roxi nodded. "Are you ready to return?"

Luke nodded and pulled Roxi in for a hug, inhaling her scent as he buried his nose in her unruly hair. "Let's go."

With confidence and purpose in his stride, Luke strode back into the soundproof room, Roxi following in his wake.

"I recognize that face and walk. Luke's got a plan," Pablo said.

Nodding, Luke tried to force the anger and sadness from his visage. "I do indeed." He turned to Alejandro. "I might have a way to help Jeremy. It's not orthodox, though. I want to speak with you before I interrupt Erin's grief."

"I'm willing to listen." Alejandro gestured toward the chair across from him with his head.

Luke sat and crossed an ankle over his knee. "How much do you know about the origin of the werewolves?"

When Alejandro shrugged and shook his head, saying he knew nothing, Luke told him the tale of their origin, the good, the bad, and the realities. Then, Luke told Alejandro about his relationship with Selene over time from the first time she looked down on him in the temple of Mithras in Antiochia in 117 CE to her guidance and compassion as he struggled to survive in the arena and after.

"You worship a pagan goddess?" Alejandro asked, looking skeptical.

"I am a pagan. I was born one, raised one, and have been one all my life. I get my strength and power from a pagan god. I've paid homage to many pagan deities over the centuries, but Selene is the one to whom I owe my loyalty. She is a kind and gentle goddess." Luke made sure he held Alejandro's gaze. "I can't promise her aid. She chooses how her power is spent, but I can ask on Jeremy's behalf, if Erin will give me permission."

"Can she heal his wound and bring him back?" Alejandro asked, hope tinging his voice.

Luke shrugged. "I don't know. It would be foolhardy to promise something I have no control over, especially without speaking to her first."

Alejandro sat back in his chair, clasping his hands over his stomach, and stared off into the distance. After he made his decision, he made eye contact with Luke. "When we're done here, I'll go speak to her."

Luke nodded and smiled. With that settled for the moment, Alejandro, Pablo, and Sam filled Luke in on all the work that'd happened over the previous twenty-four hours, detailing how the various packs had divided up the victims of the vampires' death camp, though the three American packs were bearing the weight of that burden since the border was closed, but the St. Johns Pack had offered to provide money to aid in the cause until such time as people could be safely moved. It's easy to go full wolf and jog across the border on all fours, but trying to sneak sick and unhealthy people across the border with both countries' border patrols on high alert seemed foolhardy.

The werewolves they'd rescued were being kept in Maine and, as soon as they were healthy, would be moved across the border as a way to help split up the needs of all those Luke and the local packs had rescued.

"You've been busy," Luke said.

"Yeah, it was a lot of organization, but we were prepared thanks to Sam and Pablo. We'd have been in big trouble without their aid." Alejandro nodded his thanks to Pablo and Sam before returning to Luke. "Now that you've helped us rescue our missing wolves, what's next for you all?"

Luke looked over at Sam and Pablo, then back to Alejandro. "Not sure quite yet. I think that's on our agenda after this meeting. We've been making preparations, but once we meet, we'll fill you in on our next move."

"Sounds like a plan to me." Alejandro stood and shook Luke's hand. "I'm going to head over to speak with Erin, then I'll be in touch with you if your plan is a go. You're welcome to use this room if you'd like after I go."

"Thanks, Alejandro. I think we have other plans, but your offer is appreciated." Sam gave him a hug.

They followed Alejandro out of the building, then loaded up in the SUV they'd used the other night, heading to Allagash brewing. They'd rented out the brewery's event space for their meeting, bringing in everyone from the team so they could lay down their final plans for their return to Portland, to home.

"We've got enough storage space to get all our toys, new and old, home," Owen said. "I'm expecting one more shipment of new toys from my local contacts. They've got some sort of hidden route over the border they're using to get their shipments across."

"Delilah?" Sam said. "How we looking on seats for butts?"

"We're short a couple spots right now, but I have an appointment to look at a passenger van tomorrow morning. If it looks good, we can get everyone home."

"Did we take any injuries during our little excursion the other night?" Luke asked.

"Nothing of consequence," Sam replied. "Some people are going to need to have some bullets and shrapnel removed when we get home. The usual fast healing fun and games."

Luke chuckled. "I guess I'll be in that line, too. Speaking of bullets, how goes production on replacing our anti-vamp shells?"

Pablo took his feet off the chair next to him and sat up. "Pretty good. We've got enough material. If we put a couple days of hard labor in, we'll have a decent amount, assuming we don't run into trouble."

"If nobody has anything to add, that's it for my agenda," Sam said, standing in the middle of the room. When no one had anything to add, she set down her notepad. "Keep us in the loop on your various projects, and once we have a go time, we'll let you all know."

Raising hands to hush the new round of chatter, Sam waited until the pack quieted down. "Now, Pablo and I thought it would be a good time to have a light celebration since we broke up another vampire nursery and made it out without serious loss or injury to their people, though Jeremy's wounding would dampen the mood. Our food should be coming in shortly. There's an open bar. Enjoy yourselves! We have the room for the rest of the evening. We'll make sure you all get back to your various hotels safely."

Cheers and clapping rose. Sam stuffed her notepad into her backpack then went to the door to let in the staff so they could refill drinks and get the evening started.

"Good thinking on keeping our party contained," Luke said to Sam after she procured herself a beer. "Probably best that we're not whooping it up in town with the local pack in mourning."

"My thoughts exactly. I feel terrible for Erin. Have you heard anything from Alejandro yet?" Sam took a drink.

Luke shook his head, sliding his arm around the small of Roxi's back so he could pull her in closer for a side hug. "Nothing yet. It's a lot to present."

"That's the truth." Sam chuckled. "I know it took some readjustment on my end when you first introduced us, and I'm a Shin-

Buddhist with an open mind. Why don't you two go get yourselves some beer and join your friends?"

"I am feeling a touch parched." Roxi smacked her lips and rubbed her throat.

Luke laughed and guided Roxi toward the bar, following along. With their beers in hand, they sought out Delilah and Simone.

"I haven't gotten to talk to you in a couple days." Luke said, giving Delilah a one-armed hug. "How are you doing?"

"Doing pretty good," Delilah replied.

Beside her, Simone snorted.

Delilah arched an eyebrow and turned to Simone. "Do you have something so add, Ms. Ndiaye?"

"Actually, I do. If there's anyone in this room who you could talk to, it would be Luke and Roxi." Her French accent, usually in control, grew thick with emotion. She turned to Luke. "She hasn't been sleeping—almost not at all since we got back. Bad nightmares."

Delilah's shoulders sunk as she avoided eye contact with Luke.

He reached out and squeezed her shoulder affectionately. "That's understandable. It's not something you can shake off. I slept pretty badly the first night we got back. I know I'll have nightmares of that place for a long time, and my long time is…long."

The group slowly closed their circle, forming a tight circle of protection.

Delilah finally looked up at Luke. "I can't get rid of the images, Luke. They're there when I wake and there when I dream." She sighed, her eyes watery with unshed tears. "I sometimes wish I'd listened to you all those years ago."

Luke felt for his young friend. She'd been so strong and steadfast since he'd met her, a true force of determination.

"It's a horrible thing to have to manage. But for my part, I'm glad you didn't. I'd have died on the pedestrian bridge or been thrown into Wapato and probably been tortured to death by Cassius and his goons. So many people owe you their lives. It's a terrible burden to bear, the horror of what we fight, and I won't discount your feelings. I've had them and still do on occasion. But for all the horror, it brought you to Simone."

Simone lifted Delilah's arm and draped it over her shoulder. "I owe you my life, and so does my brother. We both owe Luke, and it sounds like you saved his life. Without you, we'd both be gone. And if you had given hunting up, we'd have never met." She looked up at Delilah, her heart in her eyes, and caressed her cheek. "You're the love of my life, and sure, I'd wish there to be less awfulness in the world, but for all of that, it brought us together."

Tears sparkled on Delilah's cheeks. Thrusting her beer toward Luke, she turned and pulled Simone in tightly as soon as Luke took the half empty glass from her hand.

"Simone, I love you with all my heart and soul. I'm sorry I said that."

"Don't be sorry. It was a true feeling and an honest one. We lead a terrible life this hunting of vampires, but we have each other—and for that, I feel more blessed than words can convey."

Luke reached out and took Roxi's hand, looking over at her with a misty-eyed smile on his face. He was happy for his dear friend. Delilah deserved the kind of love she had with Simone. He also knew the psychic trauma she'd suffered being exposed to the hell of the vampire nursery. She'd likely never shake it entirely, but she had someone to share the burden with, someone who loved her and would hold her up when needed. And so did Luke in both Roxi and Maggie.

Roxi had helped prevent his descent into despair. He knew, and he guessed she did, too, that he wasn't out of the woods yet—not after that death camp, but they had each other. When they were back in their room, he'd need to check in with her so he could ensure he was providing the kind of support she'd given him. Also, he'd need to make a call to Maggie. He missed her and needed to hear her voice.

When Delilah and Simone parted, an arm still around each other, Luke handed her glass back to her. "We're all here for you, Delilah. Roxi, Pablo, Sam, and I have all lived long lives and seen more than our share of badness. We're not professionals, but we are experienced and love you."

Delilah nodded and smiled weakly. "Thank you, Luke, for everything."

Roxi raised her glass. "Here's to you, Delilah and Simone. You're such wonderful people, and I'm glad I can consider you friends. And thank you for saving Luke's life, because I got to meet him and was rescued thanks to you."

They clinked glasses and took drinks. Simone fished some tissues out for Delilah, who blew her nose before taking off to the restroom to make sure she was still in order and splash some water on her face.

"Thank you for saying that, Luke. She needed to hear it." Simone finished the last of her beer.

"She's a tough woman, but she's not always the most open with her emotions. Of course, I'm a poor mentor in that department. I'm even more closed up than she is." He chuckled and shook his head at himself.

"Dōšagīh, it looks like the food is ready. Let's go get a plate." Roxi gestured toward the chafing dishes wafting steam and delectable aromas into the air. "Why don't you come with us? We'll let Delilah have cutsies when she's finished in the restroom."

Together, they got in line and filled heaping plates before finding a table to sit at. After letting off the initial bit of emotion, Delilah seemed to feel much better, joining in the camaraderie and laughter of her closest friends as Pablo and Owen tried to top each other with outrageous stories and jokes. After dinner, people moved about, mingling and checking in on the rest of their friends and team. As the beers flowed, the room grew noisier with everyone celebrating success and surviving.

Though Luke was quiet, as he often was, he absorbed the good feelings and wishes, feeling buoyed. Pablo was in the middle of yet another story when the circle they were standing in grew quiet, Pablo included.

The group parted, revealing Erin standing with her hands held in front of her.

" I 'm sorry for disturbing your merriment, but I'd like to speak with you, if that's OK." Erin shuffled nervously as she clasped her hands, twisting them. Her eyes were dark and red.

Luke expected judgment in her voice when discussing their celebration but found none. "Of course. Let's step outside so we can have some quiet."

Erin nodded and turned to exit to the side patio. Luke followed her, holding the door, then ensuring it shut behind them. They stepped away from the windows so they wouldn't be watched, but ended up standing under the moonlight in awkward silence as they avoided making eye contact with each other.

"I'm sorry about Jeremy. How's he doing?" Luke asked, breaking the silence.

"About the same. The wound has mostly closed though, at least the skin. The skull is knitting a bit. Still no…" She stopped speaking, choking on what she was going to say.

Luke could probably guess. *"No brain activity."*

"What happened, Luke? I couldn't get any clear answer on how he got there." She looked up, her eyes filled with pain.

Luke sighed. "At some point before we left, he snuck into the back of the box van. We found him when we transferred from the passenger van to the box van for our little charade. Once we found him, we made him move to the passenger van and ordered him to stay. When Charlie went to blow up the power lines heading to the camp, he must have slipped away. After that, I don't know. I didn't see him again until after he'd been found."

She nodded, returning her gaze to the pavement between them. "Alejandro tells me there might be something you can do for him?"

"Maybe. I can't make any guarantees until I speak to her," Luke replied.

"And the 'her' is a goddess of werewolves?" Erin asked, an eyebrow raised.

"She's the goddess of the moon, Selene to the Greeks and Luna to the Romans. She and Artemis accepted the werewolves when they rebelled against their creators and fled. She is also my patron and has lent her strength to me on many occasions." Luke cast his eyes up toward the silvery moon peeking out as clouds danced past her. "If you wish, I can speak to her now."

Hope flooded Erin's eyes. "Would you? Please?"

Luke nodded and looked to the Moon. *"My Mistress?"*

"I am here, my brave soldier. How do you fare?"

"I am well."

"Not entirely. I can feel the wound in your heart. It is fresh and deep." Sympathy suffused her voice.

"It is. It is partly this that I wish to speak to you about. A young man was wounded grievously in the head." He sighed. *"He shouldn't have even been there. His mother is a new ally and forbade him to join in our assault against the vampires' camp."*

"I rarely interfere in such things save for in the instance of our hunters, and you're the last of them, although I'll claim Roxiustana now, but I will do this for you and in honor of my pact with Artemis and the children of Tutyr."

"Thank you, My Mistress." Luke bowed his gratitude.

"I shall await your word, Lucius."

When he looked down at Erin, her eyes were filled with a mix of pain and hope.

"Selene has agreed to look at Jeremy, but this may be beyond her. She isn't really a goddess of healing, nor is she as powerful as she once was. Her followers are far fewer than in days of old."

"And if she helps, what will she demand of me, of Jeremy?" Erin asked.

"She does this because I asked her to, and in the spirit of her pact to protect your ancient werewolf ancestors. She doesn't compel worship. Most who do give it to her freely out of love. She is kind and gracious."

"Is there anything I need to prepare?" Erin asked, shuffling nervously.

"Is there a window that can let in the moonlight? Or if it's possible, could we wheel his hospital bed out into the moonlight?" Luke asked.

"I'll call the doctor and have him meet us, but maybe we can get him moved outside."

Luke squeezed her shoulder and gave her a soft, sympathetic smile. "OK. Send me the address. I'll be there as soon as I go talk to the crew."

"I'll text you the info. Thank you. You don't know how much this means to me." Erin darted in and hugged him fiercely.

Though slow to react, he returned the hug, patting her back. When she released him, she left the patio and headed toward the parking lot. Luke watched her go, then turned to find Roxi watching from the doorway.

"I take it Selene is going to try to help?" Roxi asked.

Luke nodded, pulling her in close, and kissed her. "I hope she can help. I don't need another innocent life on my conscience."

Roxi caressed his cheek. "Luke. You can't let his death weigh on you. Jeremy is an adult and made his own decisions. I don't think he deserves these consequences for his actions, but you did everything possible short of sitting on him until we were done. You can't hold all the world's lives in your hand."

"I know, but it's hard. I led the mission, he got shot. I don't know if I can disconnect it in my head. It's too ingrained after centuries of leadership." He sighed, taking her hand in his and kissing her palm.

"It's what makes you a good leader and a good man, but you have to find the balance, so it doesn't weigh too heavily and break you." Her love for him burned in her eyes. "You're a strong man, but you're not as resilient as you used to be all those centuries ago. You need to develop some new ways to protect yourself. We've got a way to go yet."

Luke nodded. "You're right. Maybe after all this time, I'll figure out how to develop that skill. I need to go in and tell everyone where I'm going."

"Where *we're* going." She turned and headed back into the building, but instead of letting her hand slide out of his, she gripped it and pulled him after. "I'm not letting you face that alone with no emotional support."

He was grateful for her offer. Wondering what he'd done to deserve her, he decided to ignore that thought and just be happy she loved him. Once they found Pablo and Sam, Luke filled them in on the situation and where he was going.

"Want some company?" Pablo asked.

Luke patted Pablo's shoulder. "No, you stay here and keep an eye on the kids. If things get too mellow, you can show them how to party."

"Good luck, Luke. Call us if you need anything." Sam slipped between his arms for a hug, then stepped back next to Pablo.

When their taxi arrived, Luke and Roxi slid into the back and gave the driver the address. Twenty minutes later, they rolled up to a nondescript building near downtown Portland. Erin waited for them at the door and ushered them in.

"We use this building for a medical clinic for pack members. He's back this way. We can roll him out to the patio easily enough," Erin said.

"That will work. Let's open the door and get him under the sky." He squeezed Roxi's hand. *"My Mistress, we'll wheel the boy out shortly."*

"I shall be ready."

Erin introduced Luke and Roxi to the pack doctor, then they helped her open the French doors leading out to the patio. Unlocking the wheels on the bed, Luke helped her roll him through the doors and onto the patio.

At first, the silver glow was nearly imperceptible, but as a figure solidified, the glow intensified until Selene stood on the stone patio, resplendent in her silvery Greek dress, her dark tresses falling over a pale shoulder.

Luke and Roxi both bowed low.

"My Mistress." Luke smiled warmly at the goddess.

The goddess returned the smile, the warmth in it lessening the tension at his core. Next, she ran a hand along Roxi's cheek and jaw. "It's good to see you in better health, my child."

"It feels good to be in better health, My Mistress." Roxi looked fondly at the goddess who'd helped save her.

"This is Erin, the packleader of the Portland-Bangor Pack and her son Jeremy," Luke said.

Erin looked stunned, her jaw hanging open and her eyes wide. What had been hopeful skepticism became wonder as an actual goddess appeared out of thin air and moonbeams to stand with them, solid as anyone there, though a faint glow still illuminated the goddess of the moon, standing taller than everyone on the patio.

Selene took Erin's hand in hers and leaned forward, kissing her on the forehead. "My blessing upon you in your grief, my child."

Luke could see a little of the tension draining from Erin's stiff shoulders, though nothing could make her relax with her son laying before her grievously wounded.

"May I?" Selene asked, gesturing toward Jeremy.

Erin nodded. With a single nod in return, Selene turned to focus on Jeremy entirely. She ran her hands over him, holding them a few inches away from him at all times, though she spent a much longer time over his heart and over his head and the wound. Finally, she took one of his hands in both of hers. Bending over, she laid a gentle kiss on his forehead.

"Erin, my child, unfortunately, there is little I can do."

Erin's face fell, her shoulders slumping, as she blinked irregularly, tears forming in her eyes.

"I could heal the wound, but there is nothing to anchor to his body. His spirit has already departed this plane of existence."

Selene's voice held profound sympathy as she looked down at Jeremy's calm face.

Erin's body trembled as she reached her hand out to brace herself but found nothing there. Roxi darted forward and caught her before she could fall to the ground. Clinging desperately to Roxi, Erin wailed her grief, sinking her head into Roxi's shoulder as sobs wracked her body.

Luke bowed his head and closed his eyes as his stomach sank into a deep well of anguish for the loss of a fine young man and for his mother's grief. He stepped back into the darkness, the warmth leaving him as he stepped away from the glow of Selene. When the back of his knees bumped into a chair, he sank into it, holding his head in one hand as he stared at the floor between Jeremy's bed and where he sat.

Erin's sobbing intermixed with the steady beep of the heart monitor were the only sounds in the room. He had no idea how long he sat there or when he fled into his own mind, but warm lips on his forehead stirred him back into the room.

"Luke, dōšagīh, are you alright?" Roxi asked.

"No, not at the moment. Not at all…" He held his hand out to her, and she helped him up.

Roxi wrapped her arms around his waist and squeezed him, resting her cheek against his shoulder. "I wish I could hold your grief for you."

"I would never wish that upon you, my Roxiustana. But I'm glad you're here to be with me. Quick thinking on catching Erin."

"Quick changing of the subject, but I'll allow it. I was ready for something to happen. I'm glad I caught her before she fell." Roxi stepped out of Luke's arms and moved closer to the hospital bed and those surrounding it.

"Are you sure he's gone?" Erin asked, a kernel of hope bleeding through the grief in her voice as she held Jeremy's other hand.

"Truly. I wish it were otherwise, but this body is an empty vessel." Selene rubbed the back of Jeremy's hand.

"Can you see where his soul went?" Erin asked.

Selene shook her head. "That is not within my power or purview. I am sorry, my child."

"If I ask it, can you aid in his body's passing?" Erin's voice was so low, Luke barely caught her question.

"I can."

Erin stared at Jeremy's face. "His body is healing. He'd linger too long, and I want to remember him as he was, not as an empty shell wasting away to nothing."

"Tell me when you would like me to perform this mercy."

"Not yet, please, but could you heal the wound so he's whole again?"

Selene nodded and reached out, laying her left hand on Jeremy's forehead. "It is done."

Erin stood up and leaned over the bed, kissing Jeremy on the cheek, then rubbed her hand over his other cheek. A few tears fell from her face onto his, leaving shiny damp trails slowly descending toward his pillow.

"Goodbye, my sweet boy." She looked up at Selene briefly and nodded before turning her head so she could look at Jeremy's face while she held his hand.

Selene reached out with her left hand and laid it over Jeremy's heart. A moment later, the heart monitor flat lined, sending up its heart-wrenching tone. The young man's chest stopped rising, a last whisper of air passing his lips as gravity compressed his chest in one last exhale.

The goddess took Jeremy's hand and laid it across his chest, placing his hand over his heart. Reaching out, she ran her hand over Erin's hair, stopping on her shoulder. "I am sorry for the loss of your fine boy, my child. My blessings be upon you."

Erin nodded, acknowledging the goddess, but said nothing as tears streamed down her face, falling into the blankets of the bed. Turning, Selene looked sadly toward Luke and Roxi before walking out into the small yard next to the patio. Luke followed.

Standing before his mistress, he bowed his head. "I'm sorry for dragging you into this."

"There is nothing to be sorry for. I was able to aid his mother even if it wasn't the best of results, but she knows for certainty her son has moved on. And neither does she have to watch his body waste away before her eyes. Sometimes that is the best one can do." Selene placed her hand on his cheek and kissed the top of his head. "Thank you for the opportunity to help one of my children."

"Thank you, My Mistress." He bowed deeply to her.

"Fare you well and hold Roxi. Together you are stronger in more than just body." With that, she flared bright and luminous, forcing Luke to close his eyes. When the spots cleared from his eyes, she was gone, but his heart didn't feel as heavy as before, especially with Roxi standing next to him, her arm around him.

"Luke?" Erin said, still holding Jeremy's hand. "I know this isn't your fault, I truly do, but unless there's a reason for you to be in Portland anymore, I would appreciate it if you moved on."

"I'm sorry, Erin. We've returned your packmates and destroyed the local vampire nursery. We need a couple more days to get everything together to start the trip home, but we'll be gone shortly. Until then, I'll stay out of sight."

Erin nodded, then ignored Luke. Roxi led him back onto the patio and through the door. As he passed by Jeremy, Luke reached down and squeezed his forearm, then left the building. Roxi stuck her head out into the street, looking down the road. Tugging on his hand, she pulled him along toward the neon lights of a bar.

They found two empty stools at the bar and sat down. Roxi stared up at the liquor bottles while Luke stared at the scarred bar top.

A bald man with a bar towel over his shoulder sauntered up to them. "What can I get you?"

"Two Maker's—doubles, please," Roxi replied.

"You want rocks?" the bartender asked.

"Neat."

The bartender turned around and grabbed the bottle off the shelf and a couple of bucket glasses so scratched from use and stacking they were nearly opaque. He filled the doubles. "Sixteen bucks."

Roxi pulled out her wallet and dropped a twenty on the bar. "Keep it."

She picked up her glass and took a sip, then a deeper drink, exhaling sharply after swallowing. "Bourbon... That's a bit bitier than Scotch or Irish."

Luke nodded and picked up his glass, pouring half of it down his throat. His face cringed around the burn of the whiskey. Reaching under the bar, Roxi took his hand and held it. Luke stared into his whiskey as he swirled it lightly, watching the amber-brown liquid spin in the glass until he stilled his hand. Once the liquid sloshed back to the bottom of the glass, Luke threw back the rest of the bourbon, then set the glass down, letting the burn of the liquor soothe his numbness.

"'Nother?" the bartender asked.

"Please." Roxi finished her glass and set it next to Luke's. "For both of us." She slid another twenty onto the bar.

The bartender filled their glasses, snagged the cash, and walked away to pour beer for another customer. People standing around some slowly flashing lights caught Roxi's attention.

"Luke, there's a table in the corner that just opened. Would you like to sit there? It looks dark and quiet," Roxi asked, leaning close.

Luke nodded and slid off his stool to follow Roxi into the dark corner. Settling onto the chair, he put his back into the corner. Roxi set her glass down.

"I'm going to go feed some money into the jukebox. Anything you want to hear?" Roxi leaned over the table.

Luke shrugged. "Maybe some Zeppelin."

"Sure, dōšagīh." She reached out and caressed his cheek and smiled gently.

He watched as she walked to the jukebox, her hips swaying. While she pored over the selection, he stared at her. The corners of his lips tipped up slightly as she leaned over the box, her elbow resting on the edges of the metal frame, and brushed her hair out of her face. One thin wisp of hair refused to stay put, falling back in front of her face. Too busy pushing buttons to bother with it, she tried blowing it out of her face, solving the problem for a moment before it fluttered back into her way.

She appeared to find something she wanted as she smiled and

pushed more buttons. A moment later, Led Zeppelin's "Going to California" started playing, the beautiful acoustic guitar leading up to the plaintive sounds of Robert Plant's lyrics. Luke leaned back in his chair, picking up his glass and taking a sip. His eyelids drifted to half-mast as he watched Roxi, letting the beautiful melody soothe his ears and his attraction soothe his eyes.

She solved the problem of the errant wisp of hair by tucking it between her lips as she slowly swayed to the rhythm while looking for her next song. When the Zeppelin song ended, the mournful ring of a delta style guitar replaced it, eventually leading to Jeff Buckley's cover of Hank Williams's "Lost Highway." Her long black hair fell down nearly to her butt. She'd said it had been over three years since her last trip to the salon, well before she'd been captured.

After Roxi picked her last song, she strutted back to the table, letting her hips pop at the end of each sway. Luke couldn't take his eyes off them as the woman he loved used her hips to tease a smile onto his face. After the long guitar slide in the solo, Roxi lifted her glass and tipped it toward Luke, looking deep into his eyes. Luke clicked the thick bottom of his glass against hers and took a heavy drink, matching Roxi's.

"I figured if we're going to be drinking sad whiskey, we should have an appropriate song to accompany it," Roxi said.

Luke chuckled sadly and nodded. "It's fitting."

They sat sipping their whiskey as they listened to the last of the Buckley song. It was replaced by the smooth sounds of Fleetwood Mac's "Dreams."

"Why'd you pick this one?" Luke asked, curious after her previous selections.

She finished her glass and set the empty on the table. Sitting up straight, she slid her hands under her hair to the back of her neck and lifted her arms, her wavy black hair cascading off her fingers until her hands were empty and held them above her head.

"I just like it. That and a forty-five-year-long crush on Stevie Nicks." Roxi had a dreamy smile on her face.

Lowering her arms, she grabbed her empty glass. He laughed and tossed back the rest of his shot.

"I like that sound," Roxi said. She lifted her glass and wiggled it. "One more, then home?"

"Whatever you want."

She grabbed his glass and went up to the bar, but instead of quickly returning with a couple more glasses of Maker's, she scanned the shelves. Pointing to one, she paid and returned with two glasses of a paler gold liquid.

Luke took his glass from her hands and brought it to his nose. The strong aroma of peat nearly knocked him out of his chair.

"Ardbeg?" Luke asked.

"You have a good nose." Roxi ran her glass under her nose, smiling happily.

Luke lifted his glass and raised the corner of one end of his lips. Sighing, he sat up, lifting his glass over the table.

"Jeremy, you deserved a full life, and it was cut too short. I'm sorry I couldn't do better by you." Luke stared at his glass.

"To Jeremy," Roxi murmured, tapping Luke's glass.

"To Jeremy." He took a sip, letting the whisky warm in his mouth. The perfume of the peat and alcohol seduced his senses as he mourned a young man he wished he could have gotten to know better.

Roxi scooted her chair closer to Luke's and settled in next to him, holding his hand as they sat and watched the dive bar live. People fed the jukebox, keeping to the down beat classic rock songs. Luke wasn't always in the mood for Ardbeg, but its smoky dark complexity fit his mood and the situation perfectly. He marveled at Roxi's ability to pick the things that'd work to stop his spiral downward. Tomorrow would be another day, but tonight they mourned together.

CHAPTER
FIFTEEN

At some point, Roxi let Sam and Pablo know where they were at. He wasn't sure who ordered another round of Ardbeg, but the light pouring into the window seemed particularly rude the next morning. He groaned and rolled over, pulling his pillow over his head.

"We've made better decisions in life…" Roxi said weakly next to him.

Luke reached for his phone and typed into the group chat he had with Sam, Delilah, and Pablo. *Bring coffee and greasy breakfast food for two. And some electrolyte drinks. It's kind of an emergency.*

Pablo was the first to reply. *An emergency hangover?*

Whisky choices were made, Roxi joined the conversation.

What am I bringing over? Chorizo burrito? Pablo asked.

No. Not sure I'm trusting my hangover to an unknown chorizo burrito in Portland, Maine. Biscuits and gravy, side of bacon. For two.

A hangover is a fine time to introduce our lovely Roxi to the wonders of American biscuits and gravy. Sam entered the conversation.

"Are you sure about this, Luke?" Roxi asked.

"Too queasy to eat?" Luke asked.

"No. I could destroy a proper Full English, but I've heard weird things about biscuits and gravy." Roxi squinted at him, using a hand to block the light.

"Do you trust me?"

"Of course."

Two orders, Luke texted.

We're at breakfast now. We'll have them add a couple orders to go, Delilah replied.

We'll have your medicinal breakfast to you shortly, dude, Pablo added.

Luke slid out to close the blackout curtains then visited the restroom. He fished a couple bottles of water out of the mini fridge and handed one to Roxi. She slid out of bed and used the restroom before returning. Downing the bottle in one go, she crawled back into bed and snuggled into Luke, pulling him into the little spoon position.

"Do you think Pablo would find us a couple vampires to stake? That's a sure-fire cure for a hangover." Roxi kissed the back of his arm then gently chomped his forearm.

"Hungry?" Luke mumbled.

"Very."

Thirty minutes later, Pablo knocked on the door, leaving their food. "Don't worry," he called through the door. "We've got everything under control. Call if you need us."

Luke grabbed the bags and waved to Pablo before ducking back into the room, setting up their breakfast on the table. "Behold, the American biscuit, what Australian comic Hannah Gadsby called 'a scone that's gone rogue,' slathered in a sausage milk gravy." Luke wafted the steam toward his nose, smiling and sighing happily.

Roxi grabbed a robe and threw it over her naked shoulders, not bothering to close it fully before sitting. Luke cut off a chunk of gravy-covered biscuit and popped it into his mouth, humming in satisfaction. Roxi, being more cautious, cut a small piece and delicately put it into her mouth. After a few seconds, she smiled and cut a much bigger piece. Once they finished their breakfast, they took their sports drinks and retired back to the bed, finding a movie to watch while they let the breakfast and electrolytes handle their hangovers.

AFTER SEVERAL MOVIES, Luke and Roxi ventured out for a quick dinner and more supplies before tucking back into bed to continue their movie marathon, then called it early and went to bed.

When pounding on the door startled Luke from his sleep, it took him a second after shooting upright to recognize what was going on.

"Luke, let us in. It's important," Pablo called.

"Coming." Luke yawned and grabbed his robe, throwing it on.

Roxi sat up and rubbed her eyes groggily. Luke grabbed her robe and handed it to her, allowing her to pull it on and close it before letting what turned out to be the whole leadership team—Delilah, Pablo, Sam, and Simone along with Brutus—into their hotel room.

"What's going on?" Luke asked around another yawn.

The scared and worried expressions on his friends' faces nearly woke him the rest of the way up.

"Luke…" Sam gulped. "They turned loose their nurseries all over the world."

Luke's eyebrows shot up. "What?"

He looked to Delilah, who rarely joked about such things. She nodded back. "It's all over the news. Someone even turned up the video you recorded. And played it."

"I guess Jamaal got it loaded up effectively…" he mumbled.

"Though most news outlets are calling it a series of worldwide terrorist attacks aided by some new drug that makes people go wild and murderous," Sam added.

Pablo grabbed the remote to the TV and turned it on, searching for a cable news channel. Luke hadn't seen news personalities so shaken since September eleventh. They ran through a series of videos from around the world, showing the violent attack of vampires tearing into human flesh. They warned the audience about the graphic nature, blurred out a lot of it, but Luke knew exactly what was going on. In one video, cops unloaded their guns into a couple fangers only to be torn apart, their blood mingling with the black sludge leaked by baby vampires.

Roxi scooted into the middle, letting Luke slide in next to her.

Sam slid into the bed next to Roxi. Pablo took a chair, and Delilah and Simone sat on the floor, leaning up against the foot of the bed as they all watched in horror. Brutus curled up next to them, laying his head across Simone's lap.

"Portland?" Luke asked, his body going stiff.

He reached for his phone and found a deluge of messages. He pulled up the one from Maggie first.

Out helping with casualties. Gwen is safe with Zel. I sent them to your house to hide in the basement. Please come home. You're needed here.

He opened Gwen's next.

Safe with Zel. It's super scary. Please be safe. I miss you so much.

Suddenly, he sat up ramrod straight, finally pulling together the pieces. "Why aren't we out fighting vampires?"

"There aren't any here. We killed them already," Sam said.

Luke looked at his phone, checking the time. "What's the nearest city reporting attacks?"

"Boston," Pablo supplied.

"Luke, before you think about rushing off to Boston, it'll be close to morning by the time we get there, and most likely daylight by the time we get everyone organized. Unless you're thinking of just loading up a car with us?"

Delilah snorted. "I don't feel like fighting an entire uncontrolled horde of baby vamps with just the six of us."

Roxi squeezed his thigh. "There's nothing we can do at this point. They'll be finding places to hide for the day by the time we get there."

They sat together, watching the TV in horror as the worldwide vampire attack took place. It was as bad as any war footage, probably worse with the visceral carnage of the vampires decimating human bodies then feeding on them. The occasional crack of a gun firing at one of the monsters which only infuriated them.

"I'll have to say, the camera people are sure as hell brave and foolhardy to be out there rolling tape on this kind of footage." Pablo shook his head as he stared at the latest footage that was a mix of smartphone videos that'd been mined from social media. "I'd be more worried about becoming a snack, 'cause damn."

Roxi snuggled into Luke, while on Roxi's other side, Sam rested her head on Roxi's shoulder, holding her hand. Delilah and Simone had found the spare blanket from the closet and pressed close to each other on the floor. They all needed the touch of their friends, the warmth of human companionship, to feel safe while they witnessed the unrelenting horror unfolding before them.

Finally, Sam reached over and took the remote out of Luke's hands. "We've had enough of this." She scrolled until she found a movie to watch. "There's nothing we can do about any of this until daylight. We need *The Princess Bride* in our lives right now, because I don't know about the rest of you, but I doubt I'm going to manage any sleep after that."

They broke out the snacks and beverages that Roxi and Luke had accumulated as well as the remainder of what was contained in the mini fridge. After *The Princess Bride*, they watched *Bull Durham*. As the sun crept up into the sky, they sent out a group message to assemble for a team breakfast and their final planning session before the long and now very dangerous trip home.

WITH AIR TRAFFIC STILL GROUNDED, they assembled their caravan in an empty lot the Portland-Bangor Pack owned. Though, they'd never be able to get all their weaponry on a plane, even with inside connections—not after the worldwide disaster the vampire wrought. Alejandro had made some pack folks available to them to help them round up supplies. Luke wanted enough food for the entire group in case stopping became too dangerous. They hit up warehouse stores and bought as much ready-to-eat food as they could, as well as cases of water and other drinkables.

"Dammit, I wish we had more time," Pablo said, looking over a clipboard. "I've got the ammo teams working as fast as they can to make anti-vamp shells, but we'd planned on at least a few more days to build up our stock."

"I know. Try to organize the packing material so we can pull it out and work if we get the opportunity. You're doing the best you can, as are our people. Let them know I'm proud of their efforts." Luke patted his friend on the shoulder.

"Hey, Luke. Got a minute?" Sam yelled from across the lot, waving at him.

He jogged over. "What ya got, Sam?"

"Holly has been working the phones today."

"Wrangle up any support for us as we move cross country?" Luke rubbed his eyes and shook his head, the lack of sleep wearing on him.

"A little bit. She's gonna need to know our itinerary. If we can give her some notice, she'll get us some safe waypoints. Also, wouldn't hurt if we offered some anti-vamp training along the way." Sam gave him her most winsome smile.

He chuckled. "Sure. Sounds like more than a fair trade for some sanctuary."

"Luke? Where's Luke?" Roxi shouted.

Luke turned to find where her voice was coming from and waved to catch her attention. Spotting her, he turned back to Sam. "Looks like I'm needed elsewhere."

He met Roxi and Alejandro in the middle of the lot. "Alejandro, thanks for the use of the lot. It's making things a lot easier having a central collection point."

Alejandro shook Luke's hand. "Anything to help you out. We really do appreciate all you've done for us."

"How is Erin doing?" Luke asked tentatively.

"She's mourning. I'm in charge for a while until she's ready to come back."

"That's understandable," Roxi said.

"So, what brings you to our little lot of chaos?" Luke gestured to the hive of activity around them.

"Mary and her lot intercepted an old friend of ours—the observer from Sherbrooke."

Luke raised an eyebrow. "Oh?"

Alejandro nodded. "Along with about a dozen of his packmates. He's demanding to speak with you and Erin. Since I'm covering for

Erin, I'll go speak to him, but I didn't want to waste any of your time."

"Fortunately, my crew is more than competent." He turned to Roxi. "Let the team know where I'm at. I'll be back…"

"He's close by. I didn't want to bring him here for obvious reasons, but we brought him into town to the pack community center."

"Do we have anything that's available for me to drive, Roxi?" Luke asked, looking around.

"I'm not sure. The smaller vehicles are out on errands and the larger ones are getting loaded." Roxi worried at her lip with her teeth.

"I can run you over and back, no problem," Alejandro replied.

Luke nodded and followed Alejandro. Fifteen minutes later, they parked by the community center and strode in. The observer, Luke never remembered his name, waited for them in the soundproof room upstairs with several of the local pack members and Mary's pack members standing guard. Several had handguns on their belts.

"Hey, handsome, good to see you." Mary winked at Luke.

"Hi, Mary. Alejandro tells me you caught our little spy trying to come back south."

"Yup, with some friends, too. Says he's got important information for us." She shrugged. "Could be important. He seemed a lot less cocksure than he had when he was spying. A bit desperate, actually."

Luke nodded. "I'll see what he wants."

Alejandro nodded and opened the door. Luke stepped through, striding toward the observer. His eyes shot open wide, and he tried to scoot away from Luke, almost tipping over backward until the two people standing guard behind him grabbed the corners of the back of the chair and shoved it back onto the ground.

"I'm told you have information for me," Luke said.

The observer nodded nervously. "I do. Um… Just so you know, I didn't know what my pack was supporting. I didn't know what was going on in that camp. I've left the pack, as did those who came with me."

Luke nodded. "That's good. I'm sure you can speak to the local packs about that." He stared at the man for a few moments. "What's the reason you're here asking for me? I'm leaving. I don't care what your pack affiliation is."

"That's why I'm here. They anticipated your leaving," the man said.

"Who?"

"The Montreal, Quebec City, and Ottawa nests as well as most of the packs in and around those cities."

"They've subverted all those packs?" Alejandro blurted out.

"Yeah. Sherbrooke is only one of the packs they control."

"Shit." Luke paced back and forth for a few moments, contemplating the complications. He stopped in front of the man sitting in the chair. "What's your name?"

"Matt, sir."

"Matt, when did they deploy their forces?" Luke asked.

"The order went out last night, during all the...mayhem. The vampires headed south. As best as I can tell, Ottawa's nest sent their vamps to Syracuse. Montreal to Albany. The QC vamps," he shrugged, "I don't know. I know they're moving. I've got a friend inside the Montreal pack that's passing information along to me."

Luke's brow furrowed as he exhaled. "What about their pet wolves?"

"They started this morning." Matt's eyes flicked up to Alejandro. "Someone in Erin's pack has been passing information north." He held up his hands placatingly. "I don't know who before you ask, Alejandro." He turned back to Luke. "They reported in that you all are in high activity mode and looking to move out."

Luke gestured with his head for Alejandro to follow him. Nodding, Alejandro stepped out of the room and joined Luke in Erin's office.

Luke tried to temper his stern expression into a more friendly and sympathetic one. "I'm sorry, Alejandro. But I need you to recall all your wolves currently helping me. I can't risk my people's lives. You've got a leak, and until you plug it, I'm going to have to treat them all like they could be spies."

"I understand. I'm so sorry."

"If you can give me a minute, I need to make a call. I'll join you back with Matt when I'm done with this call," Luke said.

Alejandro nodded and left, shutting the door behind him.

Leaning against the desk, Luke sighed, rubbing a hand over his eyes. He'd been betrayed dozens of times over the centuries, yet it still hurt and frustrated him every time. Now, he had to deal with damage control and make sure his people didn't pay the price. He pulled his phone out and called Roxi.

"Hey, Luke. What's the news?" Roxi asked.

"Mind grabbing Delilah, Pablo, and Sam if they're available? I'd like to update you all at once." Luke leaned back against Erin's desk.

"Sure. Give me a minute."

When she whistled shrilly, Luke pulled the phone away from his ear and shook his head, smiling.

"Oi, Sam, Pablo, I need you for a minute," Roxi yelled in the background. "They're coming, Luke. Delilah is off site right now running a few errands."

"Good. Can you find a bit of privacy? I know it's not easy with everyone there, but at least keep it to our people?" Luke yawned and squeezed the back of his neck, the muscles tense and taut.

"You tired, dōšagīh?"

"Aren't we all? I'll bear up. I always do," Luke replied.

"What's up, Rox?" Pablo asked in the background.

"Let's take a little walk. Luke's got an update for us and wants a bit of privacy." Roxi kept her voice low for Pablo and Sam but spoke into the phone while she did it. A few moments later, she spoke again, using the same low voice. "We're away from everyone."

"If I speak at this level, can Pablo and Sam hear me?" Luke asked. He figured their enhanced wolfy hearing would let them.

"They say they can. Go ahead, Luke," Roxi said.

"Alejandro is recalling all his people. Our spy from Sherbrooke reports he wasn't the only one, though he's claiming to have left his pack, for whatever that's worth, but someone in Erin's pack is reporting our movements to the Montreal nest."

"Fuck," Pablo bit out.

"So, when they're gone, we need to sweep through everything to see if they hid any trackers anywhere."

"I'm going to be so mad if they managed to do it without ruining any of their snap-up pants," Pablo said.

Luke snorted. "Tell ya what, if our spy is wearing tear-away clothing, you can keep them. But we're not going to have time to chase them down. We're running dangerously close to not leaving until dark as is."

"Do we want to stay another night and leave at first light?" Sam jumped in.

"I don't know. I'll be back shortly. We can discuss our options then. As soon as the Portland-Bangor wolves leave, sweep the caravan."

"Gotcha, dude. Looks like they're clearing out now," Pablo said.

"See you shortly, Luke," Roxi said. "Anything else?"

"No. Love you."

"Love you, too."

Luke hung up and rejoined everyone in the soundproof room. "Do you have anything else for us, Matt?"

"No, that's all the information I have at the moment. If I get more news from my contact, how do you want me to pass it on?" Matt shifted nervously in his chair.

"Pass it on to Alejandro and no one else." Luke made to turn, then stopped himself. "Matt. Thank you. If you truly wish to atone for your actions, help fight vampires and let it be known that you're only my enemy if you're aiding vampires."

Matt nodded nervously.

"Alejandro, can you take me back to my friends?"

"Sure." Alejandro waved Luke after him.

"I'm coming, too," Mary said, falling in line with them.

Twenty minutes later, the three of them parked along the street next to the empty lot.

"Do I have your permission to enter the lot?" Alejandro asked. "I'd like to ensure my people are truly gone. Man, I feel terrible that someone we trusted is betraying us and your people."

Luke hesitated for a moment, second guessing if he could trust

Alejandro. Shaking his head—he had to trust himself—he nodded. "Of course. Vampires are insidious and very good at getting what they want from people. Fortunately, Matt gave us a warning."

When they walked onto the lot, Roxi, Pablo, and Sam came over to greet Alejandro and Mary.

"Hey, y'all! Just wanted to swing by and say goodbye and say how much I enjoyed meeting y'all," Mary said, pulling Roxi in for a hug. "You take good care of that handsome man of yours, Roxi, or I'll have to come snatch him up."

Roxi laughed, patting Mary's back. "Either way, if you decide to come visit the west coast, we'll go see about hunting up some trouble."

"It's a deal," Mary said, grinning at Roxi.

Mary deployed hugs and kisses on the cheeks of her new friends, though the kiss she gave Owen was a fair bit more serious. Pablo looked at Luke and grinned, winking at him.

"When traveling's a bit easier, I'll take you up on your invite. You can show me your boat and take me for a ride." Mary looked Owen up and down, then gave him a wink.

"I'll have to let Lauren know to take out more insurance for the pack," Sam said. "Not sure there'll be much left standing when those two cut loose."

Luke laughed. "Oof. That could be cataclysmic. Homeric, even."

"I'll have you know, I'm a perfect lady," Mary said, then reached around and grabbed Owen's ass.

He pulled her back in for another kiss.

Alejandro joined them after making a trip around the lot. "Well, looks like we're good here. It's been nice to get to know you all. Wish the circumstances had been better."

"Agreed. It would have been nice to get some friendly tours around Maine. It's beautiful up here." Sam hugged Alejandro.

"Yeah. Vampires ruin pretty much everything," Luke grumbled.

"You do seem to always find them wherever we go," Pablo said, patting Luke's back.

"Luke, it was an experience meeting you. That's for sure." Alejandro extended his hand for a handshake.

"Yeah. It was definitely an eventful few days. If things ever quiet down, come out to the other coast and we'll try some beers together," Luke replied. "Please give my regards to Erin. I'm sorry for her loss."

"I will when she's a little further from her grief." Alejandro looked at everyone. "Good luck and safe journey."

Mary saved Luke for last and pulled him in for a tight hug. "You stay out of trouble, handsome, but if you decide you want some, you know my number."

"I'll keep that in mind, Mary. You take care." Luke tried to keep his blush in check.

"It was a pleasure." Mary waved and followed Alejandro out of the lot.

"So, what's going on, Luke?" Pablo asked.

"Well, I told you about the leak, but the other piece of the puzzle is we might have some roadblocks along the way out of here." Luke looked around, perking up as Delilah and Simone walked onto the lot. Brutus jogged ahead, shoving his head into Luke's hand for ear scratches. He waited until they joined the group before continuing. "Hey Delilah, to catch you up real quick, we had to remove the Portland-Bangor people. We found out there's a spy in the pack somewhere."

"Shit." Delilah shook her head, folding her arms across her chest. "Why can't people just not be assholes?"

"Well, we only found out thanks to the apparent repentance of the asshole who was spying on us for Sherbrooke. He says he left the pack, along with some others. He's the one who provided the intelligence. But the bigger news is we might have to fight our way out of here. Several of the Canadian vampire nests have mobilized and have moved south of the border."

"How are they getting through the border? Isn't it still closed?" Simone asked.

Luke shrugged. "They're vampires. They can glamour their way around border patrol."

"How many nests are we talking about?" Delilah asked.

"Montreal, Quebec City, and Ottawa. I'm not sure if that's all the nests in those cities, but they're also moving their werewolves south with them. According to our source, that's most of the packs in that territory, city or otherwise."

"Well, fuck," Delilah said.

"That about summarizes it." Luke kicked an unoffending pebble that was within reach.

"What do you want to do?" Sam asked. "Do we stay another night and head out early? Or do we go now?"

"According to Matt, the vampires have set up at Syracuse and Albany. The final destinations of the wolves and Quebec City are unknown. I think they're expecting us to take the fastest route across the country. Down to Massachusetts, across central New York, then down along the lakes to Chicago." He exhaled, pursing his lips in annoyance. "That is the route I wanted to take, but I don't think we can afford to try to slip by or muscle our way through."

"Do we go further south and then swing over?" Sam asked.

"South…" Delilah said quietly.

"We may have to, though I'm worried it's going to be a fight the entire way…"

Delilah pulled out her phone and looked at it, then walked away, letting off a stream of curses.

Roxi cleared her throat and raised her hand. "I don't think we can afford to wait until tomorrow. Right now, the vampires and their wolves are in flux. They're not set. They're not spread out and the Quebec City nest might be behind us still. We need to move, and we need to move now. It'll be easier to get through a wall that's missing bricks and has wet mortar."

Nodding, Luke gave a tight, closed-mouth smile. "She's right. Let's take five minutes. Get reports on all the lists we were working on. If we have people out on errands, they need to be recalled immediately."

"Right," Sam said, striding into action, Pablo following along.

"What's got Delilah so agitated?" Roxi asked, redirecting Luke's attention to their tall Black friend.

Delilah hung up her phone and jogged toward them, her face scrunched up in worry.

"Luke, I need to go to Virginia." Delilah shuffled anxiously.

"Slow down. Why do you need to go to Virginia?" Luke asked.

"I've been getting a call from an unknown number. I didn't answer. You know how it is. But I called back just now. It was my granny. She bought a cell phone and has been trying to call me. There must be a vamp camp nearby. She said there are monsters everywhere. I have to go get her."

"You can't go by yourself, Delilah. It's too dangerous," Roxi said, taking Delilah's hand in hers.

"She won't be." Simone stepped up next to her girlfriend and took her other hand.

Luke pulled out his phone and opened the map app and punched in an idea. "No. You're not going alone."

CHAPTER
SIXTEEN

They'd slipped out of Portland, Maine, a long caravan of cars, vans, and a couple box vans. Each second that it took them to get moving chaffed and annoyed Luke, but they had to get their people back from their errands and everything stowed properly.

Luke rode in the passenger seat while Pablo drove, Roxi and Sam in the backseat, as they worked their way southwest through Maine, New Hampshire, and into Massachusetts. As the sun set ahead of them, they drew near Massachusetts's second biggest city —Worcester.

As Pablo slowed to match the speed of traffic on I-290, Luke grumbled at the need. "Worcester isn't that big. Why does it have this much traffic?"

"I don't know, dude," Pablo said from behind the driver's wheel. "Could be an accident. Maybe the rabid vampires have something to do with it? Maybe it's nothing. Shit's weird lately."

Roxi reached up and squeezed Luke's shoulder. Before she could pull her hand back, he grabbed it and gave it an affectionate squeeze. The touch helped to calm his nerves, though not all the way, allowing them to spike to new levels of anxiety when they were forced to a complete stop.

By the time they sat without moving for half an hour, the sun was completely gone, and they were shrouded in darkness, though not as dark as Luke's mood, especially with the glow of a city ahead of them. When they finally started moving again, traffic was being directed into a single lane by a series of flashing red and blue lights ahead.

"They must be doing monster checks or something," Sam said. "Oh, I see an Indiana license plate."

Luke shook his head and exhaled sharply, his exasperation getting the better of him.

"Chill out a little, Luke. I'm just as wound up as you. We all are. I'm just trying to manage it with a harmless a game of license plates," Sam said. "Oh, Ohio, oh!"

Roxi chuckled, reaching up to touch Luke. "Does that look like a New Jersey?"

"I think it is," Sam said.

"Is it anything like Old Jersey?"

Sam shrugged. "I've never been to England, but I doubt it."

"Sorry, Sam." Luke ran through some breathing exercises to try to calm himself down.

"Um, you got those guns covered up back there? I think our officious friends are doing a car-by-car look-see." Pablo peeked into the rearview mirror.

"Yeah. I'll spread out a blanket over them," Roxi said.

"I'll let the rest of the team know to go incognito," Sam said, fishing her phone out of her pocket.

As they crept forward, Luke's finger tapped out a steady rhythm on the armrest of the door.

"Only a few more cars, then that semi-truck, then a few more cars before us, buddy. Then we're back on track."

When Luke's gaze drifted over, he saw the grip Pablo had on the steering wheel. Apparently, his words weren't just for Luke.

"I knew one of you should have driven. I've heard about Massachusetts cops." Pablo gripped the wheel harder.

"They're looking for vampires, though they don't know it, not brown drivers." Sam reached forward and patted his shoulder.

"Doesn't mean they can't multitask," Pablo grumbled.

When the cops made it to the semi-truck, they must have asked the driver to step out. Together, a pair of cops brought the driver to the back and watched as he unlocked the latches to the box trailer.

"Luke…" Roxi said, her voice loaded with tension. "I have a bad feeling."

Luke nodded, staring ahead at the trailer of the semi-truck. "Get those guns out and pass the word."

Pablo coughed, choking on something. "But the cops."

"The cops are about to be the least of our problems. That truck is parked, but that trailer's bouncing back and forth like it's in an earthquake, and I have an itch that only comes from my vampy senses. Roxi?"

She nodded. "Yeah. Now that we're close enough. I can feel it, too."

"Oh, no… You're not saying what I think you're saying." Sam bent over and grabbed a shotgun off the floor.

"Roxi," Luke said, opening the door. "Pablo, unlock the doors."

Luke ran around back and tossed his hoodie in, quickly wrapping a scarf around his neck, pulling on his armor padding, and then his armor. He pulled on his hoodie and clipped his gladius to his belt. Last, he pulled on a beanie with a fake beard. Next to him, Roxi pulled on hers.

"You look cute in a yarn beard," Luke said as he shut the back hatch of the SUV.

"Thanks."

They walked around the car, one on each side. Pablo rolled down the window.

"Hold off on following us, but be ready," Luke said. "Officers, don't open that trailer."

The cops turned, their hands dropping to their sidearms. "Stand back."

Luke and Roxi stopped. Luke lifted his hands to chest height to show they were empty. Roxi followed suit.

"No!" Luke yelled.

The driver turned his head, the headlights of the cars gleaming off the driver's fangs. He yanked the trailer's doors open, unleashing its payload of baby vamps. Luke yanked his gladius and the rudis next to it.

"Don't let them separate us," Luke called.

The vampires swarmed the two cops, shredding them, then ran over the cars toward Luke and Roxi. Fortunately, they split off in various directions, no control, only hunger. A few people made the bad choice of trying to run away, opening their doors and sprinting down the line of traffic. Luke met the first fanger, lopping off an arm, then plunged the rudis into its heart. He yanked it free and moved onto the next one before the vamp even had a moment to dissolve. It splattered to the pavement behind him as he ducked under a clawed swipe, slicing through its knee, then finished it.

Next to him, Roxi leapt back, avoiding a swipe at her stomach. She brought her sword around, taking off its hand and then its other arm at the elbow. Pivoting, she spun and beheaded it with a back-handed slash. Behind him, the sounds of Sam's shotgun burst to life. A few guns further behind joined the action. Luke ignored them, needing to concentrate on dodging and killing. For everyone that he put down, two seemed to take their place. The only thing that kept them from being overrun in the initial wave was the baby vamp's inability to work as a team, more interested in blood and carnage as they scattered over the line of cars, some disappearing into the foliage of the median strip.

"Luke, we're coming up behind you," Sam yelled, the sound of shells being fed into the magazine accompanying her.

Sam and Pablo stepped up, one of them moving up on Roxi's outside and the other on Luke's outside. Together, they protected Luke and Roxi's flank as they advanced forward.

Grunting, Luke stumbled back as claws scrapped across the armor on his stomach, knocking the wind out of him. Roxi stepped in front of him, knocking the baby vamp back. As it stumbled out of the way, Sam blasted it in the chest, splattering it all over the vampires behind it.

"Thanks," Luke gasped out, trying to get some air in his lungs.

Taking an extra second, he tried to catch his breath but decided he'd catch it later. His friends needed his arm and his swords. Drawing in a deep breath, he stepped forward and continued cutting. Luke hadn't swung his sword in earnest for that long in a while, and his arms burned with the effort. Thankfully, the numbers of baby vamps were thinning.

"I think…we've…got them…on the run." Luke struggled to speak, though his wind was returning gradually.

Sam and Pablo fired off a few last shots as the chaos dissolved along with the remains of the last vampire.

"You alright, Luke?" Roxi asked, breathing heavily.

"I think so." He looked for a clean scrap of cloth to wipe down his sword before sheathing it.

"What now?" Sam asked. "Do we try to hunt down the ones that got away?"

To punctuate her question, the occasional gun still fired in the near distance.

Pablo shook his head. "We'd be here all night, and we're going to have to keep moving."

"Luke?" Sam sounded unsure.

"I don't like it any more than you do, but we have to think bigger picture. We need to get our people home, and if we bog down trying to fight every vampire we find, we'll never make it. We owe our families and our pack to get moving."

"Luke's right, Sam." Pablo reloaded the shotgun. "We need to keep moving. Right now, our mission is Virginia and Delilah's granny. Then home."

"It sucks. I know," Luke said.

"OK. What are we going to do about these cars and that semi-truck?" Sam asked, switching to her logistics brain.

"I think we can get around the cars, but the truck is parked wonky. Roxi, go grab our shotguns and come back here. I'll move the truck. Sam, Pablo. Get the caravan moving behind me. I'm claiming this truck for the pack since we took it from the vamps."

They scurried into action, carrying out Luke's orders while he checked the box trailer to make sure it was indeed empty after disgorging its hateful vampire cargo. He pulled the little flashlight from his belt. At this point, it was approaching Batman levels of "utility belt" with the number of things he carried these days.

"Anything more in there?" Roxi asked.

Luke jumped, dropped his flashlight, and reached for a sword. "You startled me there."

"Sorry."

"No worries." Luke picked up the flashlight and shined it into the deep box trailer.

He didn't see anything. Setting the flashlight on the deck of the trailer, he pulled himself up, scooping the flashlight before proceeding deeper into the trailer, a hand on the hilt of his gladius. Nothing. The trailer was completely empty now that the vampires had fled into the night.

Back on the ground, he shut the trailer and latched the door, his head twitching in various directions with the occasional discharge of a gun.

"Luke!" someone shouted from down the line. "Get back here."

"What now?" He took off at a jog, Roxi behind him.

When they found who'd shouted, Owen stood there with some familiar new friends and a face Luke hadn't expected to see.

"Couldn't get enough of me, Mary? Just had to follow along." Luke responded to her offered hug.

"My, you're big and brawny in your armor." She leaned in and gave Roxi a kiss on the cheek. "Good to see you again, Roxi. Thought we'd tag along and see if we could help. Figured we could back you up if you needed it and get in touch with the local packs, at the least the ones we trust not to have betrayed the living."

"Roger. I'm surprised to see you here," Luke said, shaking the hand of the New Hampshire alpha.

"It galls me to have to admit it, but I was wrong. After I saw your videos of what was happening in our neck of the woods… Well, I'm sorry." Roger held his head high even as he tried to look contrite.

Luke nodded and patted him on the upper arm. "Better late than never. Glad to have you on board."

"What can we do to help you here?" Mary asked. "Looks like we missed the party."

"Yeah. That was a nasty bit of work there. They disgorged a whole trailer full of baby vamps. Shit… Did anyone find the driver? The way the babies ignored him, he had to be a vamp. Especially with those teeth." Luke furrowed his brow.

"What was he doing out on the road so close to sunset?" Roxi asked.

"I guess we should go investigate."

"What about us?" Roger asked.

"There are some baby vamps that escaped running amok. You could hunt them down or keep your team mounted up and then roll out with us. It's your call." Luke turned and ran back to the semi-truck.

Roxi stopped at the SUV and grabbed a shotgun, then caught up with him before he could open the driver's door to the Volvo semi-truck.

"You want the shotgun?" Roxi asked, handing him the gun.

Nodding, he took it. "Can you reach the door?"

"Sure." Roxi slipped in front of Luke and grabbed the handle at the bottom of the door.

Luke nodded when she looked back at him. Yanking it open, she stepped out of Luke's way as he raised the shotgun's barrel to cover the now open cab of the truck. Switching the gun to his left hand, he cradled the butt into his shoulder and used his right arm to aid his climb. Turning his ear, he thought he heard something.

"If there's anyone in the sleeper, call out now, or I'll shoot and sort it out later." Bracing himself, he put both hands on the gun, aiming at the heavy curtain that covered the entrance to the sleeper.

"Don't shoot! Please," someone called from the sleeper.

"Stick your hands out, nice and slow. I've got a twelve-gauge trained on the curtain and a real itchy trigger finger after killing a bunch of vampires." To emphasize the point, Luke pumped a shell into the firing chamber.

"OK, OK, I'm coming out."

The curtain rustled, then a pair of hands stuck out of the crack, grabbed the edge of the curtain, and drew them back. Keeping his hands in the air, he crawled forward on his knees until he could drop a foot onto the floor between the two seats.

Switching to Middle Persian, Luke spoke up so Roxi could hear since he faced away from her. "Roxi, can you go to the other side? I'm going to send our new friend down that way so I can cover them."

"Got it," she replied.

"OK, you're going to open the other door and climb down slowly. My friend will be there to ensure you don't try anything stupid. Understand?" Luke gave a firm gesture toward the other door with his head.

"I understand." The man crept out slowly and followed the directions.

As soon as he stepped onto the ground, Luke ran around the nose of the truck, keeping his gun ready. "Now, we're going to walk to the back of the trailer."

The man nodded and walked down the length of the trailer, his hands held in the air. Once they were behind the trailer, Luke stopped them.

"Were those blackout curtains in the truck?" Luke asked.

The man nodded. "Yeah. Sealable from the inside."

"That's how they moved the vampire into place," Roxi said. "So, you were supposed to hide there while he released the newly whelped vampires?"

The man nodded again. "For all the good that would have done if one had decided to investigate."

"You're here now. Alive." Keeping his gun trained on the man, Luke turned toward the motion he caught out of the corner of his eye.

Sam ran up, shotgun ready.

"For now," the man said.

Turning back to the man, Luke said, "That all depends on you. I'm going to keep asking questions and you're going to keep answering them. Lie to me, and you'll sign your death warrant. I'm not in the mood to play. Plus, my friend here is a werewolf, and she hates lying even more than I do. A shotgun is a quick death…"

Sam affected a mean expression. "And you wouldn't like me when I'm angry."

Since Roxi was behind the man, he didn't see her grin and suppressed chuckle. Luke had trouble keeping a smirk off his face.

"Let's begin," Luke said. "Are you a thrall?"

The man hesitated for a moment. "Yes."

"Where were you trucking these vampires in from?"

"Quebec City."

Luke tried to keep the surprise off his face. "That's a bit far afield. Did you run out of local vampires?"

The man nodded but didn't elaborate.

"Since you're not saying more. Did you lose a whole camp in Maine near the border? A whole vampire breeding center?"

The man's eyes grew wide and darted around side-to-side.

"I don't know if you're looking for your masters, but they're not here. I'm the one you have to worry about." Luke stepped closer and pressed the cold steel of the barrel into the man's chest.

"Yes. Someone killed all our stock and a bunch of vampires."

"And you want to become one of those monsters you were carrying in your trailer?" Sam asked.

"Power and immortality are heady lures, aren't they?" Luke stared at the man.

He nodded.

"I'm tempted to kill you now and prevent a vampire from even being born," Luke said, his face twisted in disgust.

"You said if I answered truthfully, you wouldn't kill me." The man trembled, looking to Sam to intercede.

"No. I said if you lied, I would kill you. I didn't say anything about keeping you alive."

"He's still a human. He can still repent," Roxi supplied.

Luke looked the man up and down, sneering at him. "I doubt he's wise enough to take the opportunity afforded to him. Do you know who I am?"

The man shook his head.

"Does the name 'The Centurion Immortal' mean anything to you?" Luke asked.

The man blanched and tried to back away from Luke but was stopped when Roxi placed a hand in the middle of his back.

"He's heard of you," Roxi said.

"You're the monster, the slayer of vampires, the thief of immortality." A faint perspiration broke out on the man's forehead as he licked his lips, his eyes darting around wildly.

"I blew up your little vamp baby factory. I killed every vampire there, then all the turned humans. We killed all your baby vamps, and we just did it again a few minutes ago," Luke said. "You obviously know my reputation. Now you know from firsthand experience what I can do. So, I'll say this. Do not seek out your masters and rejoin them. This will be your one chance. If I see you again in the company of vampires, there will be no staying my hand. It will fall on your neck. Got it?"

The man's head nodded like a bobble head that somebody had just slapped.

"Good. I think we understand each other. Are there more vampire traps out there?"

The man shrugged. "I'm not important enough to know those kinds of details. I was just told where to drive this truck. But I'm guessing there will be."

The man was probably right on both accounts. He wasn't important enough to really know enough information to keep him here longer, and there probably would be other vampire traps and mayhem. Luke had no idea if it was specifically targeted at him, though they might have guessed or been fed the information by their spies. Looking at his friends, he made a decision. They couldn't waste more time pumping a dry well for information he didn't have.

"One last question. Are there any trackers on this truck?"

"Not that I know of. I don't get the impression that it was intended to be recovered."

"You've earned your life. Now, go do something with it that isn't becoming a soulless monster. And remember my warning." Luke lowered his gun and stepped back.

Sam lowered hers as well, while Roxi took a step back. The man looked around at them, first taking a tentative step, then another, followed by a third. Now that he'd cleared the little triangle he stood in, he sprinted away into the night.

"We need to get on the road. We've already wasted enough time here," Luke said.

"How we getting this truck out of the way?" Sam asked.

"Keys are in the ignition. Looks like the pack now owns a semi-truck." Luke grinned broadly. "Roxi, want to ride shotgun?"

"Sure, cowboy." She swatted Luke's butt and ran down the side of the truck to the passenger door.

"Cowboy?" Sam chuckled and shook her head. "She's picking up bad habits from Mary. I'll get everyone moving behind you."

"Stay in touch." He tossed a quick smile at his friend, then ran to fire up the truck.

The engine rumbled to life. The truck might come in handy if they needed the storage space of a forty-foot box trailer. Also, the truck would make a nice battering ram against smaller vehicles if the occasion should arise.

"I've never ridden in an articulated lorry before," Roxi said.

He laughed. "I used to own one in the 1970s. I actually stole one in Belgium. Maggie and I held up this poor Polish driver and took his truck. We needed a battering ram to get through a vampire blockade." He sighed at the thought of Maggie.

"You miss Maggie, don't you?" Roxi reached over and rubbed his thigh.

"Yeah. I do. It's been too long since I've seen her." He shook his head. "I'm surprised she's bothered waiting at all. I'm not the most convenient person to date."

"No, but she knew who you were before you started dating, and I'm sure she'll agree with me that you're worth the wait."

Luke smiled. "I hope so."

Luke put the truck into gear and started it rolling, turning to slam the corner of his bumper into the front of the abandoned cop car that had partially blocked the lane.

"Not sure you needed to hit that car," Roxi said, angling her head to watch it move past.

"Didn't I, though?"

Roxi chuckled, then buckled herself in. "Let's hope you don't have to use the bumper too much."

She was right. They'd traveled barely two hours from Portland, Maine and hadn't even made it through Worcester before they had to stop and fight a pitched battle in the middle of the interstate.

The road was long and winding, and it was going to be a long time before they made it home. He needed to get there. He hadn't had a home, a place where his heart resided, in too long. Now that he had one, he longed for it, longed to be with the people that made Portland his home.

CHAPTER
SEVENTEEN

It was nearly dawn by the time they rolled into Petersburg, Virginia. The journey that should have taken seven or so hours from Worcester to Petersburg had taken over twelve between traffic snarls caused by abandoned cars, police blockades, and various other diversions and reroutings. Through careful planning and coordinated teamwork, they'd made it through unscathed, if they discounted the sheer stress of the situation.

Delilah and Simone, Pablo and Sam, and Luke and Roxi in the semi-truck wound their way through the neighborhoods until they found a spot near Delilah's granny's house. The roads into Petersburg had been eerily deserted with abandoned cars sprinkled about, some of them on fire.

When Luke turned the engine off, he yawned and rubbed his eyes. "Damn, I am exhausted."

"We need to find someone else in the pack who can drive a lorry," Roxi said. "You can't be the only one, especially if we're trying to keep moving as much as possible. We'll have to abandon the truck."

Luke nodded and yawned again. "Yeah. You're right. Maybe Delilah's granny has coffee."

Grabbing the keys, Luke climbed down, locked the cab after them, and joined the rest of their friends at the end of the sidewalk to a small, well-kept house. Some of the slats in the fence appeared to be freshly broken, and some of the flowers running along the front fence line had been trampled.

"I called. She's up, but she's a little wary right now with everything going on," Delilah said. Brutus shuffled over from Delilah to greet Luke with a slowly wagging tail and a bump of the hand for some scritches.

An elderly Black woman poked her head out the door of the small house as they stood in front of it. "Delilah? What are you doing standing around looking shady? Get your butt in this house and bring your friends. You don't want to go and draw attention."

"Yes, ma'am," Delilah replied, waving her friends to follow.

Simone, shifting nervously and twisting her hands, fell into line last. Waiting until everyone—including Brutus—was inside, Delilah's granny locked the door, including the deadbolt and a chain lock, then set down an old double-barrel shotgun.

"Granny, what are you doing with Granddad's old shotgun?" Delilah asked.

"I'm not getting ate by some monster. Now come here and give your old granny a hug. Then you can introduce me to your friends." She gestured for Delilah to come to her.

At six feet tall before you counted her usual thick-soled boots, Delilah towered over her grandmother, who was nearly a foot shorter. When they finished hugging, her granny pulled Delilah down and kissed her cheek. "It's good to see you, Delilah."

"You too, Granny." Delilah turned and stepped closer to her friends.

"Everyone, this is my grandmother, Pearl Johnson."

They all said hello, calling her Mrs. Johnson.

"Please, if you're Delilah's friend, call me Pearl or Granny Pearl."

"Granny, this is Pablo."

"Ma'am."

"Sam."

"Hello."

"This is Luke."

Delilah's granny looked Luke up and down. "He's a big one."

Luke chuckled. "It's not all natural." He unzipped his hood to reveal the armor he still wore.

"The woman next to him is Roxi."

"Ma'am," Roxi said, giving a little wave.

Delilah stepped up next to Simone. "And this is Simone, my girlfriend."

"Ma'am, it's a pleasure to meet you," Simone said, bobbing her head.

"Oh, she's beautiful *and* has a French accent?" Granny Pearl pulled Simone into a hug. "Welcome to my home, Simone." She smiled at Delilah. "You take after your mother. She never could resist an accent and a good-looking face. Though your daddy turned out to be a good man. He loved your mama, and then when she passed, he did such a good job raising you on your own. I don't know what he got mixed up in that got him killed." She shook her head, tsking.

Delilah's brow furrowed. "Granny, that's what's going on outside. The monsters running around. Dad hunted them. He was killed by one of them. We need to get you out of here."

"Where am I going to go? I'm too old to move." Granny Pearl shook her head. "Look, I've got fresh biscuits about to come out of the oven and a mess of sausage gravy on the stove. We can talk more when we all have a full belly."

Brutus snuffled the air, his tail beating harder.

"Granny—"

Granny Pearl held up her hand. "I insist, Delilah."

Delilah ground her teeth and looked around the room. Luke gave her a nod. They weren't going to get through to Delilah's grandmother with her defenses up. She wanted to feed the young people, as she thought they all were, and it was going to be her barrier.

"OK, Granny. But afterward, we're going to have a serious talk." Delilah waved everyone into the kitchen.

"If that's what you want, baby girl." Granny Pearl followed everyone into the kitchen except Luke and Roxi, who stayed behind.

"Brutus, you stay here. I don't think Granny Pearl would appreciate you in her kitchen," Luke said. Brutus whined but laid down next to the couch.

"Mind helping me off with this armor?" Roxi asked.

Luke laughed, sounding tired. "Me, too."

In a quick couple of moments, they took each other's armor off and set it out of the way, dropping their swords with the armor.

Roxi groaned, stretching out. "I can't imagine how stiff you are. My armor at least has some give and flex to it."

"You're not wrong." Luke twisted and stretched out, then headed into the kitchen and small attached dining room.

The rest of their friends were busy opening the aluminum and Formica table and putting in the extenders. As soon as the table was ready, they set it. Delilah filled coffee cups while getting another pot going.

"Wondered where you went," Sam said, spying Luke and Roxi.

"Decided to get a bit more comfortable for breakfast, though I wish I had a clean shirt." Roxi plucked at the front of hers.

When the oven dinged, Pearl took out a baking sheet full of golden biscuits and replaced it with a sheet ready for baking.

"Oh, those smell wonderful, Pearl," Sam said, sniffing the air with a smile on her face.

Luke leaned into Roxi. "Now you'll get to try some real home-cooked biscuits and gravy."

"I'm looking forward to my second-ever helping of American biscuits and gravy, especially as good as everything smells." Roxi squeezed Luke's hand.

"Your first home-cooked biscuits and gravy?" Pearl asked, raising an eyebrow in the same manner Delilah did.

"I've lived in England for a while, ma'am. There, biscuits are crunchy cookies and gravy is brown. I only received my first taste of them a few days ago. I'm looking forward to trying yours."

When the first round was ready, Pearl gave Simone the first plate and Roxi the second, then doled out the rest. They sank into their plates, making happy sounds as they devoured their break-fasts. After a second helping for all of her guests, they cleared the table and rinsed their dishes, loading them into the dishwasher.

With a fresh pot of coffee, they refilled cups and returned to the table.

"Come to Portland, Granny. We don't get to see each other often enough with me living on the west coast. We can move you there, but we need to go. Bad things are happening. I can't protect you here," Delilah pleaded, picking up her argument where her granny had paused it before breakfast.

"I don't need protection. This will all calm down. It's just some new drug the kids are on. That's what the news said."

"Granny, it's not a drug. The 'monsters' aren't just kids out of their minds on drugs. These are real monsters. They're *vampires*, Granny."

Pearl's eyebrows shot up. "Child, are you on drugs?"

"Granny, that's what killed dad. He was a vampire hunter." She closed her eyes for a moment, then sat to her full height. "We're all vampire hunters."

"Stop playing. You're worrying me, Delilah." Granny Pearl's eyes shifted around the room to all Delilah's friends. "Are you all here to play jokes on me?"

Luke shook his head. "No, ma'am. Delilah's telling the truth. The news is lying to you to keep things covered up. The planes that crashed. The people on the streets at night attacking people and tearing them apart—all vampires." He pointed to the living room where his armor sat. "You saw what I was wearing. I don't wear this for comfort. I don't carry the sword for decoration, either."

"Pearl, this is a lot to have sprung on you like this, but we promise Delilah's telling you the truth," Sam said. "There's a lot more in the world than is acknowledged by modern science."

The oven behind them dinged again.

"That's...that's my last pan of biscuits. I can't let them burn." Granny Pearl sounded nervous and scared as she left the table to attend to her biscuits.

A minute later, the oven door banged open, releasing the scent of freshly baked biscuits. After the oven door was closed, Granny Pearl sank into her chair at the table. Delilah scooted her chair closer to her grandmother, taking her hand in hers.

"Granny, you've never known me to be a liar. I'm not one now." Looking around the table, she took a breath and let it out. "The world is bigger and darker than we're told. My friends and I do our part to fight the dark creatures that prey on humans that, until the last few days, have remained silent and secret. Luke and Roxi have been doing it longer than any of us."

Brutus growled ominously, interrupting the conversation.

"You! In the house! Come out!" someone shouted from the front of the house.

They stood up and headed into the living room. Sam waved them to a stop, then snuck up to the curtains so her shadow didn't darken them.

Sam pushed the curtain aside enough to peek out. "Of course."

"Of course what, Sam?" Delilah asked, edging in front of her grandmother.

"I think we've attracted the attention of the local welcoming committee, and they're not even being discreet." Sam shook her head.

Pablo, out of Pearl's sight, pantomimed ears on top of his head. Sam nodded.

"How many?" Luke said, moving to pick up his armor.

Roxi beat him to it and helped him on with it, then let him return the favor. After strapping on their swords, they added their hoodie and overcoat, respectively.

"I'm seeing four guys and two tall dogs," Sam said.

"Any sense if the four might shift?" Pablo pulled his warmup jacket off.

Sam shrugged, moving her head around, trying to get more angles to see if she could spy anyone else. "No idea."

"We know you're in there! Come out and there won't be any trouble." The werewolves shouted.

"Cops?" Pearl asked.

"No. Not that these guys are any better, but I guess they could also be cops," Sam replied.

"I'll step outside and see if I can scare them away." Luke pulled his gladius from its scabbard and stepped toward the door. "Sam, you take Pearl's shotgun and pepper them if they decide to move in. It'll give me a distraction."

"Don't let the cops see you with weapons around here," Pearl warned.

"He knows what he's doing, Granny," Delilah said. "I wish we'd brought the shotguns with us."

"Yeah, they're not doing a lot of good in the cars," Pablo said. "Delilah, Simone, maybe you want to take Granny Pearl to the kitchen."

Luke patted Brutus's head. "You stay with Delilah and Simone and help protect Pearl." The dog looked toward the door, then turned and joined the others in the kitchen.

Sam picked up the shotgun and opened it, pulling the two shells out and replacing them with some of their special ordnance, then pocketed the two standard shells. "I didn't see any weapons, but the four dudes have jackets on. They could be holstered."

"Right." Luke grabbed the door handle as Roxi stepped up behind him, her sword ready.

Luke opened the door and strode out and to the right, blocking the window. Roxi assumed a spot to his left. He kept his sword down and by his leg, but twisted the blade occasionally, using it to reflect sunlight. Once he saw a beam flash across the lead guy's face, causing him to flinch, Luke kept the light flicking over his face, occasionally moving it to one of his other goons to irritate them, too. He wanted them to know he was armed with a rare weapon and that he wasn't afraid of messing with six werewolves.

"So, you think you're the Centurion Immortal, huh?" the lead guy said.

Luke shrugged, unzipping his hoodie to reveal the armor over his chest. "You're welcome to try me, but if you know my reputation, you might want to consider moving on and living another day, because once I start cutting, I'm not stopping until you're all dead."

"Oooh." The man shook his hands at chest height, making a mocking face. "Big scary man. Think you can bluff your way past six werewolves?"

Off in the distance, Luke heard a mix of whiny, high-pitched motors and heavier, louder ones. He shook his head slightly and clenched his jaw.

"How about if we invite a few of our friends?" the lead guy held out his arms, hands open as motorcycles of various makes and models rolled up. "I heard you like to kill werewolves. Killed some wolves I knew who wanted to win some glory in the vampire arena. I kinda miss those guys. Think I might get me a little taste of vengeance."

"You're welcome to try. Many have, a few even lived, but I'm still here." Luke gave his sword a twirl, drawing the werewolves' eyes.

Sam stepped out the door, her shotgun raised. Pablo came lumbering out behind her—stripped down and wolfed out.

"One wolf and a couple of bitches aren't going to do much good, tough guy." He looked at his friends, an overconfident smirk on his face. "The bosses are looking for you and are paying a princely sum for your ass. You can come with us willingly, and you can see if you can intimidate your way out of their care. Or you can fight here, and I'll scrape your carcass off the grass and claim the reward. Either way, I'm going to be on a who's who list of young, rich upstarts."

Luke laughed. "At least you have dreams. It's always good to die with dreams." A flicker of light caught his eye as a line of cars, trucks, vans, and SUVs pelted down the road, led by a box van he recognized. "Last chance to tuck tail and run."

"Nah, I like our odds." The guy smirked condescendingly.

Luke returned the smirk as the van plowed through their parked bikes, knocking them over and continuing down the line. The crunch of plastic and metal raised an awful din that danced across Luke's eardrums like a sonata. Once the van stopped, signaling a general halt for the rest of their caravan, Luke's wolves piled out of their vehicles, shotguns in hands.

As they fanned out, forming a semi-circle around the local wolves, they cocked guns, pumped shells into magazines, and flicked safeties off.

"How you liking your odds now, champ?" Luke asked, sliding his unoccupied hand into his jeans pocket. Luke took a few steps forward. "Now, before you get any ideas. We're loaded up on anti-vampire ordnance." He turned his head to Sam. "You know what's so special about anti-vampire ammo, Sam?"

"It works on werewolves, too."

"Exactamundo." Luke turned back to face the interlopers. "Sam, if you wouldn't mind a little demonstration just so they know that I'm not bluffing."

"His bitch-calling face?" Sam asked.

"His knees will suffice."

"No!" The guy's muscles tensed to move, but Sam was faster.

She darted forward and unloaded both barrels a smidge higher than his knees. With a screech of agony, he collapsed to the ground, grabbing his crotch as he writhed on the ground. Luke winced internally but kept it off his face. Strolling forward as if walking through a park, he squatted next to the writhing form of the formerly confident asshole. Luke lifted his gladius and set it against the man's cheek, letting the silver of the blade hiss against his skin, adding more volume to his cries.

"Boy, that silver hurts, doesn't it?" Luke lifted his sword and stood up, facing the rest of the werewolves who'd tried to abduct them. "Now, I'm hoping you're all a little more interested in listening after you've seen that I mean business. So, here's my new deal. Drop all your weapons. Toss them over to the side on the grass here. Then, throw your wallets behind. If I hear so much as a peep from any of you ever again, I'm going find you, and when I do"—he tipped his head toward the blubbering wreck on the ground—"you'll wish you'd received what he got instead of what I'm going to deliver to you."

The werewolves looked at each other, then at their fallen leader.

Luke lifted his sword, pointing at the center of their line. "Weapons. Now."

Guns and knives emerged and were quickly tossed into a pile on Pearl's lawn. After a surprising number of weapons piled up, wallets followed.

"Good. Now, get the fuck out of here and don't ever come near me again if you want to live." Luke turned away from them but stopped. Turning his head, he said, "And don't forget to take this piece of shit with you."

Luke sat on the stairs, laying his sword across his knees as the werewolves picked up their leader, none too gently, and proceeded to hustle out of there, salvaging what vehicles they could.

"Luke—"

Interrupting Sam, he held up his hand until he judged the goons were far enough away. "They probably aren't paying attention, but I don't want a wolf with sharp ears picking up something."

Sam nodded, opening the shotgun and replacing the two empties with the two standard shells she'd pulled out earlier. "We should probably station our people on the approaching roads in case anyone comes back, wolves or cops."

"I don't imagine that tosser will be calling any women a bitch anytime soon." Roxi slid her sword into its scabbard.

"At least not without cringing in pain…" Sam smiled viciously. "I'll go get the teams organized. You go see if you can help Delilah with her grandmother."

"Pablo, probably time to head into the house," Luke called to his friend. "And take off your wolf jammies and put on some clothes."

Pablo chuffed as he walked up, then stuck his tongue out between his fangs. Stepping around Luke, he disappeared into the house and shut the door behind him.

A moment later, a scream rang out from inside the house.

Luke dropped his head into his hand and rubbed his temples.

"I think Pablo surprised Granny Pearl," Roxi said.

Luke nodded and stood up, sheathing his gladius. "Shall we?"

He and Roxi stepped into the house as Pablo put on his clothes. Following the sounds of Delilah and Simone's voices into the kitchen, Luke found them fanning Pearl, who was sitting on a kitchen chair, leaning back and rubbing her forehead.

"Is everything OK in here?" Luke asked.

Delilah rolled her eyes at him. Luke squatted down in front of Pearl and took her other hand in both of his.

"Pearl, I'm sorry our friend gave you a little fright. Normally, I'd be a bit more gentle and ease you into this, but we're running short on time, and I'm not sure how much I've bought with my little shiv-aree out there. Delilah speaks the truth—there are more things in heaven and earth than you've been led to believe. One of those things is werewolves like Pablo and most of our friends here."

"Are...are you one?" Pearl asked, her hand trembling in Luke's hands.

He shook his head. "No. I'm something else. Human still, but not exactly."

"We're still human, Luke. We're just really old and well preserved," Roxi said.

Luke smirked and shook his head slightly. "You're not helping."

Roxi shrugged. "You said it yourself. We don't have time to be too delicate. Granny Pearl, Luke and I are immortal vampire slayers. We're both nearly two-thousand-years-old, though he is slightly older than I am."

Delilah scowled at Roxi but reserved a bit for Luke, too.

"Roxi's right. It's our job to hunt vampires and protect humanity. Delilah's father was also a vampire hunter. An old associate of mine killed him. We took care of him, so he won't orphan anymore people." He'd not normally claim credit for Delilah's handiwork, but telling her granny that her granddaughter had killed a person, even it if was a vampire, might not be the best approach right now. "Delilah's right, too. We can't protect you here. Those guys or the vampires they report to will be back, and this time they won't ask us to step outside."

"But... My things. They're all I have."

Sam stepped into the kitchen, shotgun tucked into the crook of her arm. "Fortunately, we have an empty truck and a bunch of strong arms to help you out. If anything happens to the house and you can't sell it, the pack will reimburse you."

"Are you...one of those things?" Pearl asked, looking up at Sam.

Sam nodded. "I'm a person and a werewolf, yes."

Delilah squatted down by Luke. Pulling himself up on the corner of the table, he walked to the sink and found a glass for water.

"Granny, these are my friends and my family. They're good, kind people, but like people, some werewolves can be bad—like those guys who tried to start a fight on your lawn." Delilah smiled softly at her grandmother. "I'm in love with a werewolf." She looked over to Simone, love in her eyes.

"Did they make you into one?" Pearl asked.

Delilah shook her head. "No. I took a different path. My father's path. Come to Portland. We'll find a good home for you, and we can visit regularly. There are plenty of human family members of all ages in the pack. I can help you find a good church. Please. I don't want you to stay here and get hurt."

Pearl closed her eyes and nodded. "OK, baby girl, but your wolf friends better not break any of my dishes."

CHAPTER
EIGHTEEN

After scrounging boxes and packing materials from a few stores that were unsurprisingly open—commerce couldn't stop for murderous hordes of vampires, after all—they packed up Granny Pearl's small house and loaded it into the back of the empty box trailer.

"If the bar ever goes under, you can always open a werewolf moving company," Luke said as Pablo walked by, his hands full with a box.

Pablo rolled his eyes, hands too occupied to deploy his usual middle finger. "Go find a box to carry, big strong man."

With Granny Pearl tucked safely in a car with Delilah, Simone, and Sam for company, they started their westward journey, managing to get on the road a couple hours before sunset. They made room for Brutus in the back of the SUV Delilah drove. Before they left, Luke grabbed a few hours of sleep in the truck's sleeper.

"You're going to have to get more than four hours of light sleep at some point. You can't just be a 1970s trucker jacked up on pep pills," Roxi scolded Luke.

"We didn't get a chance to find someone else who could drive this beast. We'll take care of it at our next stop. And those weren't just pep pills, they were amphetamines. A lot of truck drivers were fucked up on something while moving across the country." Luke yawned. "Didn't like them. Made me too jittery. Not a good thing when you're on the hunt for vampires, riding on the back of a souped-up chopper."

"You had a motorcycle? Do tell me more." Roxi looked him up and down, leering at him like he was some sexy leather-clad motorcycle club dirt bag.

Luke laughed. "When we get home, I'll dig out some photos from back in the day."

"Sexy motorcycle Luke?" Roxi made some nummy noises. "We'll have to see about having Gwen stay the night somewhere before you break those out."

Luke chuckled. "I see."

Roxi reached across the cab of the truck and patted his thigh. "Don't worry, dōšagīh, I find you attractive no matter what your disguise is, but most of all, I love the man under them all."

Luke flushed, his cheeks heating up. "I love you, too, Roxi." He yawned. "Can you find us some music?"

While the truck wasn't the newest, at some point, someone had installed a modern stereo system. Roxi tied her cell phone into it and spent a few minutes digging through her phone until she landed on something, a broad grin shifting the muscles of her tired but beautiful face.

"How about a little classic Americana road music?" she asked, hitting play on the Willie Nelson classic "On the Road Again."

"You can't go wrong with a little Willie," Luke replied.

Roxi snickered.

Roxi's juvenile laughter got to Luke in his tired state, and he joined in, wiping tears from his cheeks after the ridiculously long laugh session. "Oh, I always forget about that British slang, but a good laugh was what I needed."

Roxi followed up Willie Nelson with the up-tempo "Going Up the Country" by Canned Heat, then went back-to-back on Canned Heat with "On the Road Again."

"Really going for some traveling road songs, eh?" Luke asked, a tired smile on his face.

"I'm a-truckin' 'cross 'Merica," Roxi said, affecting her best American accent. "Can we get me a trucker hat?"

"I'm sure you'll look adorable in one, but then, you look adorable in anything."

"You're such a sweet man with impeccable taste." Roxi's next song choice was the Talking Heads' "Road to Nowhere."

"Well, trucker mama, keep the good tunes going." Luke fought another yawn. She responded with Fleetwood Mac's "Never Going Back Again," a dreamy smile on her face.

That night, the leadership team, Roxi standing in for Luke, decided to split up at a few small town hotels in West Virginia once the wolf noses decided they didn't smell any vamps and the three who could sense fangers gave the all clear. Luke barely made it through dinner without falling asleep in his food but managed not to embarrass himself. They'd reassemble near first light and get back on the road again after a good night's sleep. They couldn't safely keep pushing and make it to their destination or be able to fight well if called to.

At first light, Luke resumed driving after a full night's sleep, though Roxi was replaced by one of the wolves who had experience driving semi-trucks. After Luke gave them the rundown, they'd switch at the first pit stop of the day, and Luke would ride shotgun to guide them along. If someone else could handle the truck, Luke would rather be in a smaller car so he could move up and down through their caravan to monitor for cars with vampires in them. Also, he missed not being with Roxi, though it would be wise to put her in a different car than either him or Delilah, so they had the three who could sense vampires spread out for maximum efficacy.

"So how long has it been since you've been behind the wheel of a big rig?" Luke asked Gabe.

"I worked construction for a while in the 1990s and drove dump trucks. Not used to having a long tail like this, though. How about you?" Gabe looked nervous.

Luke wasn't sure if Gabe was nervous because he wasn't super familiar with a tractor trailer setup or if it was from working closely with Luke. Some of the newer wolves on the team, those who hadn't known him as long, had a bit of hero worship. It was something Luke had been the subject of before, though it had reached its peak while he still led his own legion and protected the Roman Empire from the incursion of barbarians and vampires.

"A couple years ago in Belgium. We hijacked a truck to use as a battering ram and to run interference. It worked pretty great until the vamps shot our fuel tanks full of holes, and we lost all our diesel. Then Maggie and I had to hoof it all the way to the border of Luxembourg. Before that, the 1970s. I had to hunt down a vampire motorcycle gang that was rolling around preying on truckers and others on the highways."

"Did you know how to drive a big rig, then?"

"I'd had some experience with heavy machinery from the second world war. Used to steal a lot of Nazi equipment when I was running with the various underground resistances, though I paid for some lessons before I became a trucker. Didn't have any connections at that point, so I had to pass my commercial driver's license test." Luke pulled out his wallet and looked through it. "Didn't think so. The pack made me a license before the freighter incident, but I think it either disappeared when I was abducted or it's somewhere at home."

"Man, you've lived quite the life."

Luke chuckled, reaching over to turn up the radio as Social Distortion's "Ball and Chain" started. "You could say that."

THROUGHOUT THE DAY, they drifted back toward the north while keeping their westerly course. It wasn't until they breached the city limits of Columbus, Ohio that they had the first issues with one of their vehicles. The beat-up box van Owen had procured overheated, forcing the caravan to pull off and wait for it to cool down while they sent someone to get some radiator fluid and a new radiator hose; the existing one was leaking. After losing a couple hours and gaining a lot of frustration, they pulled back onto the road, splitting up into smaller groups and taking to the smaller highways of western Ohio with the intention of meeting in Lafayette, Indiana.

But as reports of more issues with the box van came back to Luke, he pulled everyone back together as they limped toward Muncie. With each dip in the speedometer, Luke's frustration grew more palpable, though he did his best to manage it and not let it boil over with a wolf he wasn't familiar with. Sometimes the burdens of leadership were to keep your cool even when you didn't want to.

Barely making any speed down the highway, they found a place where they could pull the van off the road. Sending out their location, Sam had a few vehicles stop to provide security while directing the others on to a nearby town so they wouldn't draw too much attention. When Luke stepped down from the semi-truck, he still had hopes for another reasonable repair, but when he neared the box van, he saw steam and smoke billowing from the engine. The stench of burning oil washed over him, and he bit back a stream of curses.

"That mother fucker sold me a piece of shit!" Owen reared back and kicked the tire, then hobbled on one leg as he spit profanities.

"I don't think kicking it will get it working again," Luke said, trying to keep his laughter in. He didn't think Owen would appreciate it under the current circumstances.

When Owen stopped cursing, he limped toward Luke, favoring the foot he'd kicked the tire with.

"I hope you didn't break your toe."

"It'll be fine." Owen closed his eyes and took a deep breath. "I think the engine block is cracked."

"I'm not a mechanic, but that doesn't sound good," Luke replied.

"It's not. As bad as this hunk of junk is spewing steam and oil smoke, it's not going to be a quick repair, probably not repairable at all. If we weren't so low on ammo, I'd put the damned thing out of its misery."

Luke chuckled. "I'm not sure a shot from a twelve-gauge will do much good."

Owen nodded, working his fingers under the long black ponytail to scratch his scalp under it. "What do we do? Get this thing towed into a town? See if we can sell it for some pocket change?"

"Does it have any important details attached to it? Any traceable names or contact information?" Luke asked.

Owen looked disgusted as he pursed his lips and shook his head. "I thought you respected me, Luke. This van is untraceable to any of us or our packs."

"Then wipe down the cab for prints, and we'll move the cargo to the trailer."

"Guns and granny's fine China? Why the fuck not?" Owen turned to clean out the cab.

Luke walked back to the semi and directed Gabe to pull forward so they could block the van from view of any cars passing by. They set up the other vehicles to hide their unloading and reloading as best as they could. Between everyone, they made quick work transferring their various luggage and weapons from the box van to the semi-trailer. Once the van was empty, they wiped the rest of it down and abandoned it.

Following the previous night's procedure, they split up the group around the various hotels orbiting Muncie. Thanks to Ball State University, there were plenty of places to spread their people around, so they didn't attract too much attention.

Luke and the leadership team met at Roots Burger Bar to discuss their next move, since all the best laid plans of wolves and men seemed to be going all kinds of a-fucking-wry. They left the rest of their friends to seek their own dinner adventures in Muncie.

"Why'd you pick this place, Sam?" Luke asked, holding the door for everyone as they filed into the restaurant.

"They brand the buns, and they have peanut butter pie. Once I saw what, I had a hankering that demanded a hunk o' peanut butter pie." She shrugged and grinned.

"I've never had peanut butter pie before," Roxi said.

Sam's eyes grew wide with excitement. "You're going to have a slice with me. If this were a proper road trip, we'd be stuffing you full of all the classic Americana dishes as we move across the country, but alas, we have a cruel road master." She looked at Luke and stuck her tongue out at him.

"Don't blame me, Sam. I'm not calling the tune on this one." Luke shrugged, holding his hands up to protest his innocence.

After they were sitting around a round table in a round booth, they ordered beers and perused their menus. Famished after a day spent dealing with a breaking vehicle, Luke had trouble deciding. A missed lunch had applied hunger sauce that made everything on the menu look fantastic. He ended up settling on one of the specialty burgers. Sam ordered some appetizers, wanting to sample some of the unique menu items one didn't see in Portland. Their beers arrived after they placed their order, then a few minutes later, their appetizers followed—Pollo Cracklins', Dill Chips, and Loaded Elotes Fries.

"A dill chip? Is that a fried gherkin?" Roxi asked, picking one up and looking at it before popping it in her mouth. "Yup."

They hadn't sat in a proper bar booth in a long while, not since they left Portland, Oregon. It felt good to Luke, familiar and comfortable, although instead of Maggie by his side, it was Roxi. They hadn't had much time to sit at their favorite booth at the Howling Moon Brewery, not with both of them recovering and then Roxi fleeing the compulsion that was already laying waste to her body and mental health. It was different, but also good. Yet, it also increased the melancholy piece of his heart that yearned for Maggie.

After their appetizers and burgers, they ordered dessert—the reason Sam selected this spot. The casual chatter of friends enjoying each other's company, especially after so many hard days in a row, helped to reset Luke's mind, reminding him what he fought for and why he cared about this group of people so much. They were his family, and he missed this level of important unimportance, the renewal of their ties as friends and family.

He knew they had a long way to go and no delusions about them finally being on the easy part of the trip; obstacles weren't going to magically disappear. They hadn't so far—in fact going more in the other direction. They should have been home long ago. Luke almost took it personally, but how could they know his exact flight times and plan this level of international chicanery to catch them in the air? No, it was bad timing, nothing more.

Though, he could be deluding himself. He didn't want to think that the vampire world revolved around him, but if he kept striking at their biggest operations, they were bound to strike back. Either way, it was another time he was left dancing to a tune the vampires had called. He would probably never know. Vampires weren't in the habit of telling him about their most high-level plans.

"Luke?" Roxi squeezed his forearm. "You look far away."

"He looks grumpy," Pablo said.

"Sorry, I was just fixating on everything. How my luck never seems to run good for long. We should have been home a while ago and sleeping in our own beds. We should be at the Howling Moon sharing some new concoction Pablo brewed. Instead, we're in Muncie, Indiana, waiting on our peanut butter pie to show up." Luke shook his head and reached for his beer, draining the last bit.

"That's kind of what we wanted to talk about—getting home," Sam said. "Where do we go tomorrow? Holly has been working the phones. One of the Chicago packs is offering us a safe spot."

Luke pulled up his phone. "That's only four hours away. If we're crawling across the country, it's going to take forever to get home, and it'll give the…" Luke trailed off as he saw the server coming with a tray of desserts. After they ordered another round of beers and she left, he resumed. "Our fanged friends an opportunity to try to plan something in front of us."

"Do you have any other offers coming from Holly?" Pablo asked.

Sam looked at her phone. "Well, there's one that's a bit further out." Sam's nose flared as she scrunched up her face. "Sioux Falls, South Dakota will host us for an evening."

"You don't seem to particularly like that offer," Roxi observed.

"I've been to several packleader conferences with Holly over the years, and I never got a very warm feeling from the Sioux Falls 'alpha.'" She infused alpha with more than a little disgust.

"Something specific or just don't like packleaders that use 'alpha?'" Luke asked. Under the table, he rubbed his hand over Roxi's knee and lower thigh.

"Both. I just always got a squick vibe off of him. He always kind of leered at me. He was respectful enough to Holly, but when she wasn't looking, he was always checking me out. Plus, I've heard some rumors about his pack."

Luke brought both hands above the table and leaned closer, resting his elbows on the table. "What kind of rumors?"

"Just that they weren't a pack really interested in entertaining any diversity. The packs from the indigenous reservations in South Dakota didn't seem to like him very much." She shrugged. "It's hard to put a finger on. It's considered bad form to go digging around in other packs' dirty laundry, and I've never had reason to press it."

"Do you or Holly have any contacts with packs that would give us some more information? Anyone else in the area that might be willing to take us in?" Luke furrowed his brows, weighing the information Sam had given him.

"I can see what Holly says."

"If you could, that would be helpful." Luke relaxed into the booth, cutting off a small piece of his peanut butter pie.

Sam nodded and picked up her phone to fire off some messages to Holly.

Unfortunately, Sioux Falls was the only option. Picking up on Sam's distrust of the local wolves, Luke set up guard rotations so their vehicles and rooms were watched. It wouldn't lead to a restful night, but better safe than sorry. They'd been running too many nights on too little sleep, but with few options, they kept running.

When they met the next day for breakfast, they said their thanks to the local pack and got on the road. Although nothing had happened, Luke was glad they'd set up the extra precautions.

Wanting to start the day behind the wheel of the stolen semi-truck, Sam joined him so they could plan the next evening's stop, the last they'd have on the road before arriving home in Portland. One more night, and Luke could sleep in his own bed under his own roof. He'd get to see Gwen and pet his cat, Alfred. One night and several hundreds of miles more.

"I'm thinking the Missoula Pack is a good place to stop. It's a long drive from here, but I like the packleaders there. Holly and I have stayed with them on vacation before. Jim has already said they can put us all up."

"If you trust them, Sam, Missoula sounds like a good stop. It's going to be a long day today, but that means the next day we can sleep in our own beds," Luke said.

"Yeah. I miss Holly. I'm going to snuggle her brains out when I get home."

Luke chuckled. He was too tired for aggressive snuggling, but he hoped he could at least get a hug from Maggie. That thought kept him company, warming his heart, as they drove across the flat part of South Dakota toward the Black Hills. Tonight, Missoula, Montana, then tomorrow, home.

It was late that day when they pulled off onto the highway listed on the instructions from the Missoula packleader. They'd spent the day driving through the wide-open vistas of the Big Sky state, climbing into the Rockies. They'd seen little evidence of the mayhem happening in the bigger cities, though the freeways kept them from exploring the local environs except at high speeds as they breezed through.

Despite the ease of their day, Luke couldn't help but fret over the what ifs, the lack of obvious activities grinding on his nerves. Even though it was a beautiful drive, he couldn't enjoy it. He wanted to get off the road so he could get the last night of sleep they'd have on this trip.

"I thought we'd be staying in Missoula. This seems way out here," Sam said. She'd decided to ride with Luke in the semi-truck when he took his turn behind the wheel after their last pit stop.

"Yeah. I mean, it'll be nice to the see the stars, but I'd like to have a lot more escape routes available to me." Luke yawned.

They'd pressed hard to cover the drive, harder than he wanted to, but moving forward was more important. They could rest when they arrived back home.

"Sam. I'm not sure why I didn't think to ask this, but did Missoula get attacked?"

"I don't know… Shit, I didn't even think to look." She pulled her phone out of her pocket. "Fuckety fuck. My coverage is really sketchy. I'm going in and out of one bar to no bars."

"I thought they had coverage pretty much everywhere in the US these days?" Luke asked, the pit in his stomach opening a little wider and deeper.

"Well, I'd pull up a coverage map if I had any damned coverage." Sam slouched back in her seat and crossed her arms.

Luke wasn't sure he'd ever seen Sam this angry and annoyed. If she were on the ground, he'd bet money she'd have just flounced out of a room. Seeing the uncharacteristic emotions in his dear friend further opened the pit, filling it with wriggling snakes of anxiety.

"Do you feel anything?" Sam said after a few minutes, breaking the silence.

Luke had been splitting his focus between the road and his surroundings, trying to pick up any kind of twitch or vibe that might mean a vampire was nearby.

"So far, nothing."

"That's good, I guess." Sam straightened up and checked her phone again but tossed it back onto the dash with a disgusted sound. "I lived for a hundred and fifty years without a damned cell phone, now everything hinges on the tiny pixel bars at the top."

Luke chuckled. "Right? I don't know how many times over the centuries all I had to communicate was a man on a fast horse or, if I was lucky, some sort of trained messenger bird. Now we're almost entirely dependent on a few cents' worth of plastic and a few more cents' worth of silicon." Luke let silence reign for a few minutes, then decided to see if he could coax a story from Sam. "So, Sayumi Wakamatsu, tell me about the Battle of Aizu."

Sam laughed. "Not much of a secret name if you know your history."

"It's a pretty safe name in the US where they couldn't tell you the difference between a Wakamatsu and a wakizashi. Although I looked it up, and there was a famous baseball player named Don Waka-matsu. From Hood River, actually."

"Huh, waddayou know," Sam said.

Luke thought she wasn't going to tell him her story, but eventually, she broke her silence.

"It was the first and only battle I ever fought in until I met you. Odd that it would be on a bridge again." She huffed through her nose. "The symmetry is…ironic. Let's see…"

She paused to organize her thoughts. "I was seventeen in the fall of 1868 when the emperor's troops came knocking after our forces were betrayed and abandoned by Otori Keisuke. The emperor's forces laid siege to Wakamatsu Castle. I'd trained with my brother Goro and later under Nakano Takeko. Do you know her name?"

Luke nodded. "I've looked up the history."

"She was so fierce. She was only twenty-one at the time. We all adored her, both the younger girls like me and the older women who also fought. We didn't see any real combat until near the end of the siege. By then, conditions in the castle were wretched. You couldn't even walk through the rooms set up to nurse the sick and injured, they were so full." Sam shivered.

"The Meiji troops fired their cannons all the time. Constant booms and thunder. It was near the end of the siege that we, they later called us the Joshitai—the women's army, though there were only twenty of us—marched to Yanagi Bridge. When we charged into battle, the enemy troops were ordered not to fire at us because we were women. We tore into them, laying about with our naginata. It was supposed to be glorious, but I was too scared to feel anything but terror and nausea at killing another person." Sam's voice trembled slightly.

"You don't have to continue if you don't want to. I'm sorry for forcing the story from you." Luke reached over and patted her knee.

"No, Luke, you're not forcing the story. If I didn't want to tell you, I wouldn't. I love you like a brother. I want to share this with you. Besides, you've shared enough of your life with us all. I think it's only fair you get a little in return." Sam squeezed Luke's hand.

"You know, I never had any siblings, not blood siblings. Zati and

Tigi were the closest I had to a younger sister and brother." Luke smiled fondly, remembering the Armenian brother and sister who claimed to be direct descendants of Tigranes the Great. It didn't matter. Their enemies thought they were, or at least it was plausible enough to make them a threat. It never mattered to Luke, either. They'd become his friends and then his responsibility when he talked them into fleeing Armenia and joining his family by moving in with his parents.

"They were the ancestors of your caretaker's family, right?" Sam asked.

"Ariazate, yes. I lost track of Tigran's line a long time ago." Luke paused the conversation for a moment and shifted gears down to safely take yet another corner as they climbed further into the hills. "So, first blood…"

"Yes. We'd entered battle. Although they hadn't shot at us initially, that didn't last long. They opened fire, felling several warriors, including Takeko. She'd taken a shot to the chest, though it didn't kill her. I ran to her but took a bullet in the thigh and went down. Takeko begged her sister Yuko to take her head so she wouldn't be captured. Yuko and a male samurai removed her head and brought it back to the castle."

"How'd you make it back if you were shot in the leg?"

"Yoshi helped me." Sam's tone softened and drifted toward dreamy. "I thought she'd been wounded too, but she was still strong and helped me limp back. They dug out the bullet, but the wound festered."

Sam checked her phone again but must not have had any reception and returned it to the dash. "Yoshi rarely left my side, caring for me, mopping the sweat from my brow."

"Was she your girlfriend?" Luke asked.

"Spoilers, but no. Not then. We'd only exchanged glances and the touches any woman shares with another. I was pretty delirious by the time the siege neared its end. In the quiet when they were negotiating our surrender, she snuck us out and into the woods when I was having a more lucid period." Sam cringed. "I can almost feel the pain in my leg now after all these years. Moving was excruciating. It hurt worse than getting shot had."

She reached down and grabbed her right thigh about a third of the way down from her hip. "I still have the scar. It's faded to silver now, but it's ugly and puckered. Anyway, once we were away from the castle, she scooped me up as if I were a child and carried me into the woods and hills away from both armies. She found us a little abandoned shrine near a stream and laid me in its water to cool my fever."

He'd never taken any wounds that badly before winning his immortality. He was thankful for the Roman surgeons and their practice of sanitizing their equipment in ways that were unrivaled for centuries. Though he'd suffered some grievous wounds over the centuries after leaving the empire, including one that had festered badly in Mongolia in the century before the rise of Genghis Khan.

"The water worked, lowering my fever enough that I could talk with her. I wanted to die. I asked her to help me commit seppuku—I just wanted the pain to end—but she offered me an alternative. One that would let me live. One that would let us be together. Then she showed me. She stripped naked by the stream and transformed." Sam chuckled. "I was so frightened. I thought I was hallucinating or that she'd turned into an okuri okami."

"That's a yokai, right?"

"Yup. I thought she'd turned into a sending-off wolf spirit—I guess that's the best translation—and since I couldn't get away, she was about to pounce on me, but she didn't. Although she was big and wolfy, I could still see her affection and her spirit in its eyes. When she changed back, she said she could change me into a wolf woman like her, and I'd heal from my wound sickness and be stronger and faster."

"I was quite fond of living and quite fond of Yoshi, so I said yes. She helped me into the shrine, then changed back. Yoshi bit me on the arm as gently as one can bite." She pulled up the sleeve of her shirt.

Luke was on a straightaway, so he risked a quick look. There were a pair of puncture wounds that looked like a large dog bite. He imagined there would be a matching set on the inverse side. When he returned his gaze to the road, she lowered her sleeve.

"I passed out at that point, and when I came to, I felt better. Not all the way, mind you, but better. After that, I started healing at a remarkable rate. Once I was well enough, we moved deeper into the mountains and found a quiet little village we could live near. We pretended to be sisters widowed from the war. We gardened and hunted and traded with our neighbors in the village. We didn't cause any problems, so they left us alone.

"Periodically, when we judged we'd stayed somewhere long enough, we'd move on and find somewhere far enough away that no one would recognize us. We did this until the second world war, largely ignoring the actions of Imperial Japan as we lived our happy little isolated lives."

She sighed morosely. "I think it was near the end of the war, sometime in 1944, Yoshi went out to get food and never came back. It was after the US had started its regular bombing of Honshu; bombs had landed near where we were staying. I looked all over for her, but I couldn't find her. After weeks and months, I finally gave her up for dead."

"I'm so sorry, Sam." Luke reached over and squeezed her hand.

"I was devastated. I nearly starved to death from grief, though the food shortage didn't help. Then the war ended, and the American occupation began. That's when I met Holly. She was an Army nurse. I worked at her base cleaning to earn enough to buy food. It was a frightening time, though I was learning English. When she overheard me speaking to someone, she approached me after and we became friends and then lovers, though it wasn't easy to arrange time together. But she knew a couple doctors who were secretly seeing each other, and they'd let us use their quarters.

"After we'd been together a while, she asked me to come to the US with her when she was shipped back. She arranged for us to marry the doctors so I could be a war bride. When she was shipped home, we all moved together and played happy little housewives and husbands."

"Sounds like a good situation for everyone, given the circumstances."

"Yeah. It allowed me to move to the US to be with Holly and for us to have a safe situation, for both us and our husbands. They were good men. I do miss them. My husband died in the early 1980s, and Holly's didn't last much longer."

Luke squinted, leaning slightly forward as if it would help him see further. "Did they know about the werewolf thing? I'm assuming you turned Holly at some point."

"They did. It surprised us when they refused the offer to turn them so they could continue to be together, but not everyone wants this life. I miss their friendship. And that, Lucius Silvanius Ferrata, is the story of Hara Sayumi and the Battle of Aizu-Wakamatsu."

"Thank you, Sam, for sharing."

"You are welcome. Now, sometime when we're all relaxing, maybe around a fire with drinks, you can regale me with tales about how you learned Japanese in the distant years before I was born."

"That was an interesting time for Japan and me. It'll be a fair few stories if I give you the full adventure." Luke checked the side mirrors, seeing only a line of headlights behind them. "I don't like this. We keep driving and going nowhere."

"Me, too," Sam replied.

"I'm calling a halt. Meeting at the middle, if you could send out the message." Luke pulled a couple blasts from the air horn.

"That's subtle," Sam snarked.

"We're a noisy line of bright cars in the darkness. Anyone who is in the area or is looking for us knows we're here. I just want to give a quick warning of a change."

"Fair enough. I've got replies from the rest of the leadership team." Sam pulled her coat on.

Luke stopped the truck and put on the parking brakes but left it running. He pulled his coat out as he climbed down out of the big rig and threw it on as they crunched through the thin crust of snow along the roadside.

"Whaddya call the stop for?" Pablo called when Luke came in sight.

"Got lonely. Wanted to chat. Didn't feel like driving anymore, so thought I'd call a meeting."

"Ugh. Since when did you become a useless middle manager?" Delilah asked, folding her arms across her chest.

Luke looked around, ensuring he had everyone there. In the shadows, he saw a tall figure walking up. It stepped into the light, revealing itself as Owen.

"So, anyone notice a problem?" Luke asked.

"We're still driving, and we haven't arrived at our destination?" Delilah replied. "Unless there's some other problem you're noticing?"

"That's certainly the one that concerns me most." Luke looked back the way they'd came, his brow furrowing as he squinted into the darkness.

"I don't like that look, Luke…" Pablo said.

"I thought I saw something, a twinkle of light. It's probably nothing…" Luke trailed off, stepping away from the line of cars and their headlights. "There it is again."

Delilah crunched her way to stare into the darkness with Luke. "I've got a bad feeling."

"Me, too, Dee." He continued peering into the dark woods. "What would be your plan if called on to give it?"

"Send a scout and break out the weapons in the meantime. Probably send one forward as well," Delilah replied.

"Let's do it." Luke turned to Delilah. "You want to give the order?"

"Sure." Delilah smiled as they headed back to the huddle of friends. "Who feels like putting on their paws? I need a pair to head back the way we came and two to move forward."

Owen raised his hand and started stripping off clothes. Sam joined him.

"I'll scout ahead," Simone volunteered.

"I'll go with her," Pablo said.

Soon, all four werewolves had stripped, changed to their full wolf forms, and disappeared into the dark. Owen's wolf looked like a large silver timber wolf with dark patches on his head and down his back. It was the first time Luke had ever seen any of his wolf forms, though Luke had no idea if Owen had the bipedal form. Thinking about it, Luke shrugged. He'd always assumed he did as strong and powerful as he seemed.

"Normally, I'd volunteer for scouting missions since I was trained as a scout, but I lack a horse and a decent knowledge of this land," Roxi said, shivering in the cold.

"You also lack four paws and a snoot with a great sense of smell," Delilah said. She turned her head to Luke. "Should we move the line forward, but slowly?"

"We might as well. Let's not go much faster than five miles an hour. I don't want to force our scouts to go too fast to catch up or keep ahead."

"Right." Delilah turned and headed back to the car she was driving.

Roxi followed Luke back to the semi-truck and climbed in on the passenger side. Luke wanted to keep some distance between their caravan and whatever might be following them in case it turned out to be something nefarious. Plus, it kept him busy and focused so he didn't spend all his brain power thinking up terrible scenarios.

CHAPTER
TWENTY-ONE

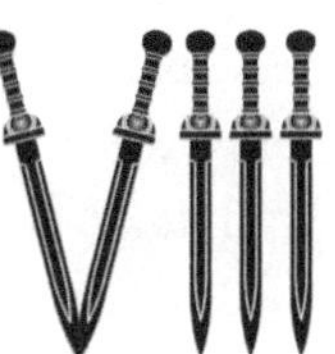

Owen and Sam, in their wolf forms, ran alongside the road up the caravan line until they got to Luke. He slowed and stopped when he heard their barks. Delilah joined them a few moments later as they waited for their friends to get dressed. It was too cold to be out in their birthday suits if they also weren't wearing their fur coats.

"So, bad news, Luke," Owen started off. "We got a line of fangers and probably some wolves as well following us."

"Shit. Any idea how many?" Luke shook his head.

"Hard to tell. They were keeping a lookout and spotted us." Owen looked annoyed by the situation.

"Yeah, they took a shot at us. Scared me. I yipped and ran off with my tail between my legs. I don't fancy increasing my body's lead content," Sam grumbled as she pulled her coat on.

"I wasn't far behind," Owen added. "I saw a lot of shadows and light reflecting what looked like they might be guns. Caught a few whiffs of gun oil, too."

"Well, we confirmed we're being followed and by whom. Think about estimating how many while we're moving forward. Let's mount up."

"Hold up, Luke. We need to delay them," Delilah said, looking around at the trees.

"I see what you mean," Sam said. "We got any axes? A couple trees across the road will force them to stop and deal with it. If we make them big enough, it'll chew up a lot of time."

"Alright, let's break out as many axes as we can. Put down as many trees as we can as fast as you can, then haul ass out of there. We'll leave a car behind so you don't have to run all the way."

"I'll manage that." Owen jogged down the line, stopping at vehicles and calling out names or demands.

Within a few minutes, he had six axes and people to wield them ready to go. A minute later, the distinct whack of an axe into a tree signaled that it was time to move the caravan. Luke got the truck moving and picked up the speed. A nervous finger tapping the steering wheel broadcast the state of his anxiety. As the minutes ticked by and nothing resembling a destination appeared, his jaw tightened until he worried his teeth might crack.

Roxi set a hand on his thigh. "Luke, unclench your jaw. We'll figure this out and get through this. It's what we always do." Reaching out, she turned the radio up, knowing music helped them both soothe. Asaf Avidan's "The Labyrinth Song" quietly filled the truck's cab.

He nodded and opened his mouth, stretching the muscles of his jaw. When a black blur moved across his headlights, he nearly had a heart attack until Roxi called out to stop. As soon as the wheels stopped rolling, Roxi popped open the door, and a naked Simone climbed in and got situated in the sleeper, wrapping herself in a blanket. Luke took his foot off the brake as soon as Roxi's butt hit the chair.

"What's the news, Simone? And where's Pablo?" Luke asked.

"He's up ahead at what is probably our intended destination, looking around. It's some kind of camp. Lots of little outbuildings and a couple main buildings. Looks like maybe logging? There's a bit of heavy equipment and a few stacks of logs."

Roxi turned to Luke, a feral grin on her face. "They didn't plan their trap very well."

"No. Give me a legion with some shovels and axes, and I can build a fort in hours. But heavy equipment and logs will do just as well." Luke poured on more speed.

The quicker they arrived at the camp and situated their rides, the quicker they could begin building defensive works. Ten minutes later, they rolled into the camp and parked their cars in an orderly double line near the back of the camp. Engines stopped, and the camp became a hive of activity as people busted out weapons and started loading. Sam sent off four people to keep a look out down the road for their impromptu logging team and their enemies.

"Hey, Luke!" Pablo waved. "Mind bringing me some clothes? It's a bit cold here. And no, I don't want to hear any comments about shrinkage."

Luke laughed and shook his head. Pablo always knew how to lighten his mood.

"Find anything useful?" Luke asked.

Pablo nodded as he pulled on clothes. "A fair bit. We got axes and chainsaws. Not much in the way of food."

"Any keys for the log crane or that backhoe?" Luke asked.

"I'm not sure. Didn't think to look. I'll be right back." Pablo turned and ran back to the central buildings.

"Check the cabs, too, in case the workers left them inside." Luke turned to find Roxi right next to him. "Can you survey the back of the camp? I want to check out the front."

"Right. I'll see what kind of defenses we can set up." Roxi gave his hand a quick squeeze then ran back past the line of cars.

Surveying the approach to the camp, they needed to block the road quickly. Making that his first priority, Luke gathered a bunch of werewolves and had them unload the trailer as quickly as possible, including Granny Pearl's belongings. As soon as the trailer was empty, Luke jumped into the cab and pulled around the camp, taking the trailer as far forward as possible. He backed it up next to a tree and pulled forward, so the trailer blocked the narrow road and had a tree at each end to keep it from being pushed back into the camp. Once the trailer's landing gear was dropped, Luke pulled the truck back around and stashed it with their line of cars.

"Luke, should we tip over the trailer?" Pablo called.

"No. Not yet. We can shoot under it if we need to."

"Yeah, but it'll be hard to tip it in the heat of battle." Pablo tossed Luke a couple sets of keys.

"True. Gather some muscle and go tip it forward." Luke didn't wait for Pablo, but turned and ran toward the backhoe.

When it fired up, he turned it off and ran to the log crane. Sure enough, they had the keys to both pieces of equipment. Now he just needed to find someone who knew how to run them. He could probably figure out the backhoe, but he didn't have the time for a learning curve, and the log crane was better left alone than to have an amateur running a machine that could lift body-pulping logs into the air. He hoped Owen had some skill with it. Sam had told him the Coast Pack used to be more heavily involved in logging and fishing before they converted to cannabis farming.

Luke ran through the group, seeing if anyone had any experience with construction or logging. He was nearly out of options and about to start a crash course when Granny Pearl flagged him down.

"I hear you need someone who can run a backhoe. I've operated them before. As long it's not some newfangled self-driving iBackhoe or something."

Luke's eyebrows shot up in surprise. "Thank you, Pearl. I was about to see if I could figure it out on my own. It looks pretty basic."

"Then I think I'm your woman," Pearl replied.

Luke handed her the keys and grabbed a stick, drawing a series of lines in the dirt to show what he had in mind. "Is that doable?"

"Depends on the soil, but I can make that happen or get as close as possible," Pearl said.

"Pearl, you're a real lifesaver." Luke wrapped an arm around her shoulders and gave her a one-armed hug.

"I don't exactly understand what's going on, but if Delilah says you fight bad people, then I trust her." Pearl headed toward the backhoe and fired it up.

"Luke! Incoming," someone called from near the trailer.

He took off in a run toward the road that led into the camp.

When he peeked around the trailer, one of their scouts ran into camp.

"Report," Luke ordered.

Charlie held up his hand as he bent over and huffed and puffed to catch his breath. "Damn, this high-altitude shit is for the birds. I miss my thick, chewy sea-level air. Anyway, we've heard a few crashes that sound like trees falling, then nothing. We thought we heard our people working their way up here, but they were going too slow. Connor and Ahmed pushed forward and left Gabe to back them up."

"Thanks, when—"

Before Luke could finish, Connor ran into camp. "Owen and his crew are coming back, but they've got an injured wolf."

"Fuck," Luke shook his head at their first injury of what was quickly becoming a race to get defenses built. "Charlie, go inform Sam and let her know we'll want to use one of the big buildings for an infirmary. Connor, work your way back down the road and see if they need anything, then come back and alert us."

They saluted and ran off to carry out Luke's orders. Before running back into camp to organize the next task, he waved at Pearl as she set up the backhoe's stabilizers. Behind him, she serenaded him with the sweet sound of the metal scoop scraping into the forest floor.

From off in the distance, Brutus shuffled toward Luke, his tail sawing the air slowly. Luke scratched the giant dog behind his ears as he surveyed the hive of activity around him. "Hey, buddy. Just stay out of the way while we're setting up." With a low woof, Brutus walked toward the central building they'd claimed as their central point.

Not for the first time, he wished he had more people. He knew his people were working hard and fast to set up defenses, but there were only so many of them, and they were already tired from days of hard traveling after a rough campaign in the woods of Maine.

Pablo was busy unloading a few chainsaws and axes from a small outbuilding that looked like a shed. He fired up the chainsaws one by one, turning them off when he was sure they were working.

"How's it looking?" Luke asked.

"We have enough equipment here for just about everyone. What we're short on is gas. There's plenty of two-stroke oil for the chainsaws, but they left the gas cans almost empty. Axes look in good shape. Recently sharpened," Pablo said.

"Looks like someone is going to have to siphon some gas from one of the cars."

"Damn it, I hate the taste of gas." Pablo stuck his tongue out and made a gagging noise.

"See if you can get a volunteer. Sucky jobs always go down the ladder of authority." Luke tried to keep the corner of his lip from quirking up.

Pablo huffed and shook his head. "I see what you did there. We'll have to be careful, though. We don't want to use all the gas in the cars—or not too much, anyway."

"That's a problem for future Luke and Pablo. Present Luke and Pablo just need to make sure we survive to have to deal with gas shortages on our vehicles."

"That's true. I'll get on that."

"Hey, Luke." Sam waved Luke down.

"Sam."

"I've got all our food stores moved inside. All our weapons are laid out and ready with ammo distributed. Owen's got some crates that are locked, though, and I can't get them unlocked. Not without potentially doing damage."

"Yeah, and his surprises often go boom with loud and damaging effects. He'll be back shortly. Just leave them until then."

"Right? I have no desire to blow myself up in one of his cheeky surprises. We have a hospital spot set up. I've been filling pans with water and boiling them while we have power and water. I'm going to sterilize some sheets so we can rip them into bandages if we need to. It's not really necessary for wolves, but it's better to be on the cautious side and prevent any issues."

"Plus, there are us humans who might appreciate a clean bandage and water that won't contaminate us."

"True. What should we get people working on next?" Sam asked.

"Stakes. Long ones we can line our trenches with. Also, probably want to make some spears. We should get a fire going so we can harden the tips. Pablo's getting more gas for the chainsaws, but we've got axes too. They'll come in handy"—Luke chuckled—"for hand-to-hand combat."

Sam smiled and shook her head. "I'll get folks organized on that. So just cut any tree?"

"Nothing too big around. We need to get it into the ground easily enough and sharpen it. Try not to fell them into the camp."

"Damn, Granny Pearl's really going to town on that backhoe."

Sam wasn't wrong. Pearl already had a decent trench leading away from the trailer with a nice berm built up on the backside. The sound of a car's motor drew Luke's attention to Owen and his crew coming into camp. Sam ran toward the car as Owen rolled down the window.

"Bring Betty. We have a hospital spot set up in that building over there." Sam ran ahead to get everything ready as two of the werewolves carried a third between them. The injured wolf had blood covering her lower left leg.

"What happened, Owen?" Luke asked.

Owen waited until they were in the building and out of hearing range. "She got distracted and her axe slipped. Stupid injury. Might have nicked the bone, but mostly a flesh wound. It'll heal up quick enough if the damage isn't too bad, mostly skin and muscle."

"How many trees did you knock down before you took off?"

"We put three giant motherfuckers across that road. It'll keep them busy, or they'll have to come the rest of the way on foot."

"Excellent. Hopefully, that gives us time to get our defenses in place. If you don't mind, can you help me gather up our leadership team? We need to have a little meeting about what's going to happen."

Off in the distance, a percussive *whoomp* sounded back down the road. At the noise, Owen grinned knowingly.

"I set up a few little surprises for our friends. Apparently, they found the first one." Seeing Luke's furrowed brows, he added. "I pulled the pins on some of those grenades, then hid them so the spoon was just held in place."

"That'll slow them down even more if they're looking for booby traps the whole way," Delilah said as she passed by.

"Nice. How many more of those grenades do you have?" Luke asked.

"Not as many as I'd like right about now, but we got a few."

Luke nodded. "We'll be sure to find them good homes. In the meantime, do you know how to operate a log crane like that?"

Owen looked over at the crane. "I've never operated that model, but I'm sure I can figure it out. What do you have in mind?"

"Can you set those logs down on top of those berms Pearl is creating?" Luke asked.

"I can, though I'm not sure I want to stand behind them. But if I take those smaller ones and set them down behind the berm and drop the big ones on top, that should backstop them."

"That's a good idea. We can always put some posts down to peg them in. Do you think enough werewolf muscle behind one of those logs would roll it down into the ditch?"

Owen narrowed his eyes, staring at the logs. "Possibly. I pity any fool stupid enough to stand in that ditch."

"Yeah. It's a way to get thinner, but I'm not sure of its medical soundness." Luke fished in his pocket for the crane's keys and handed them to Owen.

Owen chuckled, jogging over to the crane to start moving logs. While Owen worked on logs, Luke gathered Sam, Pablo, Delilah, and Simone.

"Hey, folks," Luke said. "We need to get someone to run for help. They'll need to get down where there's cell coverage."

"Who's going to come rescue us way the fuck out here?" Delilah asked.

"The pack will," Sam said. "The Coast Pack, too."

Pablo nodded. "It might be worth sending a message to Owen's friends down at Wind River."

"Anyone who will respond." Luke clenched his jaw. "We need friends, and we need them moving our way."

Delilah's brows furrowed, worry weighing heavy in her eyes. "But Portland is still a day's drive away. Wind River is probably about the same. Plus, whoever we send is going to need to get back to coverage."

"We're just going to have to hold out until they arrive," Luke said. "We've been in tougher situations."

"Have we, though?" Delilah replied. "We're a long way from home, running thin on numbers, and our friends are a long way from here.".

"This isn't the first time I've had to defend a fort while being outnumbered. Trust me, Delilah, we'll get through this if for no other reason than what other choice do we have?"

"The local yokels probably think they're badasses—all big belt buckles, cowboy boots that have never seen cow shit, and a pretty Stetson. They got a gun rack in their spotless pickups that have never seen work. They have no idea what's about to hit them." Pablo grinned. "Don't make me go put my snap-on pants on so I can—"

Chuckling, Delilah covered his mouth with her hand to stop him saying whatever was about to come out of his mouth, most likely "rip and roar" or some other egregious joke he'd been workshopping, waiting for the perfect moment to debut it. "OK, you win. We'll kick ass, but who's going to be our lucky volunteer?"

"I will," Sam said. Before anyone else could say anything, she held up a hand to forestall them. "I know how to move and survive in the mountains. I'm tough and fast. Besides, I have the biggest Rolodex here and the relationships to use it. Pablo, do you have those adjustable harness packs we've been talking about?"

"Yeah, I know right where those are. I'll be right back." Pablo ran off to fetch the harnesses Sam had requested.

"I'll go with you, Sam," Simone offered.

"No, they're going to need every fighter possible to hold this fort. I can outrun most trouble if I run into it. Now, give me a minute to fetch what I'll need. You think about anyone else we might get hold of or any specific messages you need to send." She didn't wait for anyone to say anything, taking off.

Pablo and Sam returned a couple minutes later at about the same time, Brutus trailing along with them.

"Sam, should we send Brutus with you?" Luke asked.

She narrowed her eyes and stared at the dog. "I'm not sure he can run as long or as far as I can…"

Brutus looked up at Luke, a low growl rumbling in his throat.

"OK, looks like you're staying." Luke shook his head. He didn't want the dog to get hurt, though he seemed to be able to take care of himself and had done his part to fight for the pack when he needed to.

Pablo had the harness. It looked like a harness or vest for a dog, save it was werewolf sized and had a zip pouch like a backpack. Sam grabbed it and stuffed in a set of stretch leggings, a shirt, and a pair of flip flops as well as a thin wallet, her phone, and a GPS unit. She shoved them in the pocket, then cinched it down flat so nothing could move around much.

"Anyone else we should reach out to or other thoughts you have before I shift?" Sam asked.

"Good luck," Luke said, pulling her into a hug.

Sam dispensed quick hugs to the rest of the group, then stripped down, handing her clothes to Delilah before shifting into her full wolf form. Pablo knelt down and put the harness on Sam, snugging the straps and belts until he got a quick yip, and probably some communication through their pack link, when it felt right. Standing, Pablo ruffled the hair between her ears and pulled her tail, eliciting a yip of surprise. She wheeled and snapped her jaws at Pablo, causing him to jump back. At the look of shock on Pablo's face, she wagged her tail, her tongue lolling out in a wolfy grin.

"That'll teach you to pull her tail." Delilah laughed while Simone shook her head at Pablo.

Sam turned and dashed off to the west. Soon, her bushy tail disappeared into the darkness.

"Hey, Roman! Come here. I have an idea," Roxi yelled from across the camp.

"Be right there, Parthian." Luke gave his friends a tight smile. "Let's get back to preparations."

Off to the south, another muffled explosion drifted through the trees toward them.

Luke chuckled. "Looks like they found another one of Owen's booby traps."

The small, spiteful strike drew petty grins from everyone as they returned to their various tasks. Luke went to check on Roxi's idea. He had no doubt the Parthian woman he loved had dealt with sieges, probably on both ends, both inside and out. As a spy and assassin, she'd probably infiltrated her fair share as well. Together, they'd use every trick they knew to get through this and keep their friends alive.

CHAPTER
TWENTY-TWO

Their last scout sprinted into camp, reporting the combined forces of the local packs and their vampire masters were about to enter visual range. The previous scout had brought the news of their approach a few minutes earlier, forcing Luke to call off the preparations for now, save for Pearl and Owen who were working as fast as they could to build their trenches and walls with the backhoe and log crane.

Roxi stood a dozen yards back along with a couple of burly wolves to help her operate the catapult she and Luke had hastily assembled using logs with straps from the supply shed and the semi-truck. They'd given it a few test shots to make sure it worked and to find its range. Now Roxi was armed with rocks the size of fists, small boulders closer to the size of a head or two, and some log rounds to supplement their small rock supply. All the dirt Pearl had dug from the trenches made rock collection easy.

To save on ammunition, several of the pack were in their bipedal form and armed with improvised spears. A couple had a pile of rocks they could throw once people were in range. Luke wanted to laugh at the absurdity of it all. He'd fought sieges behind the wooden walls of a Roman fort, stone castles, and later in various modern forts, but this might have been one of the odder combinations of modern weapons and a DIY hodge-podge of primitive weapons that honored their Portland aesthetic of handmade retro.

Luke pulled out his phone, now in airplane mode to save battery, and checked the time. Sam had been gone for a little over three hours now. He knew a regular wolf could make about five miles an hour at their steady ground-eating lope, but he had no idea how fast a werewolf was, though he knew it was probably faster. Plus, Sam would push it since she wasn't trying to conserve energy like a wolf on the move would be. As long as there was a town or major road somewhere near, she had to be getting close to the point where she could call in reinforcements. Then they just had to trust to the readiness of their allies and friends.

"I see them," Jung-sook said, peering through the scope of her Steyr SSG 69. "Want me to send a welcome message?"

Luke smirked and shook his head. "No. Let's wait and see if they cluster up. See if there's someone giving orders whose head you can turn into a canoe."

Jung-sook laughed. "With pleasure."

The second Steyr was nearby loaded and ready, but for now, Luke wanted to conserve their ammo for Jung-sook, who'd gone from being a great shot to downright scary after practicing almost daily for two-and-a-half years.

Luke poked his head above the trailer and put his night scope to his eyes. They weren't entirely dumb. They'd sent scouts out to sneak through the trees along the road. Behind them, the occasional flash of light or shift in the darkness told him they were moving up. Soon, the action would begin.

"Delilah, can you go check on Owen and Pearl, please? I want Pearl out of that backhoe and safely inside as soon as possible," Luke said, still looking down the dark road. They had close to six hours before the sun would start its ascent into the sky. The vampires would need to get tucked in well before that, though he had no idea if they had nests ready to go up here or if they'd brought something light tight with them.

"Right." Delilah took off at a run.

She wasn't happy about her grandma being exposed to this kind of danger but was proud of her for doing her part.

"Looks like they're gathering," Jung-sook said lowly. "Oh, no. They're actually going to stand on something, aren't they?"

A moment later, Jung-sook squeezed the trigger. Luke's answering grin looked positively vicious when the dumbass collapsed, spraying his friends with blood and brain matter. As they scurried for cover, Luke chuckled.

"Nice shot," Luke said.

"Child's play at this range on a stationary target."

"Why don't you try one of the mobile targets? I think the scouts have moved up close enough. Just one to see if his friend wants to keep moving forward. If he retreats, let him go."

"Left," Jung-sook said.

Luke swung his scope over and found the scout just in time for the crack of the Steyr followed by the body dropping. Checking back on the scout moving up on the right, it took Luke a few seconds to find the person hiding behind a thick tree. Luke stared at them while they ran through their options. Finally, they broke from cover and dashed back in the direction they'd just come, moving from tree to tree, trying to screen themselves from the wrath of the sniper.

"That seems to have stopped them." Jung-sook took a moment to pull the magazine and load a couple more bullets into it, returning it to full capacity.

"At least made them a lot more cautious." Luke watched a few heads poke out, an occasional reflection off the optics of a scope or binoculars.

When he heard footfalls, he turned as Delilah skidded to a stop. "They're getting close to finishing. After Owen drops the last log, Granny is going to pack some dirt behind them to brace them, but we should be closed up pretty soon."

"Great. Thanks, Delilah."

"Luke, do you year that?" Jung-sook called.

Tipping his ear down the road, he waited. His hearing was better than the average human's, at least when he wasn't destroying his hearing firing guns, but it was nowhere near as good as a werewolf's, even if they were in their human form. In the distance, he heard a faint rumbling.

"See anything yet, Jung-sook?" Luke tried to see if he could spy any movements or flashes of light.

"Nothing yet…oh, wait. Huh. That's not a half bad idea."

Luke raised an eyebrow and turned toward Jung-sook. "I'm not a fan of complementing our adversaries."

"Looks like a bulldozer. Yup, they've got the blade up shielding the driver. You should be able to see it soon."

Luke finally caught a glimpse of it as it rounded the corner and blocked the road, its blade raised as Jung-sook had described it. In ones and twos, people darted out from their hiding spots to tuck in behind the dozer. When they had a decent number, the dozer shuddered into motion, slowly moving down the road.

"Think you can hit the driver?" Luke asked.

The wall of the trailer rumbled as Jung-sook stood up on its thin metal sides, trying to stay close to the support beam she'd been laying on. "I can't quite get a good enough angle down, not at this range."

Dropping to the ground, she sprinted off into the trees. About half a minute later, the crack of the Steyr rang out. Luke held his breath, anxiously waiting to see if the shot had landed. A moment later, the bulldozer swerved to the side slowly until it slammed into the trunk of a tall, wide tree, sending pine needles and cones raining to the earth. One more shot rang out, sending those who'd lined up behind the bulldozer fleeing to their hiding spots again. In the middle of the road, a fresh cadaver became a bump spread in the middle of the road, abandoned by their escaping friends. Apparently, Jung-sook wanted to leave an object lesson to everyone thinking about attacking their fort.

A cracking twig alerted Luke to Jung-sook emerging from the forest. After navigating through the rows of sharpened stakes in the ditch, she handed the gun over the log barricade, then climbed up and over the berm, sliding down the other side. It wasn't the hardest setup to get through, but it was damn good for the time, number of people, and equipment they had. Besides, it would be a hell of a lot harder dodging bullets, spears, and rocks, along with fierce, battle-hardened defenders. Luke was damned proud of all they'd accomplished in the last few hours—and in the years since he'd become involved with Pablo and eventually the entire pack, including some of their neighboring packs.

He'd never thought he'd lead an army of vampire hunters again, spending the rest of his life in the lonely pursuit of his impossible goal. Now, he had the makings of a true force to be reckoned with if he could grow their numbers and train more units around the country and world. He hoped the video they'd recorded was making its rounds to the various packs and inspiring them to fight back.

He checked the time again. They'd burned another hour before sunup. "In pairs, head back to the base and grab some snacks for yourselves, then return to the lines. Refill the water if you need it. And someone take Brutus back and give him some kibble since he wants to hang out up here."

The large dog barked and jumped up, jogging back to the main building. A moment later, the lights of their camp flicked out, plunging them into the darkness of a clear forest night.

"Well, they finally cut our electricity." Luke peered down the road, waiting for the next attack to come.

"I'm glad Sam thought to fill up a bunch of pots and pans and tubs with water," Delilah said.

"You seeing anything new, Jung-sook?" Luke asked. They'd deflected the first two attempts at breaching their defenses, though Luke felt the locals weren't making an intense effort, but light, probing attacks to see what they were up against.

"Just a bit of movement among the trees back there."

"Nice little shindig you got here. Mind if I gatecrash?" Owen sauntered up to their line as if he were on a pleasant stroll through a park.

A chainsaw fired up behind them. Roxi and her wolves were cutting up a log into sizable chunks they could feed to their catapult.

Seeing Owen gave Luke an idea. "Hey, Owen, you got any more of those mortar rounds?"

"I might, if the cause is good." Owen inspected his nails nonchalantly.

"Wanna blow some shit up?" Luke asked.

Nodding and sticking his lips out, Owen stuffed his hands into his pockets. "That sounds like a worthy cause. Be right back." Owen returned a few minutes later with the mortar, then ran back to grab a few shells. "So, what're we blowing up?"

Luke handed Owen his scope and pointed down the road. "I'd rather they not try again with that bulldozer. They were trying to use it to shield their infantry."

"Yeah, and it wouldn't be too friendly on our defenses. They're solid, but not bulldozer solid." Owen rattled off some numbers for people to remember, then gave Luke his scope back.

"Now that we have walls, we need to patrol them to make sure they're not trying to come at us from the back or sides. Delilah, can you organize that, please?" Luke scooted over to make room for Owen again as he rechecked his ranges.

"Got it. I'll take a turn around the camp and see how I want to organize it. Simone, you're with me." Delilah grabbed her shotgun and threw it over her shoulder. Brutus wandered up, still licking his chops after his kibble break.

"Let's go, Brutus." Simone grabbed one for herself and jogged off into the darkness, the dog trailing behind her.

As soon as they departed, Owen smirked. "Ah, young love. Packing shotguns on a midnight stroll under the moonlight to kill the undead. Very romantic date." He made a final adjustment to the mortar. "I think it's ready to go."

"You want me to fire so you can watch the landing?" Luke asked, offering the scope to Owen. He accepted the scope, fixing it on his target. Luke grabbed a shell and armed it, adjusting the setting for impact explosion. "Ready when you are."

"Fire," Owen said.

Luke positioned the shell over the opening to the mortar and dropped it in, ducking. The loud pop sent the shell arcing high into the sky. A few seconds later, the explosion washed back over them and was followed by the cracking of a tree. Branches snapped percussively, ending in a thundering crash.

"That was fun. Range is good. Adjust two degrees to the right," Owen called.

Luke adjusted the mortar. "Ready."

"Fire."

Luke dropped in the next mortar round and ducked down as the shell flew into the night. As soon as the mortar was away, Luke ran up to the line and looked over the trailer toward the bulldozer. He'd popped over just as the mortar landed on the bulldozer, which exploded into a ball of flames. Luke clamped his eyes shut, hoping the flash hadn't tweaked his night vision too badly. When he opened them, he took the scope from Owen and smiled at the twisted wreckage of the bulldozer.

"They won't be using that anytime soon," Luke said.

"No, they will not."

"How are you looking on inventory overall?" Luke handed the scope back to Owen.

"We can't make it rain, but we can play them some marching music. I'll have to count for sure."

"OK. We've got a range. Let's adjust it a little closer to our end, not much though, and target the middle of the road."

"Can do." Owen dropped back to adjust the mortar.

"Luke!" Simone slid to a halt. "We've got someone trying to come up on the northeast side."

Luke stepped off the pile of dirt and joined Simone. "Fuck. That was fast. Is Pearl safe?"

"Yeah, Delilah's getting her inside right now." Simone fidgeted, looking back to the northeast.

"What do you need?" Luke asked.

"Three people—one with a shotgun, and two with those little machine guns should do the trick. It's not a big party."

Luke grabbed a shotgun. "Owen, Jung-sook, you're in charge here. Connor and Ahmed, grab those machine pistols and follow us." He gestured toward the north. "Lead the way, Simone."

Simone turned and ran off, Luke, Ahmed, and Connor in tow.

When they made it to the log barrier, they slowed and ducked under it, crouch walking until they met up with Delilah.

"Granny Pearl safe?" Luke asked.

"Yeah. She wanted a gun, but I talked her out of it for now."

"I hope it doesn't come to it, but we may have to if things get desperate. But she needs some rest before that. Where and how many?"

"About seventy-five yards straight back in the trees. I can't quite see how many. At least six or eight," Delilah reported.

Luke peeked over the top of the log, his scope in hand. "They're starting their advance, creeping in quick and low. Two werewolves in bipedal. A couple of vamps, at least. Not sure about the rest."

"What's the plan?" Delilah asked.

Luke ducked down. "Wait until they get closer, twenty-five yards, then open fire. Take the werewolves down first. Then I'll take the vamps."

Everyone nodded. Luke popped back up to check on their attackers. He held up four fingers on his left hand and motioned that those were coming in on the left. Five on the right. Reaching down, he flicked off the safety of his shotgun.

"Ready," Luke whispered.

Safeties clicked off around him. The shotguns already had a shell in the chamber, but the two subcompact machine guns needed to be charged. Collecting nods from everyone, he took a deep breath and let it out.

"Go."

He popped up and took aim, putting his first shot center mass on the nearest werewolf. Blood and howls of pain blossomed from the wolf as it went down, writhing in agony as silver burned under its skin. It wasn't a mortal shot; if it'd penetrated to the heart, the wolf would be making his final shift to his human form. Off to the other side, the other wolf went down and stayed down, dead. The machine guns rattled to life, spraying in short bursts. Luke's next shot took out a vampire, puffing it into dust. He fired another round, hitting someone in the knee. He couldn't tell if they were man, vamp, or human form wolf. The screams of pain were indistinguishable.

He pumped another shell into the firing chamber but couldn't find anyone still standing or running. He reloaded quickly and waited. All he could hear were moans of pain. A few people tried to crawl back into the trees. There were at least a couple vampires still alive based on what he sensed.

"Delilah, want to go over the top with me?" Luke asked.

Delilah gave him a single, quick nod.

"Behead the vampires, but don't stake them."

"What about the werewolves?" Delilah asked, reloading her shotgun.

"Let's see how they respond. If they'd like to keep their lives, we can turn them loose. Maybe it'll encourage some of the less enthusiastic of their lupine brethren to seek other adventures for the duration."

Delilah shrugged. "I guess it's your party, but since we can't afford to hold them prisoner and guard them, it's better than killing them outright."

"Vamps first, keep an eye on the wolves so they don't lash out." Luke pulled himself on top of the log and slid down into the ditch, careful to avoid the few stakes planted in the bottom of the trough.

They hadn't had time to do more. Maybe if they made it until sunrise, they could work on that next. Delilah dropped down next to him. Shifting the shotgun to his left hand, Luke pulled the gladius from his left hip and darted forward, beheading the first vampire he came upon. Delilah had thrown her shotgun over her back and pulled her jian. She had one head off and spun to take the next. With that, Luke's sense of vampire winked out.

"Wolves," Luke called out. "You may keep your lives, for now. If you come against us again, there will be no mercy for you. Dee, take a picture of them so we'll know they're one shot is spent next time we see them. If this sounds like a deal you wish to take, throw your weapons away from you."

A few of the human form wolves looked at each other, exchanging glances, then as one, they threw their weapons away, digging into pockets to find more.

"Ammo, too," Delilah added.

The only wolf that wasn't complying didn't appear to be in any condition to as he writhed and whined piteously, still in his bipedal wolf form. When their temporary prisoners ran out of weapons and ammo, they looked at Luke expectantly.

"Disarm your friend and get out of here. If any of us see you again, you die." Luke caught Delilah's eye and gestured back toward their defensive perimeter.

Together, they sheathed their swords and brought their shotguns out, keeping them aimed over the field of battle in case the wolves got any poorly conceived ideas about making a go at them. Once Luke and Delilah backed off, the wolves disarmed their friend, dodging a couple of jaw snaps, then hoisted the injured wolf up. They all had wounds, but the ones not screaming from silver would heal quickly, probably leaving some bullets embedded in their flesh.

Carrying a wounded wolf, none of them were terribly fast, but eventually they disappeared back into the woods, though they didn't seem to be angling back toward where their main group was. Luke had no idea if his threat and mercy would work, but he hoped it would sap the fighting spirit of the wolves and inspire them to sneak out.

Luke set his shotgun down, propping it against the bottom of the log, and gathered up all the weapons, handing them up to Simone, Ahmed, and Connor.

"What do you want to do with these vamps since you didn't want them staked?" Delilah stood over one of their bodies and nudged the head with her foot.

"Let's take them into the camp. Roxi and I will top up on vamp juice, but I have a plan for the heads."

Delilah raised an eyebrow and shook her head, but she helped him get the bodies over the wall with the help of their friends. They laid the bodies out of the way in case they dissolved into goo. The heads, Luke sent to Roxi to hold on to while he found a notepad.

He scrawled the same promise of mercy to wolves and the threat of true death to the vampires onto three sheets of paper. When he was done, he met Roxi at the catapult. Delilah and Simone waited with Roxi. The three women had become increasingly close the longer Roxi got to know Delilah and Simone. Despite their vast age differences, they seemed to be forming a true friendship.

"You writing love notes to me?" Roxi asked, leveling a slightly sultry gaze his way.

"Not today, but they do go with the little presents I sent you." Luke squatted down and shoved the notes, one each, into the mouths of the three vampire heads.

When he finished, he grabbed them by their hair and loaded them into the bucket of the catapult. With the help of Gabe, Luke winched the arm down, the ropes providing the torsion groaning. As soon as the bucket was all the way down, Roxi slid in the pin that kept it cocked.

"Alright, everybody clear." Luke picked up the rope attached to the pin and uncoiled it as they stepped away from the catapult. "Would you like to send a little housewarming gift to our guests, my love?"

"Ah, you're such a sweetheart, dōšagīh." Roxi's hand brushed over Luke's as she took the rope. She leaned in and kissed him on the cheek, then yanked the rope hard, pulling the pin holding the firing arm of the catapult at bay.

The whole rig creaked and groaned as it sprang to life, bucking as the arm hit the crossbar with a thwack of wood on wood. The three vampire heads disappeared into the dark night. Bark flew off the logs, settling around the catapult.

Luke smiled affectionately at Roxi. "I'm going to go see if they like our present."

"You go ahead. I'm going to reset the catapult and make sure she's holding together."

"You two are weird." Delilah shook her head, chuckling.

Simone hid a giggle behind her hand. "Let's go take another survey around the wall, Delilah. We'll take Brutus back to the main building to keep Pearl company."

Giving Roxi's hand a final squeeze, Luke jogged back to the overturned trailer and climbed up so he could look over the top, bringing his scope to his eye. He found a couple of the heads—one must have flown off course—but he was impressed that two even made it as far as they had.

"Luke," Jung-sook said, "they're sending someone through the trees to check out your little handiwork."

"You mean his heady-work?" Owen said.

Luke rolled his eyes and shook his head. The pun earned groans from several of the others standing around.

"Want me to discourage them?" Jung-sook wiggled, adjusting her aim.

"No. I want them to find them. Can you see the notes sticking out of their mouths?" Luke asked.

"The one is facing away, but maybe on the other one. It's hard to tell at this distance in this light. They're close to the heads now."

Luke watched as a werewolf in bipedal form darted from the cover of the forest to snag the two heads, then sprinted into the trees on the other side of the road.

"So, what now?" someone asked.

"Now, we wait," Luke replied.

CHAPTER
TWENTY-THREE

They didn't have to wait long. About thirty minutes after they returned the vampires, Jung-sook noticed activity through the scope on her sniper rifle.

"We got movement," she called. "Looks like a couple big pickups. They're loading people into the beds."

"Owen, get ready on the mortar," Luke yelled over his shoulder.

"Ready," Owen replied.

Luke nodded at Jung-sook. "The fire call is yours."

Jung-sook and Owen had worked out some markers so Jung-sook would spot and give timely commands. She'd done enough shooting down the straightaway to have a pretty good grasp of ranges. In the distance, the pickups pulled around the corner onto the straight approach to the logging camp and revved their engines. The sound of tires spinning out and spitting gravel alerted them to the start of the race.

"Hold ready," Jung-sook called. "And…FIRE!"

The mortar shell popped into the air. Luke held his breath as he waited to see if the shot would land, the tension rising as the pickups quickly drew closer. When the shell landed on the second pickup and exploded, turning the shiny, jacked-up truck into scrap and twisted bodies, a ragged cheer went up from Luke's forces. The first truck kept speeding toward them.

"Take out their driver?" Jung-sook asked.

"No. If they're going to keep coming, let's let them know we can defend our walls in full view of everyone." Luke turned to his crew, expectant faces looking back. "Safeties off. Wait until my command to fire. One round at a time, unless I call fire at will."

Luke pumped a round into his Winchester M12 Trench Gun. Around him, guns were readied.

"Repellers, ready your spears. Aim to kill." Luke called out.

The bipedal wolves grabbed their long spears and waited. The truck continued to pick up speed until the last moment when it locked up its brakes, tires screaming and rubber burning. As soon as it came to a stop about twenty yards from their barrier, it disgorged its attackers. Luke felt the presence of at least some vampires, though he couldn't tell how many of the dozen were fangers.

"Aim and fire!" Luke yelled.

He drew a bead on a speedy bastard he guessed might be a vampire and squeezed the trigger, splattering the fanger's nearby friends with goo as the shot struck home in the creature's heart. Around him, more shots rang out and more attackers fell, though some still charged, either bravely or stupidly, Luke didn't care. The pickup driver, seeing the swift decimation of his payload, slammed the truck into reverse and gunned it.

"Now would be a good time, Jung-sook." Luke took aim at a werewolf about to breach the walls. "Repellers, your turn."

The crack of the Steyr followed by the shattering of the windshield sent the pickup careening backward until it slammed into a tree. The growls of Luke's werewolves rang over their little battle front as they engaged, plunging their spears into the attackers; soon their screams joined the growls. Those wolves that hadn't been killed on the initial thrust were quickly dispatched. The engagement had lasted only a few minutes, but they'd come out on top again.

By now, he hoped Sam had found a cell signal and was getting the ball rolling on their relief, but every skirmish meant more ammo spent with no resupplies available. It might be best to go mostly hand-to-hand and save what they had, but that exposed his people to a higher chance of injury and death. Either way, he was left with nothing but shit decisions and few options.

"Alrighty, folks. I want the vampire heads and the bodies." Luke pulled his gladius and dropped down off the trailer.

In quick order, he beheaded the few vampires left corporeal. Working as a team, they lifted the vampire bodies over the barriers, then they took the remaining bodies and lined them across the road like speed bumps. Feeling salty, Luke darted from tree to tree, using the pickup as a screen to reach it. He popped the door open, dragging the dead driver out.

He wiped down the wheel and seat as best he could, swiping the bits of brain and skull onto the road. With a shrug, he jumped into the seat and drove forward, avoiding the corpse speedbump, and wove through the trees to leave the truck at the back of the camp. Their patrol helped him over the back barrier. With a quick thanks, he jogged to the catapult.

Roxi strolled over to him, her hands clasped behind her back. "Hey, Luke. Hope you don't mind, but I sent the heads back whence they came. I put a few notes in them."

Luke cupped his hands around his mouth. "Jung-sook, they take the heads yet?"

"Yeah, they came to collect them already," she replied.

"Want to go drain some vampires?"

Roxi laughed. "I hope someone's holding one of the heads when it goes into decomp."

They walked over to the line of headless vampire bodies, each of them pulling out their rudis, and drained the vampires one by one, recharging and healing the little aches and pains they'd accumulated since their last vampire draining.

"How you feeling?" Roxi asked.

"Tired, but vampy refreshed. You?" Luke reached out and moved a thick strand of hair out of her face.

"About the same. I could really use a nap."

Luke exhaled noisily. "Yeah. I could, too. We should probably cycle a few people out to get some rest."

"Yeah. I'm beginning to wonder if my body will ever get back to where it was before the arena."

He squeezed her arm. "I know. It seems like I can't dig my way out of that hole."

She pulled him in for a quick hug, then released him. "Not much we can do about it. Better get back to business."

Luke nodded and jogged back to the front. "Ahmed and Charlie, I'd like you to start patrolling. Run the opposite of Delilah and Simone."

"Roger that." They stood and jogged off, starting their patrol with a counterclockwise circuit.

"Jung-sook, you're in charge for a few. I need to go get some water and a snack," Luke said.

After finishing the vampires, he felt a pit in his stomach he needed to fill, not sure whether it was anxiety or hunger or most likely a blend of the two. Grabbing a water, he surveyed the ammo stocks, shaking his head and pursing his lips at the tiny stacks. They'd have to dip in soon enough, probably before the sun even broke cover. Done worrying over the ammo situation, he took a few strips of jerky and dried fruit before heading back out.

Chewing on the jerky and dried apricots at least gave him an outlet to work out some of his frustration at being stymied in his attempt to get home, a place he'd rarely had, in the spiritual sense, most of his life. He'd always had a home of sorts, a covering over his head, but few places had ever been home. As he walked under the moonlight, he thought about what had made those few homes he'd had, and it had always been the people. When he'd felt the true sense of home, it was because he felt a deep connection to a person.

Now Portland was his home because of Gwen and Maggie and his friends, Delilah, Pablo, Sam, and Simone. Home was the place he genuinely wanted to be, it was the place he wanted to take Roxi so he could have her as part of his home as well. But right now, this improvised fort was his home, and he'd defend the people in it until his last breath.

THEY'D REPELLED a couple more probing attacks around the sides of the camp. With a couple of hours before dawn, the vamps and their allies even ventured a three-pronged attack, hitting two spots at the back and one at the front, but they couldn't make it through the hardened defenders.

When the first glow rose over the mountains in the east, they all released a collective sigh of relief. The vampires would go to bed soon, leaving only whatever collection of werewolves and possibly allied humans they had. Taking advantage of the transition time, he sent Pablo and a group back to the cabins to get a few hours of sleep and sent a couple folks to relieve Delilah and Simone from their patrol so they could rest, leaving Luke, Roxi, Jung-sook, and Owen awake to handle the camp while they rested.

Luke couldn't stop yawning, some so big he felt his jaw pop.

"You should be back with them taking a nap. You're no good to us half asleep." Jung-sook dipped into her pocket to pull out a snack.

"I don't know what you're talking about. I'm as fresh as a daisy." He barely made it through the statement without yawning again.

Several people chuckled, though Luke wasn't sure if it was because he'd tried a Doc Holliday accent or because he'd yawned, graphically proving Jung-sook's point.

"I don't like the look of those clouds," Owen said, pointing off into the west.

The clouds looked dark and thick, ready to disgorge their payload over the mountains to unburden themselves before continuing their eastward journey. It was cold enough, they might get snow if the temp dipped ahead of the front coming in.

"I don't like these clouds much either." He turned to Jung-sook. "Don't worry, I'll go take a nap when it's my turn. I just want to be here for the morning shift to see if they're going to try something thinking they'll catch us with our pants down now that the vampires are out of it for the day." He pulled the last piece of jerky out and shoved it in his mouth. The chewing would help keep him awake.

Fortunately, they got the early morning off. When Delilah—Brutus in tow—returned a few hours after sunrise, Luke took the rest of the folks back for their turn to rest, leaving Delilah in charge.

Even with all the worries eating at Luke, he fell asleep quickly, his body exhausted from twenty-four hours of activity. Thankfully, nightmares didn't visit him, but wake-up time came entirely too quickly, and there'd be no coffee without coffee beans. Rubbing at his eyes, he visited the restroom before grabbing some food to break his fast on the way back to their forward position.

"Good morning, Delilah. Anything to report?"

"Not much. They've been sending out scouts but staying well-hidden enough that we haven't tried to shoot any since none of us are as good a shot as Jung-sook. They haven't gotten too close, but they haven't pulled out, either."

"Alright, why don't you take your crew for a snack break and a bit of quiet. We've got it from here."

Delilah nodded and waved for her people to follow her. While Luke and his people set up, Charlie and Gabe took off to patrol the wall. Jung-sook grabbed her rifle and crawled up on top of the tipped over box trailer.

"What do you want me to do about those people running around the woods?" Jung-sook asked. "Keep them honest?"

"Let's save ammo for now, especially if they're not closing in. Just keep an eye on them for now. I'll cover the right side." Luke pulled the scope out and tucked in at the edge of the trailer so he could watch over the right side and note where their snoops were hiding.

Other than moving about a bit, the enemy's scouts just kept to themselves. With nothing happening, the gentle noises of the forests tried to lull him into a sense of peace, but he knew death waited just down the road. The bodies left by their enemies reminded him whenever he looked down the road. It was often like this, beautiful vignettes surrounded by ugly death.

Without engines or guns firing, silence shrouded the pine forest, enticing out birds hunting for food and singing for mates. Closing his eyes, he listened to the various bird calls, a woodpecker pounding into the bark looking for bugs, the far-off scream of a raptor, and the wind moving through the bows and denuded deciduous trees. Breathing deeply, he let the crisp mountain air fill his lungs to capacity, the stretch of his rib muscles feeling good under the stiff steel bands of his lorica segmentata. When he opened his eyes and exhaled, steam blew from his lips.

"It's getting colder."

"You had to say it, didn't you?" Owen complained.

"What?" Luke asked.

"Don't you know? Once you say it, it makes it true."

"It's getting warmer, pleasantly so?" Luke tried to keep a smile from quirking the corner of his lips up.

Owen shook his head. "It's too late."

A cold flake landed on Luke's face, and he was forced to agree with Owen's assessment. "I've fought in the snow before." Luke shrugged.

"I haven't. They sent me to the Pacific and, most of that time, I was in the tropical and subtropical regions. I'd rather stay warm and not get snowed on." He stuck his tongue out and marched off, grumbling.

Luke chuckled and went in search of some more clothes to layer on. Fortunately, they'd packed for winter conditions—Belgium tended to be more rainy, though it did get more snow than western Oregon. Owen, spending most of his life on the coast, was used to cold, rainy winters, but snow was not something common under the moderating forces of the Pacific. He hoped Sam had made it through OK. She should have found a town by now. Snow would only slow her down. As they waited, Luke sent his people for another break and to grab some warmer clothes and extra socks.

His people were bearing up well, considering they were all tired with too little sleep under their belts. They'd borne up well and hadn't taken any serious wounds, but the tension of waiting was causing some to grumble. In a few moments of heat, tempers flared into sniping and short-lived arguments. They were friends, many having known each other longer than they'd known Luke, but they weren't seasoned soldiers, and they were still a long way from the home they should have been at long ago.

Luke had stopped to wait for Roxi at the catapult after she took a little break, but he was interrupted by a call from their forward position.

"Coming," Luke ran up front and pulled out his scope. "Interesting. How long have they been waving the white flag?"

"Just about a minute," Jung-sook replied.

"What new devilry is this?" Luke mumbled.

"Dork." Jung-sook grinned.

"You recognized the quote, nerd." Luke stared as someone waved a white flag from down at the end of the straightaway. "I guess we should see what they want. Ahmed, call the loafers back to the front. I want a double patrol around the perimeter. And someone bring me a white towel or a T-shirt."

A minute later, someone brought back a white undershirt. Luke shoved a spear through one T-shirt sleeve and out the other side. Handing it off to Ahmed, Luke pulled his scope out and had Ahmed wave their white flag. The other side shoved their flag into the air and waved it, before walking further out of their tree line. Three people accompanied the flag bearer.

"Should we send someone out to meet them?" Jung-sook pulled back on the bolt, loading a round in case Luke called for a shot.

"No. They can walk. I'm not putting anyone out beyond our walls unless we absolutely have to. Three or four people would be a serious dent to our fighting forces if they kidnapped them."

"Do you think they'd violate their own white flag?"

"It's a strip of cloth, and they've violated the rules of humanity by aligning with the forces of darkness. I'll trust us and no one else. Jung-sook, I want you to keep your eye on everything except the people walking down the road. You can pick them up quickly if we need to. I want to make sure they don't sneak something around while they distract us with a flag of truce."

"Right."

When the loafers reported in, Luke informed Delilah and put her in charge of watching the back half of the fort, sending her extra people in case the enemy werewolves decided to spring something. If the enemy hit hard at multiple points, they might be able to break Luke's meager defenses, but so far, they'd been largely tentative, trying a bit of trickery that wasn't fooling an old hand like Luke.

When they reached about halfway between their two positions, they stopped and waved their white flag aggressively. When no one emerged from the fort, they had a hasty conversation with a couple of the people violently gesturing toward the overturned trailer. Whoever won the argument got the quartet moving toward the fort again. At about forty yards from them, Luke popped up, pointing his shotgun at them.

"That's far enough," Luke called. "What do you want?"

A man in a western cut flannel shirt and cowboy boots stepped forward. "We're under a white flag. Stop pointing your guns at us."

"I don't think I will. The only reason I haven't wasted you is I'm curious to hear what you have to say. You're the people who offer sanctuary and betray us to our enemies. So, you can either live with a gun pointed at you, or you can walk your asses back to your line and pray my forbearance lasts long enough that I don't ask my sniper to turn your skull into a gravy boat."

The man blanched, his mouth opening and closing like a fish out of water. Eventually, he got himself under control. "We've come to ask for the surrender of the Centurion Immortal and his..." The man looked profoundly nervous. "This isn't my quote, but his Parthian bitch. Everyone else will be released and allowed to go back to their packs to show the mercy of the vampire lords to our supernatural brethren."

Pablo stepped up and looked over at Jung-sook. "What do you think? Should we give them the Centurion Immortal?"

Jung-sook smirked. "I don't know. It doesn't sound like the best offer."

"Should we see about a draft pick and a free agent to be named later?" Pablo asked.

"And a cash deal. The Centurion Immortal is hall of fame material."

Pablo looked at the men out under their white flag. "What do you say? Got any good up-and-coming lefties? We need to shore up our bullpen."

The man stood there with his brow furrowed and his jaw hanging open.

"Maybe they're not looking to swap draft picks," Jung-sook commented. She turned toward the quartet. "Are you going to freeze him in carbonite and give him to a Hutt gangster?"

"No, they were supposed to freeze young Skywalker. Then Vader made another deal with Boba Fett." Pablo shook his head. "Is this a stormtrooper deal? Where we give you what we want, then you change the terms and betray us? The Wookie and the princess have to stay here?" Pablo looked the man up and down. "You aren't smooth enough or cool enough to be Lando. You just look like some discount dime store cowboy."

"Are you people just going to make jokes at us? You should take this seriously. We know how many people you have in your little fort. This is your chance to get out of this alive. What do you care about some human vampire slayers? They're not one of us. They're not werewolves."

"No, but they're our friends, and they're people of integrity and honor. You have neither. Now run along and report to your masters like a good little doggie…maybe they'll throw you a milk bone." Pablo reached down and grabbed a shotgun, though he didn't bring it into sight.

The spokesperson clenched his jaw, his face going beet red. "This is your last chance —"

"No. This is *your* last chance. We offered mercy to the wolves we've injured if they decided they would rather live than be misled, and the offer is still good if people would rather find elsewhere to be, but for you, ya empty Stetson, there will be no mercy." He yanked the shotgun up, pumping it one handed and sending the shell flying, and aimed it toward the spokesperson. "I suggest you get moving, or I'll fill you full of buckshot like some neighborhood stray who's going after my chickens."

When Pablo lowered the barrel, aiming it at them, the three standing behind the leader started edging away. They were none too quiet or subtle about it. The spokesperson was caught between turning and running away or trying to stay and negotiate more.

When a few more people pumped their shotguns and took aim, he turned and ran after his compatriots, cursing them as he ran away.

"Chickens, Pablo?" Luke asked.

Pablo shrugged. "I didn't always live in a city."

"You were a pretty convincing tough guy there." Jung-sook reached over and patted Pablo's shoulder.

"Whadda you talkin' 'bout?" Pablo said, affecting his best cliche Italian gangster voice. "I'm the toughest." Then he flexed comically, breaking the tension and drawing laughter from his friends.

"Thanks for not trading me for a pack of baseball cards." Luke squeezed Pablo's shoulder.

Pablo scrambled, pretending to climb over the trailer. "Shit, no one said anything about baseball cards! Do you think they'd still be willing to talk?"

Luke shoved Pablo and laughed. "Be careful I don't trade your rip-away pants and your catch phrases."

Pablo's eyes went wide, and his jaw dropped. "You wouldn't…"

"Try me, fuzzball." He watched them finally disappear into the tree line. "I'm going to take a walk around the perimeter if anyone needs me."

Roxi met him on the way, sliding her hand into his as they walked. "I take it we're not being traded to our enemies?"

Luke shook his head. "No. Not today."

"It wasn't a possibility, was it?" Roxi sounded concerned, their recent captivity darkening her eyes.

"No. They won't trade us. They're family." Luke yawned. "I'm so tired. I want to collapse into a nice bed and not wake up for like a month."

Roxi snorted. "I haven't known you for centuries, or even for a few years, but you don't strike me as the kind of person who's really capable of taking it easy. At least not when there are vampires to be fighting."

"Yeah. I guess. I'd like to be a person with a hobby or two."

"You've got your garden." Roxi stopped and pulled him around, so they were facing each other. "What's bothering you, dōšagīh?"

"I don't know, Roxi. Sometimes I just feel like I'm at my breaking point. Right now, I just want to get my friends home to their families and see my own. I'm glad you're here with me and the rest of my friends, but I'm so tired of the constant struggle. We couldn't even catch an easy flight home."

Roxi stepped in closer, their armor pressing against each other. "I know. For the first time in ages, I have a place I yearn to be. I've only seen it for a couple months, but I want to get to Portland, too. I've made good friends with the people here and I want to be with you and not have to wonder where we're bedding down for the night. I want to get to know Gwen better. I want to have a cat to pet on retainer." She leaned up and kissed the tip of his nose. "We'll get there. We'll get our friends home. It's what we do."

Luke nodded slowly. "It's what we do." He sighed and rested his forehead against hers. "Thanks for listening."

"Thanks for talking." She tipped her lips up and kissed him. "Now let's walk around our little wall and hold hands like it's a walk in a park."

"The trees are quite nice. And they look lovely in the snowfall."

They turned hand-in-hand and continued their walk around the wall, nominally keeping an eye on the situation but also to enjoy the peace and solitude of each other's company.

The werewolves made a couple more hesitant pushes later in the afternoon, trying to hit them at a couple points. But they didn't send enough people or press hard enough to even make it to the walls. All it accomplished was interrupting a couple nap breaks Luke had called so they could be as rested as possible before heading into the night when the vampires would return to action.

"Where's Owen?" Luke asked, realizing he hadn't seen the man in a while.

All Luke got in return were shrugs and confused looks, so he went looking. As his worry grew, so did the speed of his footsteps until Delilah called him over, pointing beyond the wall.

"I didn't see him leave, but there he is," Delilah said.

Luke scowled. "What's he thinking not letting one of us know where he's going?"

Delilah snorted. "You can chew his ass out, but I doubt he'll give a shit."

"Yeah. You're probably right."

"Hey, you two want to help me over the wall, or you just going to complain about me?" Owen called from the bottom of the ditch.

They helped him over and followed him as he grabbed some water.

"So you gonna ask where I went?" Owen looked between Luke and Delilah.

"Sure. Why not? Where d'ya go?" Luke asked.

"Took a little stroll through the woods. Almost right up to our friends' camp." Owen looked proud of himself.

"Their patrols aren't too thorough, are they?" Luke commented.

"Not at all. I don't think our werewolf counterparts are as professional in their military training as you and those of us who've served are."

"And you've rubbed off on the rest of us who haven't been in the military. You're a bad influence, Luke," Delilah teased.

Luke chuckled. "If they're being stupid and incompetent, I'm of the mind to keep letting them be stupid."

"I was thinking maybe we should go a step or two further. Feel like taking a walk with me?" Owen fished a grenade out of his pocket and tossed it lightly into the air like he was playing with a baseball or an apple.

"I see. You want to throw them a party, eh?" Luke waggled his eyebrows.

Delilah groaned. "That was terrible. And with that, I'm going back to Simone to take another patrol."

"Let me get geared up, and then we'll go see about delivering an explosive eulogy."

Owen laughed. "You've been hanging around Pablo too much. You're starting to pick up his terrible jokes."

Luke ran over to Roxi to explain where he was going. "Let Pablo know. You, he, and Delilah are in charge while I'm gone."

Roxi helped Luke shift his sword to his back, then pulled on a bandolier of shotgun shells and snugged it down over his double layer of hoodies. He'd be able to move fast and quickly. He might not be able to run like a wolf, but on thin rations after a lot of exertion, he was nearly hungry like a wolf. He downed a bottle of water and grabbed some jerky and apricots, shoving them in his pocket to chew on as they went. When he returned to Owen, he had a handful of grenades, holding them out for Luke.

"I don't plan on carrying them in my mouth," Owen said. "It's warmer in my fur jammies."

Luke grabbed the five grenades and put them in an empty pouch on his belt. The thick clouds had dimmed the day into a soft light as snow slowly fell. He stole a quick glance at Roxi as she talked with Delilah and Simone. Save for the wildness of her hair, and even that was tamer, she looked nothing like Marpesia—but like his first wife, she was strong and confident and a fierce fighter. Though their personalities were different, they'd probably have been friends, challenging each other with horse and bow. The one thing both women had in common was that Luke loved them both entirely. And Maggie.

He'd spent most of his life alone and lonely, with only a few bright spots. Marpesia had been the brightest spot of his first few centuries of life, and now when his life had become the most hectic with his battle against the vampires, he had so many bright spots in his life, but none burned brighter than the two women he loved. He smiled at himself and shook his head.

"Don't worry, I'll bring you back to her," Owen said, a kind smile on his face.

"Sorry, was gathering wool." Luke followed.

"Dangerous thing to do around a bunch of wolves." Owen helped him up and over the barrier before following him over. "Let's go, love shepherd."

Owen stripped down and shifted to his full wolf form, dashing into the woods. When Luke found him, he was sitting on his haunches, his tongue lolling out. Under the umbrella of the fir and pine trees, the snow hadn't accumulated as much as in the open areas. Buffered by fallen needles, Luke followed Owen into the woods on silent feet. Ranging out in front, Owen blazed the path, staying just in sight, his bushy, black-tipped silver tail guiding Luke along.

As they got comfortable working together in this form, they picked up the speed, swinging west before angling to the south. He'd never explored the forests of the Rocky Mountains. In some ways, they reminded him of the forests of the Alps he'd spent years moving through as a legionnaire, though the Rockies were bigger. If they weren't on a deadly errand, he'd be enjoying this run through the woods. The crisp, cold air filled his lungs and sharpened his mind. The anxieties of poor sleep and worrying about getting his people to safety faded into the calm tunnel of a mission filled with danger that wasn't nebulous and just over the hill, but immediate and present.

Every footfall disappeared into a ground muffled with forest debris and freshly falling snow. The world had transitioned from the dark gray of a cloud-shrouded sky to the artificially bright world of light reflecting on snow, causing Luke to squint as he followed the silver timber wolf that was his friend Owen.

As they ran, Luke checked the signs to make sure they were still on the right path to angle around where he guessed the enemy camp was. He trusted Owen, but old habits died hard, especially when his own life and those of his friends were on the line.

They moved quickly, but he wanted to ensure they made it in and out before it was dark enough for the fangers to emerge from their daily slumber. Pissed off werewolves would be hard enough to evade but having wolves and vamps on their tail would be more trouble than Luke was looking to borrow.

Scanning the area, Luke nearly ran into the silver wolf crouched under a low branch. He dodged out of the way, landing on a branch that snapped loudly. With a cringe, he froze, listening for the approach of anyone looking to see what made the sound. Owen, already still, perked his ears up. Luke didn't relax until Owen did, his tongue lolled out. Luke shook his head, embarrassed at his lapse.

Owen popped up and shifted to his bipedal form. The timber wolf markings stayed true. In the dark, it would be hard to hide his fur, but in the snow and shadows, he blended in nicely.

Where earlier it had been a steady, hard run, now they crept, moving from cover to cover, ensuring every foot found a silent patch of ground to tread on before moving to the next. Luke's senses went on hyper-alert as he moved his head about trying to pick up any sound, smell, or sight that might be out of place.

When Luke heard the first murmur of distant conversation, they slowed even further until Owen crouched down behind a thick pine tree. Once Luke snugged up next to Owen and peeked around the trunk, he could see the distant splashes of color that marked pickup trucks, SUVs, and other vehicles. People in various outfits ranging from high-end outdoorsman fashion wear to camouflage wannabe warriors moved about, probably trying to look busy so they wouldn't be asked to do something.

When they heard a twig snap ahead of them, they pulled back behind the trunk and dropped to the ground, breathing shallowly to keep their breath from fogging too much. A hasty, whispered conversation took place near the snapped twig. Grabbing a wind fallen bough, Luke lifted it to cover his face as he poked his head around the trunk. Three men argued, trying to keep their words from drifting. Every few seconds, one of them would look back toward the camp they'd just left.

Something decided, they moved forward, holding a path that would lead them near the tree Luke and Owen were currently hiding behind. Darting behind a tree, the men stripped down, dancing in place as they exposed their naked skin to the falling snow and the increasingly cold late afternoon air. Two of them blurred into wolf forms, then slunk from their hiding place and continued their path out of the camp, moving by and seemingly not noticing the werewolf and human hiding mere feet away. Thankfully, the breeze was in Luke and Owen's face, carrying their scent away from the wolves. The third was tangled in his pants and fell.

Luke went perfectly still and held his breath as the man landed facing him. The man, his cheeks ruddy from the cold, blanched when he saw Luke hiding in the snow. If he yelled out, their little stunt would end prematurely and probably with an injury or worse. Hoping the branch would obscure him enough so that the man couldn't differentiate friend from foe, he reached out and settled a hand on Owen's shoulder to keep him from springing from cover and killing the man. Once Owen settled, Luke held up a finger and laid it across his lips, asking the man for his silence. With any luck, he'd think Luke was one more rat fleeing the ship.

The man used his foot to shove the pant leg down one leg, then the other foot to repeat the maneuver on the other leg. As soon as he disrobed, he blurred into a wolf and ran after his slinking friends. Pulling back and looking over Owen's shoulder, they waited until the three wolves disappeared in the distance. When they felt the coast was clear, they stood up. Luke brushed the snow and debris off himself and crouched low as he walked to check out what the men had left behind.

Kicking some tighty-whities out of the way, Luke sifted through the pockets and took a wallet. Under the clothes, he found a pistol and shoved it into a pocket before moving to the next pile of clothes. Owen posted up near the tree they'd hidden behind for their strip-and-change and kept an eye out while Luke sorted through everything. He found another handgun, but the big find was a fully kitted-out AR-15. Luke pulled the magazine and checked it—full—then put it back in. Lastly, Luke picked up a nice, heavy flannel jacket that looked like it was big enough to fit over his armor. He pulled it on and buttoned it up. The extra warmth would be nice, and if he got the chance, he might try to sneak into camp and reconnoiter the situation.

Ready, he gave Owen a nod, and they resumed their interrupted tree-to-tree sneakfest until they were within throwing range of the camp. Owen pantomimed pulling a pin from a grenade and throwing it, but Luke shook his head and held up a hand to stall him. Settling in, Luke let his calm help him bring in the distant conversations. He didn't have wolf hearing, but after juicing up on three vampires, his supernatural hearing was at near peak levels, and he could hear the words clearly enough.

"...get everyone ready. The masters will want us armed and ready to move out if they decide to attack first thing. They're not going to be happy that we haven't made any progress today," said the first guy.

"It's not our fault. They've got to have way more people in there than they led us to believe," the second guy said.

"You know they don't like excuses, and they certainly don't like the person giving them excuses, look eager and ready and keep your head down; maybe you can keep it attached to your neck."

"They're lucky we don't all slip out of camp while mercy is still available to us."

"Shhh, keep it down. They'll slit your throat if they even think you're considering fleeing. I don't know about you, but murdered by a vampire isn't how I want to go."

"Me, either, but slain by the Centurion Immortal isn't how I want to die, either."

"This is fucked up."

"Totally." He sighed loudly. "I'll go open up the ammo truck and get ready for everyone."

"Good. I need to report in to my alpha," the first said before turning and disappearing back into the camp.

Luke looked at Owen and grinned, then mouthed, "Ammo?"

Slipping out of the tree, Luke darted to the next one, keeping an eye on the guy who said he was heading for an ammo truck. Owen moved along on silent paws behind him, slipping into his full wolf form to help keep a lower profile. As close as they were, Luke was risking being spotted. His senses, already on high alert, went into overdrive. Every sigh of a bough blowing in the winds. Every whiff of cigarette smoke. Every snatch of conversation. Every movement. Luke absorbed them all, sorting through them to pick out anything that might signal a threat or put them in a position to be noticed.

The man seemed oblivious to the danger lurking yards away as he went about his task. When he made it to a series of oversized pickups, he stepped behind and unlocked a canopy, dropping the tailgate. Setting the AR-15 against the tree, Luke pulled the backpack off over his shoulders and slowly unzipped it to keep the sound down. He signaled for Owen to stay and keep watch before he slipped out of the cover of the tree and moved closer to the camp and behind the next tree.

Luke looked all over before leaving the cover of the last tree before the pickup. Standing up, Luke walked out and opted for "bold and belonged there" as his attitude. When sneaking wasn't an option, go with bold as brass.

"Hey, what are you doing back here?" the man said. "I don't recognize you."

"Sorry, I just got here. My packleader is consulting with the other alphas and I was told to report here to get more ammo if you had any for an AR-15." Luke held up his purloined AR-15.

"Dude. We got a fuck-ton of rounds for those. Half the guys here have at least one." He stepped aside and gestured into the back of the pickup.

"Nice. Got any Winchester .243 and twelve-gauges in there? Some of the boys are a bit old school with their shotguns and deer rifles."

"Sure do, brother. I'm Joey, by the way." Joey reached in and grabbed several boxes of the cartridges and shells Luke had requested.

"Nice to meet you, Joey. I'm Peter, though my buddies call me Big Petey," Luke said, picking the first common name that popped into his head.

"Well, Big Petey—"

"Yo, Joey, get your ass over here, man. The alpha wants a quick word."

Joey looked nervously at the open pickup truck, then back to where he'd just been called.

Luke plastered a friendly smile on his face. "Go for it. I'll stand here and watch everything."

"Really? That would be awesome. You sure?"

"Yeah, totally." Luke waved Joey away.

Joey nodded and dashed off. Luke wanted to laugh but kept it to himself. He loaded up on the ammo he needed. He was about to turn and go when he noticed some 9mm rounds and grabbed as many as he could fit in the limited space left in the bag. Looking down at the AR-15, they only had the one and no backup magazines. He moved some boxes, hoping to see if there were a few mags, but found none. He pulled out most of the ammo for it and replaced it with more of the 9mm, since they had the two APC9K compact machine guns and several mags for them. They'd only used them sparingly since they were running dry on 9mm stock, and they went through them quickly if the handler wasn't careful.

Shimmying the bag, he barely closed the zipper on the stuffed backpack, then hoisted the bag onto his back. His head on a swivel, he faded backward into the woods until he stepped into the thicker section and slipped behind a tree. When he heard rustling behind him, he whirled but lowered the barrel of the purloined AR-15 when he saw it was Owen in his bipedal form. He had a wolfy grin on his face, his tongue lolling out as he gestured for the grenades.

Luke pulled one from his pouch and handed it to Owen and pulled another out for himself. "Throw yours far into the camp."

Owen nodded. Together, they pulled their pins and let the spoons fly. Owen used his wolfy strength to lob it over the outside line of trucks and deeper into the camp. Luke aimed shorter, his landing near the ammo truck. He lost track as it disappeared. He tossed another one to Owen, and they chucked them in different directions, then dove behind the tree as the first round went off.

Peeking around the tree trunk, the ammo truck had been blown over, its wreckage burning.

"Shit. That ammo is going to start popping in that fire," Luke said.

Owen shot up, shifted to his full wolf, and ran away from the camp. Luke, only slightly slower, sprinted after him; silence sacrificed for speed and distance. He reached into his pocket and grabbed the last of the grenades they'd brought with them and kept it handy.

Instead of just running straight away, Owen angled them out and back in the direction they needed to go to return to their fort. Yells and screams drifted out of the camp after four grenades had gone off. Luke slid to a halt in the deepening snow and pulled the pin, hurling the grenade as far as he could. It disappeared over a row of outer tents. Not waiting to see what happened, he bolted after Owen.

"Owen, duck." Luke slid behind a thick aspen trunk just as the grenade went off. "Go!"

Reaching down, he zipped the pouch and then adjusted the straps to the heavy backpack. Soon, he was panting heavily as they continued their mad dash into the woods. Owen, despite his need for haste, kept within easy range of Luke. Once they skirted a small hill, Owen stopped and gave Luke a moment to catch his breath. The stolen ammunition would go a long way to keeping them alive, but the weight was going to slow Luke down and make the return trip a bit more laborious than he'd anticipated.

With the vampires he'd drained and his improving conditioning, Luke caught his breath quickly and took off at a steady run. Owen joined him, running alongside him in the easy lope of a wolf. Periodically, they'd stop and listen, making sure no one was following them, but the chaos of five grenades had stopped any pursuit for the moment, though order would eventually be regained, especially as the vampires woke and expressed their displeasure at what they'd awoken to.

Luke and Owen pressed as fast as they could until the shadows stretched long as the sun slipped behind the mountains. Both of them had superior night vision, but now was no time to be overconfident and twist an ankle or break a leg. Luke would have heaved a huge sigh of relief when the shadow of the fort loomed in the growing darkness had he not been struggling to catch any air at all.

"I see them," Delilah called.

Owen shifted back to his human form and hopped in the snow as he quickly redressed. Luke handed up the ammo bag, then helped Owen up the bank and log. When it was Luke's turn, two sets of hands reached down and tugged him up.

"Damn, what's in here? Rocks?" Delilah asked, hoisting the backpack.

"Even better." Luke took the bag and unzipped it enough that Delilah could see his stolen goods.

"Holy shit! It's the kind of present a woman always wants to see."

"I've got some twelve-gauge shells, 9mm rounds for the machine pistols, a few rounds for this thing"—Luke held up the AR-15—"and plenty of rounds for the Steyrs. Everything a growing army needs."

"Let's spread the Christmas cheer!" Delilah seemed genuinely delighted at the bounty of destruction Luke had brought.

"Gather everyone up. We need to talk. I'm going to go grab a bite of food and a water."

Roxi drifted over, Brutus trailing along behind her. "You should probably change into some dry clothes, too."

Luke, still hot and sweaty from the long, hard run, looked down at his wet clothes, steaming from the heat he was generating. "Not a bad idea. Let's meet by the trailer in fifteen minutes. Leave some people on patrol around the back."

Delilah nodded and barked orders to the people who'd gathered around. Roxi took his hand and lead him to the luggage so he could change, while Brutus shoved his head under Luke's unoccupied hand to collect some affection. They joined him in his brief snack.

"Are you sure they're getting reinforcements?" Pablo asked.

"Yeah. The guy didn't seem surprised when I said I'd just arrived. That's a pretty good indication, but I guess technically I can't be one hundred percent certain." It wasn't the first time Luke had answered similar questions since he'd returned with Owen.

The answer wasn't changing, but people kept hoping they'd misheard or misunderstood what Luke had said.

"Luke, something's happening." Jung-sook kept her voice low as she peered through the scope of her sniper rifle.

Luke patted Pablo on the shoulder, then climbed up so he could see over the trailer. Pulling his scope out, he peered down the road toward the enemy camp. It was hard to tell at this range. The snow, still falling lightly but persistently, made seeing difficult, as if the world far away was cloaked in static. But he saw movement as people emerged.

Their grenade shenanigans had bought them forty-five minutes after Luke and Owen made it over the wall. There was plenty of time for furious vampires to whip things into shape, especially if they weren't too kind and gentle on their minions, and vampires were neither kind nor gentle, especially to those who failed them.

"Jung-sook. Pick your shots, but you're free to fire at will once they're in range." Luke adjusted the scope, hoping to see something.

"We don't have that much ammo."

"What good is spare ammo if we're dead? Plus, what I stole will stretch us a bit further. Every one you drop before they make it to our walls is one less we have to fight, and it might inspire one of their buddies to lag behind or make a break for it. Being painted in your buddy's brains will take the starch out of their shirts. These aren't hardened soldiers."

"Right. Understood."

Unlike last night, Luke and the leadership team had shifted their strategy, using most of their shotguns. They'd interspersed their special anti-vamp shot with the standard stock they'd stolen. It might not kill, but it would do a lot of damage—especially the several boxes of slugs he'd ended up with.

Luke put the scope away since he couldn't really see anything yet. "They clustering around that tree line?"

"Not yet," Jung-sook replied.

"Feed Owen some distances. I want to lob a mortar or two down that way."

The mortar had the longest range of their ordnances, but they only had a handful of shells left. Next, Jung-sook and the Steyr sniper rifle had a max range of two miles, which was only truly effective inside half a mile. Though Jung-sook was reliable a bit beyond that, but the snow would cut down her visibility and effectiveness. A proper onager would maybe hit at just over a quarter mile. He doubted their improvised one would be effective even at three-hundred yards. The APC9K was reasonable at a hundred yards, maybe longer if the enemy came in clustered up tightly where spray and pray would be an effective machine gun strategy. The Winchester M12s were good at forty yards with standard shot, but the specialty anti-vamp shot cut the effective range down to twenty-five to thirty yards.

Luke and the leadership team had marked out the area around the camp at twenty-five, fifty, seventy-five, and a hundred yards to ensure everyone waited for the appropriate time to open fire.

"Hey, Luke. I've got the range set. Do you want them both on the same spot, or shift?" Owen asked.

"Put one dead center, then give me a one-degree shift left and drop it in as soon as you're set. I'm hoping we'll catch them flat-footed, then hit some more after they've jumped out of the way."

"You're a mean son of a bitch, Luke. I like it." Owen chuckled and readied his two mortar rounds.

"You don't win battles by being polite. I aim to get all you home safe if I can, and I'm not going to do that by being nice." Luke pulled up the other Steyr to use its scope. Also, he was a decent enough shot that he could take a few rounds once the enemy breached the quarter mile line.

"On your mark, Luke," Owen called.

"Mark." A wicked grin slipped across Luke's face.

The first round popped into the air. Luke held his blink, wanting to see how it hit. It plunged to the ground just behind the tree line, exploding and sending up a gout of flames and smoke. The light illuminated bodies scrambling away. The second mortar rocketed out of the mortar tube. Luke looked to the left of the original spot, waiting for the second round to hit. He chuckled quietly when he thought he saw a body fly, propelled by the explosion. Not normally a bloodthirsty individual, Luke wanted to make his enemy think twice or even thrice about making their next attack.

"Looks like they're either rallying or fleeing," Jung-sook commented as she squeezed the trigger. "Got him."

Luke set down the Steyr and slid off the trailer and down onto the dirt berm behind it. "Roxi, you got one of those fire rounds ready to go?"

"Sure."

"Might as well see what our range is, plus it'll give us a good marking point." Luke leaned against the trailer to watch Roxi work.

"Arm the catapult!" she called.

The two werewolf assistants pulled the firing arm down, holding it in place until she could slide the pin through the loops.

"Load a fire log."

She'd borrowed some gas from the vehicles and had soaked the fire rounds for most of the day.

"Torch," she ordered.

Simone lit a torch with a lighter, then handed it to Roxi, who picked up the firing rope, held the torch to the gas-soaked log, then leapt back out of the way.

"Clear!" she yelled, then yanked the rope, pulling the pin. "Let's arm it again and get some dirt in the bucket to nip those flames."

The blazing log flew into the air, sending a flaming arch down the road until it landed, bounced, and rolled further, settling near the edge of the road.

"Nice shot, Parthian."

"How far did it go?" Roxi asked.

Jung-sook looked back at Roxi. "About a hundred and sixty yards on the first hit, with another twenty yards on the roll."

"That'll work." She inspected the bucket to make sure they'd snuffed out the flames and to ensure they hadn't done much damage to it. "What do you want on our next round?"

"Let's hold until we see if they're going to try a vehicle or infantry," Luke said, smiling at the beautiful Parthian woman in her gleaming armor.

"Luke, I think the vamps reasserted control of their troops. They're moving forward."

Luke spun around, bringing the scope to his eyes. "Fire round! Owen, Give me a half mile straight down the pipe."

A row of pickup trucks sped around the corner and were making their way toward their barriers.

"Owen, fire!" Luke yelled.

A mortar popped into the air.

"Roxi, ready?"

"Ready."

The mortar slammed down in the middle of their caravan, sending a truck flying and spilling mangled bodies. The truck behind it slammed into the tumbling wreckage, twisting to the side as it rolled over. The truck behind them jammed the brakes and maneuvered to the opposite side of the mayhem and made it around.

"Roxi, fire!"

The arm of the catapult groaned and slammed into the cross-beam, sending its burning payload into the night sky.

"Reload and fire immediately!" Luke ordered.

A few seconds later, Roxi called clear and sent a second log into the sky. The first one fell, bashing into the hood and smashing the windshield. The pickup appeared to buck and buckle just behind the cab, tossing some passengers out from the bed as it swerved into the trees, slamming into one at a dangerously high speed. The second one landed on the ground and took a weird bounce, missing the truck it was on target to hit.

"Damn," Luke mumbled. "Reload with anti-infantry."

Beside Luke, Jung-sook and her Steyr went into action, shots in quick succession cracking out into the night. She started with the drivers, then anyone that was still on their feet and trying to run, leaving the wounded to writhe in the middle of the road. A few people made it into the trees to find hiding spots.

While Jung-sook hunted for targets, Luke looked down the road toward the tree line. In the shadows cast by the flickering flames of their initial mortar rounds, Luke saw people moving forward, using the trees as cover to advance toward Luke's fort.

When gunfire ripped the silence behind him, he spun around, seeing muzzle flashes near their northwest corner. "Bravo team. Reinforce at the northwest corner."

The people who'd been assigned to Bravo team split off from the front line and sprinted toward the back. A couple minutes later, the team on the east started firing into the woods.

"Shit. Shit. Shit," Luke muttered. "Charlie team, eastern wall, on the double."

They were spread thin with fighting at three points. If they hit them at a fourth, they might not stand. A fifth spot would probably bury them.

Simone sprinted up and yelled, "Help! East wall. Almost here," then dashed off.

"Jung-sook. You're in charge of calling the shots. Roxi, you're with me."

Luke grabbed a Winchester M12 and ran toward the back of the fort. A few werewolves in bipedal form had made it over the walls and were battling with Luke's people. He yanked the wooden-bladed bayonet from his belt sheath and fixed it to the end of the shotgun and charged into battle.

Roxi hadn't bothered pulling her shotgun around, opting to yank her sword free. Starting from the catapult position, she hit the fight before Luke, savagely raking the sword across the hamstring of the first werewolf she came to. With a pained yelp, the wolf crumpled backward. Luke leapt out of the way and plunged the bayonet into its heart, killing it and sending it into its final shift. Another yelp, more a scream of death, signaled Roxi's next victim as it made its last shift.

With the addition of Roxi and Luke, they pushed back the last of the wolves, sending them fleeing back over the wall and into the woods save for one poor bastard who landed on one of the sparsely placed wooden spikes. It struggled to pull itself off the spike that had driven through its guts, yelping as it tried and failed. Luke lifted his shotgun and aimed for its heart, putting it out of its misery.

"Luke…" Roxi said, grabbing his hand. "Do you feel that?"

He concentrated for a second, then it hit him like a truck. Vampires. Lots of them.

"Charlie team, you're with me and Roxi. Follow us." He spun and ran across their compound toward the western side of their fort, angling to the north where he'd sent Bravo team earlier. Along the way, Brutus sprinted from the central building to join them. Before Luke could stop him, the dog plunged into the vampires, snarling and snapping, ripping out throats and severing hamstrings where he could.

Homing in on the vampires, Luke dashed into the battle. The vampires had made it over the wall. Several were armed with hand-guns and were firing haphazardly. Too many of Luke's people bled from wounds. He couldn't tell how bad they were. They'd have to assess the injuries after they repelled this attack.

Finding an isolated vampire standing back, Luke pumped a shell into his shotgun and took aim, dusting it. Roxi still hadn't brought her shotgun out, diving into battle with her sword slashing and stabbing, her enhanced speed making it look like blurs of silvery light. Her first priority was helping the injured wolves, or those being ganged up on. Parting limbs and heads, she looked for any opportunity to turn the tide.

Luke swept along the wall, finding angles he could pop off shots from. After he'd drained his magazine, he'd dusted two more, and gooed a third. Sprinting up behind a vampire drawing aim with a pistol, Luke plunged the bayonet into his back, sending him splattering to the ground.

Seeing Luke between their exit and them, the fangers fought desperately to disengage from the rest of Luke's friends to charge him or to get around him. He dropped the shotgun behind him, kicking it up against the log and dirt wall, and pulled his gladius from his scabbard and waded in.

With his shotgun, he was dangerous; with his gladius, he was a surgeon. He could carve into his enemies with a preciseness he couldn't achieve with the shotgun or even the bayonet and, at this range with so many of his friends nearby, precision was his priority. With the addition of Roxi and Luke plus Charlie team, they pushed back the vampires, killing them to the last.

Luke found a clean-ish shirt and wiped his blade down and sheathed it, tossing the rag to Roxi so she could clean hers. Picking up his shotgun, he brushed the snow and dirt off of it, smearing mud along the barrel and heat shield where it had melted the snow. With a deft hand, he shoved shells in quickly until it was full again as Brutus found a clean patch of snow to roll, probably hoping to cover up or clean off the vampire blood he was covered in.

"Luke, get back to the front. I've got things handled here," Delilah called.

"Charlie team, help Delilah until she dismisses you and then back to your station." Luke, still breathing heavily from the fight, nodded at Delilah, then jogged forward, Roxi behind. Delilah, as she became more comfortable with her new abilities, was becoming a fierce fighter and a true terror. Her speed and skill served as an inspiration for her team.

Charlie jogged up next to Luke. "Do you think Sam made it?"

"She should have by now," he replied as they jogged back to the front. They wouldn't know until she showed up with the reinforcements. They'd decided not to have her sneak back, not with the area becoming a hot zone. He just hoped she was OK.

Roxi squeezed his hand before peeling off and returning to her catapult crew.

"Report," Luke said, climbing onto the dirt berm and peering over the top of the trailer.

"They're working up, but not where we can get too many good shots. They're staying off the road. A few of the injured have pulled themselves into the trees," Jung-sook said.

"Depending on their healing ability, we could be seeing them again, though I hope they decide to feign heavier injuries and retire from the fight." Luke pulled out his scope and looked the scene over.

Jung-sook fired, dropping someone who'd been too slow between trees. Behind them, Charlie team rolled up, a few people lighter.

"We've got three people down. Granny Pearl is seeing to them the best she can, though they'll heal in time. Delilah kept a few of us back to reinforce her position," Charlie reported.

"Alright, refill your ammo and catch a breather until you're needed again." Luke returned to observing the front until he had an idea. "Roxi, can you turn the catapult about thirty degrees?"

"What direction?" she asked.

"Either. Let's drop some rocks on them and see what happens."

They'd rigged up some basic skids for the catapult, but it would need a lot of muscle to move it. Fortunately, werewolves packed a lot of that. They quickly unloaded the catapult and released the arm before moving it for safety's sake. With it ready to move, she called over some help and got it turned in the direction she wanted. In a half a minute, she had it cocked and loaded. Giving Luke a pleasant smile, she raised her eyebrows and tipped her head questioningly.

"At your leisure." He gestured off in the direction of the woods.

"Clear!" Roxi called, then stepped back. After she determined the catapult was clear enough, she yanked the rope and sent a load of fist-sized rocks sailing into the night.

If nothing else, the cacophony of rocks crashing into trees would probably scare the shit out of anyone nearby, but Luke hoped that at least a few rocks would plink-o their way down to land on the heads of a few people. Watching the general area, Luke smiled as people scrambled around, breaking cover. Jung-sook took advantage of the chaos and fired off three shots in quick succession.

"Damn, missed one," she cursed.

"Let's try a flame log," Luke called back to Roxi.

"Right," she replied.

A few moments later, a flaming hunk of wood soared into the air. Luke tracked it the best he could through the trees. Out of the corner of his eye, Jung-sook tracked it as well. When it crashed to the ground, it provided enough light to see around it in a reasonably clear manner. Jung-sook opened fire, downing four people in quick order. People near the log tried tossing snow at it to put it out.

"Roxi, to the other side, if you please."

"On it."

Soon, Roxi and her catapult crew launched more rocks and flaming logs into the forest. Luke thought he heard a scream but lost the thread as more gunfire broke out toward the back of their camp. Sighing, he jumped to the ground and waved Charlie team after him. It was going to be a long night, and he just hoped they had enough people and ammo to last it out. The reinforcements Sam had ordered had to be coming soon. They had to…

It was well after midnight, closer to two a.m. They'd repelled several more attacks, though not without cost—several injuries, one that looked quite bad. Luke tried to put it out of his mind for now, no matter how hard it seemed. The best thing he could do was keep the camp protected until sunlight when their adversaries would be once again reduced to the werewolves who didn't seem too eager to mount big attacks unaided during the day.

His people weren't the only casualties. Four of the Winchesters had broken and would need some love. The catapult's crossbeam had cracked, rendering it useless. And they were nearly out of all ammunition at this point. What remained had been parceled out to a few people. Luke and Roxi had been leading the vanguard of their attacks, swords blazing. And somehow, Brutus kept active, particularly enjoying tearing vampires to shreds, though he never did much more to werewolves than distract them or sever a hamstring if needed.

Luke and Roxi topped up on downed vampires as often as they could to keep their bodies moving at peak speed and power, but after a certain point, it couldn't hide the mental and spiritual exhaustion of constantly fighting for their lives and the lives of their friends. Roxi, despite a limp from a shallow slice in her calf, still sprinted in, screaming her war cry. Luke, covered in sweat and drying blood from the cuts he'd taken and healed, followed close behind, unwilling to give an inch and to ensure Roxi wouldn't be swarmed. Brutus was never far behind.

Most of Luke's werewolves were fighting in their bipedal forms now, using what was left of their supply of improvised spears. Luke would have to teach them some proper spear wall techniques for the future, assuming they ran into a similar situation. But they still did well, holding back waves of vampires and enemy werewolves long enough for the remaining guns to take down a few intruders before Luke and Roxi plowed in.

On the other side of the camp, though Luke had joined to help with bigger surges several times, Delilah's blade carved its own path of destruction, the fierce woman dealing death with precision and grace. Few vampires wanted to challenge the human that should have been an easy target. Though she didn't have a way to refuel from vampires like Roxi and Luke did, she must have some other way to keep fighting at the speed and power she did. Ọ̀ṣọ́ọ̀sì's young hunter was quickly becoming a demon to the vampires—and one that inspired her comrades to excel and fight hard.

Sitting on the ground, his back propped against Roxi's, they took a brief breather while they had the opportunity. They'd repulsed yet another attack, sending the vampires and their now less-than-eager werewolf minions scurrying back over the side, though Luke and his team ensured the vampires were the first down. It seemed to be the best strategy. As the vampires lost numbers, they lost their heart to fight the ferocious defenders, and when the vampires fled, their wolves had no desire to keep the fight going.

Bodies of their fallen enemies were nearly impossible to avoid at this point. The snow inside the fort churned red and brown from feet mixing the sludge of dead vampires into the mud.

"How you doing, Rox?" Luke said, breathing hard.

"Alive for now."

Delilah staggered up to them and bent over, her hands on her knees, as she tried to catch her breath. "They're...massing. A lot."

Luke struggled up and helped Roxi to stand, pulling her into a tight embrace and a brief kiss. He mouthed, "I love you" to her. "Where at, Dee?"

"North side. Looks like all of them." Delilah stood straight, placing her hands on top of her head.

"Take everyone. Roxi, you go with her, then report back. I'm going to check the other side…" He staggered toward the south wall with its tipped over trailer to find Jung-sook still on top, taking shots. He'd almost forgotten about her, the constant noise turning her shots into white noise. "How you looking on ammo?"

"Not good. Down to seventeen rounds." She tracked some movement and squeezed off another shot. "Sixteen."

"What's going on here?"

"Not sure, everyone seems to be heading north along either side," Jung-sook answered without taking her eye away from her scope.

"Shit. They're massing on the north side. Keep an eye out here, but don't get caught. I'll send someone if I need you to move, or if you feel you need to meet up with us."

"Got it. Leave me a spotter if you can."

Luke pointed to one of the werewolves taking a breather and tossed him the scope from his pocket. "Your Jung-sook's spotter. Make sure no one sneaks up on you."

Luke stopped by Owen at the mortar station. They hadn't had the opportunity to use the remaining rounds, but Luke had him hold ready if needed.

"Owen, you can throw a mortar round, can't you?"

Owen nodded. "Yeah. If we're desperate."

"I think it's now desperate o'clock. Grab the rounds you have and let's get to the north wall."

Owen grabbed a bag and tossed it to Luke. "Last few grenades." Then, he grabbed the tubes of the three remaining mortar rounds and followed Luke as they dashed to the north side.

"Jung-sook says everyone is filtering around to the north," Luke said.

"Yeah, I think they're going to try one massive push to overwhelm us," Roxi replied as she squinted out into the dark, her sword hanging naked and ready in her hand.

"Everyone, spread out. Ready your spears along the walls. Remaining guns, spread out evenly. Owen, you and I will be in the middle. Stay down so they don't hit you with a pot shot." Luke moved toward the front barrier and crouched down low, laying out the grenades where he could reach them easily.

Owen sat next to him, handing Luke tubes. He held the tube as Owen pulled them out, setting them carefully on the ground.

"You know how to arm these with a mortar?" Owen asked.

Luke nodded. "Set the explosion setting, pull the pin, strike the firing mechanism on the bottom and chuck them hard."

"Right. Be careful because it's armed. If you hit the nose, you'll set it off."

Luke's eyes went wide. "I'll be sure to handle them with care."

"Please do. I want to get home to my sister and my nephew." He crouched down next to Luke. "I'll handle them for now, but if I call for it, you arm them and hand them to me. I can probably throw them further."

"Sounds good." Luke peeked over the log. "Damn. Gave my scope to someone."

Delilah dug into her backpack and pulled out some binoculars, handing them to Luke.

"Thanks." He examined the woods to the north.

All he could see were shadows moving about in the trees about a hundred yards out. They'd adapted, learning the hard way the effective range of the weapons inside the fort.

"How far do you think you can throw those things?" Luke asked.

"I'm not sure. It's not like they're footballs and I'm a quarterback, but far enough, I guess," Owen replied, squinting into the woods. "Not that far, though."

"Let's wait until they get in to about fifty yards. That work?"

Owen nodded. Luke ducked back down behind the log, looking around at the nervous and scared faces of his friends. They all looked stretched past their point of resilience, yet they held on and fought. He was proud of every one of them. They just wanted to survive the night and win the possibility of going home. That's all he wanted, too. He'd fight until his body failed to give it to them.

"Looks like they're getting ready," Owen said. "Yeah. They're moving through the trees. Spread out wide."

"Stay down until the last minute everyone," Luke called out as he popped back up to watch, Delilah's binoculars over his eyes.

The massed vampires and werewolves let out a ragged yell, some howls mixed in, and surged forward.

"Steady…" Luke called as he reached down and grabbed a grenade, pulling the pin.

Owen grabbed a mortar and got it ready to go.

"Owen, you and me… Now!" Luke popped up and hurled the grenade into the center, bending to grab another.

Owen slammed the bottom of the mortar shell onto the top of the log and threw his toward the left of the line.

Gunshots rang out at the two people popping up behind the fort's walls. Luke had the second grenade in the air when the first went off. The mortar shell joined it with a louder explosion. The screams of downed wolves and vamps rang out into the night, the sound raising a small cheer from Luke's friends. Grabbing the last two grenades, Luke hurled one, then the other, dropping to the ground. Owen lobbed the last of the mortars and joined him behind the log.

The speed of the charge necessitated the last throws be much closer than Luke liked, but the thick log against their back provided a good defense, though his ears still rang from the concussive detonations. When the last explosion mowed down anyone near it, Luke poked his head over the log to watch.

"Now!" Luke yelled.

They all yelled as they stood up holding their weapons in place. The wall suddenly looked like a hedgehog that spit out occasional bursts of machine gun fire or shotgun blasts, taking down more vampires and wolves, yet they still came, too many to be deterred.

Luke stood up and pulled his gladius and his rudis, readying for the first surge to hit their wall. Letting out a primal scream that was equal parts terror and aggression, the vampires and werewolves hit the line, an occasional shot answering their own.

Luke's sword blazed into action, stabbing and slashing. Taking limbs and heads if he couldn't kill. Near him, Brutus's vicious snarls buoyed those around him as he tore into any vampire in range. With each swing, his arms burned, and his lungs heaved for oxygen to feed his body, yet the flow kept sweeping over the barrier, pushing Luke and his people back until the enemy had established a beachhead inside their wall.

Seeing a group of angry vamps and wolves surge toward the right side of their thin line, Luke feared it would collapse if they were cut off from the rest of their line. "Delilah! Swing your wing back toward the center."

He worked his way down the line to help cover their movement backward. The beachhead was quickly growing. They couldn't hold their line anymore.

"Roxi! Delilah! Fall back," Luke yelled, carving with his weapons as they backed up.

The sound of the Steyr entered the fray, a vampire or wolf dropping with each shot fired. Spears snapped as they bent beyond their tolerance and in their place, the jagged ends were thrust forward as his people backed up steadily, fighting desperately.

With each step backward they took, the deeper Luke's anger grew until he stopped backing up. Tapping into the well of his power, he cut into the front line of his enemy, felling anyone brave or stupid enough to get within reach. A shot rang out and a line of pain burned in Luke's arm, but he kept cutting. Another hit him in the chest, knocking him back a few steps as the air fled from his lungs, but he straightened up and moved forward, forcing his lungs open to pull in air.

Next to him, he heard the grunts and low screams of Roxi as she joined him. Together, they stemmed the advance of the vampires and werewolves with their sheer will and the brutal speed of their swords.

"Luke! Roxi! Fall back. Now!"

Delilah's voice filtered through to his mind despite the fog of action. Instead of halting the tide, he moved backward, step-by-step, blades still flying with deadly precision. Risking a quick glance to his left to ensure Roxi was still by his side, he continued his steady retreat.

"Roxi, now!" Luke yelled, turning and sprinting as fast as his legs would carry him.

He slid to a halt in front of the doors to the main building and stood to face the advancing line of their enemies as Roxi darted past him into the doorway.

"Luke, get in here!" Delilah yelled.

Luke turned, his eyes going wide as he dove through the doors and slid forward on his stomach, the remaining spears thrusting over him to form a barrier of death at the doorway. Luke slid his swords away from himself, crawled back to the doors on his hands and knees, and pulled them shut, barring them and chaining them quickly.

Placing his hand along the wall of the entryway, he staggered the rest of the way into the main room, his legs and arms trembling as he tried to keep upright. Someone darted forward and slid a hairy arm around his back to hold him up as they guided him to a chair. He sank into it, gasping for air, sweat and blood running down his face. He wiped at it, pulling back a red-stained hand.

Roxi sank to the floor next to him and wiped his face gently with a damp cloth. Panting hard, Brutus shuffled over and flopped down onto his side, his sides working like bellows.

"Here. Let me." Pablo took the rag from Roxi. "Your hands are trembling. Someone get a chair for Roxi, please?"

Pablo dabbed at Luke's head. A chair clunked to the ground next to Luke, then Simone helped Roxi into it. Luke took the time to catch his breath and let his lungs fill his body with much needed oxygen.

"Looks like you got a pretty good cut on your forehead. Shit. You're bleeding from several spots. Did you get shot?" Pablo shook his head. "For fuck's sake, buddy. You'd give the battery bunny a run for his money."

Luke laughed weakly. "I'm the human Timex. I take a licking and keep on ticking."

"Sorry, dude. I may be a werewolf, but I'm not grooming you with my tongue." Pablo stuck his tongue at Luke, then grinned.

The sound of something heavy bashing into the door choked

Luke's laugh, killing it before it could be released. Luke hoped the doors would hold for a while. The building was built strong. This was grizzly country, and the building was built to accommodate that fact.

"Everyone accounted for?" Luke asked. "Team leaders, report in."

Simone looked around frantically. "Has anyone seen Delilah? Delilah!"

Groaning in pain, Luke forced himself onto his feet, steadying himself on the arm of the chair. "Someone, find something for me to wrap around my head." He took the cloth from Pablo and held it over his forehead, allowing the sting to mark the spot.

Delilah would be standing here if she were in the building. He sighed, dread filling his heart and opening a pit in his stomach. Beyond all hope, he prayed she was alive and not another victim of the vampires he'd led to their death.

Simone, tears running down her cheeks, checked everywhere in case Delilah had stepped into one of the rooms. "I can't find Delilah."

Each of Simone's tears was like a dagger in his heart.

"We're also missing Gabe and Charlie," Jung-sook said.

"Did anyone see what happened to them?" Luke called out.

He whipped his head toward the sound of breaking glass as a stone shattered it, slamming into the wood covering it. The quick motion made him wobble on his feet. He closed his eyes for a moment to let his head stop spinning. Taking his hand off his forehead, someone wrapped a bandanna around his forehead and over his cut.

"That should hold you," Jung-sook said.

"Hey! You, in the main house! We have your friends," someone shouted.

Simone rushed to the door, but Jung-sook stepped in front of her and held her back.

Luke walked slowly toward the door, stopping before the entry way. "Are they alive?"

"For now."

"What are your terms?" Luke yelled back.

"Open the doors and we promise a quick death. Keep fighting, and we'll make it long and painful."

"That's not much of an offer." Luke spat blood out onto the ground.

"Is it though? You're all supernaturals. Your lives can be extended for a long time, and you can endure a lot. A quick, merciful death is all you can hope for right now."

"Let me talk it over with everyone."

"I'll be magnanimous. You may have five minutes."

Luke flipped off the door and stumbled before catching himself as he turned to talk back to his friends.

"We're not going to surrender, are we?" Pablo asked, his arms crossed over his bare chest. "I'd rather die taking as many of them with me as possible."

Looking at his friends, he received near unanimous nods and affirmative grumbles. He knew they wouldn't take the offer, but it was their lives to spend how they saw fit.

"How long can we hold in here?" Roxi asked. "Can we hold it long enough to get us to sunrise?"

"What time is it?" Luke asked as he patted his pockets, looking for a cell phone that wasn't there.

"Almost three a.m."

"Fuck. Three hours. They'll tear this place down around our ears in three hours."

"Can you...uh...ask for some divine intervention?" Pablo asked. "I know you don't like doing that all the time, but this seems like a time that you should."

"He's right, Luke. Call to Selene." Roxi squeezed his hand.

Luke nodded, holding Roxi's gaze with his. All these years of doing Mithras's bidding and it was Selene they were calling, and Selene who always responded. Someday soon, there would be a reckoning between the god and him.

"Everyone who is willing, join hands," Luke said.

Luke closed his eyes and held out his other hand. A large, strong hand slid into his and squeezed it. He gave everyone a few moments to join in and grab a hand.

"Selene, My Mistress. I and my friends are in danger, surrounded and outnumbered with too much time until the rays of your brother once again bathe the land. We need your aid, anything to help us hold out. Help is coming, but we may not make it until then."

"I see you, my brave soldier."

Selene's words sounded in his head and heart, reducing his bone weariness and returning a bit of steel to his spine.

"Help does come, but so does the darkness," Selene said.

Luke slumped. "We have even more trouble. The dark entity is coming." He returned his focus to Selene. *"Is there anything you can do to aid us?"*

"I cannot shield you all. My strength has yet to recover to that point, but I can be your shield. I can strengthen your arm. And that of your beloved. Together, you can buy the time you need."

Selene sparked an ember of hope inside him. Opening his eyes, he made eye contact with Roxi. She nodded once. Selene had included her in their conversation.

"Selene has an option, but you probably won't like it," Luke said, preparing protests. "She can aid Roxi and I enough to create a distraction so the rest of you can flee. She says aid is coming, but she gave no details."

"Please don't argue," Roxi rested her hand on Luke's shoulder. "Thus far, they've wanted us alive to give to their masters. It'll buy us time if we're captured."

Several people looked like they wanted to argue, but the determination on Luke's and Roxi's faces stalled them.

Pablo straightened his spine and caught the eyes of their friends. "OK, Luke. Where do we go?"

"South. I think their camp is nearly abandoned. Get over the wall and go wolf."

"What about Granny Pearl?" Jung-sook asked. "She can't go wolf."

"I'll carry her," Pablo said.

"I'm not leaving without Delilah." It was the first time Pearl had spoken up since they'd been forced to retreat into the camp's main building.

"Pearl. We need you free and clear," Luke said. "Roxi and I will free her, but she'll need to know you're safe and getting away. It's the best option of all the bad options we have right now. Pablo can carry you whether you go willingly or not, but it'll be easier for everyone if you cooperate."

Pearl opened her mouth, then snapped it closed and gave a reluctant nod.

Nodding back, Luke turned his eye to Brutus, who still lay on his side panting. "Someone is going to have to carry Brutus. I think he's reached the end of his strength."

"I'll take him," Simone said.

"It is done. What next, My Mistress?"

"Your friends will need to stand back. The light I will infuse you with will be harmful to Tutyr's children as well. Form it how you will. Fight hard and hold out as long as you can. I will be with you, my children."

CHAPTER
TWENTY-SEVEN

Selene's power thrummed through Luke. Standing by the door, he formed a scutum and helmet in his mind, letting Selene's light solidify into a giant rectangular shield and a helmet that was the match to the one he'd left in Portland. His gladius, in his hand and ready, lengthened as he formed a silvery blade around its blade. Giving it a couple swishes through the air, the addition to his weapon left a blurry trail but handled like it was nearly weightless.

Roxi, like Luke, used her power to bring a shield to hand, though hers was an oval type with notches in the middle of both long sides that were favored by the Persians and Parthians. Her helmet had a pointed top and silver hair streaming out of it along with cheek guards.

Their lupine friends stayed clear, watching Luke and Roxi with a broad sense of caution. As they readied to flee, all of their friends stood back, though they had their spears ready to thrust out after Luke and Roxi engaged the awaiting enemies. Luke knew they were ready; he could always rely on them. Looking over at Roxi, he gave her a wan smile. He reached out and tapped his glowing sword against hers, igniting it with the silver light.

"Ready?" Luke asked.

Roxi nodded. Together, they touched the tips of their swords to the doors and pressed out. The doors exploded out of the frames, plowing into the rows of werewolves and vampires lined up outside, waiting for what they thought was an orderly surrender. The glowing shrapnel of the doors sliced through their targets, maiming and killing anyone who it touched—the light infusing it with a deadliness beyond steel and glass.

Not allowing their enemies to recover, Luke and Roxi surged forward, reaping death and ruin with their moonlight-enhanced blades. In the back of Luke's mind, he wished the swords would make a humming sound like a light saber.

Luke waded straight through the crowd while Roxi pressed to the right, hoping to open up a lane for their friends to escape through. The shock of their attack caught the vamps and their pet werewolves completely off balance. With terror in their eyes, anyone within reach of Luke and Roxi's blades died or tried to run away. Anyone who dared counterattack was quickly mowed down. Soon the crowds began to disintegrate at the back end as those out of reach of the vengeful vampire hunters chose feet over fists and made their best efforts to save their lives.

"Luke!" Delilah cried out.

His ears pulled his head around, finding Delilah and Charlie tied up, wolves and vampires abandoning their hostages. Luke pressed forward, ignoring the burn in his arms from swinging his sword and lashing out with this shield. When he made it to his friends, he slashed through the ropes binding Delilah's ankles, then cut the ropes around her wrists, the silvery light leaving her unharmed. She leapt to her feet and grabbed a dagger from Luke's belt and freed Charlie, since the light would hurt the werewolf.

"Go, run. To the south. Pablo has Pearl. They'll be waiting for you." Luke darted to the side and took a machete on his shield.

The light slithered down the blade and singed the hand of the wielder, forcing him to drop it. Following with a quick slash, Luke removed the head of the werewolf who'd been dumb enough to fight back. Delilah snatched up the machete and ran, tugging Charlie after her as they fled to rejoin the rest of their people.

"Luke!" Roxi shouted.

He could feel it—the encroaching darkness. Luke turned to the north. A dark column of shadow advanced toward the north wall from outside their breached fort. Vampires and werewolves alike fled before it, scattering to get out of its way and leaving Luke and Roxi alone in the center of the camp.

"Do we run?" Luke asked.

"We need to buy time for our friends." Roxi, breathing hard, strolled up next to him and stopped.

He let out a ragged exhale. He'd tangled with the dark entity before and barely survived the encounters. He feared his luck might not hold for a third time. Every muscle in his body burned from wounds and fatigue, but he'd have to find a reserve somewhere. "I was afraid you'd say that, but you're right."

They looked at each other, love in their tired eyes. They'd fought side-by-side before and come out victorious in the arena. Now they were much stronger and in better condition, though the nearly forty-plus hours of battle had drained them both. But they had little choice. At least they had the backing of Selene and her strength to bolster themselves.

"I don't know what he's bringing, but be very careful," Luke said.

"We can do this. You and I, dōšagīh."

He loved it when she called him dōšagīh. It calmed the turmoil inside and brought a kernel of peace into his heart.

Luke didn't recognize the man at the center of the dark column when he finally made it over their log barricade. It wasn't the same body he'd seen in Wyoming and Belgium. He didn't know if the entity had picked a new host, modified the old one, or merely picked this one out of convenience and need. Either way, it didn't matter. The body was incidental in comparison to the entity that drove it.

It stopped, staring back and forth between Roxi and Luke, then formed a blade of darkness in one hand and a round shield of similar substance with the other. Its face remained unmoving and emotion-less save for the eyes that slowly moved back and forth between Luke and Roxi, weighing them against some terrible scales only it knew of. Not waiting to offer its usual banter, it charged in, targeting Roxi.

She parried its vicious overhead slash and darted around to the side, shoving it toward Luke with her shield. With the entity off balance, Luke knocked its sword aside and slashed into its torso. Instead of blood, it leaked black smoke from the wound for a brief moment before the cut sealed itself. Roxi took advantage of the distraction bought by the wounding to thrust forward into its lower back where the kidneys should have been. This time, the creature let out a shrieking scream like a wounded Nazgul and arched its back around Roxi's sword.

Luke spun to the front and delivered a vicious backhanded slash to the entity's throat, cutting off the ear shattering screech, then danced back. Roxi pulled her blade out and opened up space. Despite what should have been two mortal wounds, or at least debilitating wounds on a vampire, the cuts spewed that same oily black smoke, then sealed.

Luke's eyes widened and his face sagged as the empty pit in his gut widened and deepened. So far, their attacks could hurt, but they couldn't kill. He couldn't tell if the wounds sealed just as quickly or if they took longer. He wanted them to take their toll. If they couldn't do any lasting damage, they'd eventually tire, even with Selene's strength, and make a mistake, possibly a life-ending mistake. At least the wounds had earned them a moment's reprieve.

"No mercy," Luke called to Roxi.

"No quarter," she replied.

As the last wisp of smoke from the entity's throat disappeared on the breeze, a terrible growl rumbled up from its core as it peeled its lips back into a snarl.

Before the creature could take back the lead, they reengaged, striking and creating more wounds as they knocked aside ineffectual sword thrusts and shield blocks. Somehow, the entity and the new body didn't seem to be entirely in sync yet. The dark nimbus would draw back its sword arm to strike, but the body would be a split second behind, moving in a slightly different manner. With each tiny miscue, entity flexed and squeezed, forcing the movement. But instead of increasing its link, it only exacerbated the issue. Luke wanted to keep the two parts of it fighting with itself to prevent it from achieving mastery over its stolen vessel. Luke pressed harder, striking more deadly blows but only getting brief puffs of smoke in response.

Unfortunately, they didn't appear to be doing enough damage, and the entity was gaining control of the body. Soon, Luke and Roxi were struggling to land blows, instead forced to block and dodge. Raising his shield to take a particularly savage slash from the entity, Luke lost the top quarter of his moonlight scutum, the slivers dissolving into the night sky. Leaping back, he reformed his shield, though it felt thinner, as if he'd lost part of the substance and had less to work with. Even the moonlight blade was taking nicks. When he lost that, he'd have to hope his silver and magic infused blade would hold out.

Falling back on his nimbleness and training, he tried to avoid taking more direct hits to his shield, using his sword to parry and shield to divert instead of outright block.

As he leapt away yet another time, he stumbled slightly, his muscles burning with fatigue. He barely raised his shield in time to catch another brutal attack from the entity. He lost another chunk of shield and staggered back. Roxi, who'd been darting in and out, charged in, slamming her shield into the side of the darkness. She knocked it away from Luke, then slashed low, catching it across the hamstring before slipping away.

Her move bought Luke the time he needed to regain his footing, but instead of reforming his shield, he formed a matching sword for his left hand. The substance wouldn't have made a thick enough shield, and a paper shield was nothing to stand behind.

Shifting back to the attack, Luke rained blows down on the entity, slashing high and low, thrusting where he could. Though he didn't land any of the big hits he had earlier, he opted for a death of a thousand paper cuts, landing shallow slices and thrusts in less vital areas. The speed and power of his counterattack opened up gaps for Roxi to land harder blows. It seemed to work; the wounds taking longer to seal as they belched oily acrid smoke.

When the entity caught a hard hit on its shield, Luke noticed it begin to throb and expand until it exploded outward in a three-sixty radius, knocking Luke and Roxi away and to the ground. Luke struggled to get up, pushing himself away from the entity. Roxi seemed to be having a similar struggle.

Luke's chest heaved, and his brain throbbed as he tried to catch his wind and get his muscles to respond, but they felt sluggish and unresponsive. Fear bordering on panic surged through him as the entity stalked toward him, its face an emotionless mask, though the dark column seethed with hatred. Luke barely blocked the slash it directed at his head. The blow shattered the moonlight sword, sapping Luke of more of Selene's strength as he tried to scuttle away from the being stalking toward him.

Sitting on his butt, he blocked another attack toward his head, though his light enhanced real sword held up to the strike as he thrust it away. If he didn't get to his feet, he'd be dead. Desperation fueled his movements as he parried another attack, then another, forcing all his will to survive into keeping the entity from skewering him.

Behind the entity, Roxi had abandoned her shield and had pulled all the light inward, forming a cavalry bow. When she drew back the string, an arrow of pure moonlight formed and lanced out, streaking into the entity's back. As it hit, she drew back again, releasing another bolt of moonlight.

The shots halted the entity's advance toward Luke as it shrieked in agony at the pure moonlight arrows piercing its body. Instead of disappearing, the arrows formed bright lances of light, smoke pouring from the wounds. With each arrow launched, Selene's glow around Roxi diminished. Closing his eyes and putting his faith in Roxi and Selene, he pushed the goddess's strength toward Roxi, save for a small portion he pulled into himself to stave off utter exhaustion. The glow around his gladius blinking out.

With the added power, Roxi continued pounding arrow after arrow into the entity's back until the creature's screams became raspy gurgles. And yet she didn't stop shooting until the last arrow representing the borrowed power of Selene, pulling the energy from the bow as it flew, plunged into its back and the bow winked out.

Forcing himself to his feet, Luke staggered toward the creature, marshaling the last of the retained light and pushing it through to the gladius, lighting up the moon and star on the side dedicated to Selene as it set the cutting edges to glowing. Luke reached out with his left hand and grasped the hair of the entity. Roxi, who'd gotten to her feet after filling its back with arrows, kicked it in the back of the legs, sending it to its knees. With a harsh yank to expose its neck, Luke hacked into its throat, black, oily smoke pouring from the deep cut as Luke forced the blade the rest of the way through until the headless body flopped to the ground, leaking a fetid black ooze that stank of death and things worse.

Despite not having a body, the eyes stared at Luke, its mouth forming into a hateful snarl as the same black ooze leaked from the stump of its neck. Luke drew back his sword and plunged it into its eye, twisting hard before removing his sword and ruining its face and destroying the brain. Finally, the mouth and jaw went slack, hanging open. Luke tossed the head onto the body.

"Roxi, grab one of those gas cans, please." Luke's voice was rough and weak, his body near the end of its ability to keep him upright and moving.

"Right." Roxi, looking just as tired as Luke felt, stumbled her way to one of the sheds and grabbed a gas can they'd prepared for the chainsaws.

Unscrewing the lid and the air valve, she dumped the entire can on the body, then tossed the can away, moving to stand by Luke. He rummaged around in his pouch until he found the small box of matches. Striking one, he tossed it on the body, igniting the gas — except the body itself went up as if it were as flammable as the gas Roxi had doused it in.

As it exploded, sending out a dark wave, Luke and Roxi were thrown backward by the palpable edge of the destructive shock wave. A column of light-eating blackness launched into the sky above the burning body until all of the entity had fled the body, the last of it disappearing into the night.

He forced himself over to Roxi and pulled her head onto his lap, cradling it gently. Roxi, with the last of her strength, reached up and grabbed his hand. Just before Luke lost consciousness and tipped over, he saw the werewolves that had fled his wrath earlier pouring back over the wall. At least at this last moment, he held Roxi.

SOMEONE OR SOMETHING jostled Luke's body and his arm flopped to the side, dangling in the open air. Forcing his eyes open, he was greeted by the worried face of Sam. The sight of his friend quirked up the corners of his mouth.

"You can go back to sleep now, Luke. You're safe." Sam squeezed his hand.

"Roxi?" Luke whispered weakly enough that Sam probably wouldn't have heard him if she weren't a werewolf.

"Alive, but unconscious." Sam appeared on his other side and picked up his arm, setting it next to him. "You should try to rest."

"OK." Luke closed his eyes and let his total exhaustion carry him to sleep.

When he next woke, he felt the gentle sway of the road under him and heard Antony and the Johnsons's cover of "Knockin' on Heaven's Door" playing over the speakers. He tried to move but was strapped to a gurney, much like he'd been after his rescue from the arena. He turned his head. Roxi lay across from him, also strapped down. She smiled weakly at him.

"You're awake," she said.

"As are you," he replied.

"You should both try to get some more rest," Maggie said, stroking Luke's hair.

"Hi, Maggie. I kept him alive for you," Roxi said. "Although he's a little worse for wear."

"Thank you, Roxi. I'm glad you came back. Did you solve your problem?"

"I didn't. Luke did. He threatened a god for me."

Maggie chuckled. "That sounds like something he'd do. Try to get some rest. We're still a ways out from the farm."

The farm. There was no place he'd rather be, save for home. It would be the perfect place to rest and regain his strength. He was curious how things had gone after he'd passed out, but if they were driving home, it mustn't be too bad. Though he wanted to ask, the gentle movement and sound of the road lulled him back to sleep.

By the time they arrived at the farm, Luke still felt nearly unable to move, so Maggie set him and Roxi up in one of the pack's small cabins. That way, he wouldn't have to navigate the stairs to get to his room.

Over the next few days, Maggie nursed them back to, if not health, at least the ability to move around a bit. Since he'd not been able to use his rudis on a vampire, he'd have to heal the old-fashioned way for now, and he had plenty of it to do with a series of stitched-up cuts and other smaller wounds—though the real wound was the exhaustion and the aftereffects of another battle survived against the dark entity.

Several of the wolves were being sent to the farm to recuperate after surgeries to remove bullets and other debris that had been healed over in the heat of the action. Luke knew his turn would come to go under the knife, but the pack doctors wanted him stronger before scheduling his surgery. He imagined the same held true for Roxi.

Maggie, after giving them both yet another physical exam, handed out cookies she'd baked. "You two are ready to move into the house. Be sure to use the handrails on the stairs and don't overdo it, but you're on the mend."

"Thanks, Maggie, for everything," Roxi said, swinging her feet onto the floor. "I don't mean to be ungrateful, but do you have a spare room I could have? I could use a little alone time. I'm still not used to being with this many people all the time." She winked at Luke.

"We have plenty of spare rooms in the farmhouse. You're welcome to have one to yourself," Maggie said.

"In that case, I'll go see about getting one." Roxi gave Maggie a quick hug, then squeezed Luke's hand before leaving them alone.

"Oh, Maggie, I've missed you so much." Luke smiled softly at her, hoping his nerves didn't show in his eyes.

"I missed you, too, Luke."

He took a deep breath and plunged ahead. "Maggie, may I stay with you? I mean, if you're still… If you'd like…" Not sure why he was having trouble finishing his thought, he closed his mouth.

Maggie nodded. "I'd like that. It'll give us a chance to talk and check in with each other."

Luke sighed in relief. "I'd like that." He sat up and caressed Maggie's cheek, a content smile spreading over his face.

"I think there's lunch ready and people who want to see you." She took his hand and led him out of the cabin and back up to the farmhouse.

As soon as he stepped through the door, Maggie moved aside and made room for Gwen. Although much gentler than a younger Gwen, she was just as excited to see him.

"Oh, it's good to see you, little one."

"I'm glad you made it back. I missed you, Luke." After her hug, she stepped back, clasping her hands in front of herself awkwardly.

"Tell you what. Let me shower and have lunch, and we'll sit down and play some cribbage, and you can tell me everything you did while I was away."

Gwen smiled and nodded. "OK, I'll set up the board."

"Hey, Luke! Glad to see you moving," Sam called from the kitchen. "I've got some potato soup ready for you when you're done showering."

Luke poked his head into the kitchen. "Hey, Sam. Are we meeting soon to fill in Holly?"

"Tomorrow, if that works for you?" Sam replied.

"Tomorrow it is." Luke waved and headed upstairs for a shower.

They'd kept all news from him while he recovered. He knew they thought it was for the best, and they were probably right. He'd worry about whatever news and become anxious and agitated. Still, he wanted to know what had happened. He'd only have to wait for one more night.

CHAPTER
TWENTY-EIGHT

After an afternoon of light activity, Luke fell asleep early, missing out on a chance to talk with Maggie. The next day, they met around the kitchen table over pastries and coffee. Roxi had tea.

"How you doing, buddy?" Pablo asked as soon as Luke shuffled into the room.

"Still tired. How about you?" Luke sipped his coffee.

"About the same. That was one hell of a trip home."

Luke snorted. "You could say that."

Holly walked into the room with Sam and stopped by Luke, giving him a one-armed hug before heading to the coffee pot. "I'm glad you're up and about, Luke."

"Me, too. It's good to see you, Holly."

After everyone got situated with food and drink, Holly cleared her throat and called the meeting to order. "I guess we should get started."

"Can you get me and Roxi up to date since we've been out of commission for a bit?" Luke asked, then sighed. "What were the casualties?"

"We lost two wolves. Gabe and Amelia. We'll be holding their memorial services in a couple days," Pablo said, sounding tired.

"We've got more surgeries to perform to extract bullets and other junk, but that's more annoying than a true danger. Charlie may lose an arm. The surgeons have done all they can, now it's just a matter of time to see if he can heal."

Luke nodded, moving his hand over his eyes for a moment. He knew, all things considered, those were light casualties for as badly outnumbered as they were. All the same, the logic of it didn't help. He'd lost two friends. Those two people left families and more friends—two holes ripped in the fabric of the pack. The memorial service would be the first step in patching the holes, but it would never be the same, never whole again. From Portland, Maine to Portland, Oregon, death had followed him. He didn't want to think of the numbers, the names of those who'd lost their lives since Jan's betrayal. Even one was too many, but he knew the list was far longer.

"I'd like to speak at the memorial," Luke offered.

Holly smiled sadly. "That would be welcome. Gabe's partner wants to talk with you when you're feeling up to it."

Luke nodded. "Give me a couple more days, and then I'll be at their disposal." He took a deep breath and let it hold before releasing it. "What else happened? Did Pearl make it out safely?"

"Yeah. She did. She's at my place, resting up," Delilah said.

"Where do you want to start?" Sam asked.

"For one, what the hell happened in Montana? The last thing I remember is passing out after fighting the entity and then seeing a bunch of werewolves coming over the walls. I thought we were done for."

"That was us." Sam lifted her cup and tipped it toward Luke. "Let's see. After I left, it took a while to get to cell coverage. I called Holly, and we called in all our allies and potential allies. Fortunately, a goodly number decided to help. All the Portland area packs joined us, of course, and the gang from Wind River, too. They called in some friends from the reservations around Wyoming, Idaho, and Montana. By the time all was said and done, we had a pretty good little army."

Luke's eyes were wide as he nodded appreciatively. "Damn, I'll say so."

Sam chuckled. "Although everyone was a bit disappointed that you all had done such a thorough job that there wasn't much for us to do. I mean, it was fine with me. I'm tired of fighting and just wanted to get us home."

"I'll have to extend a personal thank you to everyone." He stood to refill his cup.

"What was that you were fighting when we arrived, Luke?" Holly asked.

"That was our friend from Wyoming, the one who blew up the arena."

"And Belgium, when you rescued me," Roxi added.

"Do you still not know who it is?" Holly leaned forward, resting her elbows on the table.

"No. Selene and Mithras are still working on it. He's a slippery customer. He's been avoiding the detection of several gods since who-knows-how-long. They're pretty sure it's not the dark one, Ahura Mazda's counterpart." He turned to Delilah. "Has Òṣọ́ọ̀sì any ideas who we might be up against?"

"No. At least not that he's told me." Delilah leaned against the counter, a cup held in both hands.

Holly shook her head. "It still baffles my mind that you all toss around the names of gods and goddesses that were all supposed to be pagan myths."

Luke shrugged. "I am a pagan myth. So are werewolves, for that matter. The creation of werewolves wasn't an evolutionary aberration, it was an intentional creation of gods, just like me and Roxi."

"I believe you, it's just strange is all," Holly replied.

Roxi chuckled. "I've lived it, and I still find it strange. I was even raised as a pagan, and I'm just barely used to it."

"So, we have some unknown powerful entity who is in charge of vampires and using them to corrupt werewolves into fighting by their side," Holly said.

"Fighting *under* them might be more accurate. Every instance of werewolves working with vampires has been in a subservient roll, and the vampires aren't particularly kind to their allies either." He turned to Sam. "What happened with the Missoula pack? You said they were friendly."

Sam made a disgusted sound. "They were, but the same thing happened that's happened with other packs. The packleaders were overthrown by those who had less than savory motives. After I got hold of Holly, I wandered down to Missoula to see what was going on. I found the old packleader jailed, but they didn't leave that many guards, so I broke him out."

Luke's eyebrows rode up his forehead. "You were busy."

"Let's just say I don't like being betrayed, and I wanted to get to the bottom of it. They forced him to invite us up to their logging and hunting camp. His family was being held hostage. After I freed him, we went and remedied that situation."

"What's going to happen with what's left of his pack?" Roxi asked.

"I'm not sure exactly, but there were more local packs there than just Missoula. He's reaching out to the affected dissidents. If they can form a power block, they may reassemble into one pack. Since you all killed the more belligerent members of the local packs, they may forgive those who were forced to fight." Sam shrugged. "But it's not my place to tell them how to run their packs. Jim is a good leader, though, so I imagine he'll make the best of the situation. I'm guessing we'll be hearing more from him once things get situated. I don't think he appreciates having vampires interfering in his pack."

"Good. We need more allies. This is getting big, fast," Luke said.

"Speaking of which, I have Jamaal working on setting up some servers and sites so we can keep distributing those videos you took." Holly sat back, grabbing Sam's hand. "I'd like you to keep making them. Training video. Informational videos. Anything to keep spreading the word."

"Why would we need that on our own servers?" Luke asked.

Holly chuckled. "The videos were a touch too violent for YouTube."

"I bet the government didn't want them circulating either," Pablo said.

"The feds still toeing the 'terrorist' line?" Delilah asked.

"Yeah. Still no word on when they'll be restarting air travel," Holly replied, "especially after the atrocities the vamps committed by releasing the young vampires."

"Have they released any more? Are there still baby vamps on the loose?" Luke's brows furrowed as he leaned into the table. When he looked around the kitchen, all his friends appeared disturbed—brows furrowed, lips tight—by the raw inhumanness of the vampire's ploy.

"It's hard to tell. The random killings are down, but there are still plenty happening around the world that we can probably attribute to the vampires. How long does it take before they stop being so brutal?"

"I have no idea. Days. Weeks. It depends. If they haven't released any more freshly turned fangers, then we could be seeing some of them mature into their control, leaving fewer out-of-control ones to commit heinous butchery."

The usually jovial Pablo looked a bit green around the gills, an uncharacteristic frown cutting a slash across his face.

Holly chewed on her thoughts for a moment. "So, what do we do next?"

"I like your plan. Let's step up the social media campaign. We can record more videos. Also, we'll need to increase our politicking. We need to get every wolf pack we can allied with us, so we don't have to fight them with the vampires. The fangers are formidable enough without having tanked out werewolves providing shock troops."

"It might be time to revisit a national wolf council," Sam said.

"I don't know. It's never worked before. American werewolves are too independent." Holly sounded frustrated.

"Things are different. A lot of packs have lost people to the vampires and their instigated rebellions. If coming together to do the right thing isn't motivation enough, losing power and assets might inspire them to choose an official alliance instead of risking every-thing on their own, especially with vampires gunning for them. It's got to be worth a shot to try, Holly."

Holly pursed her lips and nodded. "You're probably right." She sighed. "I'll get some emails going first thing in the morning."

"Anyone heard from Pieter?" Pablo asked. "I thought he was supposed to be here."

Holly pulled out her phone. "Yeah. He said he's running late and to start without him, but he should be here soon. Let's take a bathroom break."

"I'll get some more coffee ready," Pablo volunteered.

While they took care of their various needs, Pieter arrived, running upstairs to stow his bag in a room. Luke, having refilled his coffee, returned to his seat as Gwen came through to grab a cup of tea and another pastry. The teen had grown even taller in the months he'd been gone, stretching her out into a skinny adolescent. He'd missed so much of his time with her. When they had some time and privacy, he'd need to sit down with her and discuss their future together. He didn't want her to feel obligated to stay with him, but he didn't want her to go either. Maybe together they could figure out a compromise that worked for both of them. He wanted to come up with a solution that let them spend more time together, but still allowed her to be safe and have a childhood, such as in a world where vampires weren't making their presence known.

Gwen, with Brutus close behind, popped her head into the kitchen. "I'm going to take Brutus for a walk. I'll be back in a bit."

Luke smiled at her and nodded. She grinned back, then headed toward the door, the dog following her, his tail wagging slowly. When the door shut after her, more footstep sounded across the wood floor of the entryway.

"Hey, Luke. Glad you're moving about. You were looking a bit rough there for a while," Pieter said, placing his hands on Luke's shoulders.

He pulled Pieter in for a hug. "Yeah, that seems to be a bit too common these days, but I'm alive and mending, so I guess I can't complain too much."

The last few people trickled in and settled as Pieter pulled out a chair next to Pablo.

"Any news from Europe?" Luke directed the question to Pieter.

He scowled, letting out a low growl. "No. Jan is still on the loose. No one has seen him since he escaped in Paris. He's proving hard to track."

"That's troubling." Sam pulled the tea bag from her cup and set it in a tiny dish.

"Yeah. Pieter, do you have any photos we could send around? Might be worth letting folks know to keep an eye out for him," Luke said.

"That's a good idea. I think we'll up the security around Amiata and Olivia, too." Holly drummed her forefinger on the table as she thought about the situation. "I'll let our allies know as well. Is he the violent, vengeful type?"

Pieter stood up and paced along the back of the kitchen near the cabinets, wiping his hand over his eyes. "I guess so. Three years ago, I'd have never guessed he would have murdered our father and betrayed our pack, but you can't know what's truly in the heart of someone." His voice cracked, and he paused for a moment to collect himself. "I think for everyone's safety, we should assume he's going to be gunning for vengeance. Our European allies are on high alert and will be feeding me regular updates."

"I guess that's all we can do for now. It'll take him a while to get here without flights, but it's not an impossibility," Holly replied.

"Given Jan's history of working with vampires, I wouldn't put it past him to seek out other vampires to aid him in his quest for revenge," Pieter added.

"Hey, buddy. You keep winning friends and influencing people, don't ya?" Pablo teased.

"That's Luke," Roxi said. "Though his enemies don't stay alive for very long once he's decided to do something about it." She reached under the table and patted his knee.

Luke chuckled and shook his head. "There's no shortage of enemies right now—all the vampires, some of the werewolves, Jan, Flavius Constantius, Eusebius, the dark entity. The list grows long these days."

They sat in silence, contemplating the trouble Jan could cause if he showed up in Portland looking to take revenge on all those who'd contributed to his downfall.

When no one spoke up or added anything, Holly cleared her throat. "If there's nothing else, let's call it for the day. I have some more calls and emails to make for the welcome home celebration and the memorial service. We've got a table reserved at The Birk for dinner."

"Good. The pack could use a party," Sam said. "It'll help everyone find balance after the hell we've just been through."

"It'll be all our local allies as well. It's going to be packed." Holly stood up. "Pun not intended."

Gwen poked her head into the kitchen and wiggled a cribbage board. "Anyone want to play? Luke? Maggie? Roxi? We could play teams."

Luke smiled at his ward. "That sounds good. I'm still feeling a bit tired to do much else."

Maggie and Roxi nodded.

"OK, I'll go set up the board in the other room." Gwen disappeared, the sound of moving furniture announcing her efforts to set up a four-person game.

Although he still felt weary and wrung-out, being here with his friends and family went a long way to restoring his sense of self and place. Sitting down to do something as simple as playing cards with Gwen, Maggie, and Roxi sounded like the best balm for his tired spirit.

There would be more fights and maybe bigger ones, but he and the pack were doing what they could to make sure they came out on top. They were the bulwark against the encroaching darkness, fighting tooth and nail to protect humanity and werewolves from the evil machinations of the vampires.

EPILOGUE

VIII

The pack started a long weekend with the memorial service to honor their fallen packmates. Normally a private affair kept strictly to members of the North Portland Pack, dignitaries from the other local packs were invited, particularly those who'd joined forces with the North Portland Pack to bring their people home. Though security was increased to ensure any undesirables stayed far away from the isolated town of Birkenfeld, people tried to put aside the ever-present dangers of the vampires to celebrate their packmate's lives and their community.

As requested, Luke spoke, though he felt his words wholly inadequate. How could one say anything profound enough to assuage the sadness of losing a loved one? He just hoped his words helped a little.

When the service ended, they retired to tents set up to keep the early spring rains off and toasted the memories of their friends with wine, food, and Howling Moon beer. Many of the pack businesses were closed or running on light staff, so the human employees, mostly those who'd been rescued from the vampires and had become trusted friends of the pack, could cater the weekend.

On his way to fill his plate, Zel stopped Luke. "I'm glad you're back." They pulled Luke in for a hug. "Magdalena and Gwen missed you."

"Thanks for taking such good care of them both, Zel. I appreciate you."

Zel reached up and patted Luke's cheek. "You're a good lad. Now introduce me to this Roxi Maggie's told me about."

Roxi, overhearing the conversation, stood from her seat at the bench and waved nervously at Zel.

"Zel. This is Roxiustana Surena, daughter of the Parthian General Rustaham Suren and my fellow vampire hunter. Roxi, this is Maggie's partner Zel. They've been helping with Gwen while I've been away."

They politely shook hands.

"Pleasure to meet you, Zel," Roxi said.

"Ah, that's a familiar accent. London?" Zel asked.

"Yes. Luke mentioned you were from London. Where did you live?"

Zel took Roxi's elbow and directed her toward the food line as they chatted about the London neighborhoods they'd lived in. Roxi was several inches taller than Zel and leaned down to listen as Zel talked.

Maggie stepped up next to Luke, taking his hand in hers. "That'll keep Zel busy for a while. They loved London."

"It's been too long since I've lived in London to be able to usefully contribute to that conversation." Luke smiled at Maggie. "Shall we go get some food?"

"That sounds delightful. After that, we can take a walk."

Together, they strolled to the line and grabbed some plates of food and a couple of the latest creations from Pablo's brewery, though they were the recipes of his new head brewer since Pablo had been away for a while. Luke hadn't met them yet, but the new brewer was very talented. Pablo had done well on finding someone to take over the bulk of the duties. When Luke and Maggie finished, they stepped out of the tent and headed toward one of the forest trails.

"I'm sorry we haven't had a chance to really talk much. I've just been so tired," Luke said. He felt unaccountably nervous. It had only been a few weeks since he'd seen Maggie in Paris and sent her home with the bulk of their forces, but he wanted to ensure they reconnected and continued working out the new dynamic of him being in a relationship with Roxi.

"That's OK. Just being next to you is welcome. How are you feeling?" Maggie asked, a soft smile on her face. He thought he saw a bit of trepidation in her eyes.

"A bit better. It's good to be up here. It feels rejuvenating."

Maggie chuckled. "You've sure spent enough time up here recovering from various wounds and ailments."

They walked along in silence, holding hands.

"So," Maggie broke the silence, "how are things going with Roxi?"

"Good. Though it certainly hasn't been a typical courtship. I mean, unless you count international vampire wars as normal dating stuff."

"I would not consider that a normal dating situation. Do you want to keep dating her?" Maggie sounded tentative and nervous.

"I do. I think at this point it's gone beyond just dating."

"How do you feel about it?"

"Good. I love her, Maggie."

"I'm happy for you, Luke. You deserve to have a partner."

Luke nodded. "I still want to keep seeing you, too. I mean, if you still want to keep seeing me. I know I'm not the easiest person to date. You know, with everything I'm involved with." He gestured vaguely around him.

"I love you, Luke. I don't want to stop seeing you, but how does Roxi feel about it?"

"She's known since the beginning that I'm involved with you and that I love you. We've talked about it. She has no opposition to polyamory." Luke chuckled. "She's probably like I was before you and I started dating. I don't think she's had any relationships in a long time. So, she is not inclined to seek out another relationship, but who knows when she gets settled what she'll want? Right now, she wants to be with me and is happy for the relationship you and I have."

Maggie stopped and stepped in front of Luke, reaching up and holding his cheeks in her hands. She tipped her head up for a kiss, which he gladly reciprocated.

"I was worried that since you'd found someone so compatible, that you might not be interested in seeing me anymore," Maggie said.

"I love you, Maggie. I want to be with you."

"Good. That makes me happy. I never wanted to deny you a primary partner. I'm so thrilled for you. Roxi seems to adore you. We can work out the details to make sure everyone is satisfied." Maggie kissed him again.

"I missed your lips." Luke, his eyes hooded, gave her a soft smile.

Maggie quirked up an eyebrow and one side of her lips. "Just my lips?"

"I missed everything about you, Maggie."

"If your energy holds up, we'll have to see how much you missed me."

Luke laughed at her audaciousness. "I'd like that very much."

Stopping periodically to kiss, they walked around the trail until it reemerged back in the meadow next to the farmhouse. Luke stopped for another round of beers for him and Maggie, then joined her at the table where Zel and Roxi were talking animatedly in a language Luke didn't know, though he guessed it was one of the many languages spoken in the South Asian subcontinent. It appeared they'd hit it off. Watching them brought a smile to Luke's lips. He hoped they'd become friends.

Luke looked around the table at the people he considered his family—Gwen, Pablo, Sam, Delilah and Simone, Maggie, and Roxi—and felt the last of the spiritual weariness that had plagued him for a while wither. He'd nearly lost them all, nearly lost everything. They still might lose everything, but for now, he put those thoughts away for when they could be more carefully examined.

Right now, it was good to be home.

Luke Irontree will return in Ancient Sword Unyielding
Available Now!
Keep reading for a brief excerpt

LUKE IRONTREE WILL RETURN IN

ANCIENT SWORD UNYIELDING

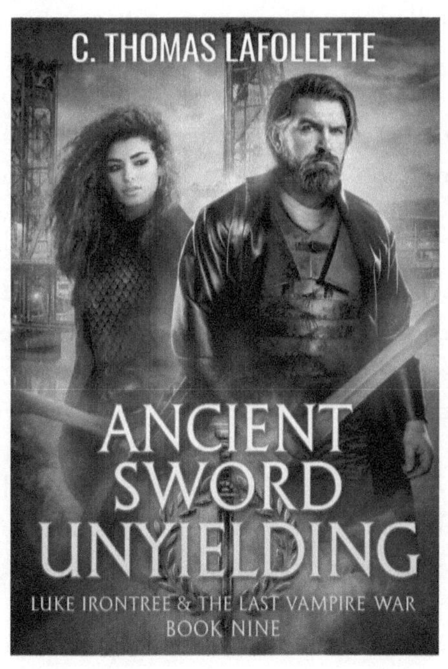

NOTE: THIS IS AN UNPROOFED SAMPLE.

CHAPTER ONE

Luke stared out over the sagebrush and bunchgrass from the ranch's observation deck, his heart beating faster than it had a right to while standing still. Next to him, Gwen raised a set of binoculars to her eyes.

"She's going awfully fast…" a woman said, a tremulous note in her voice. "Are you sure she's an experienced rider?"

"Very," Luke replied, curtly. He inhaled, then sighed quietly. Trying to be patient with the woman, he reminded himself that their request was a bit unusual. It was a riding and archery school, but they usually required a person to already own their own horse. "She's a highly skilled equestrian and archer. Your horse is in good hands."

He'd offered a sizable payment to grease the wheels with the owners of the ranch so Roxi could use one of their horses, though it had been conditional on their final approval after meeting them.[[A sizable payment to do what exactly? Just a hint would help us to understand what they're working on here.]]

Roxi weaved through the junipers and the ponderosa pines, she and the horse hitting their stride as they neared the first target. He looked up at the monitor affixed to a post, along with a bank of several other monitors showing targets spread out over the course.

His chest tightened as he held his breath. Roxi, her curly black hair flying out from under the rim of the riding helmet, rose in her saddle, her legs absorbing the motion of the smooth gait of the horse. As she approached the target, she drew back smoothly and released. Exhaling explosively, he smiled as the first arrow plunged into the center of the target. Gwen squeaked and clapped a few times, returning the binoculars to her eyes to follow Roxi to the next target.

Flying through the course, her control of the horse and the terrain complete, Roxi smoothly bullseyed one target after another to the mumbled approvals of the owner of the ranch. Once she reached the end of the course, she smoothly slowed the horse and guided it along the trail back toward the deck.

When she drew close enough, Luke smiled, responding to the broad grin on Roxi's face. Gwen clapped and waved at Roxi.

The owner of the ranch, Wanda, joined Gwen, clapping enthusiastically. "I don't know if I've ever seen anyone that fast or on target, and certainly not on their first go through the course."

Luke smirked but kept his eyes firmly planted on the woman he loved.

"Can you ride and shoot like that, too?" Wanda asked.

"No, I never had the knack for horse archery. Lance and sword were my weapons of choice," he mumbled.

"What? I'm sorry, I didn't quite hear you."

He shook his head at himself, focusing himself before he revealed any of their other oddities. He'd gotten used to being around people who knew who he was, people he didn't need to hide who he was from.[[The only thing miss is a short beat somewhere in here that gives us a nice hint of the what happened before versus this moment here. Has Roxi been working hard to regain her strength to get to this? Is Luke nervous to see her ride again, or just happy to be enjoying a moment of calm? This will help us understand the world beyond this moment and what it took to get here.]]

"I said I never could get the knack for riding and archery. And she's a better rider than I am. She was practically born in a saddle. I came to riding later in life."

"Hmph," Wanda vocalized, her attention switching back to Roxi. "You were brilliant, dear."

Roxi dismounted, stroking the horse's neck as she walked to the railing and tied it down. "Thanks! I felt rusty out there. It's been long time since I've had the opportunity to ride and shoot."

Wanda chuckled. "If that's you rusty, what can you do when you're in practice?"

"I'm faster, and I can put two or three on target," Roxi replied, removing her helmet and wiping the sweat from her brow.

"What?" Wanda furrowed her brow, then laughed nervously. "Oh, you're joking."

Roxi smiled indulgently, then laughed along with Wanda. Neither Roxi or Luke would be winning points for fitting in and acting like normal people today.

"Well, if you're ready, we can saddle up a couple more horses and start the lessons," Wanda said, nodding toward Gwen.

Gwen looked nervously between Luke and Roxi.

The corner of one side of Luke's lip quirked up knowingly. "Would you mind if I let Roxi show me around the course while you get Gwen started?"

"Not at all," Wanda replied.

Luke squeezed Gwen's shoulder. "Be sure to pay attention to all the steps and listen to Wanda."

"Ugh. I know. I'm good at following directions," Gwen said.

He could practically hear the eye roll in his sixteen-year-old ward's voice. "I know."

"She's in good hands, Luke," Wanda said, a reassuring smile spreading across her face. "As long as you take good care of my horses…"

"I may not be as exceptional as Roxi, but I'm a very experienced horseman," Luke replied.

"I'll keep an eye on him for you, Wanda." Roxi caught his eye and winked at him.

Wanda chuckled and led them down to a trio of waiting horses. One was hers while another—described as slow, patient, and steady—was set aside specifically for Gwen. A tall roan gelding waited Luke with a calm but slightly wary eye.

Luke pulled an apple from his pocket, cut it in half with a pocket knife, and held out one half on his flat palm. The gelding quickly lipped it into his mouth, crunching it up while eying the other half. Stroking the horse's cheek, Luke let him finish the remainder of his bribe.

"He knows how to earn trust," Wanda commented.

Soon, Luke settled the blanket on its back and had the saddle cinched tight. Roxi, who'd already untied her horse and led it away from the deck, waited for him patiently. He cast a final glance toward Gwen who was listening raptly as Wanda introduced her to the horse she'd be riding before he untied his gelding and led him toward Roxi. When he drew abreast of her and her mare, he stepped into the stirrup and settled himself into the saddle, nudging the gelding into a walk as Roxi set her horse to walking next to him.

She waited until they were out of earshot of the young werewolf before speaking. "Didn't want to watch her lesson?"

"No, I did, but I think she was nervous about being bad in front of us, so I decided it would be better to leave Wanda to it."

"But she let you teach her how to fight, and she didn't know anything then, right?" Her brow furrowed in question.

"Yes, but she's not an eleven-year-old girl with nothing going on in her life, anymore. Also, after your blazing display of speed and skill, she was a bit intimidated about trying to ride in front of you."

"Hmm." Roxi said, staring forward as she nudged her horse up to a trot. She remained silent for a while. "I figured she'd want us to teach her since we're both far more experienced than Wanda."

Luke chuckled. "Though, I've never taught a young girl to ride before. I've only forged horse soldiers."

"You taught her the sword."

"Yeah, but the situation has changed. Maybe when she feels a little more comfortable after a few lessons, she'll be ready for us to take over."

Roxi nodded, picking up the speed of their ride again. He looked ahead but flicked his eyes toward Roxi to check on her. He'd picked up disappointed notes in her voice. Maybe he'd underestimated Roxi's desire to teach Gwen how to ride, though it was probably more the chance to bond she wanted over the specific need to relay the skill.

"I hate these western saddles," Roxi mumbled.

"If we're going to do this regularly, we can see about getting some proper saddles, assuming we can even find what we're looking for in the US."

Roxi snorted. "I'll just make my own. It'll be cheaper and fit better."

"I didn't know you knew how to make saddles."

Shrugging, she laid her hand on the horse's neck. "It helped pass the time."

He nodded along knowingly. During a nearly two thousand year life span, he'd learned all kinds of skills to burn time and keep his mind occupied, though saddle making had never been one of them. If he needed a new saddle, he'd just pay someone to make him a custom one.

"I'm going to take another pass through the course." She pulled the bow from her hip case along with a handful of arrows and set the horse to running, pulling away from Luke.

He gave her a few moments to gain a lead before he nudged his horse into a run, following her at a respectful distance to allow her time to work through whatever she needed to at the moment. Maybe after punching a few arrows into targets she'd be ready to talk to him.

She'd settled into his house relatively easily, though they'd both been exhausted and needed further time to recuperate after the injuries they'd sustained fighting the vampires, their werewolf hench-people, and the dark entity in the mountains of Montana. They'd both needed the time and had settled into a lazy domestic bliss, though it had taken all three of them time to get used to being in the house and developing a schedule that worked for the two unem-ployed adults and the kid currently attending high school.[[Good start, but a few specifics would also help, such as names for those s vampire head honchos they faced most recently, or the thunderdome, etc. Don't be afraid to lean into these two both being beaten down and tired.]]

At the insistence of his friends, he'd taken the time, letting them handle rounding up any vampires they could find, though he did regularly join in their planning sessions and the higher level meetings so he was fully updated on the goings on in the post-vampire attack world of hijacked airplanes and unleashed baby vamps. He hadn't even made a big fuss over stepping back, unlike the Luke of yeast-eryear. He'd only stepped forward when they'd finally found an actionable piece of intelligence in the laptops they'd taken from Le Mousquetaire's mansion.

So far, their social media campaign was going well with their vampire and vampire hunting videos racking up millions of views, though Jamaal had been forced to increase his tech team to keep ahead of the constant hacker attacks and other attempts to shut down their servers or block people from accessing them.[[Have they gotten any further backlash from this? And have they been able to manage it? Blowing the lid on vamps is pretty huge, I like that its casual but we need to keep the consequences in view as well. That will keep this grounded and real.]]

People seemed to be interested in the videos, though the governments still maintained that the various tragedies and violent outbursts were related to drugs of terrorists. But he didn't know if the people watching were just there for kicks or actually trying to apply the skills in real life.

With a quick shake of his head, he focused in on Roxi's hair flying out behind her as he followed . On a speeding horse moving through trees was no time to get distracted. Taking a deep breath, he held it before exhaling, trying to push out the tension in his chest that had started to tighten as his mind drifted toward the things he was trying to escape during this little vacation to Bend and central Oregon. Soon enough, he'd have to focus on the next stage in their war against the vampires and the dark god that drove them.

Ahead of him, Roxi had found another gear and peppered the targets, managing two shots per. Sometimes, she'd delay until she passed the target, then turn and take the famous "Parthian Shot," nailing the target as she retreated from it.

He loved seeing her in her element, though she seemed to be using the opportunity to ride and shoot to deal with something else other than relaxation. When they reached the end of the course, they pulled up, slowing their horses to cool them down.

"That was some spectacular shooting," Luke said, reaching out to pat her near leg.

Roxi grunted, shaking her head, then sighed heavily. "Thanks."

"Penny for your thoughts?"

She rode in a silence for a bit before answering. "Who even uses pennies anymore? Do you even have a penny?"

He chuckled. "I'm sure there's one in a change jar somewhere around the house."

"I don't know, Luke. I'm just feeling restless. It seems like we've been fighting for our survival non-stop since we met, and before that individually." She gestured around to the trees and sagebrush. "Now we're taking a lovely ride and playing in the woods while others do the fighting."

Nodding, he pulled up on the reins, stopping his horse. Roxi turned her horse and stopped so they faced each other.

"I know. I had to force myself to pay attention instead of letting my mind drift toward my responsibilities. But as my friends have reminded me more times than I can count, I need to take some time off and let others bear the weight of our test for a while. You and I have been doing this for centuries, often on our own. They're right. It's better for us to take a little time to recharge."

"I guess so," Roxi mumbled.

"We're still plugged in. We know what's going on, we're just not doing foot soldier stuff at the moment. Besides, it's good to delegate and let others grow more skilled and confident. Then we can diversify the leadership team so that no matter what happens to us, the work can continue."

She chuckled and shook her head. "Yeah, yeah, yeah. I know you're right, but it's a hard habit to break."

A series of beeping tones emerged from Luke's pocket, his hand drifting towards the it.

"If you take out that phone, I'll snatch it from you, toss it in the air, and put an arrow through it. I thought you were supposed to have it turned off, anyway."

Shrugging, he snorted and rested his hand on the saddle horn. "I didn't even figure we'd get reception this far outside Bend."

"You can check it —" Her own phone interrupted her.

Luke smirked, an eyebrow rising. "I thought we were supposed to turn our phones off."

"We can check them when we get back into town. Let's enjoy a quiet ride while Gwen gets her lesson, then we can return to our regularly scheduled lives after our little holiday."

Reaching out, he grabbed Roxi's hand and squeezed it. "OK."

He nudged his horse forward, Roxi pulled hers around and settled in next to him. The real world could wait for a few hours longer. For the moment, they'd pull in what tranquility they could while they had the opportunity; it would be needed and no doubt too soon.

Luke Irontree will return in Ancient Sword Unyielding
Available Now!

NEWSLETTER

The Centurion Immortal is a Luke Irontree prequel novella and is exclusive to the Dispatches from C. Thomas Lafollette newsletter. Please sign up for your free copy and you'll also receive a twice-monthly newsletter with news, book updates, recipes, drinks tips, and other fun stuff. Your email will never be given out, rented, or sold.

CThomasLafollette.com/newsletter/

ACKNOWLEDGMENTS

I'd like to thank all the people who made this book possible.

Suzanne, your editorial eye has made this book and series infinitely better. Your belief in my vision for these characters has made this a kick ass team effort.

Ravven, your covers are amazing and really capture the essence of Luke and his world.

Amy, you're my alpha reader and my proofreader. These books wouldn't be possible without you.

Alan Silverwood, you're copy edits have really polished this book.

To my critique group, thank you for all your hard work. Your eyes and efforts have made my writing better.

ABOUT THE AUTHOR

C. Thomas Lafollette is a student of history and a world traveler. He's dined with a Prime Minister, read poetry with Yevgeny Yevtushenko, and drank beer with monks. He's the author of the action-adventure urban fantasy series Luke Irontree & The Last Vampire War and the forthcoming Red City Reaper series. Besides reading and writing, he loves a good action movie, be it a Hollywood blockbuster or a classic Samurai flick, as well as the occasional rom-com. He lives in Portland with his partner – the devastatingly talented author Amy Cissell – his stepdaughter, and their two jerk-face cats.

ALSO BY C. THOMAS LAFOLLETTE

Luke Irontree & The Last Vampire War

Book 0 - The Centurion Immortal

Book 1 - Dark Fangs Rising - March 22, 2022

Book 2 - Dark Fangs Raging - April 19, 2022

Book 3 - Dark Fangs Descending - May 17, 2022

Book 4 - Blood Empire Reborn - August 23, 2022

Book 5 - Blood Empire Avenged - September 20, 2022

Book 6 - Blood Empire Infiltrated - October 18, 2022

Book 7 - Blood Empire Burning - November 15, 2022

Book 8 - Ancient Sword Falling - March 21, 2023

Book 9 - Ancient Sword Unyielding - August 22, 2023

Book 10 - Ancient Sword Shattering*

The Luke Irontree Historical Adventures

Rise of the Centurio Immortalis - April 5, 2022

Fall of the Centurio Immortalis - May 31, 2022

The Moonlight Centurion*

The Highway Centurion*

Red City Reaper - A Dark Urban Fantasy Adventure

Book 1 - A Shot For Death* - Winter 2024

Book 2 - Death Orders a Double* - Winter 2024

Book 3 - Death on the Rocks* - Sprint 2024

*Forthcoming

Titles and release dates may be subject to change.